DAPHNE DU MAURIER
MARY ANNE

Books by Daphne du Maurier:

THE HOUSE ON THE STRAND
REBECCA
FRENCHMAN'S CREEK
HUNGRY HILL
THE KING'S GENERAL
THE PARASITES
MY COUSIN RACHEL
KISS ME AGAIN, STRANGER
THE DU MAURIERS
DON'T LOOK NOW
THE SCAPEGOAT
THE BREAKING POINT
THE FLIGHT OF THE FALCON
THE INFERNAL WORLD OF BRANWELL BRONTE
THE LOVING SPIRIT
I'LL NEVER BE YOUNG AGAIN
THE PROGRESS OF JULIUS
THE GLASS-BLOWERS

DAPHNE DU MAURIER

MARY ANNE

A DELL BOOK

Published by
Dell Publishing Co., Inc.
1 Dag Hammarskjold Plaza
New York, New York 10017

Dell ® TM 681510, Dell Publishing Co., Inc.

ISBN: 0-440-15208-9

Reprinted by arrangement with Doubleday & Company, Inc.

Printed in the United States of America

January 1987

10 9 8 7 6 5 4 3 2 1

WFH

ACKNOWLEDGMENTS: My grateful thanks to Sir Walter Peacock for his Notes on Mary Anne Clarke, which gave me much valuable information; to Oriel Malet for long hours spent at the British Museum and the Public Record Office; and above all to Derek Pepys Whiteley for his tireless research through books, papers, and documents of the period, and his most helpful advice on the necessary works to be consulted.

To

MARY ANNE CLARKE

my great-great grandmother,

died Boulogne, June 21, 1852

and

GERTRUDE LAWRENCE

who was to have acted

the part on the stage,

died New York, September 6, 1952

IN MEMORY OF BOTH

Mary Anne Thompson—m.—Joseph Clarke
(1776–1852)   (–d. 1836)
|

Ellen Clarke—m.—Louis Mathurin Busson du Maurier
(1797–1870)   (1797–1856)
|

George du Maurier
(1834–1896)
|

Gerald du Maurier
(1873–1934)
|

Daphne du Maurier
(1907–)

PART ONE

ONE: Years later, when she had gone and was no longer part of their lives, the thing they remembered about her was her smile. Colouring and features were indistinct, hazy in memory. The eyes, surely, were blue—but they could have been green or grey. And the hair, knotted in Grecian fashion or piled high on top of the head in curls, might have been chestnut or light brown. The nose was anything but Grecian—that was a certainty, for it pointed to heaven; and the actual shape of the mouth had never seemed important—not at the time, or now.

The essence of what had been lay in the smile. It began in the left corner of the mouth and hovered momentarily, mocking without discrimination those she loved most—including her own family—and those she despised. And while they waited uneasily, expecting a blast of sarcasm or the snub direct, the smile spread to the eyes, transfiguring the whole face, lighting it to gaiety. Reprieved, they basked in the warmth and shared the folly, and there was no intellectual pose in the laugh that followed, ribald, riotous, cockney, straight from the belly.

This was what they remembered in after years. The rest was forgotten. Forgotten the lies, the deceit, the sudden bursts of temper. Forgotten the wild extravagance, the absurd generosity, the vitriolic tongue. Only the warmth remained, and the love of living.

They remembered it one by one as they sat alone at different times, figures shadowy and indistinct to each other. And though the paths of some of them had crossed, there was no friendship between them; the link binding them together was involuntary.

The strange thing was that the three she had loved most all went within a year of one another, while the fourth did

13

not lag far behind; and each remembered the smile before he died. They heard the laugh, clear and strong, with nothing ghostly about it, ring in some sound-box in the brain; and memory, like a sudden haemorrhage, flooded the mind.

Her brother, Charles Thompson, was the first to go, and this was because he lacked patience, and always had, ever since he was a little boy and had stretched up his hands to her, saying, "Take me with you, don't leave me behind!" He had thereby entrusted himself into her care forever, so that never, then or in his adult years, was he free of her or she of him, which had brought them both to disaster.

It happened, the end of things for him, after a tavern brawl, when he had been talking big as usual—about himself in the old days, the most promising company commander in the regiment, due for promotion. Out came the old story once again; his ill-health, the spite of his colonel, the animosity of his brother officers, the manifest unfairness of the Court Martial, and—to crown all—the petty revenge of the Commander-in-Chief, who, by disgracing the brother, sought to revenge himself upon the sister.

He looked around him, expecting sympathy, but nobody cared very much or bothered to listen, and anyway it had all happened so long ago, what did it matter? They turned their backs upon him and began to fill their glasses, and Charles Thompson rapped his upon the table, an angry spot mounting to his cheek, and said, "Listen to me, damn you! I can tell you things about the royal family you wouldn't credit. If you knew, you'd heave the whole House of Brunswick across the Channel."

And then somebody amongst them who could remember back sixteen years or so softly whispered a crude verse that had been sung about that time in the streets of London, unflattering to Charles's sister. The fellow intended no harm, he meant to be funny. Charles Thompson thought otherwise. He stood up and hit the man on the mouth, and the table fell over, and Charles hit somebody else, and all was clatter and confusion, noise and blasphemy, until he found himself out in the street, with the blood pouring down his cheek and the derisive laughter of his late companions ringing in his ears.

14

The moon was shining and the dome of St. Paul's stood clear against the sky, and without realising it some long-lost sense of direction took him through the maze of streets to their old childhood home, the existence of which he would have denied amongst his friends of the tavern; or, as his sister so often did, he would have invented for it a new locality, Oxfordshire, perhaps, or even Scotland. But there it stood, dark and cramped amongst its fellows, at the head of Bowling Inn Alley, not even a slant from the moon to light the windows where they had knelt together as children and planned the future. Or rather, she had planned it and he had listened. People were living there still. He heard a child cry and a woman's voice, faint and fretful, call up to it in anger, and then the door of the dark house opened and somebody came and threw a basin of slops on to the flagged stones, shouting abuse over his shoulder.

Charles Thompson turned away and the ghosts followed him. They followed him through the streets to the river, where the tide ran fast and high in the Pool of London, and he realised he had no money and no future and she was not with him any more, and the blood she would have wiped away from his face was running into his mouth.

Some children dabbling in the mud found him, but that was a long time afterwards.

It was William Dowler, faithful to her for twenty-five years, who identified Charles Thompson's body. A sick man at the time, he came up from Brighton to London to do so, a letter from her solicitors telling him of the discovery in the London river. Certain details tallied with descriptions of the missing brother, and Dowler, in his capacity of trustee, braced himself to the task. He had never cared for Thompson, and when he stared down at all that remained of him in the mortuary, he thought how different life might have turned out for her if only the brother had drowned himself after he was cashiered, seventeen years before. Different for Dowler, too. She would have turned to him, brokenhearted, and he could have taken her away to forget all about it, instead of which bitterness and anger drove her to revenge. Well,

15

there he lay, the cause of so much trouble. Her "precious brother," as she used to call him, her "darling boy."

Back again in Brighton, Dowler wondered if his dislike of Thompson had been jealousy all the time. He had accepted her many friends, they never seemed to matter—sycophants, most of them, courting her for what they could get. One or two more intimate, perhaps, but he had shut his eyes to that. As to the Duke, after the first shock to the emotions he had looked upon that relationship as a necessity, a matter of business. Nothing he might have said would have stopped her.

"I told you that I aimed high," she had said to him, "and the arrow's found its mark. I shall still need you in the background."

And in the background he had remained. He waited on her when she summoned him. He gave her advice, which she never took. He paid her bills when the Duke forgot to do so. He even took her diamonds out of pawn. The final degradation of escorting her children back to school had been thrust upon him, while she followed His Royal Highness down to Weybridge.

Why had he done it? What had he got out of it all?

Staring at the sea that broke so serenely on the Brighton shore, William Dowler thought of the weeks they had shared there together, before the Duke appeared upon the scene. Of course she had been in search of quarry even then—Cripplegate Barrymore and the Four-in-Hand gallants—but he had been too much in love to notice or to care.

Hampstead had been the happiest—she had needed him then, running to him on impulse from her sick child's bedroom. Later, when the Duke left her, she had needed him even more. Hampstead revisited, he had believed at that time she had no thoughts for anyone but him, but with her restless mind he could not be sure.

Finally, was it emotion that sent her to him that night in Reid's Hotel, barely an hour after he had arrived from Lisbon, travel-stained and weary? She had flung a cloak round her shoulders—there was no attempt at disguise. "You've been away too long," she said. "I've wanted your help so much!" Or was her visit exquisitely timed to catch him unawares, knowing his weakness for her, certain in

16

her intuitive mind that he would make a most valuable witness for her before the bar of the House of Commons?

There was no answer to that, or to any other questions. No matter, the smile remained. William Dowler turned his back on the sea, and he stood still for a moment with the other promenaders, his hat in his hand, as like an echo to memory a carriage drove past containing a stout, elderly gentleman and a little girl.

It was the Duke of York and his niece, the Princess Victoria. The Duke had aged lately—he looked a great deal more than sixty-two. Still the same high colour, though, the same stiff military bearing, his hand half raised in a salute as he acknowledged the passers-by. Then Dowler saw him bend and smile down at the child, who looked up to him, laughing, and for the first time in his life he felt a stab of pity for the man he had once envied.

There was something pathetic in the sight of the old fellow sitting there in the carriage in the company of the child, and Dowler wondered if he was very lonely. Gossip said that he could not get over the death of his last love, the Duchess of Rutland, but gossip could say anything, as Dowler knew too well. There was more likelihood of truth in the rumour that dropsy would carry him off before many months were past, and when that happened the more scurrilous newspapers would rake up the old mud of the Investigation, and side by side with the black-edged obituary notices Dowler would see her name splashed once again.

He was spared this ordeal by dying himself just four months before the Duke, and it was the Duke who read Dowler's obituary tucked away in an old number of the *Gentleman's Magazine*. He was sitting in the library of the house in Arlington Street, wrapped in a grey dressing-gown, his swollen, bandaged legs propped up in the chair in front of him. He must have fallen asleep—he tired very easily these days, though he said little about it, even to Herbert Taylor, his private secretary; but everyone told him he was very ill and must rest, from his brother the King down to the useless muddling doctors who called every morning.

Dowler . . . What did the magazine say? "The death

17

occurred at Brighton on the 7th of September of William Dowler, Esq., late Commissioner of His Majesty's Forces." And the Duke was not sitting, crippled and useless, in Rutland's house in Arlington Street any more, but standing in the hall of the house in Gloucester Place, taking off his sword belt and throwing it to Ludovick, and then mounting the stairs, three steps at a time, as she called to him from the floor above. "Sire, I expected you hours ago!" The little ritual of ceremony meant nothing at all— it was just in case the servants should hear—and while she dropped her absurd curtsey (she adored doing this, no matter how she was dressed, from ball gown to night attire) he kicked the door open with his boot, slamming it behind him, and in a moment she was in his arms, undoing the top button of his tunic.

"What kept you this time? The Horse Guards or St. James's?"

"Both, my darling. Try and remember we're at war."

"I never forget it for a moment. You'd get through your business quicker if you'd kept Clinton as your M.S. instead of Gordon."

"Why not run the office for me?"

"I've been doing so, behind the scenes, for the past six months. Tell your tailor he makes these buttonholes too small, my nail's broken."

Dowler . . . William Dowler . . . that was the chap. He'd found him a job in the Commissariat. Stores and Provisions, Eastern Command. He could even remember the date, June or July 1805.

"Bill Dowler's a very old friend, sir," she had said. "If he gets this appointment he will show his gratitude to me."

He was half asleep at the time—it was the last glass of port that did it. Always fatal. Her head on his shoulder, too.

"How will he show it?"

"By doing whatever I tell him. He could pay the butcher's bill, for instance—it's been outstanding for three months. That's why you had fish for dinner tonight."

God! How the ghost of her laugh came echoing out of the past to haunt him. Here, suddenly, in Arlington Street, that held no memories of her. He thought they were all

18

buried long ago, hidden away in the dust and cobwebs of the empty house in Gloucester Place.

At the Investigation it turned out that Dowler had given her a thousand quid for that appointment, and had been her lover, off and on, for years. So they said. Probably all lies. What did it matter now? The havoc she had caused in his life was only temporary. He had lived it down. And there had never been another woman to touch her, though Lord knows he had done his best to find one. They all lacked that indefinable quality which had made those brief years in Gloucester Place so memorable. He used to go back there in the evening after an interminable day at his headquarters, and she made him forget all the frustration and obstruction and annoyance that inevitably fell to his lot as Commander-in-Chief of an army fifty times smaller than that of the enemy. (He had got all the abuse and none of the praise, and it hadn't been easy dealing with a lot of nincompoops and struggling to put the home defences in order while the enemy squatted across the Channel waiting the right moment for invasion.) But once he was inside that house the irritation went from him and he could relax.

She fed him so damn well. Knew his hatred of big dinners. Everything just right. And then to be able to stretch himself full length before a blazing fire and drink his brandy, while she made him laugh with idiocies! He could remember the very smell of the room, the slight disorder everywhere that made it a home, her painting attempts on the table—she was always taking lessons at something—the harp in the corner, the ridiculous doll that she had brought back from some masquerade perching from the chandelier where she had thrown it.

Why had it ended? Too hot to last, or that meddler Adam interfering in the affair and making mischief? Or the drunken sot of a husband with his threats? He must have finished in the gutter. Dead, probably. Everyone was either dead or dying. He was dying himself. He pulled the bell for his personal servant Batchelor.

"What's the movement I hear going on outside in the street?"

"They are laying straw, Your Royal Highness, in Picca-

19

dilly, so that you won't be disturbed by the sound of the traffic. Sir Herbert Taylor's orders."

"Damn nonsense. Tell 'em to stop. I like the sound of traffic. I hate silence."

There had been a barracks at the back of Gloucester Place. They used to look down on the Life Guards, riding, from the window of his dressing-room. There was always life in that house, and laughter, always something afoot— singing as she dressed her hair; calling to her children, who had the run of the top floor when they visited her; hurling abuse at the maid when she put out the wrong pair of shoes. It was never silent, like this, never dead.

The damned old idiot, Taylor, ordering straw to be laid in Piccadilly . . .

The husband whom the Duke of York had called a drunken sot preferred silence to the sound of traffic. It was softer to the backside to fall on heather than in gutters. Not that he fell often. Sutherland the farmer, with whom he lodged and who looked after him so well, took good care of that. He kept the whisky locked up. But Joseph Clarke had a private store hidden away under the floor boards of his bedroom, and now and then, when melancholy descended upon him—and the winters in Caithness were very long—he held what he called a little celebration all to himself, and when he was well lit, but still in the first stage of his bout, he solemnly drank the health of His Royal Highness the Commander-in-Chief.

"It's not everyone," he said aloud, with no one to listen, "who has been made a cuckold by a prince of the blood."

Unfortunately this mood was not one that lasted long. Self-pity followed. He might have achieved so much, but the fates were against him. He'd had ill-luck from beginning to end. He knew so well the kind of work he would have done, but there was never a chance to show it—he could not get going, something always happened to prevent it. If someone would only put a hammer and a chisel into his hand now, and stand him before a block of granite six feet high, or perhaps six foot three, the height of the Commander-in-Chief, he would . . . he would create the masterpiece she had always asked him to create. Or else break the stone to blazes, and finish the whisky.

There was far too much granite in Caithness anyway. There was granite all over the country. That's why he'd been sent there in the first place. "You were bred a mason, weren't you? Well, get on with it." A mason? No! An artist, a sculptor, a dreamer of dreams. All three combined, after a bottle of whisky.

Yet she had had the face to stand up in the House of Commons and tell the Attorney-General, and the whole crowd assembled there to listen, that he was nothing.

"Is your husband living?"

"I don't know if he is living or dead. He is nothing to me."

"Was he in any business?"

"He was nothing. Merely a man."

And they laughed when she said this. It was written in the paper. He bought it and read. They laughed. Merely a man.

He forgot the insult with the third glass of whisky. Throwing the window wide so that the Scotch mist filled the cold bedroom, he lay down on the bed and stared at the ceiling. And instead of the heads of saints he might have carved, remote, austere, with blind eyes looking to heaven, he saw the smile and heard the laugh, and she was holding out her hand to him in the early morning as they stood in the little churchyard of St. Pancras.

"Something fearful has happened," he said. "I've forgotten the licence."

"I have it," she answered; "and there has to be a second witness. I thought of that too."

"Who is it?"

"The gravedigger at Pancras church. I've given him two shillings for his pains. Hurry. They're waiting."

She was so excited that she signed her name before his on the register. It was her sixteenth birthday.

Nothing but a man. Though he got his obituary too. Not in the *Times*, nor in the *Gentleman's Magazine*, but in *John O'Groats Journal*.

"Died, on the 9th of February 1836, at the house of Mr. Sutherland, of Bylbster, Parish of Wattin, in this County, Mr. J. Clarke, generally believed to be the husband of the celebrated Mary Anne Clarke, remarkable for having acted such a conspicuous part during the trial of

His Royal Highness the late Duke of York. He had for some time been addicted to intemperate habits, which, together with the severe domestic misfortune he had been subjected to, had visibly affected his mind. Several books, it is said, were found in his possession, in which was written the name of Mary Anne Clarke."

So the last link went, wafted to eternity in a haze of alcohol, and nothing was left of any of them but bundles of letters and scurrilous pamphlets and old newspaper reports dingy with dust. But the owner of the smile had the laugh on them, right to the end. She was not a ghost, nor a memory, nor a figment of the imagination seen in a dream long vanished, breaking the hearts of those who had loved her unwisely and too well. At seventy-six, she sat at the window of her house in Boulogne, looking across the Channel to an England that had forgotten all about her. Her favourite daughter was dead, and the second lived in London, and the grandchildren she had nursed as babies were ashamed of her and never wrote. The son she adored had his own life to lead. The men and women she had known had passed into oblivion.

The dreams were all hers.

T W O :   Mary Anne's first memory was the smell of printer's ink. Her stepfather, Bob Farquhar, used to come back with it on his clothes, and then she and her mother would have a job with it in the wash. However hard they scrubbed the stain remained, and his shirt-cuffs never looked clean. He never looked clean himself, for that matter, and her mother, who was spotless and very refined, continually grumbled at him. He would sit down to the evening meal with ink-stained hands—the stuff even got under his fingernails, turning them black—and Mary Anne, quick and watchful, would see the pained expression on her mother's face, the gentle face of the martyr, the long-sufferer; and because she was fond of her stepfather and disliked to see him nagged, Mary Anne would pinch one of her brothers under the table to make him cry out, and so cause a diversion.

"Shut your mouth," said Bob Farquhar; "I can't hear myself eat." Noisily he would slop the food into his mouth, drag a stub of pencil and a roll of copy out of his pocket with his left hand, the copy still wet and reeking from the press, and so he would eat and correct all at the same time, the smell of the ink mingling with the steam of the gravy.

This was how Mary Anne taught herself to read. Words fascinated her, the shape of the curling letters, how some, by repeating themselves more often, had importance. They had difference of sex, too. The *a*'s, the *e*'s, and the *u*'s were women; the hard *g*'s, the *b*'s, and the *q*'s were all men, and seemed to depend on the others.

"What does that mean? Spell it out!" she said to Bob Farquhar, and her stepfather, easygoing, good-natured, put his arm round the child and showed her how letters

23

formed words and what could be done with them. This was the only reading matter that came her way, for her mother's books and possessions had been sold long ago to supplement the small income Bob Farquhar earned from Mr. Hughes, owner of the printing-press where he worked, who, employed by certain anonymous scribblers, turned out a spate of pamphlets at a halfpenny a sheet.

Thus Mary Anne, at an age when most children would be learning their catechism or spelling out proverbs, sat on the doorstep of the cramped house in Bowling Inn Alley, poring over attacks on the government, outbursts on foreign policy, hysterical acclaim or equally hysterical denunciation of popular leaders, the whole mixed up with a profusion of dirt, scandal, and innuendo.

"Look after the boys, Mary Anne, and see to the dishes for me," her mother would call, tired and fretful, and her small daughter, laying aside the grubby sheets of newsprint that her stepfather had left behind him, would get up from the doorway and wash the breakfast things, or whatever meal it was that her mother, pregnant again, could not face: while Charley, her own brother, helped himself to the jam, and her two half-brothers, George and Eddie, crawled on the floor under her feet.

"Behave yourselves, and I'll take you out," she commanded—but softly, so that her mother in the bedroom upstairs could not hear. Later, when the dishes were washed, the table set for the next meal, and her mother tucked in bed for an hour's rest, Mary Anne picked up one boy and straddled him on her hip, gave her hand to another, and let the third tag behind hanging on to her skirt. Then away they went, out of the dark alley where the sun never shone, through the maze of small courts adjoining, and so into Chancery Lane and down into Fleet Street.

This was another world, and one she loved, full of colour and sound and smell, but not the smell of the alley. Here people jostled one another on the pavement, here the traffic rumbled on towards Ludgate Hill and St. Paul's, the carters cracking their whips and shouting, drawing their horses to the side of the road as a coach passed, spattering mud. Here a fine gentleman would step out of his chair to visit a bookshop, while a woman selling lavender

24

thrust a bunch under his nose, and there on the opposite side a cart overtipped, spilling apples and oranges, tumbling into the gutter a blind musician and an old man mending a chair.

It came to her in gusts, the sound and the smell of London, and she felt part of it, caught up in the movement and the bustle, the continual excitement that must surely be leading to something, to somewhere—not only to the steps of St. Paul's, where the boys could play safely, out of the stream, and she could stand, watching.

Adventure was here. Adventure was there. Adventure was in picking up a posy dropped by a lady and offering it to an old gentleman who patted her head and gave her twopence. Adventure was in gazing into pawnbrokers' windows, in riding in wagons when the carter smiled, in scuffling with apprentice boys, in hovering outside the bookshops, and, when the bookseller was inside, tearing out the middle pages to read at home, for prospective purchasers never looked at anything but the beginning and the end.

These were the things she loved, and she did not know why. So she kept them secret from her mother, who would have scolded her and disapproved.

The streets were mentor and playground, teacher and companion. Rascals picked pockets on the streets, beggars were given alms, goods were bought, rubbish was sold, men laughed, men cursed, women whined, women smiled, children died under wheels. Some men and women wore fine clothes, some wore rags. The first ate well, and the others starved. The way to avoid rags and starvation was to watch, to wait, to pick up the coin dropped on the pavement before anyone else, to run swiftly, to conceal quickly, to smile at the right moment, to hide at the next, to keep what you had, to look after your own. The thing to remember was not to grow up like her mother, who was weak, who had no resistance, who was lost in this world of London that was alien to her, and whose only consolation was to talk of the past, when she had known better days.

Better days . . . And what were they? Better days meant sleeping in linen, meant owning a servant, meant possessing new clothes, meant four-o'clock dinner, things without reality for the child, yet because she had heard her mother speak of them they became real in her eyes. Mary Anne saw the better days. She saw the servant, she saw the clothes, she ate the four-o'clock dinner. The only thing she did not understand was why her mother had given them up.

"There was no other choice. I was a widow. I had you and Charley to support."

"How do you mean, no other choice?"

"Your stepfather asked me to marry him. There was nothing else I could do. Besides, he was good and kind."

Then men were not dependent upon women after all, as she had thought—women were dependent upon men. Boys were frail, boys cried, boys were tender, boys were helpless. Mary Anne knew this, because she was the eldest girl amongst her three young brothers, and the baby Isobel did not count at all. Men also were frail, men also cried, men also were tender, men also were helpless. Mary Anne knew this because her stepfather, Bob Farquhar, was all of these things in turn. Yet men went to work. Men made the money—or frittered it away, like her stepfather, so that there was never enough to buy clothes for the children, and her mother scraped and saved and stitched by candlelight, and often looked tired and worn. Somewhere there was injustice. Somewhere the balance had gone.

"When I'm grown up I shall marry a rich man," she said. This was one day when they were all sitting round the table having supper, not four-o'clock dinner. It was midsummer, and the hot air from the alley came in from the open door, smelling of decaying vegetables and drains. Her stepfather had hung his coat over his chair and was sitting in his shirt. Great hoops of sweat showed under his armpits and, as usual, he had inkstains on his hands. Her mother was coaxing Isobel to eat, but the child, fretful from the heat, turned her face away and cried. George and Eddie were kicking each other's shins under the table. Charley had just slopped his gravy on to the cloth.

Mary Anne looked at them all in turn and then made her pronouncement. She was thirteen years old at the time. Bob Farquhar laughed, and winked at her over the table.

"You'll have to find him first," he said. "How will you set about it?"

26

Not the way her mother had found him, thought the child. Not waiting in patience to be asked. Not turning into a drudge to mind children and wash dishes. She reasoned like this with her mind, but because she was fond of Bob Farquhar she smiled and winked back at him.

"By making a fool out of someone," she said, "before he makes a fool out of me."

This delighted her stepfather, who lit up his pipe and chuckled, but her mother was not so amused.

"I know where she picks up that language," she said, "following you in the evening, listening to you and your friends."

Bob Farquhar shrugged his shoulders, yawned, and pushed back his chair. "What's the harm?" he asked. "She's as smart as a monkey, and knows it. No girl got into trouble that way."

He threw a roll of copy across the table and his step-daughter caught it. "What happens if I pull the monkey's tail?" he asked.

"The monkey bites," said Mary Anne.

She ran her eyes down the copy. Some of the words were long and she was not sure of the meaning, but she knew her stepfather wanted her to correct it because he was putting on his coat and making for the door, and he pulled one of her straggling curls as he passed by her chair.

"You haven't told us how you'll find your rich husband," he teased.

"You tell me instead," she answered.

"Why, stand on the pavement and whistle to the first fellow you fancy. You'll get anyone with those eyes."

"Yes," said Mary Anne, "but the first fellow I fancy mightn't be rich."

She heard him laughing as he strolled down the alley to meet his friends. She had often gone with him, she knew just what he would do. First, stroll the alleys and byways and pick up his cronies; then take a turn in the streets, laughing, joking, and watching the people; then, in a bunch of six or seven, they would go on to a tavern and blithely and heatedly probe the affairs of the day.

Men's talk was better than women's. Never food, never babies, never sickness, or boots needing mending, but

27

people, what happened, the reason. Not the state of the house, but the state of the Army. Not the children next door, but the rebels in France. Never what broke the china, but who broke the treaty. Not what spoilt the washing, but who spilled the beans. A Whig was a patriot, a Frog was a Frenchman, a Tory a traitor, a woman a whore. Some of it was puzzling and some of it was tripe, but all of it was better than darning Charley's socks.

"Thirsty weather?"

"Thirsty weather."

Solemnly they clinked their glasses, solemnly they drank, and riotously the reputations of the famous tore through the smoky air, dropping pieces of themselves into the lap of a listening child—but not tonight. Tonight there were stockings to mend and shirts to wash, the boys to mind and mother to console, and even at bedtime, when she had a moment to sit down by the window and look at the copy that had to go to press tomorrow, Charley would come to the door, Charley would claim her.

"Tell me a story, Mary Anne."

"I'll box your ears first."

"Tell me a story."

Anything served. The beat of a drum. The bells of St. Paul's. The shout of a drunkard. The cries of a hawker. The shabby tinker who came knocking on the doors crying. "Pots an' pans. Any ole pots an' pans t'mend?" stumbling over Eddie and George, who were sailing a paper boat in the open drain. Even the tinker's drab, familiar figure, turned from the door by their mother, could be changed into a prince to dazzle the eyes of Charley.

"Tell about the Forty-Five, and the silver button."

Prince Charles had lost the battle, and the Duke of Cumberland had won. She never mentioned the fact in front of her mother, who had been born a Mackenzie. One of the Mackenzies possessed a silver button worn by the Prince. That was enough.

"What happened to the button?" she had asked when five years old. Her mother did not know. Her branch of the Mackenzies had come south when she was born. They had lost touch with the clan. So Mary Anne wove a fabrication for Charley and herself. They had only to find the button, and the fortunes of the family would be restored.

28

"When we have found the button, what shall we do then?"

"Have candles everywhere."

Candles that filled the room with light, and not with grease. Candles that did not have to be hoarded until they spluttered and went out.

Mary Anne told Charley the story of the silver button. Then she lit the candle, and taking the roll of copy in her hands, she stood reading it aloud, beside the small mirror on the wall, listening to her own pronunciation. Her mother had told her that she spoke badly, and Mary Anne could not get it out of her mind.

"How do you mean—I speak badly?" she had asked, on the defensive.

"It's not your voice—it's the sound. It's the way they speak in the alley. You've picked it up from the children there. Your stepfather doesn't notice it. He speaks that way himself."

She was branded again. Branded with her stepfather, and the alley, and the streets. The Mackenzies from Scotland had been different. Likewise her father, Mr. Thompson, of Aberdeen.

"Was he a gentleman, then?" She snatched at the straw of romance, the link with better days.

That was not enough. Not enough the better days, and the dining at four. Not enough plain Mr. Thompson of Aberdeen. Not enough that he had lost his life in the American wars.

"Do you mean he commanded troops?"

"Not quite. He was attached to the Army."

An adviser, perhaps? A weaver of plans? A go-between? The pamphlets gave hints of such people. Sometimes they called them spies. Mr. Thompson, who had given her mother better days, was no longer so dull. He smiled, he bowed, he listened; he whispered strategic secrets behind his hand; he was clever; he was cunning. Above all he was a gentleman who spoke with a cultured voice. He did not speak broad like the children in the alley.

"Listen, Charley. Listen to my voice."

"What's wrong with your voice?"

"Never mind. Listen."

The *"h"* was all-important. Her mother had told her

29

that. The *h* and the *o* and the *u*. And the *o* and the *l* when together.

" 'We have it on the highest authority that His Majesty's Government, which will search around for any available stick to beat the Opposition dog and lame it during the present session, and not content with the stick, pick up the mud . . .' "

"What are you reading, Mary Anne?"

"Tomorrow's copy."

"But I don't understand it."

"No more do I. But that doesn't matter. Father says the readers don't either. Don't interrupt. 'We have it on the highest authority . . .' " And out came her pencil—the *r* of "authority" was broken.

"There's someone knocking on the door down below."

"Let them knock."

But the boy was off the bed and craning his neck out of the window.

"It's some men . . . they're carrying Father . . . he's hurt."

And suddenly they heard her mother's voice, calling out in alarm, and Isobel crying, and George and Eddie came running upstairs.

"All right. Easy now. No cause for alarm."

They were laying him down between two chairs in the living-room, and his face was mottled and queer.

"It's the heat."

"The doctor will bleed him."

"He fell at the street corner."

"He'll be himself again directly."

Her mother stood by helplessly. Mary Anne sent Charley running for the doctor, packed the other two boys and Isobel upstairs, and shut the door on them. Then she fetched a basin of cold water and sponged her stepfather's head, while his friends went over the story in detail once again to her mother.

Presently Charley returned with the doctor. He looked grave, he murmured something about apoplexy, he sent Mary Anne and Charley out of the room—children were in the way when there was sickness.

Finally Bob Farquhar was carried to bed, and after the bloodletting and the purging the children were told that it

30

was not apoplexy after all, that he was not going to die, but that he must rest. He must on no account go to work, not tomorrow, not next week, not for several weeks. While the doctor explained the ritual of nursing and feeding to her distraught mother, Mary Anne slipped into the bedroom and took hold of her stepfather's hand. He had recovered consciousness.

"What's to happen?" he said. "They'll find someone else to do my work at the printing-house. A sick man's no use to them."

"Don't worry."

"You'll have to take a message. Someone must go and take a message. Ask for Mr. Day, the overseer." He closed his eyes—talking was too much for him.

Mary Anne went downstairs. Her mother looked at her hopelessly.

"This is the finish," she said. "They'll pay him for this week's work, and no more. It may be months before he is well again, and his place will be filled. How do we live meanwhile?"

"I'm to go down to the printing-house in the morning."

"You must tell them the truth. That your father is sick."

"I'll tell them the truth."

Mary Anne rolled the copy carefully. She must take the chance that every word was correct. She knew all the signs by now, the small marks in the margin, but never before had copy been delivered back to the printing-house without her stepfather glancing at it first. She knew his hand well. The sloping *R*. The curl to the *F*. She signed at the foot of the copy, "Corrected, Robt. Farquhar."

Early next day she washed her face and hands and put on her Sunday frock. The straggling curls looked limp, making her childish. She snipped at them with scissors and then stood back to see the effect in the mirror. Better, but lacking in something, lacking in colour. She stole softly into the next bedroom. Her stepfather was asleep. She opened the press where her mother kept her clothes. A gown was hanging there that she never wore in Bowling Inn Alley, a gown which belonged to the better days, with a bunch of red ribbons on the bodice. Mary Anne threaded the ribbon through her hair and looked at her reflection once again. Yes, the ribbon was the answer.

She stole out of the house before her mother or the boys could see her, and, the roll of copy under her arm, went down to Fleet Street.

THREE: The doors were open and she could go where she pleased. No one took any notice of her. The press was at work, and she caught a glimpse of the great wooden contraption in a long, narrow room, with two men beside it and a boy holding rolls of paper that he passed to the men. Two other men were standing nearby, talking, and a second boy kept running up a narrow stairway to a room above, returning with fresh paper. The men raised their voices to make themselves heard, because of the clanking sound the rollers made as the sheets of paper passed through the press.

Another door, marked "Private," stood opposite the pressroom across the passage. Mary Anne knocked at the door. Somebody shouted, "Come in," but the voice was irritable. She went into the room.

"What do you want?"

The owner of the irritable voice was a gentleman. He wore a good coat and silk stockings, and his powdered, curled wig was tied with black ribbon. The other wore his own hair and his stockings were worsted.

"I've come with a message from my father. He's sick."

"Who's your father?"

"Robert Farquhar."

The gentleman turned away with a shrug. The plainer man, with the worsted stockings, apologised. "Bob Farquhar, Mr. Hughes. One of our best men. Compositor and corrector. What a piece of ill-luck."

He turned to the child. "What ails your father?"

"He was taken ill last night. The doctor says he won't be well enough to come to work for some weeks."

"Strike off his name," said the irritable gentleman. He

33

was cleaning his nails by the window. "Easily replaced. Give the child the week's pay, and let her go."

The plainer man looked worried. "I should be sorry to lose him for good, sir. He's been with us for some years."

"Can't help that. Can't afford to keep sick men."

"No, sir."

The man sighed, and opening a drawer in the desk, pulled out some money. "Tell your father we're very sorry, and if he comes to see us when he's well again we may be able to find something for him, but we can't promise. Here is his pay for the week."

"Are you Mr. Day?"

"Yes."

"I'm to give the copy to you."

She handed over the precious roll and watched him carefully as he skimmed over it. She saw him glance at the signature at the bottom.

"Your father did this last night before he was taken sick?"

"Yes."

"That's another loss, Mr. Hughes. Bob Farquhar takes copy home to correct. It saves paying wages to a second man."

"The copy must be corrected here, then, by one of the others doing extra. Give the child the money and get rid of her."

Mr. Day handed the money to Mary Anne. "I'm sorry," he said.

Mary Anne took the money and left the room. She did not start back home. She went out of the building and stood a little way off, watching, until she saw Mr. Hughes leave and walk away up Fleet Street. Then she returned. She knocked once again on the door marked "Private" and was told to enter. The overseer was writing at his desk. He looked up, surprised.

"You again?" he said. "I gave you the money."

Mary Anne shut the door behind her.

"Was that copy all right?" she asked.

"What do you mean, was it all right? It was clean enough. Had you dropped it in the street?"

"No. I mean, was it correct?"

"Yes. It's gone through into the pressroom."

"No mistakes?"

"No. Your father's very thorough. That's the reason I'm sorry to lose him. But Mr. Hughes is a hard master, as you saw."

"If one of the men corrects the copy here, it will keep him late, won't it, and he will ask for extra money?"

"Yes. But the extra he asks won't be as much as what we now pay your father for his full time."

"The extra would keep my sick father and the rest of us from starving until he's himself again."

The overseer stared at the child.

"Did your father tell you to say this?"

"No. I thought of it myself. If I fetch the copy every evening here, and take it home for him to correct, and bring it back in the morning, that would suit you, wouldn't it, and nothing need be said to Mr. Hughes?"

Mr. Day smiled. The child also smiled. The red ribbon was certainly becoming.

"Why didn't you suggest this when Mr. Hughes was here?"

"Mr. Hughes would have told me to get out."

"How old are you?"

"Thirteen."

"Do you go to school?"

"No. My father doesn't earn enough to send us."

"You could go to the church school."

"My mother says the children there are common."

Mr. Day shook his head in reproof. "You'll grow up very ignorant if you don't go to school. Every child should learn to read and write."

"I can read and write. I taught myself. Can I go back and tell my father you will pay him for correcting copy until he is well again?"

Mr. Day hesitated. His eye was caught again by the red ribbon, the large eyes, the strange self-assurance.

"Very well," he said, "we'll try it for a week. But I don't see how a sick man is going to correct copy. It's not work to be skimped, you know."

"No, sir. I understand that, and so does my father."

"You think he will be well enough in himself to do it? He hasn't got heat stroke, or fever, or anything like that?"

"Oh no."

35

"What is it that's wrong with him, then?"

"He . . . he broke his leg. He fell off a ladder."

"I see. Well, if you come back this evening I'll give you some copy to take to him. Good morning."

When Mary Anne returned home her stepfather was still in bed with the windows closed and the blinds drawn, to keep out the noise and the smells from the alley.

"The doctor's been," said her mother. "He says there's nothing for it but rest and quiet. Did you see Mr. Day?"

"Yes, he said not to worry. He'll pay five shillings a week while father is sick."

"Five shillings a week for no work? That was generous."

"He said father was one of their best men."

The child went upstairs and hid the scarlet ribbon.

During the next three weeks Mary Anne corrected copy and took it backwards and forwards to the overseer without her family knowing. Then, at the beginning of the fourth week, after she had been out in the streets with her brothers one afternoon, her stepfather called to her from his stuffy, airless bedroom, "Mr. Day was here just now."

"Oh."

"He seemed very astonished. He thought I had been laid up with a broken leg."

"I told him that. It sounded more hopeful than apoplexy."

"I didn't have apoplexy, either. I had heat stroke."

"You can't correct copy with heat stroke."

"Exactly."

Mary Anne was silent. Bob Farquhar had caught her out.

"Mr. Day thanked me for correcting the copy. I told him there'd been no copy to correct. Then I guessed what you'd been up to. Did you think of the risk when you did it? Two, three faults might have slipped by, but not half a dozen."

"I went over it four times, and again in daylight, before I took it down to the printing-house."

"No faults?"

"No. Mr. Day would have told me if there had been."

"Well, he knows now that it was you."

36

"What did he say? What will he do to me? Will you lose the work?"

"You're to go down to the printing-house and see him."

She changed into her Sunday frock and put the red ribbon in her hair. Charley, her shadow, watched her anxiously. "Mr. Day's found out what you did. He'll beat you."

"No, he won't. I'm too old to be beaten."

"He'll do something."

She did not answer. She ran out of the alley and down Chancery Lane into Fleet Street, her heart thumping. What if Mr. Hughes was there? Mr. Hughes would certainly order her to be beaten. He might even beat her himself.

Mr. Hughes was not there. There was only Mr. Day, the overseer, in the room with the door marked "Private."

Mary Anne stood meekly, her hands behind her back. Mr. Day had rolls of discarded copy in his hand. Perhaps there had been mistakes after all.

"Well, Mary Anne," he said, "I see you've been trying to make fools of us here at the printing-house."

"No, sir."

"What made you deceive me?"

"We needed the money."

"Your father tells me you'd been correcting copy for some time, even before he was ill. Why did you do it?"

"It was something to read."

"This stuff isn't written for little girls."

"That's why I like reading it."

Mr. Day coughed and laid aside the rolls of copy. Mary Anne wondered what he was going to do. Obviously he intended to punish her.

"How much of it do you understand?" he asked.

"I don't know."

"What did we say about the Prime Minister last week, for instance?"

"You said Billy Pitt held the reins too firmly to be shifted from the saddle, and Charlie Fox had better go play tennis in St. James's Street with the Prince of Wales and Mr. Mucklow who keeps the court. I think that has two meanings, but I'm not sure."

37

Mr. Day looked more shocked and disapproving than ever.

"At least you don't understand the slang in the paper!" he said.

"I know what it means to pick up a flat."

"What does it mean?"

"It's really a term in tennis. But when you print it, it means to hoodwink a chap who doesn't know his onions."

Mr. Day raised his eyebrows.

"I have had a long talk with your father," he said, "and I agreed we should like him back here when he is well. But you are not to correct copy any more. At least, not for the present. You are going to school instead."

"To school?"

"Yes. Not to your parish school, but to a boarding school for young ladies that I know about at Ham in Essex."

Mary Anne stared at Mr. Day in bewilderment. Was he mad?

"I can't go there," she said. "My father hasn't the money to send me, and my mother won't spare me from home."

Mr. Day stood up. He did not look disapproving any longer. He was smiling.

"I have offered to pay for your schooling," he said. "I think you are worth educating. I have a daughter your age at this school at Ham, and I'm sure you'll be happy."

"Does Mr. Hughes know?"

"This is a private matter. It has nothing to do with Mr. Hughes."

The overseer frowned. How peculiar that the child should think of that. He was certainly not going to tell Mr. Hughes, because Mr. Hughes had an unpleasant mind, and would tell his overseer that he had been beguiled by a young baggage who looked more like fifteen than thirteen and wore a red ribbon in her hair with enchanting effect.

"It's very kind of you indeed," said Mary Anne, "but what exactly do you expect to get out of it?"

"We will talk about that in two years' time," he said. He took her to the door and shook her gravely by the hand.

"If the boarding school in Ham is for young ladies,"

she asked him, "does that mean I shall become a young lady too?"

"Yes. If you learn what they teach you."

"Shall I learn to speak proper, not broad?"

"By all means."

Excitement filled the child. This was the beginning of something, the start of adventure. Leave home, leave the alley, become a young lady, and all because she had done something that she was not supposed to do. She had deceived Mr. Day, and Mr. Day was going to educate her. It paid, then, to deceive.

"I will call on your parents again in the course of the week," he said. "And by the way, I understand Bob Farquhar is not your real father, but your stepfather. Your real father was called Thompson. Which name do you prefer to go by when you are at school?"

Mary Anne thought rapidly. The gentleman from Alberdeen. The gentleman attached to the Army. The gentleman who had given her mother better days. This could all be explained to the young ladies at Ham, if only the name were not Thompson. There were so many Thompsons. Mary Anne Thompson. Mary Anne Farquhar. Farquhar sounded better, while in the background loomed the clan Mackenzie.

"Mary Anne Farquhar, if you please," she said.

FOUR: When Mary Anne was fifteen and a half the good woman who had charge of the young ladies' boarding school at Ham told Mr. Day that his protégée had completed her education and there was nothing more they could teach her. She read well, she spoke well, she wrote a fair hand. She was proficient at history and English literature. She could sew and embroider, she could draw, she could play the harp.

But she was mature for her years, and this had caused a certain amount of concern to those who were responsible for the young ladies. Miss Farquhar's appearance was such as to draw attention outside the precincts of the school. She was stared at in church. Bold looks followed her in the street. Messages had been thrown to her over the wall. Someone who should have known better signalled to her from a window in the house opposite, and it was said that Miss Farquhar had signalled back. These things made for anxiety in a scholastic establishment. No doubt Mr. Day would appreciate the fact and remove his protégée to the care of her parents, who could supervise her themselves.

Mr. Day, who drove down to Ham by post-chaise to fetch Mary Anne, was not surprised to hear that people stared at her in church. He found it hard not to stare at her himself. She was not a beauty, but there was something about the eyes, the expression continually changing, and the tilt of the nose that made for great liveliness and charm. Maidenly modesty was not one of her qualities. She rattled away to him in the post-chaise without the slightest embarrassment, and pumped him as to his journalistic progress.

"We were allowed to see the *Morning Post*," she said,

"but it was too dry for my liking. The *Public Advertiser* has all the news. I used to buy that, when we went into town, and hide it under my pillow. I missed your pamphlets, all the same and the Court gossip. I hear the Duke of York is going to marry a German princess with flaxen hair. No more duels for him. And the King doesn't like Mr. Pitt as much as he did, and the Tories are in a state of agitation about the French chopping so many heads off in case the habit is catching and we start doing it over here."

Mr. Day thought to himself that his protégée was going to find life very cramped at home, and he couldn't possibly risk her coming to the printing-house to read copy, or the press would stop working and the paper would never get printed at all. The best plan would be for the young woman—for really he could not call her a child any longer—to act as his housekeeper. He was a widower, and his own daughter still at the boarding school in Ham. Mary Anne would make a most presentable housekeeper, and possibly, as time went on, if his feeling became a little warmer, he would consider taking further steps. He would not rush her with any of these ideas at present. She must go home and see her parents first. But he was persuaded she would soon become tired of life with them.

Three years had seen changes in the Farquhar household. They had left the cramped old home in Bowling Inn Alley for a roomier house in Black Raven Passage, off Cursitor Street, owned by a Mr. Thomas Burnell, a well-known carver in stone and Master of the Masons' Company, who kept a room on the ground floor as an office but let off the rest. The three boys were at school all day, and only Isobel remained with her mother, while her stepfather, Bob Farquhar, though still affectionate, easygoing and good-natured, was now fatter, coarser, and lazier than ever, and very often the worse for drink.

Mary Anne tried to discuss this with her mother, but her mother, proud and reserved, would not be drawn. "Men have their faults," was all she would say. "If it's not one thing, it's the other."

The other, Mary Anne supposed, must be women. Her stepfather sometimes came home very late at night and when he did creep in, sheepish, tipsy, winking an eye at

41

her as he had done when she was younger, she would feel like boxing his ears. Her mother wore a martyred look. She complained without words, and Mary Anne found herself divided between the two and sorry for both. She was young and gay and bursting with life, and she wanted everyone about her to be happy. Meanwhile the days had to be spent in dusting for her mother, and teaching Isobel multiplication, and walking up and down Holborn looking in the shops. Her fine education seemed to be wasted. Charley was still the companion, the favourite, but even he seemed young to her grown-up eye, and when he begged her for stories the romances of Ham in Essex took the place of the silver button and the "Forty-Five."

"What happened then?"

"I didn't answer his note, of course. I threw it away."

"Did you see him in church?"

"Not him. The other one."

"Which did you like best?"

"I didn't fancy either. They were only boys."

Yet waving from a window had been amusing enough, and there was no one to wave to in Black Raven Passage.

After Christmas Bob Farquhar, who had been coming home at three in the morning for several weeks, did not come home at all. Nobody had seen him. He had not turned up at the printing-house, nor at the coffee house, nor at the taverns. An accident was feared, and enquiries were made, but without result. Finally, eight days afterwards, when his distraught wife was preparing to buy crêpe and a widow's bonnet, a laconic note came from the culprit, saying that he had left home for good, and the printing-house too, and had gone to live with a woman in Deptford.

Mrs. Farquhar collapsed. She confessed that she had suspected something of the sort had been going on for years. She had scraped and saved to put aside a little sum that would help them in the eventuality that had now come. But the sum would not last many months. Something would have to be done.

"But he *has* to support you," said Mary Anne. "The law will make him."

"No law can make him do what he doesn't want."

"Then the law should be changed," said Mary Anne.

Injustice—there was always injustice between men and women. Men made the laws to suit themselves. Men did as they pleased, and women suffered for it. There was only one way to beat them, and that was to match your wits against theirs and come out the winner. But when, and how, and where?

"If I could find a rich man, I'd go to him tomorrow," she told Mr. Day.

Mr. Day did not answer. She looked very bewitching as she said it. It was tempting to make some sort of a proposal immediately, but he was cautious. He must feel his way. And he did not want Mrs. Farquhar and a great brood of unruly boys under his roof. That was not his intention at all.

"Of course," he said, "your mother, as a married woman, can plead her coverture when tradespeople press her for bills."

"What do you mean, plead her coverture?"

"The husband is liable for all payments for goods, not the wife. No claim can be made against the wife."

This at least was something. But it did not help much, because as soon as tradespeople knew that her stepfather had deserted her mother they would no longer supply her with goods. If no rent was paid either, Mr. Burnell would turn them out. She must see Mr. Burnell. Something might be done with Mr. Burnell.

"Meanwhile," she pleaded, "will you let me correct copy for you again? I did it once, I can do it now."

She was very persuasive and Mr. Day agreed, but he made the stipulation that Charley should fetch and take back the copy. It was not pleasant for a young lady to hang about Fleet Street.

Mary Anne's next move was to ask Mr. Burnell if they might remain on in Black Raven Passage.

Mr. Burnell possessed a good town house in another part of the city—he used the office because it was handy to his stoneyard in Cursitor Street—and, having won renown for his fine carvings in several churches, he had just been appointed mason to the Inner Temple. This plum had long been his ambition, and he knew himself to be the envy of all his colleagues. Word had already got round of his appointment, and he was receiving congratulations from callers when Mary Anne descended the staircase from the floor above. A busy man, he had little time to notice the Farquhars. They seemed a good sort of people, and gave no trouble, and paid their rent, which was all that was necessary. He had nodded to the daughter home from boarding school when he had passed her in the entrance, but had never observed her closely. This must be she, then, joining in the congratulations and speaking so enthusiastically of his future appointment.

"Is it Miss Farquhar? Yes, it is. I was not sure. Yes, thank you indeed. Very gratifying."

Quite a young lady, surprising. The father seemed a common sort of fellow. So she knew about the monuments at Culworth, and at Marston St. Lawrence? Had read about them in a newspaper? Fancy remembering. Yes, the stonework at Culworth had proved most successful.

Before he knew how it happened the other callers had gone, and Miss Farquhar was telling him about her rogue of a stepfather, who had disappeared without leaving an address, so that it was impossible to get any money out of him to pay the rent.

"So I was wondering, Mr. Burnell, now you will be having so much work in the Inner Temple, whether you expect to employ several apprentices who will have to be housed and boarded? I know my mother would be delighted to lodge them for you, so close to your yard in Cursitor Street. If we did that, then we could pay the rent just the same as before, and you would have none of the bother of wondering what to do with the house yourself."

She spoke quickly, with a disarming smile, and he found himself agreeing to everything she said. Certainly he would be employing more apprentices. How many rooms could they spare? Actually, only two, she admitted, but then taking only two lodgers would ensure greater comfort. Any more than two would make a crowd—Mr. Burnell would understand that—and they might be rowdy, and naturally that would never do, for it would reflect upon Mr. Burnell.

Mr. Thomas Burnell was given no time to disagree. She had it decided, had paid him a quarter's rent in advance (borrowed from Mr. Day) to seal the new bargain, and had taken herself upstairs again to inform her mother of the transaction before he had given the matter two minutes of serious thought. He supposed it would work out in practice, and it was really of not much importance. What happened in the Inner Temple meant more to him than a little trifle about lodgings in Black Raven Passage.

Mary Anne experienced rather more difficulty with her family. Her mother, as with any new suggestion, looked apprehensive.

"Lodgers!" she exclaimed. "Coming in with dirty boots and throwing their things all over the place."

"The boys do that already. Two more won't make any difference."

"Besides, which rooms shall we give them?"

"There are two good rooms in the attic."

"I shall hardly know how to feed them. They will be bound to have large appetites."

"They will be paying for their appetites, don't forget that."

"I don't know what to say, Mary Anne. Lodgers. It's hardly genteel."

"It's hardly genteel to starve in the street. If we don't take lodgers, we shall."

"I think you should ask advice from Mr. Day."

"Mr. Day has nothing to do with it."

Mrs. Farquhar protested, the boys grumbled, but Mary Anne had her way. The attics were scrubbed, curtains were hung at the small windows, and strips of matting ordered from a shop in Holborn and placed to the account of Mr. Burnell.

"Very nice, very pleasant," said Mr. Burnell after a hasty inspection of the two attics, and without an idea that he was expected to pay for the carpets. "And, of course, the whole thing only in the nature of an experiment. James Burton, who is doing very well in the building trade, needs temporary accommodations—a Scot, like yourself, Mrs. Farquhar. I have suggested that he come here to lodge. And a young apprentice, Joseph Clarke, son of an old friend of mine—you may have heard of him, Thomas Clarke the builder on Snow Hill. Very respectable men, both of them, you shouldn't have any difficulty with either."

45

He bustled off to his business in the Inner Temple, leaving Mrs. Farquhar a prey to nerves.

"These gentlemen won't expect attics," she said. "They will take one look at the rooms, and go away."

"Nonsense!" said Mary Anne. "The Scot will think only of his pocket, and board cheaper with us than elsewhere. If the other is young he'll sleep sound, and the harder the bed the sweeter the dreams. But please don't refer to them as the attics. The rooms are on the third floor."

A few finishing touches, a picture or two, a twist to the curtain, a flick to a mirror. It only remained for the boarders to arrive.

Unfortunately Mary Anne was not in Black Raven Passage at the exact moment when Mr. Burton and Mr. Clarke chose to install themselves. She had it all arranged that she and her mother would receive them in the parlour (no longer called the living-room—nobody had talked of a living-room at Ham), and after a few minutes' polite conversation she was to escort the boarders to the third floor and leave them to unpack. After which dinner, not supper, would be served at six o'clock.

Fate willed otherwise. Mary Anne, having called on Mr. Day at the printing-house in Fleet Street to borrow a further loan, money being a little tight until the lodgers paid the first instalment, returned home later than she expected, to find her mother in a fluster.

"They've come," she said, " and I hardly knew what to do, so I took them to the rooms at once. One of them came down almost immediately and said he was dining out and did not want any dinner. The second is up there now, and he has called to me twice. Once to say there was not a wardrobe fit to hang his clothes, and the second time to know who was going to brush his boots for him. I suppose it was weak of me, but I told him he must wait until my daughter came home, that she had made the arrangements."

Mrs. Farquhar was flushed from running up and down the stairs.

"You were perfectly right," said Mary Anne, "if he's going to make trouble, I'll deal with him." She paused, her hand on the banister. "What do they look like?" she whispered.

"The one who went out I didn't notice," said Mrs. Farquhar, "but the one upstairs is tall and dark."

A thumping sound came from above. The lodger was banging the floor. Mrs. Farquhar looked anxious. "That means he wants something," she said, "that's what he did twice before."

Mary Anne went upstairs, a light of battle in her eyes. Before she arrived at the third floor the door of one of the attics opened and a young man, without a coat, wearing a fine linen shirt and busily tying a silk cravat, looked down upon her.

"Ah!" he said. "Just in time. I was afraid I should have to wander down all those stairs in my stockinged feet. My boots are dusty. Will you please shine them for me?"

Mary Anne looked at him. She wanted to smack his face, and smack it hard. The fact that he was the best-looking young man she had hitherto seen in her life was of small importance. Business came first, and her status.

"I can get your boots cleaned for you," she said coldly, "but that is not included in the board and lodging. It will cost you extra." She would bribe Charley, or George, or Eddie. The boys could take it in turns. They could clean them in the back kitchen, out of sight.

"I don't mind who cleans my boots," said the young man, "as long as they clean them well. I happen to be rather particular." Her cool gaze was disconcerting. He had expected a servant. This was something very different, and for once he was at a loss for words.

"I beg your pardon," he said, "but whom am I addressing? My name is Joseph Clarke. At your service."

"I am Mary Anne Farquhar," she replied. "I make all arrangements in this house. I gather your friend has gone out to dinner. Will you be dining out too?"

He hesitated a moment. He glanced back over his shoulder at the disorder of his room, the choice of coats, cravats, the preparations for a night on the town. Then he glanced once more at Mary Anne.

"No," he said. "If convenient to you, I should prefer to dine at home."

FIVE: Joseph Clarke made it quite clear to them all, this first evening, that there was no necessity for him to earn his living. His father was a rich man and he could lead a life of leisure if he chose. But he had talent, and his father did not like to see this talent wasted. Hence his apprenticeship to Thomas Burnell.

"But of course," he said carelessly. "I am not tied in any way. Not like your usual apprentice. I can leave Burnell when it suits me to do so, and perhaps set up on my own. I have not made up my mind."

The Farquhars watched him with interest. The boys, with scrubbed hands for once, and parted hair, were silent from respect, young Isobel from awe. Their mother, on edge from sudden entertaining after a lapse of years, tried to remember at what point to serve the wine, and whether it was vulgar to put cheese upon the table. Luckily, any faults of etiquette were covered up by her daughter. A boy who stretched his hand across the cloth was slain by a frown. A boy who suddenly hiccoughed had his shin kicked beneath the table. Isobel's second helping was whisked from under her nose and handed to the boarder with a smile.

The boarder noticed nothing. He was too busy talking about himself.

"My father has retired," he told them, "and my brothers carry on the business at Snow Hill. They make a very good thing of it. My youngest brother has just gone to Cambridge. He intends to become a parson. Have you ever met an uncle of mine, Alderman Clarke? He expects to be Lord Mayor of London one of these days."

The boarder drank the wine: he was appreciative. He refused the cheese: he was fastidious. Yes, indeed (in

48

answer to a question from Mrs. Farquhar), he feared he never touched fats of any kind. His digestion would not stand it. The delicate child had grown into the delicate young man.

This was another reason why he was unable to work long hours—he tired easily. Surely it would be better, then, to live in the pure air of the country? The boarder wrinkled his nose in disgust. Certainly not. He would be bored to death in the country. What were his pursuits? He confessed to a fondness for games of chance, but only against skilled players and for high stakes. He had a mild interest in the turf. Last season he had persuaded his elder brother to buy a curricle. They had raced it to Brighton for a wager, and won two hundred pounds. He liked music, singing, going to the playhouse. Politics were not his line, and the affairs of the day not worth discussing.

"We were put into this world to enjoy ourselves," he said, "to do what pleases us best. Miss Farquhar, don't you agree?"

Miss Farquhar *did* agree. Before the meal was over she had forgotten the original request to shine his boots. This young man with his mournful eyes, his Roman nose, his languid manner, his aristocratic ways was another matter from the pimpled fellow who had stared at her in church, or the lanky youth who had waved to her so ardently from the house opposite the boarding school in Ham.

This was the type who was having his head chopped off in France. He might have stepped straight off a tumbril. There was romance in every gesture. Later, as the evening wore on and they were alone together in the parlour, her mother having vanished discreetly to the kitchen with the boys and Isobel, he admitted to her that he had been unhappy under his father's roof ever since his mother died.

"My father makes no excuse for temperament," he said, "elation one moment, despair the next. The only thing that counts in his eyes is solid achievement. Sometimes I have been prostrate with fatigue. He calls it idleness. I need the stimulation of good company. He terms this riffraff. The plain fact is, I am misunderstood."

Mary Anne listened, enraptured. For three years she had heard nothing but female chitchat, the only male voice the rector of Ham's when he visited the school on Sunday.

The tavern gossip of her stepfather and his cronies had been good in days gone by, but this was different. For the first time in her life she had a handsome young man all to herself, only too ready to pour out his heart. The head could be forgotten. The soul was all.

"When I saw you on the stairs this evening I felt an instant sympathy between us, a bond of recognition. You felt it too?" he said.

She had wanted to slap his face, but no matter. That was over. Wine, to which she was unaccustomed, loosened the tongue.

"To tell you the truth, I care for no one in this neighbourhood," she answered. "Keeping house for my mother is a dull occupation. I want much more out of life than that."

What did she want? She did not know. But as he stared at her in admiration something hitherto unawakened stirred within her. The combination of artist and young gentleman of leisure was intoxicating to a girl fresh from school. The genteel ways of Ham had temporarily softened the sharp perception of the cockney child. At fifteen, emotions ripened, the pulse quickened, but intuition flagged.

Mary Anne was ready for her first love affair. At this moment almost anyone would have sufficed. A printer from the house of Mr. Hughes, a butcher's boy with bright eyes up the passage, a stranger alighting from a coach in Holborn and raising his hat at sight of her—all these laid the foundations of a dream, and here was the dream personified in the person of Joseph Clarke, aged twenty-one.

Propinquity was all that was necessary, the sharing of a common roof. Black Raven Passage was not so much broader than Bowling Inn Alley, but the full moon looked better from the doorstep. The sky had fulness, the drains were more discreet. It was possible to see the stars from an attic window, even with a jealous young brother thumping the ceiling of the room below.

James Burton, the other boarder, gave no trouble. A man of thirty, hard-working, with many friends, he returned to his lodgings to sleep, and that was all. Joseph and Mary Anne were thrown together.

The first kiss took her by surprise and startled her. Scuffles there had been before, with playmates in Bowling

50

Inn Alley, sniggers and pinches and boxings-of-ears. Tomboy foolery. Now she was faced with reality. Joseph Clarke, an apprentice still, had yet to prove his worth as a carver of stone: he needed no credentials as a lover. Neither rough nor brusque, he kissed with determination. The apologetic peck was not for him, nor the murmur, "Forgive me."

Mary Anne experienced in full measure the torment and ecstasy of the first embrace. She went to her room bewildered, happy, but instinct warned her, "This is one of the things I keep from Mother."

From Charley too, who watched, suspicious, at half-open doors, who noticed that Joseph's socks were mended and not his own, that the boarder had the white meat from the fowl and he the leg.

Mary Anne was in love. She had no thought for anyone but Joseph. The day was interminable until he returned from the stoneyard; so interminable that she was forced to pass it two or three times during the course of the day, on invented errands. He would break off from his work to come to her, advancing with that slow and easy step she found so irresistible, and while they talked by the wall she knew that the other apprentices were watching her, appraising her, coupling their names together, thus adding to excitement.

Yet the adult world was hostile to first love, frowning, disapproving. First love was something to conceal from prying eyes.

"You were very late to bed last night. I heard your door. What were you doing?"

"I was chatting to Joseph Clarke."

"Was Mr. Burton with you?"

"No . . . He had gone out."

There was silence, a chill air. Nothing further was said, but in a flash Mary Anne was reminded of former silences, former chills, when Bob Farquhar had seized his stick and sauntered down the alley to take the air. Now she sympathised and understood. There must be secrecy.

"Mrs. Farquhar, ma'am, would you permit Miss Mary Anne to take a walk with me this evening after dinner? It's a pity to stay indoors on such a fine night."

"A walk? I had rather expected her to stay with me.

51

There is so much sewing to be done, and she knows my eyesight is poor."

"Mother, the sewing can be done in the morning, when the light is better."

"I don't know why anyone should wish to take a walk when they would be more comfortable at home."

The mute reproach, the sigh, the weary stretching for the workbasket. How could her mother know what it was like to walk up Ludgate Hill on the arm of Joseph Clarke, to see the dome of St. Paul's by the light of the moon? She signalled with her eyes to her lover, impatient to be gone, and presently, when her mother was intent upon the sewing, Mary Anne slipped from the room and joined him.

"Can I come with you?" asked Charley, sullen, reproachful too.

"No."

"Why not?"

"We don't want you." And then, relenting, "Well, just as far as Fleet Street, but no further."

The walk, troubling and exciting amongst the crowds who frequented the taverns and the coffeehouses, served as an excuse for the late return. The narrow courts and alleys gave them shelter, dark doorways a haven from a shower, St. Paul's, sounding midnight, an echo to stammered words. "Mary Anne, I can't live without you."

"But what can we do? Where can we go?"

The first exuberance, the thrill of discovery, passed to guile and all the complications of secrecy—the terror of the creaking door, the hazard of the dark stair, a footfall too loud, a clumsy stumble. These things awakened a sleeping house. Moments that should be prolonged were hastened through fear; finesse and the tender approach were skipped to achieve finality.

Unfortunately facilities did not improve as appetite increased. There was no alternative to the parlour in the small hours. Here they were found, one April morning, by Mrs. Farquhar, who, on pretence of hearing rats in the wainscot but inwardly suspicious for many nights, descended at last the creaking stair.

Escape was impossible, bluster out of the question. They were caught. The immediate result was tears—not from Mary Anne, but from her mother.

52

"How *could* you behave so? After all I have taught you and impressed upon you. Creeping down here in the dark like one of the little sluts in the alley. And you, Joseph Clarke, you call yourself the son of a gentleman, accepting board and lodging from me, knowing full well that Mary Anne has no father to protect her."

The whole house was roused. The boys came tumbling from their beds.

"What's happened? What have they done?"

James Burton, seizing the situation in a glance, retreated, with raised eyebrows, to his room.

This, then, was shame. This was something that should never be. She had been found out, discovered, made to look guilty and foolish and young.

"I don't care," said Mary Anne loudly. "I love him. He loves me. We are going to be married. Aren't we, Joseph?"

Why did he not answer at once? Why did he stand there with that odd, sheepish look on his face? Why did he stammer something about not knowing his prospects, he was uncertain of getting his father's permission, they were both rather young to marry, he was sorry for Mrs. Farquhar being disturbed, they had heard rats, they were doing no harm?

"But it's not true. We were not looking for rats. We do love each other. And of course we intend to be married."

Mary Anne, passionate, outraged, turned to her mother. Joseph stood dumbly, the weak, ineffectual smile marring the handsome face.

Some latent strength came to the aid of Mrs. Farquhar, perhaps the memory of Mr. Thompson and the better days. She held herself with dignity.

"There is no question of marriage. Joseph Clarke leaves my house in the morning with a letter to Mr. Burnell. Mary Anne, you are not yet sixteen and are under my care. Please go to your room."

The moment of storm was over. The aftermath set in. Mary Anne went to her room and locked the door, and now it was she who wept, and not her mother. Her tears were not for the discovery, but for the memory of Joseph, anxious, awkward, unable to say a word in defence of love.

She stayed in her room all day. She heard the sounds of removal, of luggage being bumped downstairs. Isobel, with a scared face, brought her some food which she did not touch.

No longer was she Miss Farquhar, who made all the arrangements for the house. She was a child of fifteen, hurt, disgraced, and most painfully in love.

It was like a house of mourning. Voices were hushed. Callers came. First Mr. Burnell. Next Mr. Day. Would the third be the principal of the boarding school in Ham? Was she to be sent back there at once?

"I won't!" she said to herself. "I shall run away."

She longed suddenly for her stepfather, Bob Farquhar. He would not have scolded. He would have understood. He would have patted her shoulder, with a twinkle in his eye, and said, "So the monkey slipped. Where's her rich husband now?"

There was only one answer to her turmoil of mind. She must find Joseph, and once he was alone with her she would obtain his promise of marriage. His father's permission did not matter, for Joseph was of age. He had told her repeatedly that money played a small part in his life. His father was rich. Joseph could work or not, just as he pleased. He could leave Mr. Burnell and set up on his own, or do nothing. It did not matter. Once she and Joseph were married, everything would be all right. What had seemed like deceit would be looked upon with favour. A married woman could do no wrong. Her mother would relent.

Mary Anne's natural optimism returned. She had only to gain her mother's consent and find Joseph, and the future was assured.

It was not, however, this kind of future that Mrs. Farquhar had in mind. Her plans were very different.

"I am not going to speak of what has happened," she said that night to her daughter. "I am to blame for permitting lodgers under my roof. I always disliked the idea, and my dislike was well founded. Joseph Clarke has left here for good and he has left Mr. Burnell also. Mr. Burnell, like the true gentleman he is, was horrified at his conduct and has written to his father. We are all of us well rid of him."

"Where has Joseph gone?"

"I did not enquire. And if I knew I should not tell you.

His whereabouts do not concern you because you are also going away."

"If you mean I'm to go back to Ham, I refuse. I'm grown-up, I'm too old for school."

"I was not speaking of school. There is no question of that. You are to go as housekeeper to Mr. Day."

Mary Anne burst out laughing. "You must be mad. I should never consider such a thing. I have seen his house, a stuffy, mournful place in Islington, and I don't much care for Mr. Day, a pernickety, preaching sort of man."

Her mother looked at her in disapproval. This was her daughter's answer to all her benefactor had done for her. A pernickety, preaching man.

"Mr. Day has behaved very generously. I told him what had happened and he agreed that you are in need of protection, of a father's protection. By becoming his housekeeper he can give you just that. After what happened last night, it is too much responsibility for me."

"Very well."

The sudden change of mind should have warned Mrs. Farquhar. But she was too anxious to have her daughter out of harm's way to question her further.

To Mary Anne the solution was simple. She could do as she pleased at Mr. Day's, and as soon as he left for the printing-house in the morning she would look for Joseph. Nothing was easier.

The atmosphere of mourning departed from the house. The boys whistled once again, all except Charley, who wept and refused to be consoled.

The following day Mary Anne left for Islington in a hackney carriage. She was received by Mr. Day, a little graver than his custom, perhaps, on first meeting, but presently unbending, and later, when he handed her the keys of the store-cupboard, positively cheerful.

"I think we shall suit one another very well," he said. "No homesickness, I trust, and no regrets."

She asked him at what time he would want his breakfast before leaving for the printing-house in the morning.

He looked at her in surprise.

"Didn't your mother tell you?" he said. "I have retired from the printing-house. I made up my mind to it some time ago. I intend to spend my days at home, with my

55

books and other interests. These things we can share. We shall get on capitally. Later, when my daughter returns from school, you will have her companionship too, but in the meantime my company must suffice."

He smiled, he bowed, his manner was altogether gallant. This was quite ridiculous. Mary Anne had not bargained for a Mr. Day at home. She had hoped to shut the door on him at half-past eight in the morning. It was all part of a plot, then, between him and her mother, so that she should not escape supervision.

Mary Anne did her mother an injustice. The plot was Mr. Day's. It was true that he had left the printing-house and had done very well for himself. But Mrs. Farquhar's account of her daughter's lapse from grace had fired his imagination. The young woman needed discipline, but discipline of a kind they might mutually enjoy.

Far from Mary Anne shutting the door upon him at half-past eight in the morning, she found herself locking the door on him at half-past ten at night. She had retired early, worn with the emotions of the preceding days, and, hearing his knock, thought something must be wrong, that he was ill, that the house was burning. She saw him standing there, candlestick in hand, a nightcap on his head, a foolish, hopeful, unattractive figure.

Then she knew. She slammed the door in his face and turned the key. Clothes did not matter. A drainpipe close to her window served as exit in the first light of morning. So that was why he had educated her at Ham. But he had not reckoned on Joseph. The final touch was his.

SIX: She had enough money for a hackney carriage. She would leave Islington in style, as she had come—no trudging of streets in the small hours, with every passer-by a potential Mr. Day. The lesson had been learnt. The trouble was that no one would believe her story, least of all her mother. The respected Mr. Day a wolf in sheep's clothing? Never! Mary Anne must have imagined the whole thing. Mr. Day would have his own version. A man past forty was to be trusted before a girl of fifteen.

Jogging back to Holborn in the hackney carriage, Mary Anne decided upon two things. The first, to remember in future that face value counted for nothing, that every act of apparent generosity hid an ulterior motive, and one motive only, when the benefactor was male. The second, not to return home until she was married, when, flaunting a ring and her marriage certificate, she would have the whip-hand over her mother. Mary Anne would be the benefactress then. The daughter-in-law of rich Mr. Clarke of Snow Hill would have a very different status from Miss Farquhar of Black Raven Passage. No necessity for lodgers any more. Her mother, Isobel, the boys would appreciate at long last the better days. Mrs. Joseph Clark would keep them all.

She had nothing with her but the clothes she wore and a few shillings in a small purse, but she was young and her hopes were high.

She stepped with dignity from the hackney carriage and paid the man his fare. Then she went to find James Burton in the Inner Temple. Yes, it was true. Joseph had left Mr. Burnell. There had been, said James Burton, a devil of a scrap. Joseph had torn up his articles of apprenticeship and thrown them on the ground at Mr. Bur-

57

nell's feet. Mr. Burnell had called Joseph a waster and a seducer of young girls. Joseph had called Mr. Burnell a bully and a miser.

"Yes," said Mary Anne impatiently, "but where is Joseph now?"

"In lodgings in Clerkenwell," said Burton. "I can give you his address. He is full of wild ideas of going to America. I took him on the town last night, and he got very drunk. We ended up at the 'Ring O' Bells' at three. Joseph had the luck to win ten pounds at hazard. If you go to his lodgings now you'll find him asleep."

The lodginghouse in Clerkenwell, though situated in a street and not in a passage, was a different affair from Mrs. Farquhar's trim dwelling. The front door stood wide open. Anyone could pass in. A thin child on her knees scrubbed the dirty entrance, watched by a lounging woman with painted cheeks. The place had an air of shabby, stale neglect.

"Clarke? Second floor back, first door," said the woman, jerking her head.

Mary Anne went up the narrow stairs, high spirits momentarily damped. If Joseph was too proud to return to his father's house, surely he might have chosen somewhere better than this in which to lodge.

He was asleep, just as James Burton had surmised. If he had really been drunk the night before he showed little sign of it. His face was flushed, perhaps, but the flush was becoming. He had the childish look of innocence that Charley wore when sleeping, and Mary Anne knew that she loved him more than ever. She tiptoed about the room, restoring the disorder, the clothes flung anyhow on the floor, then lay down beside him on the bed.

When Joseph awoke to find Mary Anne upon his pillow, any ideas he may have had of sailing to America died a natural death. Propinquity had its instant fatal effect. And they were no longer under the parental roof. Creaking stairs held no menace in a lodginghouse where questions were not asked.

By midafternoon nothing mattered in the whole world but that they were together again. The future was theirs. They could do what they liked with it.

"Nothing but this," said Joseph dreamily, "day after

day, night after night. No rising early, no Tommy Burnell, no plans."

"We have to eat," said Mary Anne, "and I don't think much of this room. There is no blind to the window and the bed's too small."

He told her she had no temperament. She told him he had no common sense. At half-past seven they went out to dinner.

If Joseph's idea of a lodginghouse was below his station, his idea of where to eat was distinctly above. Not for him a hole-and-corner tavern off one of the alleys. They must dine in splendour in the Strand. Nor would they go on foot, they must go by chair.

Mutton and ale? Good heavens, what a suggestion. Sweet-breads, and a light French wine. A duckling to follow, but it must be tender. His manner of ordering was magnificent, his manner of paying better still. Servingmen bowed low before him. If he was unsteady when he stood upon his feet in the open air it did not really matter— he looked so handsome—and it was such an easy matter to summon another chair.

"What now? The Opera?" he suggested, jingling his change. The thought was tempting, but how much was left of the ten pounds he had won at hazard? Mary Anne shook her head. "Not tonight," she said, and was just in time to catch him as he fell. It was, after all, a very good thing that no questions were asked in the lodginghouse at Clerkenwell.

During the days that followed Mary Anne realized that she must be the practical one of the two. She must take charge. Joseph, rejoicing in his freedom from apprenticeship, wished for nothing more than to lie abed until after midday, and then to saunter abroad and take the air. "Why look ahead? Why plan?" he used to say, then fall to discussing where they might dine that night. Money? Pooh! No worry. He had plenty for the time being. Later, if he found himself short, he could always win another tenner at hazard, and if the worst came to the worst, and pride must be humbled, he would condescend to approach his father. Meanwhile, it was so pleasant to be idle, to make love.

While Joseph slumbered on her shoulder, Mary Anne

planned the moves ahead. The first step was to make her whereabouts known to Charley, so that the boy could act as go-between, fetching clothes, necessities, even food, if possible, from the house in Black Raven Passage. This was easy. Charley, stifling his jealousy, gave way to adventure and romance. If the descendant of the clan Mackenzie could not crawl in the heather with a dirk between his teeth, he could at least slip out of his mother's house with loaves in a basket, and receive a shilling for his pains.

He reported shock and alarm at home. Mr. Day, primed with his own version of the night at Islington, had declared Mary Anne a baggage. Mrs. Farquhar had posted her daughter missing. Descriptions of both Mary Anne and Joseph had been forwarded to the newspapers. The same descriptions had been nailed to the doors of shops, taverns, eating-houses.

"You'll have to shift lodgings or you'll be caught," warned Charley. "And then you'll both be brought to trial and sent to prison."

"We can't be sent to prison for being in love," said Mary Anne.

"You can if you're not married," returned Charley. "I heard Mr. Day say so. They call it living in sin, and he should know."

He should indeed. A bunch of housekeeping keys was the answer to him.

"We'll have to get married. That's all there is to it. Joseph, do you hear?"

Joseph, his feet over the bedrail, his head pillowed in cushions, was manicuring his nails. A pleasant, soporific occupation. He yawned. "I know nothing of legal affairs," he said, "and I care less. But you are under the age of consent—you are only fifteen. So how do we get over that?"

This was the poser. Her mother held the trump card still, unless . . . What if Bob Farquhar could be found? And, once found, bribed, cajoled, coaxed, threatened, blackmailed into giving his consent as legal protector? Here was the germ of an idea, and once it took root in her mind it expanded and grew.

The search for Bob Farquhar had never been thorough. It had been left entirely to Mr. Day. And now she knew

Mr. Day better, Mary Anne could well believe his interest had lain in quite an opposite direction. It would never have suited Mr. Day to find her stepfather. She could imagine the familiar wink, the well-remembered chuckle.

"Housekeeper? Fiddlesticks!" he would have said.

Mary Anne pulled the pillows from under Joseph's head and dragged him to his feet. He stared down at her, yawning, useless, reluctant, but impossibly handsome.

"What now?"

"Hurry and dress yourself. We're going to Deptford."

Bob Farquhar was elusive. He was slippery. He was sly. It was not for nothing that he had printed scandal sheets for twenty years. He knew all the ropes—where to disappear, where to hide, how to prepare for himself a comfortable nest with an amiable companion, and so escape responsibility and a reproving wife.

Yes, he had been seen at the Crown and Anchor, but not for three weeks. A square, heavy fellow with a twinkle in his eye? Yes, but not at the Crown and Anchor, at the White Hart. Five days, eight days ago. Lodging after lodging was tried in vain. Deptford knew him not. Finally, the last inn on the London road had firmer news.

"Farquhar? A party of that name was here two nights ago. Man and wife. Room Number Four. They took the coach to London, and the daughter too."

Wife and daughter. It was not living in sin. It was bigamy. If you were found committing bigamy there must be punishment for that.

"Did they say where they were going?"

"No. But I heard the daughter talk about Pancras Fields."

Back to London, the other side of town. And while they were about it, she and Joseph, would it not be wise to flit themselves?

The painted sloven who kept the lodginghouse in Clerkenwell had stared after them suspiciously that morning, and she had a copy of the *Advertiser* in her hand. Charley must be go-between again. Charley must be sent to collect their few belongings and bring them to the next address. The next address was Pancras, on the outskirts of town. If her stepfather were in this district he should be easy to find. It was hardly more than a village, and there were only two taverns.

"But this is the end of the earth," protested Joseph. "I can see a farm across the way, and cows grazing. We shall bore ourselves to death in such a spot."

A kiss, a word of love, a rumpling of his hair, and he was as easy to handle as Charley. She left him hanging his cravats in a line from wall to wall.

Bob Farquhar was at neither tavern. The second one gave her the hint, and she found them sitting down to a homely meal of bacon, bread, and cheese in a small house the other side of Pancras Fields. Opposite him was a stout, comfortable woman of his own age who could never have known better days, and a very plain-looking girl who, oddly enough, bore a strong resemblance to Bob Farquhar.

Whoever hits hardest always wins, thought Mary Anne. She prepared her blow.

"So we've found you at last," she said. "I have the whole family outside in a hackney carriage, and two lawyers. What do you propose to do?"

To her chagrin her stepfather did not seem disturbed. He leant back in his chair and pulled out a newspaper from his pocket.

"I can always read them the *Advertiser*," he said. "Missing from her home since April the seventeenth, Mary Anne Thompson, alias Farquhar, daughter of Elizabeth Mackenzie Farquhar, of 2 Black Raven Passage, Cursitor Street, being fifteen and three-quarters years of age, blue eyes, light brown hair, fresh complexion, neat in person,' etc., etc. Or have you seen a copy of this already?"

He tossed it across to her and she caught it from habit, as she might have done the pamphlets in old days, in Bowling Inn Alley.

"Since we've both given your mother the slip, let's call it quits," said Bob Farquhar. "Meet Mrs. Farquhar Number Two, or Mrs. Favoury, as she used to be called, and Martha, the hope of our declining years."

Dignity was out of the question, further pretence impossible. In a moment Mary Anne was sitting with them, eating bread and cheese. "The point is," she said, "if I give you away you do the same to me. There's nothing in it. We're dependent on each other."

"That's fair sense," he answered.

"You're a bigamist."

"And you need slapping."

"I've only known Joseph eight weeks, but he's the one man in the world for me."

"I've known Mrs. Favoury seventeen years, and it's taken me that long to decide between her and your mother."

"You went backwards and forwards between them?"

"I could hardly fix both at the same time."

Mrs. Favoury, not in the least put out, drank tea and beamed upon them. Mary Anne, remembering the silent reproach of her mother, thought it odd that her stepfather had taken as much as seventeen years to come to his decision. Still, he had made the best of both worlds. And it was no longer remarkable that Martha had his nose and eyes.

"So you've set your heart on this fellow?"

"We've set our hearts on each other."

"Prospects good?"

"He has a rich father."

"That's more than you have. Will his father play fair?"

"He will when he meets me."

"H'm. Marry in haste, repent at leisure."

"Marry at length, no youth together."

She was not going to wait seventeen years for Joseph Clarke, whatever her stepfather might have done for Mrs. Favoury.

"All right. What do you want me to do?"

"Give your consent, as my father."

"Who'll pay the licence?"

"Joseph will. He does as he's told. I'll arrange it. We can be married here, in Pancras. I saw the church from the road."

Bob Farquhar sighed. "We'll have to flit again afterwards," he said. "Once I put my name to your marriage certificate here they'll find me. Your mother will demand her dues."

"I'll take care of Mother."

"Come along, then, and let's take a look at your fancy fellow."

Mutual suspicion made both men wary. The contrast

between them was great. The one tall, elegant, disdainful; the other short, thick-set, and bluff. They eyed each other like two dogs before a fight. It was no moment for parlour talk, for pleasantries, for exchange of views. The situation called for an immediate visit to the nearest tavern. They remained within for two hours, and emerged like brothers.

"Remember always, my dear," said Mrs. Favoury to Mary Anne as they watched the two men coming towards them arm-in-arm, "there is nothing in life that can't be settled with a glass. Or perhaps two glasses. It opens the heart and deadens the brain, which is just what we women want with our men. You can take it, the marriage is on."

She was right. Consent had been given. The following day, while the two men slept off the effect of the bond between them, Mrs. Favoury and Mary Anne bought the licence and saw the curate of St. Pancras church. Mrs. Favoury agreed that neither she nor the round-faced Martha, her eyes agog with excitement, should be present at the ceremony, for fear of disclosure. Mary Anne slipped two shillings into the hands of the gravedigger, who agreed to act as witness on the day. Nothing remained but to bring the bridegroom to the altar.

"Joseph, wake up! It's our wedding morning."

"Wet or fine?"

"Fine. Not a cloud in the sky."

"All the more reason to stay in bed. The day will keep." He yawned, he stretched, he permitted himself to be dressed. That shirt, the cambric one, not worn before. No, no, the satin waistcoat. Cravats? But it would take him half the day to match that waistcoat. He had seen just the thing in a hosiery shop in the Strand. Could they not take a hackney carriage and drive to the Strand before going to the church? Impossible. The time was fixed. The curate waited.

"Do you like my gown? I bought it yesterday. Mrs. Favoury was generous."

"I think it enchanting. But why pink? Pink will clash with the salmon of my cravat."

"No one will notice. Not in the early morning. Please make haste."

It was the nineteenth day of May, seventeen hundred and ninety-two. They walked across the fields to the little church of Pancras in warm sunshine, hand in hand. It was not only Mary Anne's wedding morning, but her sixteenth birthday.

Halfway to the church Joseph clapped his hand to his coat pocket. "Something fearful has happened. I've forgotten the licence."

"I have it. And there has to be a second witness. I thought of that too."

"Who is it?"

"The gravedigger at Pancras church. I've given him two shillings for his pains. Hurry. They're waiting."

Bob Farquhar, a flower in his buttonhole, was standing in the porch with the minister by his side.

"We thought you'd changed your mind after all," he said.

Mary Anne held on to Joseph's arm and smiled. "Never in this world," she answered.

Her stepfather looked at them and wondered. The young dandy, with his remote, disdainful air. Mary Anne, flushed, excited, radiant in her new pink gown. "Let's hope you feel the same about him in ten years' time," he said.

The Reverend Sawyer led them into the church. It was very simple, very plain. A gleam of sunshine filtered through the stained window to the whitewashed walls. Outside they could hear the birds singing from the cluster of elms beside the church, and the distant baaing of the sheep in Pancras fields.

Mary Anne made her responses in a clear, decided voice. Joseph was inaudible. Afterwards, in the vestry, she signed her name first, above his, in the book.

"And the honeymoon?" enquired the minister, charmed to have made the innocent couple man and wife. "Where is that to be spent?" He passed the marriage certificate to Joseph and awaited the reply. Joseph turned enquiringly to his bride. The honeymoon having gone delightfully the past five weeks, surely there was to be no change? Life was to continue as before—driving, dining, spending in the busy whirl of London, bed long after midnight, rising around noon.

Mary Anne smiled. Curtseying to the Reverend Sawyer, she took the marriage certificate from Joseph's hands.

"We are going to Hampstead," she said. "My husband is in need of rest, fresh milk, and country air."

She stared steadily at Joseph. Joseph stared back at her. Bob Farquhar chuckled and nudged the gravedigger in the ribs.

It was the first challenge.

SEVEN: They had been into the subject again and again, but nothing ever came of it. Argument was useless: they had reached an impasse.

"Then you lied to me all along?"

"I never lie. It's far too much trouble."

"You told all of us, that first evening in Black Raven Passage, that you had plenty of money."

"So I had, at the time. It went very fast. I can always make more."

"How do you propose to do that?"

"By cards—by speculation, by backing horses. Something will turn up."

"But your father. You told me your father was rich, that you could always get money from him!"

"It's a little involved."

"What do you mean, involved?"

She put her hands on his shoulders and turned his face towards her. Why always the careless laugh, the apologetic shrug of the shoulder?

"Joseph, you must tell me the truth. Now, and have done with it. I love you. I promise I won't be angry."

They had been married six weeks, and although she had had her way with him—they had lived quietly in lodgings, and the air had brought some colour to his cheeks, so that he had lost his dissipated look—he still refused to discuss the future, and, when she asked if he had written to his father, he changed the subject.

The quiet of Hampstead was beginning to pall. She wanted to return to town, to see her mother and the boys, to parade as Mrs. Joseph Clarke, daughter-in-law of the well-known builder, to enjoy to the full the honest status of a married woman.

Already they owed two weeks' lodging, and it was ridiculous to live in this shabby, furtive fashion when a word to Joseph's father would establish their footing and bring them respect wherever they chose to go. Mary Anne wanted the usual perquisites of a bride—the wedding presents, the congratulations, the gifts of linen and silver, the settling into a house of her own (it needn't be large, to start with). What was the sense in being married if none of these things was yet hers?

There would be a baby in the autumn, too—she was certain of it now. Nothing but the best would do then; Joseph must understand that. She looked at him closely again. The dark eyes flickered and would not meet hers.

"What is it, Joseph?"

Suddenly he put his hand in his pocket and brought out a letter. "Very well," he said, "you win. I saw no sense in spoiling our amusement with it before. You had better read it."

There was no beginning to the letter. It was dated the twenty-third day of May, four days after their wedding, and headed "Angel Court, Snow Hill":

Since you have proved a continual disappointment to me from your early boyhood, I was not surprised to hear of your disgraceful conduct from Thomas Burnell. I would remind you that it is not the first, nor the second time that you have misbehaved in such a fashion, and it was the hope of keeping you out of mischief that caused me to apprentice you to Burnell in the first place. I never had any belief in your talent, which Burnell confirms is negligible. Your only hope, as far as I can judge, is to earn an honest pound or two as a jobbing mason, under supervision. I note you have married the young person whom you seduced, which, knowing your character, surprises me, but the matter is of little interest as I have no intention of receiving either of you. For the sake of your mother I will allow you, for your lifetime, the sum of one pound a week, or fifty-two pounds annually, but you may expect nothing further from me than this, and at my death what money I possess, and the business also, will go to your brothers.

Your father, Thomas Clarke

Joseph watched his bride as she read the letter. Would she keep her promise that she would not be angry? Her temper was quick, he knew that. Already there had been scenes, battles, words of anger, which, so far, he had been able to disperse by acts of love.

But what would she say to the reference "misbehaved" in his father's letter? "Neither the first, nor the second time." That was the poser. Must he confess to the unfortunate affair of the innkeeper's sister? Or the more lamentable business of the waggoner's wife? Must he face reproaches, tears, a storming from the room, followed by a slamming of doors and a return to her mother?

Joseph did not know his bride as well as he thought he did. The allusions to his former conduct left her unmoved. His method of approach the first week at Black Raven Passage had explained, without words, all she wished to know about his past. One sentence above the others in the letter hit her hard: "I never had any belief in your talent, which Burnell confirms is negligible." This alone mattered. And the suggestion for the future, "A jobbing mason, under supervision." Was this the only outlook for the years ahead?

She tore the letter into pieces and smiled at her husband. "So much for your father," she said. "What about your brothers?"

He shrugged his shoulders. "John is the eldest," he said, "the son of my father's first marriage, and years older than the rest of us. Married, with a family, and living in Charles Square, Hoxton. We get along well together. Thomas is my father over again, hard-working, careful, always suspicious of me. James has nothing to do with the business—he is at Cambridge, studying to be a parson— and I have a sister, too. But what's the use of discussing them? I'm the black sheep. They've always had it so." It helped his mood to disparage his family. By throwing the blame on them he absolved himself. Nothing was ever his fault.

"What about your uncle?"

"What uncle?"

"You told us, at home, that your uncle was Alderman Clarke, who might be Lord Mayor of London one day?"

"Oh, that." Joseph shrugged his shoulders again. "In

point of fact the relationship is very distant. I don't know him at all."

Every word he uttered confirmed her worst fears. The truth was, she realised it now, he had misled her all along. The Clarkes were not the wealthy family she had imagined them to be. They were tradespeople, like hundreds of others, with no very great connection, living in a small way. She had been so much in love with Joseph, and so blinded by his charm that it had never entered her head to question him deeply. *Had* been in love. Was she already thinking in the past? No . . . never . . . never . . . she thrust the thought away.

"There's only one thing we can do," she said, "and that is to approach your brother John. Better leave it to me."

Her natural optimism returned to her, as it always did when she had something to think about, something to plan. She would outwit Brother John, just as she had outwitted Mr. Day, when he had allowed her to take back copy to read to Bowling Inn Alley. And quite a lot would depend on Brother John's wife.

She went to Hoxton alone. She chose a Sunday afternoon, when Brother John, mellow from his morning in church and his Sunday dinner, would be comfortably at home, in the bosom of his family.

Charles Square, pleasant and quiet, the houses lately built, gave forth an air of stolid respectability.

"We could have the top floor," she thought. "There must be two rooms in front, another at the back. No rent to pay."

She wore her wedding gown of pink muslin. She looked very innocent and very young. The door was opened by Brother John himself. She recognised him instantly. He was an older, flabbier, less elegant edition of Joseph, and, she decided, even easier to manage.

"Forgive me," she said, "I'm Joseph's wife," and burst into tears. The effect was like magic. The brotherly assistance to the parlour, the anxious summons to his wife (thank heaven, a motherly face), the curious eyes of children, hastily thrust from the room, and, when calm had been restored and a cordial given, she told her story.

"If Joseph knew I had come, he would never forgive me. I told him I was going to see my mother. But I knew,

70

from the way he has spoken to me about you both, that you wouldn't turn me from the door. He has such an affection for you, but you know his pride."

They doubted his affection and his pride, but when she smiled at them through her tears she turned doubt into sincerity.

"He nearly broke his heart over his father's letter. You know about it, of course?"

They knew. It was distressing, but nothing could be done about it.

"The marriage was all my fault. I made him run away. I was unhappy at home, and my mother sent me to be housekeeper to a man called Mr. Day."

She told the story of Mr. Day. The forcing—no mention of his diffident knock—the forcing of the door at ten o'clock at night, the escape to Joseph.

"What would you have done in my place?" She turned to Mrs. John.

Mrs. John expressed horror, shock, concern. Poor child, what an experience.

"I knew my mother couldn't protect me, and my brother Charley was not old enough. I had to go to Joseph, whom I could trust. It was improper to live together, so of course we were obliged to be married. My stepfather gave me permission."

She realised, with growing wonder, that her story was really true. The forcing of the door was the only fabrication, but somehow it made all the difference.

"And where is your stepfather now?"

"He has gone to Scotland. We owe two weeks' rent at our lodging in Hampstead, and they'll turn us out by next Saturday. If only we had somewhere to go. You see, in the autumn . . ." She looked at Mrs. John. Mrs. John understood.

In less than a week Mr. and Mrs. Joseph Clarke had moved into Charles Square. The top floor was theirs. It was not what she had expected, standing before the altar in Pancras church, but no one need ever know that except herself. And the neighbourhood was superior to Black Raven Passage. This gave distinction. She was able to assume a little air of condescension when she called upon her mother for the first time.

71

"So you see, it really suits us very well. The two house-holds live separate, but we are there, if they want company. Joseph, of course, has his allowance from his father, and is quite independent."

It was a different story from the one Mrs. Farquhar had heard from Thomas Burnell, but it served. She had missed her daughter. All was forgiven. The only thing she did not understand was the sudden reappearance of her own husband, who had chosen to vanish again after the wedding.

"How am I to live? What is to become of Isobel and the boys?"

"You must continue to take lodgers."

"But how could you let your stepfather go? Surely you could have detained him, so that I could have some redress through the law?"

"Useless. He hasn't a penny."

Bob Farquhar was dismissed. He had done what was required of him, and could be forgotten. He did not fit into the picture of Charles Square. Neither the John Clarkes nor the Joseph Clarkes sat down to dinner in their shirt-sleeves. Appearance and good manners before all. Mary Anne was prepared to thrust her stepfather out of her mind forever, but she had reckoned without the round-faced Martha.

Martha arrived one morning to an advertisement in a paper for nursemaid to the baby not yet born. Mary Anne seized hold of her and took her upstairs to the top floor, before Mrs. John had sight of her.

"What are you doing here? Who told you to come?"

"I saw the bit in the paper. I guessed it was you."

The creature stared at her. The expression was stolid, dumb worship. Could she be slightly mental? Were the eyes a trifle vacant?

"Does my stepfather know you are here?"

"They didn't want me no more. They said I must earn my living. So I've come to be servant to you."

"How much do you want?"

"I don't know. My keep, I suppose."

Yes, she could cook. Yes, she could wash. Yes, she could mend, she could darn. She knew how to shop in a market.

"If I take you, you must never mention my stepfather or your mother, nor the fact that you saw me at Pancras. You will be Martha Favoury, my servant. Do you understand?"

"Yes."

"If you do anything to displease me, I shall send you away at once."

"I won't displease you. I'll do just what you say."

In a moment Martha had found herself an apron. In the next she was scrubbing the hearth. A nod and a smile at Pancras had made her a slave on sight. Yes ma'am, no ma'am. No wages, only her keep.

Mrs. Joseph Clarke had a servant. Mrs. Joseph Clarke could say to Mrs. John, "If you like, I can spare you Martha for the afternoon." A touch like this cancelled obligation. Mrs. Joseph and Mrs. John could meet on equal terms.

Mary Anne and Joseph lived two years in Charles Square, and during that time two children were born to them. The first died soon after birth. The second, a girl, lived, and was baptised Mary Anne like her mother. When the third was on the way, Mary Anne declared that the top floor of Charles Square could hold them no longer. They must have a house to themselves, but who was to pay for it? Joseph's father had died, but he had kept his word. Not a penny more than the annuity of fifty-two pounds a year came to Joseph. The business on Snow Hill prospered, but without the second son. The second son shrugged his shoulders. He had a pound a week, a free roof over his head, and did not even have to pay wages to the servant, so why worry? They could live on at Brother John's indefinitely.

"Don't you want to be independent?"

"I call this independence."

"Don't you want to be respected, looked up to, spoken of as a craftsman, like Thomas Burnell? Wouldn't you like to see your own name, Joseph Clarke, above your own business?"

"I prefer to live like a gentleman."

But was it living the life of a gentleman, lounging on the third floor of his brother's house, and suggesting, more often than not, that they shared his brother's dinner? Was

73

this not the first step in the direction of someone shabby, down-at-heel, pitied, who eventually bore the stigma of "poor relation"? If only he had one ounce of drive, one particle of ambition.

"Brother John, we are crowding you out of your house. Now your family is growing up, you need our rooms."

"Nonsense, my dear. There is room for us all."

"But Joseph needs work, needs occupation. The talent is there, if he had the chance to use it. The will was unfair, unjust. Joseph has a right to share in the family business."

Brother John looked worried and upset. His father's death had made a difference to all of them. Already he was at loggerheads with his other brother Thomas, who had inherited the brains and most of the capital. John had fallen from favour because he had befriended Joseph. Sometimes he wondered whether it would not be better to split altogether, and leave Thomas to carry on in his own way, while he retired.

"Joseph asks for nothing," said Mary Anne, noting the crease of anxiety, the frown of indecision. "I am asking for him. It would take such a small sum of capital to set him up in business, and naturally, as soon as he made any profit, he would repay you the original loan. Have you heard, by the way, that Brewers of Golden Lane are selling up? The house is in good repair, and the yard is behind it. If Joseph had one apprentice to help him, a boy in his first year . . ."

Charley would do. No outsiders. Profits all in the family. No wages paid to strangers.

"It would start, don't you think, as a branch to the business in Snow Hill? But Thomas would have no say in the matter; it would be entirely in yours and Joseph's hands, as you both agree so well."

In the Christmas of 1794 the Joseph Clarkes moved to Golden Lane . . . At last Mary Anne had her own front door, her own staircase. No more tumbling over Brother John's children on the stairs. Her own new curtains hung at the windows; her own new carpets covered the floor. Martha, in a print dress, cap and apron, gave the orders to the butcher's boy. There was a perambulator for Mary Anne the second, a bassinet for the baby on the way, paid for by Brother John, who had quarrelled with Brother Thomas.

"How are we doing? Very well indeed. An order for a monument at St. Luke's. Another from St. Leonard's. Joseph has really more work than he can manage."

Show visitors upstairs. Show them the rooms, so spick and span, and the well-clad baby daughter, and the respectful serving-maid in the kitchen. Every sign of prosperity, of success. But keep the door to the stoneyard firmly closed, to hide the slabs of granite not yet touched, the tools lying neglected in the loft, the master absent.

"Is Mr. Clarke at home?"

"I'm sorry, he's out on business. Some important order."

And later, much later, Martha calling in a whisper from the kitchen, "Master's back."

Joseph, with his hands deep in his pockets, would be kicking at the slabs of granite. No need to ask where he had been: the flushed face, the unsteady hands, the immediate attempt to take her in his arms and kiss away her stare of accusation told their own story.

"I'll work tomorrow, but not today. Today we must have a celebration. To hell with work."

She must not nag. She must not threaten. Nor must she show reproach. These things had sent Bob Farquhar from her mother. Smile, then, and laugh, and drive with gay assurance through the town. The spirit of bravado must be maintained before Mrs. John, who during the course of the summer would often visit her, each time with an added problem to discuss, and finally in tears.

"John made a great mistake to break with Thomas—he acknowledges it now. He's a child where money is concerned, and his share of the capital is going fast. Until the yard here in Golden Lane shows a profit we must depend upon speculation, and John knows nothing of the City. Can't you prevail upon Joseph to work harder?"

"He does work hard, but business is slack, what with sickness during the winter, the war, the uncertainty of the times." Mary Anne seized upon any excuse to save her husband's face. "And speculation isn't necessarily a risky thing, if you know the right people. A friend of Joseph's made a fortune the other day—I believe he introduced

75

him to Brother John. If his advice is followed we may all of us wake one morning to find ourselves rich."

Never be apprehensive. Never dread the future. A hopeful heart wins three quarters of the battle, and duplicity the rest. There must be no more borrowing from Brother John until his speculations in the City came to success, and in the meantime Mr. Field, the silversmith in Golden Lane, was willing to advance loans on terms suggested by herself. "My husband is a nephew of Alderman Clarke, and in the event of my husband's business not making an immediate profit, the Alderman will help us later on. But perhaps a small loan temporarily?" Temporarily, there were few silversmiths who would not have obliged at sight of the elegant, newly furnished house a few doors down the street, the whole presumably backed by a future Lord Mayor of London.

James Burton, too, could be touched—not financially as yet, perhaps, but for workaday advice. He was now a successful builder, and could see in a glance the faults and omissions of the stoneyard in Golden Lane.

"A word from you, Mr. Burton, would mean so much. Joseph is reserved and shy. He will not push for orders. For old times' sake . . ."

Old times? She smiled upon him. He had long left her mother's lodgings in Black Raven Passage and lived in a house built by himself in Bloomsbury, but from the way she talked, half teasing, half nostalgic, it was as though she had dallied with him three years ago, and not with Joseph.

"I should have done better" was hinted, was thrown in the air, but never admitted, never put into words.

For old times' sake, therefore, he obliged with orders, but the work was skimped, was poor, was left undone. Gradually he withdrew his patronage. Why should he employ a mason without skill, who was seldom sober and worked as though doing a favour?

"The trouble is, Mrs. Clarke, your Joseph drinks."

"It's worse than that, Mr. Burton, he has no talent."

The father's statement was fully borne out by now. Not merely negligible, but nonexistent. She had married a man without any purpose or will. Yet she loved him still. He was young, he was hers, he was handsome. She held their

76

first son in her arms, one hot summer's evening—Edward, with eyes like her own, the same mouth, the same features. She showed him to his eighteen-month-old sister, to faithful Martha, to the smiling midwife; but Joseph, who should have been with her, was not there.

It was the twenty-eighth of July, 1795. Birth of a son and heir to Golden Lane. She lay alone, staring at the ceiling of her bedroom. If he had chosen this night to get drunk she would not be silent. Silence could go so far, but had an ending. She wanted his understanding as never before. Tomorrow she would be strong, ready to face the future and to take command. But—for pity's sake—peace and tenderness tonight. When he came he was not drunk but very pale, and he did not glance at the baby in the bassinet but straight at her.

"The venture's failed," he said.

She sat up in bed and stared at him as he stood there in the doorway.

"What venture? What do you mean?"

"The venture in the City," he said, "the risk, the speculation. I went to Charles Square as soon as I heard the news. I arrived too late."

He flung himself down by the bed and started sobbing. She held him as she had held their son an hour before.

"It's never too late. I'll plan. I'll find a way," she told him.

Joseph shook his head, his face disfigured with weeping. Whatever she might scheme and plan could not mask his own incompetence now. His had been the advice, taken as expert by the trusting brother.

"How much did your brother John lose?" she asked.

"His savings. All he possessed. He learnt of it in the City this morning, and didn't return home. He shot himself at noon. They found his body in a chaise in Pentonville."

EIGHT: The important thing was to keep face, to
show a bright façade, never to betray how near they stood
to bankruptcy. John had committed suicide; they survived.
Therefore profusion, painted panels, polished floors, silk
hangings, gay attire. Sprigged muslin for the children. A
spinette, hired by the month, not paid for, sheets of music,
books with leather bindings, candlesticks of plate. Fashion drawings spread upon a table, playhouse bills, em-
broideries in frames, the latest pamphlet from the press, a
gross cartoon. A puppy with long ears, sporting a ribbon,
two lovebirds in a cage. The whole dolled up to portray
ease, prosperity, to suggest that Golden Lane bore no
resemblance to Bowling Inn Alley.

Take away the trimmings and the bones were bare. The
skeleton of poverty grinned from the walls. Cover the
falling plaster with a damask sheet—the neighbours saw
the frills and not the fissure.

Alone, lying in bed beside a drunken husband, she saw
her life merging into that of her mother, repeating the
same pattern. A baby every year. Malaise, irritation. The
four little faces round the table mimicking the past—Mary
Anne, Edward, Ellen, baby George—dependent upon her,
never upon Joseph. Joseph turning into her stepfather Bob
Farquhar in nightmare fashion, sleepy-eyed, blotched, always an excuse upon his lips. How break away, escape?
How defeat her mother's image?

Mrs. Farquhar visited her daughter every Sunday and
the talk was women's talk, dragging, tedious—the price of
fish, the fads of a new lodger, Isobel now helpful in the
house, a cure for rheumatism. But somewhere beneath the
chat complaints lay unuttered a mute reproach that this
love match, so desired by Mary Anne, had not brought

affluence. The terrible "I told you so" was a spectre between them. So much promised from this union with the Clarkes, nothing fulfilled. Mary Anne's half-brothers had gone away to sea, to serve in the Navy—but as ship's boys (this was never mentioned); and both of them had been drowned at the battle of Cape St. Vincent. Charley was living in Golden Lane, apprenticed to Joseph but feeling it a dead end, leading to nowhere, threatening to quit, to join the Army.

"You said we'd all be rich. It hasn't happened."

The orders that came their way were humiliating. A plain gravestone for a cheesemonger up the lane, or a simple scroll for a butcher dead in Old Street.

Always contriving, pretending, covering up inefficiency. But if it continued through the years, what then? There must be some way out, and not stagnation. She remembered the old scandal sheets, a halfpenny a copy, thumbed by grubby fingers in the taverns. Hot for a few nights only, sniggered at, discussed, then used to wrap a cod's head for the cat. Found later, sodden, in the gutter. This was the stuff produced by Mr. Hughes, by Blacklock in the Royal Exchange, by Jones in Paternoster Row, by countless others up and down the town. Who wrote the smut? Some third-rate scribbler with an ailing wife. Why not a woman? Easy enough to persuade Joseph to an outing, to seek out eating-houses where the publishers met. Easy to mix with them, chat, and throw out hints, discover their dingy names, their drab addresses. And while Joseph rattled dice, talked big, and played the gentleman, she learnt the tittle-tattle required, the stuff which fed the market.

Sydney from Northumberland Street, Hildyard from Fetter Lane, Hunt from Beaufort Buildings in the Strand: they knew the ropes. The cunning pen flattered their reader first, threw in a classical tag to top a page, and assumed a knowledge not possessed by either the one who wrote or the one who read. Prosed his beginning, laboured his paragraphs, then smack! came the innuendo, the dig in the ribs. For this the halfpenny was spent, the sheet was smudged. The higher the rank the greater the interest taken.

"Where did you learn your fireworks, Mrs. Clarke?"

"In the cradle. I had a hot squib for a rattle."

She scribbled the trash in bed while Joseph snored, and nobody guessed the truth, not even Charley. It served its purpose, and five bills got paid—out of five dozen. Besides, it took her mind off household cares. Croup and convulsions, fever at midnight, holes in the carpets, Martha's sulks, burnt puddings, Joseph's embraces, now no longer wanted. How to avoid them? That was a pressing problem. Feign illness, feign fatigue, go to the limit of all lies and feign frigidity. But no more children, hiccoughed to conception. Four was enough. But how she loved them when she held them first, heavy-lidded, helpless, the head out of all proportion, lolloping, loose. The tight-closed eyes, the waxen hands; hers, never Joseph's. Given security, she'd bear a dozen, but not as things were. No paupers for the parish.

Yet where was the alternative to Golden Lane? How beat the brokers? Scribbles by candle grease would never keep them all, nor spare her mother, nor make a man of Charley. There were too many people dependent on one woman's wits, and that one three-and-twenty.

She fought a losing battle. The brokers came. They took away the tables and the chairs, they took away the lovebirds and the beds. Not enough dying tradesmen needed gravestones, or if they needed them they scorned them plain. Joseph was bankrupt and the yard was sold. Even Martha had to go, with tears, with protestations, and take a place as nursemaid down in Cheapside.

This happened in the summer of 1800, and a hasty makeshift plan had to be formed. No hope from Brother Thomas of Snow Hill, but how about the younger one, the curate? The Reverend James Samuel, late of Cambridge? He had a house too big for him in Bayswater, and had already given asylum to Mrs. John. Room could be found for more if tightly packed, so the Joseph Clarkes decamped to Craven Place. In time, perhaps, the curate would be a bishop, but meanwhile the children were housed, which was all that mattered, and Joseph was forced to pull himself together—what happened round the corner did not matter, as long as he sobered up to dine at five.

Neighbours were pleasant, Craven Place a suburb, the curate, hospitable, kept open house to all, and Mary Anne was hungry for new faces. The Taylors at Number Six were her great find. Three brothers in the Army, two in the Navy, and the eldest daughter a namesake, Mary Ann.

"There mustn't be two Mary Annes. I'll call you May."

Once more, as in school at Ham, she had a female friend, someone to joke with, giggle with in private, swap hats and dresses and ribbons with, quiz every male acquaintance without mercy. Nonsense was balm, an antidote to marriage. And May Taylor had connections who might be helpful, for if Mary Anne was to keep her children clothed the editors of Fleet Street must be fed. There was a Taylor grandmother in Berkeley Street, whose seminary for young ladies was well known, the prospectus saying, "Mrs. Western's classes are for the pious tuition of tender misses, and for the practice of more experienced dames."

When the misses were packed off to bed and the dames forgathered, Mrs. Western sometimes lapsed into indiscretion.

"I can tell you what goes on in high society. The very best families send their pupils to me."

Young Mrs. Clarke who had come to rub up her French, took notes of a different sort, in printer's shorthand. The notes were not shown to the curate, or to the Taylors, but found their way to Paternoster Row. Result, a pelisse for Ellen, a pram for George.

There was a Taylor uncle in Bond Street, Great-uncle Thomas. As shoemaker to the Royal Family, he was better value still. There was nothing he would not reveal after two glasses of port. But only to friends and relations, within four walls.

"As my niece's best friend, Mrs. Clarke, I can say this to you." He could and he did, to the glee of the Grub Street scavengers. Rubicund, round, bald-headed, with a nose like a parrot, his hobby was draughts by the fireside, with stomach well lined.

"Your move, Mrs. Clarke."

"No, yours, Mr. Taylor."

"You've missed it, I huff you. But what was I saying?"

"The Princess Augusta . . ."

"Ah! Yes, in her boudoir. It happened at Windsor."

"And no one discovered it?"

"The lady-in-waiting. She's out of the country now, packed off and pensioned."

"But who was the lover?"

"Ssh! Bend your head closer."

Great-uncle Thomas was one in a thousand, rubbing this monstrous nose, with the draughtboard set, but sometimes it crossed her mind that he had suspicions.

"Did you see the remark in last week's *Personalities*?"

"No, Mr. Taylor. My brother-in-law, the curate, doesn't take halfpenny pamphlets."

"Curious, that the anecdote about the Princess should have got repeated. I asked myself this morning, who blew the gaff?"

Ah, who indeed! She set out the pieces and then let him win the game, to allay suspicion. He told her, *en passant*, that she should buy her shoes from him. Bond Street, Number 9, close to Piccadilly.

"You charge too much. I couldn't afford your prices. My husband hasn't the money, Mr. Taylor."

"But I understood from my niece that he lived upon his fortune?"

"A small annuity, left him by his father."

"You must have difficulty, then, in getting by, with four children on your hands."

"It isn't easy."

"Fond of your husband?"

"We've been married for eight years."

He fiddled with the draughtsmen and rubbed his nose. The hubbub in the Taylors' parlour lent them privacy. She wondered what he was getting at with his questions. He pushed his first man forward, she followed suit. He hummed under his breath, then spoke in a whisper.

"It's always possible to increase your income. A young woman like yourself, good-looking and smart. I've helped several of them, similar cases to yours. Don't mention it to my niece, she doesn't know."

She doesn't know what? Why was the old man whispering? Did he mean he lent money out at three per cent?

"Very good of you," said Mary Anne, "but I hate to be indebted."

The humming again. The fiddling with the draughtsmen, and a glance over the shoulder to see who was near.

"No question of that, the gentlemen pay the costs. It's all a matter of accommodation. I have two or three reception rooms over my Bond Street premises. Discreet and silent, no possible fear of disclosure. Only the cream of society have the address. The Prince of Wales himself is amongst my clients."

She had it now. Good God! Who on earth would have thought it? Old Uncle Tom and a *maison de rendezvous*. She'd have to be pretty hard up before she tried it, but how amusing—no wonder he heard all the gossip. A shadow fell between them and the board. Little May Taylor stood with her hand on her shoulder.

"What are you both discussing so intently?"

"The price of leather. Your uncle says that when my present shoes start to pinch, he'd be pleased to fit me." She rose from the board and curtseyed, meeting the old man's eye. No harm in letting him know that she understood.

"I mean it, my dear," he said. "You never can tell. Your shoes may start to pinch at any time."

He handed her his card with a bow and a flourish.

THOMAS TAYLOR
SHOE-MAKER TO THE ROYAL FAMILY
9, Bond Street, London

"You've printed it wrong," she told him. "Shouldn't it read, Thomas Taylor, Ambassador of Morocco at the Court of St. James's? By the by, do you make to measure? Or do I have to take the first shoe offered?"

His small eyes gleamed, his large cheeks creased into folds. "My dear young lady, I assure you a perfect fit."

His niece swung around in delight and called to her friends, "Mary Anne is going to buy shoes from Uncle Tom."

They all applauded and laughed and joined in the discussion.

"Take care, it will cost you something."

"Frightfully dear!"

"Surely special terms for the family, Uncle Tom?"

The old man hummed and smiled and didn't answer. Nothing improper had been suggested, no harm done. He turned the subject to music, and to singing. Shoes were forgotten, and the end of the evening came. Mary Anne was escorted home, two doors away, by a Captain Sutton, late of the Grenadiers, and an army acquaintance of one of the Taylor brothers. As he said good night he held her hand for a moment, and then, with an odd expression in his eyes, he asked her, "When, Mrs. Clarke, are we likely to meet again? In Craven Place or Bond Street?"

Was it a feeler? She shut the door in his face and ran upstairs. Past widowed Mrs. John, past the curate's sanctum. Past the prayer books laid in rows for tomorrow's service. Through the children's bedroom, where the four lay sleeping, bland, unconscious, part of herself, dependent. Into her own room, to a sprawling Joseph. He'd missed the bed and fallen on the floor. She wondered that the curate hadn't heard him. At least he had spared her the shame of fetching her from the Taylors', had saved her from that sudden entry with stumbling footsteps, silence, followed by chatter to cover confusion and a good-natured Taylor brother holding his elbow.

She bent to turn out his pockets and found a shilling—he had three guineas when he left the house. Tomorrow there would be the usual excuses and apologies, a few games of hazard, drinks with a couple of fellows. She put a pillow beneath his head and let him lie.

Where was her scrap paper and her pen? What could she feed the vultures with tonight? Nothing from Mrs. Western now for days. The last had been a baby at Devonshire House, body wrapped in a facecloth and found in a closet. Said to be the kitchenmaid's, but rumour had it . . . Anything new about Mr. Pitt? She racked her brains. Premier seen to stagger in the lobby. A couplet from Pope to give it a double meaning. Always remember the sting comes in the tail. She scribbled for twenty minutes, then closed her eyes.

No sound from the sleeping Joseph, except his breathing. A child cried once and was coaxed to sleep again, the blanket tucked in the cot, the pillow smoothed. No rest for her active brain, but only conjecture.

The appraising, quizzical glance of Captain Sutton. "Craven Place or Bond Street, Mrs. Clarke?"

NINE: One week there was a return of hospitality. The Taylors came to the Clarkes', the object music. And the day before there was a note from Captain Sutton. "I ran into a friend of mine at noon, Bill Dowler, on the Stock Exchange. May I bring him along to dinner?" Answer: "Delighted." It was one of those chance encounters that alter life.

Excited and on edge before the party, a demand from Joseph setting the evening awry, Mary Anne's taut nerves demanded stimulation—and found it. A stranger in their midst, he sat beside her. She liked his looks, his blue eyes, medium height, and fair complexion. The chatter of the other guests gave these two excuse for exploration. Badinage passed to agreement, agreement to understanding. The mood of the moment found them in tune. The result was a chemical fusing, disturbing to both. Here was a complication upsetting plans and scruples, this sudden advent of a man she liked too well. How must she deal with the danger? Desire, now dead to Joseph, quickened to Dowler. The one was all the other failed to be. Protective, not demanding; dependable, not weak; low-voiced, never strident. No shallow patter, boasting of what had been. Words were considered, thoughts were weighed, and afterwards expressed. Strength lay in those hands, and in those broader shoulders . . . She realised now too well her great mistake, the pseudo polish that had caught her at fifteen. This was quite different.

"If we had met before, what would have happened?"

Said by a thousand lovers, and now said again. He was not forcing the pace, but was quiet, reserved, fanning her flame still further, making her think—shocked by her own emotions, pride outraged—"I want this man. How do I set about it?"

What hope of answer, under the curate's roof? There lay instant damnation. The trouble was Bill Dowler's sense of honour—hence, possibly, his attraction. There would be no midnight prowls for him, nor creaking boards. If dinner was at five, he would leave at ten—agony for both, but honour saved. To compromise a woman was not done. The only son of fond and gentle parents, his code was theirs: fear God, and shun the devil.

A party to Vauxhall? Of course, delightful. But they went in a six, or even an eight, never in pairs. Shoulder touched shoulder, as they watched Punch and Judy; hands brushed against hands, pointing to Bruno Bear; laughter was shared, and looks exchanged, and all the warmth of intimacy suggested. But what, at the turn of evening, did it bring? A jog back, four to four, in a chaise to Bayswater, when a curricle for two might have wrought wonders.

Hints, thrown by May Taylor, brought compassion and speculation to his eyes.

"Her husband's a perfect brute, didn't you know?"

"I guessed as much from Sutton. How distressing!"

Concern was in his voice and in his air of protection. But there was no flinging of caps over windmills, no attack—merely a couple of volumes of poetry, verses marked, a pat on the head for Edward, a doll for Ellen.

"If there's anything I can do, will you let me know?"

Do? Good God! Did he think she was made of marble? Must she sit demurely, and bow her head, and endure? Or behave like the girls at Ham and tear daisy petals? He loves me, he don't. He'll have me, he won't. This year, next year, some time, never. And meantime, night after night, the sleeping Joseph, the wasting weeks, the high tones of midsummer.

It was Joseph himself, in the end, who forced the decision. Perhaps he had guessed, for all his blurred condition, that it was not only fatigue that turned her dumb; perhaps he had sensed what lay behind the yawn, the averted head, the implied resistance.

"What's happened to you lately? Why have you changed?"

"Changed? What do you expect? Look in the mirror."

No veiled reproaches, but a stab direct. The tone of disgust told him how far he had fallen, and he stared in the glass and saw his own reflection, a monster aping what he once had been. The features smudged, the whole complexion mottled. The dark eye narrow in the puffed, full face. The trembling hands, the bending, stooping shoulders. A twisted mouth, as if a bee had stung him. A wreck of the self long known, and not yet thirty.

"I'm sorry. I can't help it."

Shame came in the morning, with pity and clinging hands, a cry to be forgiven, a prayer for mercy.

"I've had no chance, no luck, the world's against me."

Talks with his brother, the curate, were no use. The solemn "May God in His infinite mercy give you peace" was followed by tears and a vow to behave in the future, but he knew too well in his heart that she despised him, and by afternoon no hope of salvation remained. One little glass to steady shaking hands, a second to restore the loss of pride. A third to lend a swagger to the step, a fourth to give the world a garish colour. A fifth to trounce them all, to be God Almighty. A sixth to blot the brain and bring oblivion. At last a total loss, and the devils had him.

"It will take months of nursing, Mrs. Clarke. I have seen others recover, in this condition. But never, for one moment, can you relax. One drink, and the whole breakdown will be repeated. It is a burden to carry on your shoulders for a lifetime, especially with young children."

The physician told her this in the curate's study, where all of them held a family consultation—Mary Anne, the Reverend James, and Mrs. John. At last the horror was faced and the fact admitted. No longer did they try to cover up or brush aside.

"You call my husband a dipsomaniac. I call him a drunk. If I am forced to choose between him and the children, I choose the children."

The alternative was to be chained to his bedside forever, and at intervals put him to grass, like a bear with its keeper. A lumbering monster, padding, with lolling tongue. The children parcelled out amongst relations, the girls to her mother, the boys to Mrs. John. The invalid and herself kept by the parish. She thrust the picture aside and turned to the curate.

"I've stood this for nine years, and that's six too many. This all began before we left Charles Square and the final rot set in at Golden Lane. Better now, for himself and all of us, if he'd put a bullet through his head like your brother John."

The curate begged her to postpone decision. Parables sprang to his lips about prodigal husbands and erring lambs and sinners that repented. "There is more joy . . ." he began, but she cut him short.

"In heaven, perhaps," she said, "not on earth, to a woman."

He reminded her of the marriage vow, and the ring she wore, and the blessing. For richer for poorer, as long as they both should live.

"With all my worldly goods I thee endow. He said that too, once, and he gave me nothing. Except infection, and because of it I lost a baby. Respect for your cloth forbids the sordid details."

Shocked and aghast, they pressed her no further. The physician, a man of sense, was on her side. He advised withdrawal out of town, for a time at any rate. Rest . . . fresh air . . . a sedative to nerves. The husband to be left at Craven Place, a male nurse in attendance.

The curate wavered, hoist with his own petard. The prodigal husband was also a prodigal brother, and Joseph was Esau, without his mess of pottage. John had been driven to suicide, and Joseph must be saved; perhaps in time the marriage could be mended. But a young woman alone in the world, with four small children? Blushing, he forced himself to words of warning.

"Are you strong enough, Mary Anne, to withstand temptation?"

She wasn't. That was the point. Temptation beckoned, and she wanted to yield and forget. She wanted to wallow.

"I can take care of myself, and the children also."

No need to tell the curate of the note, already written but not yet despatched, to be sent by private messenger to Dowler.

The bewildered children were bundled into a coach, and, with May Taylor and Isobel as companions, the little party set forth to lodgings in Hampstead.

"Where's father? Is he sick? Why was he shouting?"

Young Edward was quickly silenced, and anyway the journey made a distraction. The cool sweet air of Hampstead was an antidote, and the Yellow Cottage, owned by a Mrs. Andrews, looked out upon Haverstock Hill and the budding heather. Joseph must be forgotten, lying in Craven Place with shuttered windows. The scene was now set for escape and for romance. Tomorrow would bring an answer to her note, or Dowler in person. She would say to him, "Why not stay? You can have May Taylor's room, she's got to go. She can't be spared any longer from Craven Place. And Isobel—well, Isobel's with the children. So good with Ellen, fretful in the night . . . Have you brought me books? I'm lost without books and music."

Then, with the candles lit and the curtains drawn, a man would be a freak of nature if . . . ? She lost herself in sleep and speculation.

Day brought disaster, not what she had planned. Mary Anne the second woke to a high fever, coughing, delirious. By afternoon a rash was on her face and chest. The little girl kept calling for departed Martha, Martha, who had quitted them now a year. Her mother, kneeling by her bedside, could not quieten her.

"I want Martha. Please get Martha."

The child tossed and turned, the name was repeated. A doctor, summoned by Mrs. Andrews, shook his head. A bad attack of measles, very infectious. The rest would get it; there was nothing to be done. Cupping was no use, warm milk the only treatment.

"Isobel, where does Martha live now?"

"At the same place, in Cheapside, isn't it? A Mr. Ellis."

"Go there at once with May. Take a hackney carriage. Don't mind the expense, that doesn't matter."

"But how can you get her back, when she's been gone a twelve-month?"

"Tell her I want her. She'll come to me at once."

Retribution. Agony. The glazed eyes on the pillow were no longer the child's, but Joseph's. The two merged into one, the husband, the daughter. Vainly she offered prayers to a Power offended. What have I done wrong that this should happen? Take my life in exchange, but spare this child.

Cold to the burning forehead, but no use. Minutes were

hours, and hours eternity. Charles Square, then Golden Lane, a baby laughing. Something had gone wrong in marriage, but whose was the fault? And why must it bring this child to a burning pillow?

"I've come, ma'am."

"Martha!"

She clung to her, weeping. There was hope in that rounded face, that solid figure, in the shawl—a gift on parting—and the wicker basket, something so reassuring in her manner, the way she set the basket down, took off her shawl.

"What did you say to your master?"

"I don't mind him. I told him my mother was ill."

Bob Farquhar's smile, Bob Farquhar's wink of the eye.

"Here's Martha, love. Here's Martha come to look after you." She knew the flight of panic, the sudden ease of the heart, cessation of all feeling save fatigue, aching fatigue rotting her as she stood.

She looked through the open door and saw Bill Dowler.

"What are you doing here?"

"I received your note this morning. I came at once."

"My note?"

Everything was forgotten because of the child. The baited hook, despatched from Craven Place, belonged to another time, to another era. The Yellow Cottage was a lazar house, not a hiding-place for lovers.

"You've come too late."

He did not know what she meant, and did not enquire. She was suffering and exhausted, and that was all that mattered. He held out his arms and she went, like a child to a father.

It was an odd comfort, never before known and quite unplanned. No evening magic, working to its climax. He led her downstairs to Mrs. Andrews' parlour and they sat by the open window, hand in hand. In the garden leading to the heath Isobel chased a truant Edward. May Taylor picked flowers with Ellen, the baby George tripped on his pinafore.

"I thought you might need help. I came provided."

"My brother-in-law, the curate, gave me money."

"It may not be enough."

Enough for what? For sickness, death, disaster, for all troubles unforeseen, for future trials?

Suddenly he said, "Have you left your husband?"

"Yes."

"I mean, forever?"

She did not answer, for she didn't know. If she said, "No," then sitting there meant nothing. He'd rise, and go, and travel back to town. If she said, "Yes," the child in the room upstairs would become a hostage.

How, if she made a pact with God, could she be sure He would keep faith and not confuse the issue? Fear was the driving force, and guilt the master.

"If my Mary Anne gets well . . ."

She did not finish the sentence. He understood. His fate depended on the child's, and hers as well. Measles, to her mind, was now a symbol, a signpost with two pointers, right and left. If the child recovered, duty, gratitude, and stern resolve would take her back to Craven Place and Joseph. This was the moment's mood, harrowed by sickness. Besides, fear blunted inclination.

Fear worked the other way with him, and sharpened longing. To see her anxious and distraught doubled the craving. Prudence had made him wary up to now, the husband, a shadowed figure, blocking the path. The curate's roof had helped to keep instinct dormant, but here the ground was neutral, killing convention. It was strange that the teasing flirt who mocked him at Vauxhall, pressing his knee and fluttering a fan, should pale in beauty to this woman with set eyes, unhappy and fearful, thinking of her child.

"You'll stay the night, then? Please, you're such a comfort. I know Mrs. Andrews has a room to spare."

She did not even say good-night to him, but went at once, drawn like a magnet to the sick child's room.

"How is she, Martha?"

"Better, I think, ma'am. Not so restless. You get some sleep. I'll watch by her tonight."

"If anything should happen, wake me instantly."

To bed, then, and to sleeep. To total darkness. No thoughts, no dreams, nothing till morning came—and then the sharp, swift torture of waking life. She seized a wrap and ran, barefoot, to Martha, and instead of the black

91

vault, a curtain pulled aside, found a smiling Martha and a small head raised on the pillow, with large, bright, conscious eyes.

"The fever's all gone. She's almost herself again."

"Oh, thank God!"

But why the wave of feeling, the flood of emotion, the instant longing, so that she must run, hair flowing, straight to his room, the pact with God forgotten, nothing remembered, only this surging neeed to be shared and fostered?

"I love you dearly. I have wanted this so long."

To whom the gratitude? To God in heaven? It made no sense to her, nor to Bill Dowler. What had been was no more; this was the present. Isobel went home, so did May Taylor. The lovers had the cottage to themselves. The children caught the infection, but what did it matter? A few spots on the face, a cough for a night, with Martha and Mrs. Andrews willing nurses.

"You'll not go back to your husband?"

"Never . . . never."

But Edward caught the measles last, and died.

TEN: She did not reason deeply. The mood of the moment caught her, made its mark, seemed like the answer to the heart within, but the mind came up in conflict, splitting emotion.

Joseph was to blame for death and tragedy. She had followed heart and instinct, and he had failed her. Had he been successful, like his master Burnell or like James Burton, disaster would never have overtaken them. They would now be affluent, happy, with Edward living.

She could not separate success from peace of mind. The two must go together; her observation pointed to this truth. Failure meant poverty, poverty meant squalor, squalor led, in the final stages, to the smells and stagnation of Bowling Inn Alley.

A woman old before her time, dragging, fretful, with unruly children—this was the picture she had of herself in ten years to come, and all through a husband who had failed. The man provided. The man held the purse. Therefore go for the man foolish enough to yield it, and acceptance would be revenge for what had been.

Striving, bearing children, making do, keeping face had brought no ultimate thanksgiving, no reward—a husband, in the charge of a keeper, a dead son. So go for everything denied her hitherto, and then fight, if failure threatened.

The Hampstead idyll had been a panacea to pain, the body's purge. Dependence and desire went, when the too small coffin, hiding a waxen boy whose smile, whose laugh, whose touch must now be projected into the baby George, was lowered, covered with a spray of lilies, into a yawning grave.

Bill Dowler, lover, answer to all yearning, merged to

Bill Dowler, provider and friend, though lover still, as and when mood proposed. His status was stamped, accepted without question; no longer Mr. Dowler, but Uncle Bill. She made no bones about his future rôle. As long as money lasted, he sufficed. If love should falter, and his purse as well, she'd look elsewhere. There was no chance of marriage, with a husband living, but marriage was not all, in a man-made world. The shoemaker of Bond Street—Uncle Tom—loomed like a shadow in a dark recess that might, or might not, promise treasure.

He called on her at Hampstead, with his niece and nephew. She knew why he had come; she saw his eyes. The excuse, of course, was conventional and trivial. Sympathy, condolence, a fatherly pat on the arm. But, the two of them alone for the space of a moment, she sensed his appraising glance, thoughtful, cold-blooded, and she wondered if he looked thus choosing leather, balancing weight and texture, before purchase.

"I gather," he said, not meeting her eyes direct, but staring at some point above her head, "from some chance remark of my young niece on our way to Hampstead, that you don't return to Craven Place?"

"Correct."

"And that you are, if I may venture to say so, for the moment suited?"

"I'm no longer dependent on my husband's annuity or on his relations, if that's what you mean."

"Quite so—quite so. A temporary measure. The assistance of a friend." His murmur, courteous but scathing, cast doubt upon the future. Old bird, she thought, calculating, wise, he knows his world.

"Stock Exchange," he muttered. "Risky, of course, with this country in its present anxious state. Fortunes easily won, but more easily lost. Unless you're an expert in the game, it's one best left untouched."

No name was mentioned, but she knew he referred to Bill. Boldly, she said, "Well, what would you suggest?"

"A settlement, of course," he said. "There are no loopholes then. Young women like yourself must have protection. A fixture in the bank and you're independent . . . Unless . . ."

"Unless what?"

94

"The lease of a house might be better," he murmured; "in your name, naturally. Money can quickly go, but property remains. In your circumstances that might be wiser."

She pictured him with strings of dancing dolls. Do this, my pretty, twirl, and show a leg. Easy, now, gently, here's the way to catch them. She looked across the room and saw Bill in conversation with May Taylor. Steady, reliable, and yet . . . John Clarke had risked his all in speculation, then blown his brains out in the chaise in Pentonville.

Not that, perhaps, for Bill, cautious and prudent, but quiet withdrawal to his doting parents. A safe life in the country. And now, with churchgoing, law-abiding parents, could there be a place for Mrs. Clarke and children? The boats were burnt, once a woman left her husband. All right, then, let them blaze. To hell with subterfuge.

"Tell me," she said, "what *is* my market value?"

This time he looked at her direct and did not waver, the middleman, controller of the trade, who knows his business.

"How old are you?"

"Twenty-five."

"Might pass for twenty, but they like them younger. That is, for general taste. Doesn't always follow. Married how long?"

"Nine years this summer."

"That's a subject to avoid. The premium drops. Married two years, and suddenly a widow. It can be a magnet, with the bloom scarce bruised—depends upon the client, and the passing fashion."

"What is the fashion now?"

"Anything lively. Quick and smart as paint. Dumb innocence has been out for a number of years. The Prince set the tone, of course, with Mrs. Fitz. The sheep all follow. Heard of Lord Barrymore?"

"I've seen his name in print."

And seen it smirched, she thought, in the muddied pamphlets. Or was that Richard, the seventh Earl, who ran off to Gretna Green with a sedan chairman's daughter, then tripped up over his own musket in the Berks militia and that was the end of him? "Surely he's dead?" she added.

"One of them is, the Prince's particular friend. There are three brothers, all as wild as hawks. He gave them nicknames—Hellgate, Cripplegate, and Newgate. The sister's Billingsgate. His Royal Highness told me once she outswore her brothers. I'm thinking of the present Earl. He'd do your work."

Her work. Was she then a field to plough, and Taylor, the farmer, picking his team of horses?

"Married an Irish girl in '95," he said, "but she's always skitting back to Waterford, leaving His Lordship loose. He's got a gammy leg, but that don't worry him. One of my top clients, in point of fact. Just say the word—I'll fix the introduction."

She saw Bill Dowler's eye wander towards her, the fond eye of a lover, happy, possessive. The question was, how long did emotion last?

"You said something about a lease," she murmured softly, "a house in town. I see it would be an advantage. I have friends in the building trade who might be useful."

James Burton, old acquaintance, might help with that. He was building houses every day, mapping the whole of Bloomsbury with his products.

The trouble was, could Bill produce the money?

The shoemaker must have read her thoughts, for he paused an instant, flicking an eye to Dowler, measuring, then back to her, patting her on the knee. "No business there," he said, "merely affection."

"You mean a friend in need, but not in deed?"

"Exactly. If you fancy him at the moment, go to it, by all means, and have your fun. I don't see him signing on the dotted line, that's all. I tell you what . . ."

"Yes?"

"We understand each other well enough. See your building friends and choose your house. I can advance you money."

"On what security? Isn't it a gamble?"

He laughed, and tapped his nose.

"You're not a gamble, you're a certainty," he said. "Don't fear, I'll get my money back, with dividends. Have you got a mother?"

"Yes, and a sister too, and one young brother."

"Mother's the card to play, and younger sister. Have

them installed, it gives a certain cachet. Young widow, living under mother's wing. It sounds good and proper, whips the appetite. Now, that's enough. You know where to find me when the moment comes."

He fumbled in a capacious pocket and dragged out a sugar stick, two sugarplums. He waved them, smiling at her solemn children.

"Who wants a sweetmeat from old Uncle Tom?"

Walk up . . . walk up . . . She saw him at a fairground, thumping a loud tattoo upon a drum. Curtains tightly closed, a crimson colour. What lies behind? Pay cash, and you'll discover. The children, lured by the sugarplums, pressed closer to him. George, with sticky lips, danced on his knee. Old ogre, baiting babies . . . Angry suddenly, she went to Dowler.

"Take me away," she said. "I can't endure it."

He stared at her, perplexed. What, now? This minute? These people were here for the day, it was a sort of party. A moment ago he had seen her intent and laughing, chatting ten to the dozen with that garrulous old chap Taylor. Tears for her dead boy were long since spent—she never mentioned him, nor cried at night upon a shared pillow. Why then this look of anguish, as if ghosts pursued her?

"Of course I'll take you away, whenever you want," he answered. "Tonight, or tomorrow, or the day after. What's the matter?"

She might have said, "The spinning globe's the matter. You may walk out and leave me flat. No, not on purpose, but through circumstances. Those parents down at Uxbridge, in their dotage. They have first claim upon you, haven't they? Or else you'll marry with some squire's daughter, and fall to breeding sons with pudding faces. Well, if you do, I'll come under the hammer, wielded by that old toad in the corner there. What price a shop-soiled mother of three children? Anxious to serve. Full value guaranteed."

Instead, she smiled at him and said, "I'm bored."

So that was all. She hid it most successfully. No shrugs or yawns. And yet . . . the way she said it was a challenge. "Make up to me for what I've lost," she implied. He'd done his level best, what more was wanted? Always at her beck and call, instantly granting her whims, her children

97

amused, and Mrs. Andrews paid. Had she been free to marry . . . No, there'd be trouble. Much as he loved her, would continue loving, there was something about the old home down at Uxbridge, his father's face—however, she wasn't free, therefore the argument couldn't arise. Perhaps, though, later on, there might be a cottage; a decent small-sized house on a friend's estate, handy for visits. And when his parents died everything might be solved and no hearts broken.

Meanwhile he'd take her out of all this jumble, sister and friends and convalescing children, and get her to himself.

"I know a village," he suggested. "Chalfont St. Peter's, not twenty miles out of town. A little inn, few people. Fields, and woods, and quiet, deserted lanes." The blank look on her face showed him his error.

"St. Peter's what?" she asked. "I'm not a pilgrim. For heaven's sake, let's see a bit of life. We'll go to Brighton."

Lucky, he thought, if that's what's in her mind, that I had the windfall on the Stock Exchange. Brighton's expensive, whereas St. Peter's . . .

She had it planned before five minutes had passed. Her mother would come to Hampstead and take her place. She'd make a jaunt to town tomorrow to buy a gown. She was not fit to be seen, her hats all out of date. Isobel could go with her, and May. It was the end of the season, with everything going cheap.

"And shoes?" asked Uncle Tom Taylor.

Bill Dowler wondered at the look she flashed him. The old fellow spoke politely, meant no harm; and seeing it was his trade, and May his niece, perhaps he hoped to help and save her pocket?

"I'll get myself shod at Brighton," said Mary Anne. There was no need to speak so sharply. She turned her back. The old man smiled and handed out more sweet-meats. He'd offended her in some way perhaps, thought Dowler. Women could be so tricky, unaccountable.

Love was returned that night as never before. Why, then, the trek to Brighton? Whence the boredom? Better to ask no questions but stay mute. Carry the parcels, write and engage the rooms, be Uncle Bill and shoulder a child to its breakfast, turn a deaf ear while sisters talked of fashion. Were feathers out or in, were bosoms covered? One final puzzle—was the to-do for him? He thought so, when they found themselves at Brighton, strolling the promenade with the Upper Ten. Her smile was all his own, her eyes, her laughter, despite the many stares in her direction.

Jove, he was proud of her. Hair in a mass of curls, the latest fashion, a stylish gown (Not paid for? Let it pass), the hat, covered with feathers, stuck at an angle. No cares in the world, her sorrow forgotten. Poor child, she deserved this treat after what she had suffered. That brute of a husband, spoiling her finest years.

"Happy?" he asked, as he looked at her dancing eyes.

She squeezed his arm and nodded, but did not reply.

"The air is doing you good, you've got more colour."

Colour—rubbish! she thought, but did not say so. This was the sort of crowd she'd always wanted. It had nothing to do with ozone or the fresh sea breeze. This was the world of the pamphlets, the world of fashion, the higher stratum read about since childhood, the world of the halfpenny scandal sheets, the men and women she'd joked at, with nobody knowing. Here they were in the flesh just as she'd pictured them—flashy, affected, futile, and ripe for the plucking.

There went the drivers of the Four-in-Hand Brigade, spanking along the front with a call and a flourish. Bill Dowler pointed out the famous figures. Lords Sefton, Worcester, Fitzhardinge, Sir Bellingham Graham, and wasn't that "Teapot" Craufurd and "Poodle" Byng?

"The best whip of the bunch is Barrymore," he told her. "I met him once at Almack's. Not my sort—the devil of a rip. That's the fellow there."

The coach-and-four passed them at a smacking pace. The driver, with a dahlia in his buttonhole the size of a cabbage, turned his head and stared, then muttered a remark to his companion.

So that was Cripplegate, old Taylor's client. Did he whip his women as he whipped his horses, forcing the pace, hating his women slow? "All right, my friend," she thought, "not at this moment. I'll meet you at Number 9 Bond Street one of these days. But leave your buttonhole behind. I can't stick cabbage. Nor am I partial to a whip with thongs."

Aloud she said, "Let's walk a little further. We might see the Prince of Wales." Instead, by a stroke of fate, they met James Burton.

"By all that's strange and surprising. Mrs. Clarke!"

"Mr. Burton! How delightful. Do you know Bill Dowler?"

No Joseph mentioned. So that was the lie of the land. Burton grasped the situation and wasn't astonished. She was bound to go off the rails, and why not Brighton?

"Let's meet tonight in the Assembly Rooms," he said. "We'll pick up each other's threads. It'll be quite like old times."

Old times? Nothing could be more different. How compare the glitter of the Rooms to Golden Lane, the creaking stairs of Black Raven Passage, and Burton making himself scarce for the playboy Joseph?

She looked very well, he thought, and deuced attractive, and was it intentional the way she gave her escort Dowler the slip that evening so that he and she could have a chat together?

She came to the point at once, straight and direct.

"I want a house," she said, "a house in London."

"How much can you afford? Do you want to purchase?"

"A lease of ten years was what I had in mind."

He looked at her and wondered who would pay. This fellow Dowler, or had she other quarry?

"You may as well know," she told him. "I've left Joseph for good. I shall be on my own, with my mother and my children."

In that case the coast was clear. A shot into the blue might find its mark.

"I've houses going up in Tavistock Place," he said. "The lease would cost a thousand, or fourteen hundred."

"Rent paid in advance? Six months or quarterly?"

He smiled and shook his head. "I won't be trapped. Things can be arranged at leisure with an old friend like yourself."

"How soon could I move in?"

"Some time next spring. If you're put to it meantime, I

100

can pull strings in Brighton. The season's gay enough until December."

Time to look round, she thought, to make my mark. To be seen, to be met, to be known. Then London to follow.

"I'd like the house in town soon after Christmas," she said, "but keep the plan under your hat. For the moment, at least."

"You don't want your friend to know?"

"I'll tell him later."

The vista, he thought, was even more alluring. Dowler was not provider after all. In which case business could be combined with pleasure.

"And what about me?" he asked. "Any 'perks' for the builder? I ought to inspect the roof from time to time. The state of the paint, the need for ventilation. I'd drop you a line, of course, before I called."

The look in his eye spoke volumes. She knew what he meant. In other words, she could forget the rent. The fourteen hundred pounds might be overlooked. A ten-year lease in exchange for a romp on the side. Oh, well . . . he was a friend of ten years' standing, presentable enough. Married not long since, he would give no trouble. Family life would claim him most of the time. If she lived rent-free, there would be no need to approach Uncle Tom. She could give Bond Street a miss and make her own connections. She lifted her glass to Burton and met his eye.

"As architect," she said, "you'll have the entrée."

No more was said. She knew the lease was settled.

"I've taken the plunge," she thought, "and there's no returning. I'm out for what I can get, and I'll see that I get it. I'll pay back in kind, I won't cheat, I won't be dishonest. No one will claim I haven't earned my money. Value given for value received. It's one trade like another, the butcher, the baker, the candlestick maker. We've all got to live."

The point was, this way she'd make money. Not money to pinch and save, but money to spend. Hack-writing never brought in enough. At last she could buy what she wanted—gowns and wraps, trinklets, ridiculous bonnets, clothes for her mother and Isobel, toys for the children. No guineas going to waste in Joseph's pockets. A house of her own, with furniture to her taste. New faces, new people, new friends. A raffish enjoyment, begrudged by no one living and earned by herself.

The months in Brighton brought their own reward. Acquaintances grew thick, the circle widened. When Bill Dowler came to claim her at weekends he found, for the first time, competition. Cards from Four-in-Hand Coachmen graced her mirror. "See you at noon," she would say, or "See you at supper," and off she would streak to the races with Johnny Brunell; and then when noon came he'd find her with Charles Milner.

"Who gave you this model of a whip in diamonds?"

"What, that? Oh, Cripplegate Barrymore. He meant it as a joke."

"Expensive sort of joke."

"He can afford it."

She was always in somebody's curricle, somebody's phaeton. When questioned she passed it off lightly, evading the issue.

"I've never before had amusement. I'm having it now." In other words, he must lump it—or get out. They had had their moment and now the moment was gone. He could make his windfalls on the Stock Exchange or toddle home to Uxbridge, whichever he chose.

The trouble was, the windfalls were too few. Markets were all to pieces and he was losing money. He'd have to go home to Uxbridge, or go bust. It was late autumn when he broached his plan.

"I know of a snug little cottage, not far from home. There's just room for yourself and the children. How about it?"

She thought, "Here we go. Face the facts. All cards on the table." She stood up and put her arms around his neck, then kissed his eyes and his neck and his waistcoat button.

"I'm moving to Tavistock Place," she said, "in town. I've got a house from Burton, going cheap. I don't want to live near Uxbridge, or hide in a cottage. I'm out to make a splash, and this may achieve it."

So . . . Brighton had been an experiment, a rehearsal. Now he must stand and watch the full performance.

"Not to mince matters," he said, "you mean you're for sale?"

"Winner takes all," she said. "It's the luck of the game.

102

Your windfalls won't last, you know it, there's no use pretending. I must make my plans before that, and I must have my freedom."

"Freedom for what? To go jigging about in a phaeton?"

"I do that already. There's more comfort in Tavistock Place."

"With Burton providing the house, and Cripplegate calling? Spending the night and leaving you two hundred guineas?"

"Two hundred and fifty, I hope, concealed in a dahlia."

She laughed and kissed him again. He knew he was beaten.

"Did you ever hear of Kitty Fisher?" he asked. "Lucy Cooper, Fanny Murray? They took the same road, and ended all three in the gutter."

"Very low-class," she replied. "I aim rather high."

"That's why you've finished with me—I haven't a title. My father was only a merchant. Wine, as I told you before, was the family business."

"But now sold, Bill, and father retired, so it doesn't attract me."

"When he dies, I'll inherit."

"You'll inherit false teeth and a wig, and I'll be bald-headed. I have to live now, and not count on some date in the future."

"And what about love?"

"I'll probably love you a lifetime. Love isn't business."

"I'm to take my share, then, when Cripplegate's had his? What will you put on your door? 'Inspection Invited'? 'Old Friends at Quarter-Cost'? 'Music included'?"

"I thought of sending cards to all the clubs. 'Mrs. Clarke, At Home. But not on Tuesdays. Tuesdays reserved for Mr. William Dowler.'"

She kissed him again, making the whole thing a jest. But it wasn't a jest, and he knew it, and so did she. Here at last, round the corner, were the better days, and the splendour, and the fairy-tale nonsense she'd spun in the past for Charley. She pretended to mock at it all and make fun of her suitors, yet deep in her heart she was flattered and gratified. Bill Dowler had never suggested champagne for breakfast, or given her roses at midnight, or diamonds at dawn; but the Four-in-Hand Coachmen did their stuff with a flourish, and it pleased her to sit wrapped in furs with a peer for a driver, it all seemed so far removed from Bowling Inn Alley.

Of course she would love Bill a lifetime, that wasn't the point. The point was, a cottage at Uxbridge was out of the question. Her taste had matured, and ambition ran high, and to hell with emotion. Emotion was a thing of the past, except when the moon shone or somebody tickled her fancy at three in the morning.

This new life was easy. No cares and no worries, and, the first shock to pride overcome, the next step was simple. Men were straightforward, direct, and grateful for little. Amusing to talk to at supper, but generally tipsy. After nine years with Joseph the last was really no hardship—a few clumsy embraces, followed by snores on a pillow. The snores of a peer grated less than the snores of a mason, and a peer was lavish with presents, which tipped the scales higher. The point was, she made her own choice and took whom she wanted. It wasn't a question of waiting, and hoping for callers. Two dozen cards in the mirror, and all invitations, so what was the best proposition? It was as simple as that.

A letter from the curate was answered briefly.

I shall never return to Joseph, nor will the children. Please explain this to him, in whatever way you please. If he ever attempts to find us, he won't be successful. Thank you for all you did, but forget us in future. Yours in all sincerity, M.A.C.

The envelope was the last she ever closed by the simple method of stubbing the seal with her finger. The paper bore no mark and no address, simply a date in February 1802.

Next time she wrote to her friends—but not to the curate—her note paper was headed "Tavistock Place," and the seal upon the envelope wasn't a finger, but the clear imprint of Cupid riding an ass.

PART TWO

ONE: A white front door, scrubbed steps, gay window boxes, the knocker a woman's head with one eye closed—where had she come upon that, the stranger wondered? It gave the game away to those who knew. He knocked, and pulled the bell. The front door opened.

"Is Mrs. Clarke at home?"

Loud voices proved it. So did the greatcoats, the Malacca canes, the cocked hats tossed upon a table and two or three other hats with curling brims. A growling bulldog, tethered by a leash, lay on the floor of the hall, his jowl between his paws. Beside him were a pair of overshoes, a sword in slings. Visitors in plenty, plainly male.

The youth who had opened the door must be a servant, yet he wore no livery and his face was familiar.

"I've seen you somewhere before?" the stranger ventured.

"Yes, sir. I used to live with Captain Sutton. He sent me here to wait on Mrs. Clarke."

So that was it. The stranger laid down his cane. The youth who passed as Sutton's natural son, but was nothing of the sort—it sounded better. One way of getting rid of him, of course, passing him on as footboy to this house.

"Please to go up, sir, and announce yourself."

It was all most informal, just as he'd been told, even to the sound of scampering feet and shrill, delighted laughter. Children *en évidence*. This was to make the customer unbend—or to hoodwink innocents. He mounted the stair and entered the drawing-room door. An elderly lady, thin and rather nervous, came towards him, bony hands extended.

"I'm Mrs. Farquhar. Do make yourself at home. My daughter hasn't yet arrived from Ramsgate."

107

A glass of wine was offered, and biscuits, handed by a gawky girl in middle teens who flushed to the roots when he thanked her, and then disappeared.

"Isobel, the gentleman may prefer port to sherry."

"No, madam, I assure you. Sherry is delightful."

The babble in the room made talking difficult. The old lady was in a fluster—just as well. If he hadn't known the truth, he would have sworn he had come to the wrong address, and this suburbia. The noisy children romping on the floor, straddling the sofas, climbing the backs of chairs; all the owners of cocked hats and curling brims (some of them he knew by sight, young blades about St. James's) who romped with the children, too, gave pickabacks, tossing them on high—it lent the whole atmosphere a bourgeois setting, really most amusing to discerning eyes.

He thought of old Tom Taylor and his message, scribbled from 9 Bond Street late one evening: "I tell you she's the goods. Don't fail to call. Between us we can mould her for you-know-whom."

There came a sudden stir. The whirlpool livened. The children rushed to the door and the young blades crowded. Through the commotion laughter teased the ear, and a voice to waken interest.

"Darlings, don't smother me . . . George, your disgusting hands. Coal's great fun in the cellar, not upstairs. Ellen, your drawers need mending, run to Martha. . . . Mother, you'll hardly credit it, five hours from Ramsgate, it's never been so long, two horses lame. I could have murdered Cripplegate. Where's Isobel? I'm famished, I must have some food . . . Who's here? Johnny, how are you? Lovely to see you . . . Harry, too . . . And Bobby . . . Fitzgerald, you're a monster, you let me down last Thursday. We'd better have that party on Friday night . . . let's go to Sadler's Wells, Grimaldi's back, and the jokes are unrepeatable. I love him so. Who's that standing in the corner there? I don't know his face."

The stranger was confronted, bowed, kissed her hand, muttered a phrase or two, and gave his name. He handed his card, begging to be excused for the formality.

The blue eyes scanned the card, then searched his face. "She's wondering what the deuce I want," he thought.

"Old Taylor's right, though; this is the type we need. Quick-witted, and a climber. Just our stuff."

"Ogilvie? I think I know your name . . . I heard it quite recently, I can't think where."

"You might have heard of me through Captain Sutton."

This puzzled her. She stared him up and down, measured the beef and brawn, then raised her eyebrows.

"Forgive me. But you don't look quite his type. He always has curly-headed boys about him. I have one as a footman, Sammy Carter."

"Madam, you mistake me. My business with Captain Sutton has been professional."

"For that part, so has mine." Eyebrows still raised, she glanced at his card again, and read—beneath his name—his occupation.

"Oh! Now I know where I am. An army agent. That explains all. You must be very busy, with war any moment and young men shouting for commissions. I know dozens."

The dazzling smile shone out. His credentials, then, had been accepted. But the card, he noticed, was kept for further scrutiny.

"A charming house," he murmured. "Burton's product?"

She glanced at him coolly. She did not turn a hair, but she must have understood the implication.

"Yes," she replied. "He built it and he's my landlord, too. Burton's a Scot, you know, so is my mother. Burtons, Mackenzies and Farquhars, we're all very clannish."

Clannish was putting it mildly; he knew the connection. Taylor had tipped him the wink that she was living rent-free.

"Tavistock Place is very central," he said. "I always like Bloomsbury. The hub of the world all about you, yet quite an oasis. You must have a wide circle of friends who drop in of an evening?"

He thought to himself, "If that doesn't shake her, she's tough."

Her glance never wavered. She helped him to a biscuit.

"Close friends are welcome," she said, "but they come when invited."

A barb in the tail? Well . . . perhaps. He poured her some sherry.

"Your door knocker's most entertaining. Where did you discover it?"

"A junk shop in Hampstead, chosen by George, my son. He was five on St. Valentine's Day . . . just a little precocious."

"It gives quite an air to the house."

"Delighted you think so. Did you like the white paint on the door? It gets very dirty, of course, but shows up in the evening.

All right. Tit for tat. He knew where he was, and enjoyed it.

"You mean," he replied, "stray callers can't miss the colour?"

"Stray callers don't come. Nor do hawkers, or gypsies with brooms. They might bring fleas to the children. I tell all my friends that the house is next door to the chapel. You must have noticed that, too. Very handy for matins."

She smiled and passed on, leaving him stuck with the mother. Handy for matins, indeed! Very handy for Burton. For Barrymore, too, and the rest of the Four-in-Hand drivers. But the deuce of a drag from his Saville Row Agency office.

"More wine, Mr. Ogilvie?"

"Thank you, ma'am, no. I've sufficient."

"My daughter has so many friends. We're quite flooded out on a Wednesday."

Flooded all week, so he'd heard, but nearer to midnight, the old lady in bed by that time, tucked up with the children. Just as well, too, if Cripplegate Barrymore called. He showed no discretion at all, so Tom Taylor lamented, in Bond Street—used to drive up in a tandem, blowing his horn and bellowing "Tally-ho" for the windows to open, shocking the neighbouring tradesmen and waking their wives. All Bond Street complained, and poor Tom Taylor nearly closed down. He was forced to lie low for a while and send clients elsewhere.

"Do you want to help bathe the children, Mr. Ogilvie?"

Heaven forbid! He had not come for that. Some of the fellows were prepared for anything. Young Russell Manners was rolling up his sleeves, and the Irish lawyer, Fitzgerald, who should have known better, was gambolling with a child upon his back and making already for the

110

stairs. Was this the customary routine upon a Wednesday? If so, Tom Taylor might have warned him.

"The fact is, ma'am, I'm not very used to children."

This worked with the old lady. Not with the daughter. The blue eye fixed him from across the drawing-room.

"Nonsense, Mr. Ogilvie. There's nothing to it. Soap in a lather, and a scrubbing-brush. As any army agent, it should be part of your job. Think of all those cornets in the Light Dragoons."

Damn it, she put a brat into his arms. A wriggling little chap with sticky hands, who dug his heels into his ribs and yelled, "Gee up."

"What's your first name, Mr. Ogilvie?"

"William, ma'am."

"There, George, do you hear? Another uncle for you. We've got a Bill already. This can be Uncle Will."

It was useless to protest, and the brat was kicking. A stampede up the stairs, the whole crew following. Young Manners stumbled against him, red, perspiring.

"Cripplegate started this, God's curse upon him. Said it kept him fit, in perfect training. Saved him a packet at gymnasium, too."

"Why not refuse?"

"And be thrown out? No bloody fear."

Manners's reward, then, was worth ordeal by water? He'd won his spurs, and Ogilvie had not. He threw the screaming boy into a tub.

"Darling, let Uncle Will sponge handies first."

Handies be blowed. He couldn't hold the brat. The water was in his eyes, his mouth, his hair. Smack!! came a cake of soap across his chin, and shouts of triumph from another tub. A wild-eyed girl had caught him with a towel. "We're winning, George, we're winning. You'll be last."

Howls from the squirming eel with coal-black hands.

"Rub harder, Mr. Ogilvie. George hates to lose."

The cool voice murmured in his ear, the shoulder touching. Turning his streaming face, he saw the smile, amused and mocking, revelling in his pain. Tom Taylor could look elsewhere with his wily schemes, the agency in Saville Row go bankrupt, bust; William Ogilvie had had enough.

"I'm damned if I'll play nursemaid. Rub him yourself."

She seized the little brute from his useless hands and

111

smothered its head in a towel to stifle the screams. While he stood dripping, flushed and angry, she said, "Idiot! What made you call at five, and on a Wednesday too? These boys will stay to dinner, then they'll go. Come back at ten o'clock and I'll be alone."

Slowly he dried his face, his soaking cravat. He reached for his coat, streaky with splashed water, then looked down upon her, kneeling on the floor, coaxing endearments to her struggling son.

He said, "I shan't forgive you for ten minutes of acute distress. I'm drenched to the skin, and I loathe children anyway. What do I get if I come back tonight?"

She straightened her back, shaking a damp curl from her eye, and answered: "Sam—or the pirate's *drapeau*, take your choice."

He stalked downstairs, deafened by children's cries, and picked up his hat and cane. The bulldog snarled. Sam Carter, footman, discarded playmate to Captain Sutton, late of the Grenadiers, opened the door for him and bowed farewell. At the drawing-room window Mrs. Farquhar waved. It was exactly four and a half hours to ten o'clock. By then the curtains would be drawn and the candles lit, shaded, no doubt, and dim, the drawing-room screened. The mistress of the house would be alone and waiting. A pity his call must be a business one, but there it was, and anyway a partnership, if partners they were to be, precluded intimacy. A step in the wrong direction would be fatal. So, all things considered . . . He strolled towards Russell Square.

When he returned at ten the house was shuttered, but a glance at the drawing-room windows showed a light. Yes, she was right about the white front door drawing the eyesight like a magnet; it had the attraction of a blind man's cane. He rang and knocked with confidence.

This time a serving-maid opened the door, squat and round, her features almost hidden by a mobcap big as a mushroom. No Sammy Carter.

"Good evening. Where's the footman?"

"He goes to bed at nine. The mistress says he's still a growing boy and needs his sleep. I always listen for the bell at night."

"Your mistress is very thoughtful."

This time no bulldog, and no other hats. The hall was in darkness save for a single lamp.

"And what's your name?"

"Martha, sir. I'm housekeeper by rights. They call me Mrs. Favoury in the kitchen."

"Quite right, too. It shows respect. Shall I go up?"

"Please, sir. You'll find the mistress in the drawing-room. She said you'd let yourself out, later on."

All well arranged, no doubt. An evening ritual—the caller to the first floor, Martha to the basement. What did Martha make of it all, he wondered?

"Are you on duty like this every night?"

"Oh no, sir. Only when a stranger like yourself's expected. Mr. Dowler, Mr. Burton, and His Lordship all have keys."

Did they, by jove! What if all three arrived together? Then there'd be confusion, to say the least, and possibly bloodshed. No doubt she had it taped and knew their movements. The mobcap vanished. He climbed the polished stair and thought he heard, behind the closed drawing-room doors, a woman humming. He knew the song—the rage-hit at Vauxhall. All London was singing it this spring:

"Tomorrow's a Cheat,
Let's be merry today."

It sounded better here than at Vauxhall. Humming was a pleasing pastime, soothing, after a busy day, to a hard-worked man in need of relaxation. Oh yes, she'd do the job he had in mind, and hold it, too. Laughter, though! Did she laugh when she was alone? A cough, a manly cough. Now, what was brewing? Frowning, he knocked firmly on the door. There was a sort of scuffle, a whisper, padding footsteps. The door of the back drawing-room closed and then her voice rang out, clear and unperturbed, "Won't you come in, Mr. Ogilvie?"

He entered and looked about him. No one there except themselves. The scene was set just as he had pictured it. the lighting dim, discreet, the mistress of the house upon a sofa, in negligee, backed by a heap of cushions.

"Someone was with you?"

There was suspicion in his voice, and accusation. Eavesdropping was a game he much disliked, unless indulged in by himself, a master at it.

She looked up and smiled. She threw aside the buffer polisher with which she had shone her nails, and held out her hand for him to kiss.

"No one but Charley. That's my brother. I've sent him off to bed, he knows his place." She patted a spot beside her on the sofa.

Suspicious still, he glanced over his shoulder. "Are all your family under this one roof?"

"Yes, but they won't disturb us. I told you we were clannish. It's our Scottish blood; a kind of homing instinct keeps us together."

He looked at her closely. Complexion very good, neck and shoulders shown to advantage in this lace affair. Twenty-six or twenty-seven, old Taylor had said, and married to a drunk for near nine years. She must have had guts, standing it that long.

"Look here," he said, "I'm going to be very plain. I've come here for a business talk. No more."

"Thank God for that. I spent last night at Ramsgate."

"Lord Barrymore?"

"Yes, do you know him? Such a dear, but oh! so hearty. Leaves me blue with bruises. Lord knows why. Do you want anything to drink? What about brandy?"

"Thank you."

Now she knew the form she changed position, sat up a little straighter, clasped her knees. She threw aside the languor and looked alert.

"Well, begin," she said. "I'm all attention."

He filled the brandy glass and sat beside her.

"How long have you been living here?"

"A year."

"Doing well?"

"Not badly, but it's chancy."

"Anything put aside?"

"Good heavens, no. I live from day to day, as most of us do. I have no rent to pay, which saves my bacon."

"No regular sum from Burton?"

"Don't be absurd. James is a Scot. I'm lucky to get the house."

"What about His Lordship?"

"Cripplegate gives presents, mostly diamonds. The trouble is, I like to wear them, not put them into pawn. The chaps don't realise that it's cash we need, all ready to the hand, to pay the butcher."

He nodded. "It's the same in any business. Credit, as much as you like, but cash tomorrow. Who else is steady?"

She hesitated. "You wouldn't know Bill Dowler. A very devoted friend, but depends on his father. He's just lost a packet on the 'Change, with this talk of war. I won't bleed a man I love, it isn't honest."

Ogilvie sipped his brandy, crossed his legs, and flicked the minutest thread from his white silk stocking.

"I take it you pose as a widow?"

"Who told you I wasn't?"

"Tom Taylor. I'd better be frank. It was he who prompted this visit. We work closely together—it's only a step across Bond Street to Saville Row. Half the clients who go through his hands he passes to me: any young officers wanting promotion, lieutenants, captains, majors, colonels, I know the right strings, when to pull them and whom to approach."

She reached for a cushion and settled it against her side. Then she stretched for the buffer once again and flicked it back and forth over her fingernails. "If Pitt gets his way and we're plunged into war, then you'll be in clover?"

"In theory, Mrs. Clarke, but not in practise. Too many of us in the game these days, and Greenwood and Cox are squeezing us out of business. They have the Household Troops, Dragoons, and half the regiments of the line. Small firms, like my own, don't get a chance. War or no, it's only a matter of time before I'm bust—that is, officially. My aim is to work behind the scenes, in private. Which is where you come in."

She glanced at her polished nails, then up at him.

"But how?"

"By certain influence." His voice was abrupt; he had no intention of giving much away.

"You mean, give little dinners to my army friends? And tell them, 'Buy promotion from Will Ogilvie, he'll offer a cut price, and see you through? They wouldn't listen. Besides, I don't know many army men. A few nice boys come here to play, that's all. And one old footling general, who should have been superseded years ago. Calls himself Clavering."

Ogilvie shook his head and put down his glass.

"Oh, I know Clavering. He's no use. No, Mrs. Clarke, that's not what I mean at all. The fountainhead is what we want for this."

"The Wellesley brothers? Don't be ridiculous. They're so stiff-backed they can't remove their boots, let alone their breeches. No white front doors for them, they'd pass straight on to the chapel."

"I wasn't thinking of the Wellesley brothers."

"I know Jack Elphinstone and Duncan Mackintosh, both colonels in the 60th, but what of that? No fountainheads for them, they're always hunting. I met old Amherst once, on Brighton beach. He used to be C.-in-C. before the Duke of York. A drivelling old dotard, nearly eighty. It's no use, Mr. Ogilvie, you must find someone else to help the falling fortunes of your firm. Now, had it been the Navy . . ."

She looked reflective. The First Sea Lord had made an offer once, then lost his nerve, and fled to Portsmouth.

Ogilvie smiled. Odd that she hadn't twigged. She'd mentioned the very name, and it hadn't clicked. He'd best leave finalities to Taylor.

"Listen, Mrs. Clarke. If we found the man—and when I say 'we' I refer to you, Tom Taylor and myself—and got him snared; in other words, if this man, whom I needn't name, fell for you good and proper, would you play?"

"But play at what?"

"Go shares in what you earned. And you would earn plenty. That is, if you learnt the elementary rules, all of which I could teach you in a very few weeks."

She stared at him, eyebrows raised.

"And what could you teach me that I don't know? Are you such an expert? You intrigue me."

He shook his head impatiently. "I'm not referring to your own profession, ma'am. In that you hold every trick, I well believe. I meant, I would instruct you in the rudiments of mine: army lore, not love."

She shrugged her shoulders.

"Become an office boy, you mean? Oh yes, I could do

116

that. I enjoy men's shop, I always have, since a child. Political, medical, hack-writing, what-you-please. And if it brought me money into the bargain, so much the better. I have three children, as you know, to keep, and the rest of my family besides. Which reminds me, my brother needs a job. How about making him an office boy as well?"

"Excellent. 'Routine' work for him, finesse for you. But you do understand, Mrs. Clarke, if this goes through—this plan of mine—it may mean leaving here? Almost certainly will."

She sat up straight, horror in her eyes.

"My lovely house? But it's all so comfortable, with everything to my taste, and I've built a connection."

"If we get our man, Mrs. Clarke, you won't need your connection. He'll give you a house three times the size of this. Good-bye to Burton, Barrymore, and the rest. Small fry, the lot of them."

Now he had her on the end of a line. The blue eyes narrowed, widened. He could see her busy mind leaping through the peerage to the premier dukes; but she still hadn't hit the nail upon the head.

"If you mean real security," she said, and she spoke slowly now, choosing her words, "there's nothing I wouldn't do to achieve just that. You met my mother, Mr. Ogilvie, this afternoon. Trembling, nervous, old before her time. Left by two husbands, no one to protect her. Luck was on my side or we'd have starved. I won't end like that. Nor will my children. I had a son who died . . . I made a vow. I'll play any game in the world that a woman can; if it's sordid, or dirty, or mean, I don't give a damn. But by God, that little boy you put in a tub tonight, bawling his head off, and his sisters too, they must grow up secure, they must be safe. Whatever I've done in the past, or shall do in the future, will be for them; and heaven help any man who lets me down."

She got up from the sofa and walked across the room. The smile had gone from her face. She pulled the curtain, stared out of the window at the falling rain. Was he dismissed? He put down his glass of brandy.

"You can trust me," he said. "I'll be a friend. My life hasn't been easy, neither has yours. Both born in this city of London, weren't we? Right! Then we've got the same sort of wits, the same sort of brain. And here, right under our nose, is a certain class, a certain stratum, known as the 'Upper Ten.' Inherited wealth, idle, useless, and vain. You've had some of the pickings, so have I. Well . . . let's go in for a rather larger share. And here's luck to your children."

He finished his brandy and kissed her hand.

"And what do you want me to do now?" she said.

"Call on Tom Taylor. Bond Street. Number 9."

"I know the address. I've never been there yet. I hoped somehow to avoid it, I don't know why."

"I understand the feeling. Let it go. You won't regret the visit, I'm sure of that."

He moved towards the door. She stood and watched him.

"What time? Which day?"

"Friday. At eight o'clock. The evening, naturally. We'll send a carriage for you."

"Will you be there?"

"No. Taylor will. He'll be watching from the window—you won't have to wait. And by the way, pack a small bag, in case . . ."

"In case of what?"

"You might be asked to spend a few nights out of town."

She frowned, then smiled, laughed, and opened the door.

"You make me feel like a child before factory work. Shawl, and clogs, and dinner, all wrapped in a hankie. When I was thirteen, Mr. Ogilvie, my stepfather fell sick. He was corrector to the press, and I corrected the copy for him and took it down to the overseer, and pretended it was my father's. He never guessed the truth for three whole weeks. I did my first job well. It wasn't skimped."

"I bet it wasn't. Nor will this be, either. Good-night."

"Good-night."

She watched him cross the street and waved her hand. She put back his brandy glass upon the tray, patted the cushions, and blew the candles out. She went upstairs to bed, but didn't sleep. Another turning-point had come, but there was no Joseph snoring on the floor to force her hand. No Edward, silent forever, in his cot. No Bill to cling to,

118

weeping, on the pillow. Charley, upstairs, was too young and ignorant.

"My God," she thought, "a woman can be lonely, when she's the one to earn the daily bread. Men never count the cost. They're used to it."

Friday came. A day like any other, with things to see to. Some tradesmen in the morning, bringing bills and put off with an excuse. Meals ordered with Martha. The doctor to her mother's rheumatism. Shopping with Isobel, who needed stockings and gloves. Dinner at six with the children, as a treat. George rather fretful, sickening for something . . . If so? "It's nothing, ma'am," said Martha. "Too many apples."

Charley at a loose end, wanting money. "Some fellow's asked me to play tennis. Can I?"

"Of course you can. Don't be so helpless, darling."

The house was settled, then, at last. Her packing was done, a dark cloak covering her evening gown. The carriage stood at the door, Sam Carter waiting. And suddenly, for no reason, a nerve pain tautened in the belly.

"Sammy, wish me luck."

"What for, ma'am? Where are you going?"

"That's just what I don't know. But wish it, Sammy."

"Yes, ma'am. I always will."

"Then shut the door. Tell the man Bond Street, Number 9."

It was dark in the streets, a night in early April. Spring was somewhere round the corner, but late as always. There was a party in Hanover Square, with carriages stopping. She wished hers could be among them, gay and friendly, not streaking to an unknown rendezvous. She remembered the hackney carriage, and Islington, and Mr. Day in his bobbled nightcap outside her door. Eleven years since then, and so many bridges . . . The carriage drew up in Bond Street. She muffled herself in her cloak. A light shone at a first-floor window—Uncle Tom, furtive, peeping, leering, all agog. Oh well, it was too late to turn; the die was cast. The street lamp, murky, showed letters above the shop. "Taylor, Shoemaker," and the coat-of-arms, "By Royal Appointment," made the firm's status clear. The ambassador of Morocco believed in the *double-entendre.*

of colour on the white, and it's easy to adjust. The whole thing slips . . . I thought so most convenient." He stood back, measuring the road example.

"Your fellow allowance inside," she told him. "You want to put good . . .

TWO: Tom Taylor was waiting in the hall to welcome her, dressed to the nines in a peacock velvet coat, hair powdered, buckled shoes.

"My dear, I'm so delighted. It's such a long while since we met. I haven't clapped eyes on you for quite three months, not since the party you gave for my little nieces. How are your children? Beautiful as ever? And you? But I needn't ask. Blooming, like a peach."

The old man kissed his fingers to the air and led her to the stairs. "I ought to be angry with you," he continued. "How long have we known each other? Over two years? And you've never before paid Uncle Tom a visit. Not even to buy your shoes."

"I told you in Craven Place—you charge too much."

"Nonsense, my dear, all nonsense. To you, a double discount."

His staircase was impressive, deeply carpeted, gilt mirrors at every angle, and on the landing, ready to take her cloak, a chocolate-coloured page with sash and turban.

"Where are we meant to be?" she asked. "In Istanbul?"

He smiled and rubbed his hands, but ignored the joke, his beady professional eye upon her gown.

"Charming," he said, "and just the right décolletage. So many foolish girls make the mistake of showing too obviously what should be guessed, and therefore dull the edge of anticipation. But you, a subtle hint of the great divide, and the rest all promise. Did you bring long gloves?"

"No. Why should I want gloves? Are we to go to some reception?"

"Gloves give the final polish. But never mind. I have some I can give you." He touched the lover's knot, caught on her shoulder. "That's good," he said. "I like the touch of colour on the white, and it's easy to adjust. The whole thing slips? I thought so, most convenient." He stood back, measuring the *tout ensemble*.

"You follow the wrong trade," she told him. "You ought to deal in silks, not leather, knowing so much about the cut of gowns."

"You'd be surprised," he said, "the things I've turned my hand to in emergency. I've had girls come here looking like angels from heaven, but dressed disastrously, prinked up for Sunday school. Old Uncle Tom doesn't fail them. I've gone around with my scissors snipping at ribbons and laces, opening up tight corsets, trimming curls that bunch too heavy on the neckline. Without the necessary grooming the girls wouldn't have clicked. They never fail to thank me. This way, my dear, in here—a little refreshment."

She looked about her, watchful, critical. This was the room with the bow window that faced the street. Red velvet chairs, red candles, a carpet even thicker than the one she had trodden downstairs. A sofa like her own in Tavistock Place, next to a table, and the table set with glasses, a magnum of champagne, and the number of glasses, she was swift to notice, three.

Screens were dotted here and there, easy to handle and fold, and pictures of cupids lolling in billowy clouds. A large mirror on the wall reflected the sofa and table. The effect was a trifle garish, she thought, and crude. If this was the clients' taste she didn't think much of it. Perhaps the cupids jogged the slow-of-mind and whipped up doubtful appetite to take a chance. Then, with the crimson candles . . .

"You'll take champagne, my dear?" said Uncle Tom.

"If that's the custom."

For two pins she'd go home. The setting bored her. A rabbit's snare to catch some tipsy general, then sit there, blowing bubbles. Better by far to stick to the friends she knew and bounce about with Barrymore at Ramsgate.

"Now tell me all your news." His small eyes gleamed.

"My news. I haven't any. Life's very full; the house, the children, my mother, you know what it is, and now this talk about war unsettling things. My Whig friends are despondent, shaking their heads, and the Tories, of course, all exultant and whooping with joy. I don't care one way or the other; it doesn't affect me. You know Burton, my landlord? He's turned patriot, very excited. Says he'll raise a regiment of builders, in case of invasion, and command them himself. He pretends he's appalled at the thought, but of course he adores it."

"And how is Lord Barrymore?"

"Sailing for Ireland tomorrow, and sick at the prospect."

"His lady's expecting, I hear."

"So she says, but I doubt it. These Irish women will ride . . . quite fatal for babies."

"Is Mr. Dowler in town?"

"I saw him last week. Very down in the mouth, and disheartened. He's had to leave the Stock Exchange and run to father. I liked your William Ogilvie, but what's it all about?"

Tom Taylor laid his finger on his mouth. "Some other time," he murmured, "not just now," then louder, filling up her glass again, "What else have you to tell me. Any gossip?"

"Nothing by word of mouth, only what I read. Do tell me, is it true, that report in the *Post*—you should know, with so many royal clients coming to have their feet squeezed into shape—is it true that the Duke of York has sacked his brother, that there's been a botch-up at Gibraltar and Kent's recalled?"

Tom Taylor turned dark purple, choked, and spluttered. The champagne seemed to catch him in the throat. She hit him between the shoulder blades, but, seeing it did not work, reached for a sandwich.

"The nose trick? Have some cucumber, that'll settle it. All down your peacock velvet . . . what a shame."

She seized his voluminous handkerchief from his pocket, dusted him down, and put it back again. He made a violent motion with his hands—she did not get it. He pleaded with his eyes—she did not see. Suddenly ravenous, the champagne whetting hunger, she ate and talked at once, her mood improving.

"He's becoming quite a tyrant, is Frederick Augustus. Drops the poor Duke of Kent, and refuses to give a command to the Prince of Wales. The trouble is, I suppose,

122

he's the old man's darling, and can do what he likes when the old man's loose in the tile. What a tribe they are, though—confess it, as bad as the Bourbons. A few more mistakes, and whoops! go the heads in a basket. Thank God I'm a Scot, and don't owe any allegiance. These sandwiches are good. Are they made in your kitchen?"

Without waiting for his reply she seized another. "Mark you," she said, "the Stuarts weren't all that clever. Boy Charlie looked good in a kilt, but that's about all. I dare say he ran like a hare at the sound of a musket. My mother would kill me for this, but even when small I fancied the sound of the Butcher. Red coat and trimmings. I like my men big, incidentally, and he was no chicken. Isn't it time you came clean and told me my fate? Who is it that's going to pop out of your hat tonight? I warn you, if it's some Old war-horse past his prime I just won't tackle him, not if he offers me a string of medals."

She sat down on the sofa, smiling and happy. Champagne was pleasant, after high tea with the children, and the room was not so bad, the cupids harmless.

"Well, what about those gloves?" she said. "Let's get to work."

Her host, his face a study in discomfort, backed to the door.

"I'm very much afraid they won't be needed."

"All to the good. I'd only get the cramp."

"You misunderstand my meaning. I wish to infer . . ."

The chocolate page came in, pulled his sleeve, and whispered something in an undertone. Tom Taylor bent to listen, stomach bulging, then hurriedly left the room with the page beside him. Suddenly suspicious, she rose from the sofa. "Oh no," she said, "you can't run off and leave me, not without giving me full instructions first. What *is* all this, and why that child in a turban, the nonsense about gloves . . . ?"

A horrible thought occurred. Her fate was *coloured*. An elderly Indian rajah, strung with rubies . . .

"My God!" she called. "If he's black, you can take him yourself."

She heard a sound behind her. The screen was moving, the whole thing folding back, displaying doors—and doors that were open to a room within. Leaning against the

123

doors, a man was standing, hands in the lapels of his coat, legs crossed. Height about six foot two, florid complexion, prominent blue eyes, a largish nose, age—roughly —forty. His face she recognised at once with a sinking heart, seen fifty, a hundred times, in papers, pamphlets. A face that was waved to from a crowd of a thousand others, the wave acknowledged, salute to the hat, and finish. Now it was far too close and personal for comfort. Frederick Augustus, Duke of York and Albany.

"Not black," he said, "and even if I were I'm damned if I'd take Tom Taylor down to Fulham. Where's your coat?"

She stared. She could not answer. Humility and rage fought for possession. That Ogilvie, that Uncle Tom, could dare to spring this upon her, unprepared. White gloves . . . of course . . . and not this year-old dress but the new one, not yet worn . . . earrings . . . brooches. And here she stood like a kitchenmaid, wide-eyed, gaping.

Hating herself and him, she bobbed a curtsey. Martha could have done better, gone lower down. Her shoes weren't right for this, they pinched her heel. Everything learnt in the past three years was forgotten.

"I'm sorry," she said. "Uncle Tom's made a botch of this business. Or rather, we both have between us. I wasn't prepared."

"Prepared—for what?" he asked, and took a sandwich. "Don't you like my looks? I haven't had time to change, came straight from the Horse Guards. Been up since six, and chained to my desk until eight, with two hours' dusty interlude in a barracks square. Not dined yet, nor have you, and I'm bloody hungry. We'll have dinner and supper in one when we get to Fulham. Be quick—where's that page-boy with your coat? Did you bring a bag?"

"Yes, it's below."

"Well, come on down, it's as hot as an oven in here. The old fool always keeps the windows closed, cooking the champagne to the boiling point. Don't drink any more of the stuff, you'll be tight as a tick."

He laid a large hand on her shoulder, pushing her ahead, seized the cloak from the turbaned page-boy on the landing, and threw it over her.

"Where's Taylor? Gone into hiding? Tell him we're off."

She made for the stairs. "Not that way, here at the

back. Private entrance in Stafford Street, behind. Here, give me your hand." He led her to a passage past a door and down a narrow stairway, two at a time. She nearly tripped and fell, her high heels slipping.

"Don't you know this way?" he asked. "It saves a lot of bother. I can't come charging up Bond Street in a barouche and stumble into some duchess buying shoes. All fellows in the know use Tom's back door."

What did he think she was, some slut from the corner?

"I've never been here before," she said, "and shan't come again. The thing is a misunderstanding from first to last." After all, she had her pride. If he wanted a girl for the night he could go out and get one. There was no finesse in this method, no sort of technique.

He bundled her into the carriage and sat down beside her, taking up most of the room; she was pinned in the corner. He straddled his boots on the opposite seat and pulled her towards him.

"It's quite a fair drive down to Fulham, so let's get to know you."

She sighed and relaxed on his shoulder, resigned to the worst, with resentment boiling within her and vows for revenge—not against him, poor brute, he knew no better—revenge against Ogilvie and Uncle Tom. Had she but known for one moment what they had planned . . . She would have seized the initiative, worked the whole business. Got in a chef for the night, and two or three servants; found out in some manner his taste, and what he liked eating; hired a couple of boys for music and singing, rearranged the drawing-room and had the guest-room altered . . . By the time he was ready for breakfast—he might leave before—he'd have had the best out of the evening, and all she could give. Cripplegate always told her that Tavistock Place was by far the most comfortable house he had ever been in, the dinners were good, the wine was well chosen, the beds were a dream, and a word from him, weeks ago, would have set it all working. But instead . . . bumped about like a trull, in a carriage to Fulham. No chance to show off her points—how she talked, how she moved, her whole method of getting her men, and why they admired her. This sort of thing could

125

be handled by any young skit, or any old drab, for that matter, prinked up for the purpose.

"Well, that was refreshing," he said. "Now, what about supper? Here's Fulham Lodge, on the right. I'm as famished as Moses."

There were footmen, discreet, who did not look at her. One of them took her bag, another her cloak, and preceded her upstairs to a large, square room. Everything was laid out, everything ready—brushes, pin-cushions, combs, and bottles before the mirror on the dressing-table. A curtained bed, with nightgown, wrapper, slippers. Grudgingly, she found herself admitting, she couldn't fault the style, the preparations. Had the boot been on the other foot—if he had come to her at Tavistock Place—she wouldn't have thought of the nightshirt, or the slippers. Shaving tackle, of course, and combs, in the closet, but hardly this . . . She took a peep at the linen. Scented with lavender, soft, and fine as a handkerchief, it was a pity her mother couldn't see it, she set such store by good linen, and believed in that tag about running it through a wedding-ring.

"If you are ready to descend, ma'am, His Royal Highness is waiting."

He was, was he? Well, let him wait a bit longer. He misunderstood his bird if he thought she'd sit down to eat with her hair in a frazzle, all mussed up from that carriage—decency first. A squirt of the scent from that bottle, it smelt pretty good and ought to be good, for God's sake, when provided by princes. Tom Taylor was right, gloves would have looked better, they gave the right finish; but since gloves didn't seem to be part of this bedroom equipment, she must take it on trust that they didn't mean much to His Highness. She stalked downstairs with dignity and grace. Here was a chance to show him her stock in trade. He didn't notice; he bustled her in to supper, then roared like a bull because the soup was cold.

"God damn it, how often have I had this happen? Three times in one week. I must sack the cook. My stomach yawns for food. Bring me some bread."

The soup plates were removed. Steaming new rolls were presented, followed at once by freshly heated soup.

126

"Service," she thought. "I'll hand it to his staff. Had it been Martha!"

He lapped his soup as George did, like a puppy, and for lapping she always sent George from the table. A fig for royal manners and behaviour. Was she supposed to talk, or sit like a dummy? At any rate she could eat, not wait for him. He demolished sole *bonne femme* in a couple of mouthfuls, so she played with her ears, guessing a roast would follow. It did. A saddle of lamb, with all the garnish. Whilst he was attacking this with relish, his waistcoat burst, and a button flew like an arrow across the table. Prince Charlie . . . the clan Mackenzie . . . the fallen fortunes. This was an omen, and one she couldn't resist.

"Do you mind," she said, "if I give that to my brother?"

She saw the footman stiffen behind his chair, as she reached and picked the button out of the salt. The Duke looked up and grunted.

"What's the idea? The buttons only fit these waistcoats, which are specially made by hand by some fellow at Windsor, who knows the measure of my solar plexus."

"I didn't mean to wear . . . to have as a symbol."

"Symbol of what? Increasing *embonpoint?*"

"My brother's only twenty, and slim as a reed. No, perhaps to wear on a watch chain, a sort of charm." She wondered, should she tell him, or would it be tactless? Hanoverian feelings were still raw, perhaps, after fifty years.

"You see, we hail from Scotland, the clan Mackenzie. And one of our forebears had a silver button, a personal present from the Young Pretender, unfortunately lost, but supposed to be lucky. This isn't quite the same, I know, but still . . ."

"Can't do you any harm? I'm not so sure, if you're a Jacobite."

"Oh, but I'm not."

"You Scots are all alike. Bad as the Irish. Give you a chance, you'd stab us in the back. I'd shoot the lot."

"How very bloody of you." Seeing the servant's face, she added quickly, "Bloody in the sense of being warlike, truculent. Of course it's your profession, the way you're trained." It wouldn't do at this juncture to rouse his anger. Now she was here she must see the thing through to the end, be gay, be accommodating, earn her night's lodging fully as an honest woman.

"I gathered from your chat in Taylor's rooms," he said, "that we're not long for survival. Booked for the tumbrils at an early date."

"Listeners hear no good of themselves," she began, then swallowed: she must remember whom she was with. "Listeners like myself"—she changed the sentence—"hear lots of nonsense, and read drivel too, all in the daily papers and in the pamphlets. I merely echoed this nonsense to Uncle Tom."

How fatal if he turned her from the door at this late hour, the horses unharnessed and bedded, and expected her to foot it home to Bloomsbury! How did a woman gauge the royal mood and sense if she'd lost favour? Perhaps a ride in the carriage was all he demanded? Supper, and out . . . Different from Cripplegate, and Burton too. She flashed a look at his face, the third course finished. He seemed unmoved, and mellow. Ready to eat quince tart and drink sauterne.

"So," he said, fixing his eye upon her, "you think I'm a tryant, do you? Down on my brothers?"

He had heard—every word. Missed nothing, soaked it in. Hell's bells, there was nothing for it but to be honest and take what came. If he flung her out on her ear she had only herself to blame.

"You must admit," she said, her arms on the table, "it's hard on the Prince of Wales to have no command. If the old man . . . if His Majesty gets lightheaded again, then the Prince of Wales, as Prince Regent, can turn all the tables; and you'll be the one in search of a job not him."

The footman filled his glass, and hers as well, and she caught a glimpse of the fellow's face in passing. His eyes were glazed like a fish whose life was ebbing.

"It's nothing to do with me," said the Duke; "the King commands. I merely obey his orders, and pass them on."

"I see," she said. "Well, in that case, it's rather a problem. If His Majesty digs his toes in, you can't do a thing."

"Got it in one," he answered. "So tell your friends, when they indulge in palace chitchat, to read the rules and learn what Commanders-in-Chief are permitted to do. Your ignorance is abysmal, so is theirs."

128

Quince tart had disappeared. On came the Stilton. Another button burst from the tight-stretched waistcoat, and he flicked it across the table without a word. She placed it with the first—in her bodice.

"Go on," he said. "I like to hear my failings."

What with the sweet sauterne on top of claret, hock—too much of it—with the sole *bonne femme*, and warm champagne at Uncle Tom's followed by the rough-and-tumble in the carriage, her head was not as clear as it might have been. As a rule, when on business bent, she never drank, but tonight things had gone amiss from the very start. She leant her chin on her hand and gazed at the candles. Reality merged to a dream, and nothing was concrete.

"I'm sure you've done right in Gibraltar, bringing Kent home. He was never the man for the job; why on earth did you send him? His frightful attention to detail . . . a martyr to his duty, and all his men loathe him, I really have that at first hand. I had naval friends at Gibraltar at the time of the mutiny who mixed with the wretched battalion that got all the blame . . . Who were they? The Royals? I've forgotten . . . It wouldn't have happened if Kent had only possessed one ounce of reason. Naturally men get bored, stuck in a garrison with no fighting to do—there's bound to be lighthearted mischief. And what does Kent do but put the whole town out of bounds, and close all the wineshops, and lock all the boys up in barracks! My God, I'd have raised merry hell, if I'd been a soldier. They all adore you, by the way, they think you're a hero, though of course there have been times when . . . when things haven't gone quite as you planned."

She drew herself up and tried hard to focus the candles. What on earth was she saying, and was it amounting to treason?

"Such as when?"

"Well . . . surely in Holland?" She tried to remember. What was it she'd read in a pamphlet, or written herself, soon after Mary was born? The Dunkirk fiasco, or round about then, was the time. "I'm not doubting your courage," she said. "You're as bold as a tiger; but boldness can botch a battle unless there's a plan. And now I remember, wasn't that when the critics got busy—you hadn't

129

a plan, and that's why they whistled you home? Courage
. . . Lord, yes! You'd stand up all day to be shot at. But
wouldn't you say it's a tiny bit lacking in foresight. and
asking for trouble, to expose your backside as a target?
Lucky, in fact, you survived. But you did . . . and here's
to you."

She drank the last drop of sauterne, and when she had
finished she flicked the glass over her shoulder. It splintered
to pieces. A trick of the Four-in-Hand drivers, she'd been
taught by an expert, and it always gave such satisfaction
to feel the stem break.

Well . . . now she supposed she was for it. He'd summon the guard and bundle her off to serve a long sentence
at Newgate. In a way it was worth it, and something to
tell her descendants, a spill and a scramble on the Fulham
Road, followed by dinner and two waistcoat buttons.

He stood up from the table and gave her his hand. She
steadied herself and awaited the word of dismissal.

"I suggest early bed for us both," he said, "but I'll join
you at breakfast. We shan't be disturbed—we can spend
the whole day on manoeuvres. I admit I'm dull in the field,
and I want to learn tactics. On Sunday I must go to
Windsor, but I'll be back to dinner, and on Monday I'll
have you fixed up in a house in Park Lane; I keep one
fully furnished, for certain occasions. If we suit one another I'll see about something larger. Tom says you have
two or three children, and you may want 'em to stay.
Now how about walking upstairs, or must you be carried?"

She took a long breath, and sank to the ground in a
curtsey. If she never got up, at least the gesture was made.
The Stuarts could all rot in their graves . . . this man was
an angel.

"Your Royal Highness," she said, "overwhelms me."
She couldn't believe it. She wanted to laugh, she wanted
to cry, she wanted to hang out the flags and shout, "Brunswick forever!"

"Got both your buttons?" he asked her.

She showed him the place of concealment, and he
helped her to rise.

"Good-night, then. I'll see you at seven, or maybe before. I'm on top of my form in the morning, so sleep while you can."

"Good-night, sir. And thank you."

At seven . . . at dawn if he wanted. This treatment would guarantee service if anything did. Her rudeness forgiven, a house in Park Lane, something larger to follow. Ye gods! What a future.

She lay in the curtained bed and thought of Charley. They'd have the buttons mounted in a silver frame with royal arms entwined and interlaced, and beneath them, in a circle, "1803."

Ogilvie was right. This meant good-bye to Burton, good-bye to Cripplegate, and good-bye to Bill. Fair shares for all? Not with a prince for a lover. She'd play him fair and square, he needn't worry.

"I've arrived," she said to herself. "I've reached the top. I'll be second in precedence now to Mrs. Fitz. The question is . . . how long can I hold the job? I can't go easy. I can't relax for a moment . . . It'll take all the tricks I know to keep him hooked."

One lesson to bear in mind when danger threatened. When faced with a doubtful decision . . . audacity first.

THREE: "Martha?"

"Yes, ma'am."

"Martha, bring the slate, and let's see about food. Bring the list of my engagements too—I left it in the drawing-room."

She reached for her shoulder wrap and heaped the pillows high behind her back, then balanced her breakfast tray upon her knees, with writing paper, notes, and pen beside her to the left, on another pillow. This was the second breakfast, less hurried and less breathless than the first. The first was at seven-thirty, a scrambled affair of tea and rolls before he left the house: he in and out of the room, half-dressed and talking, shouting to Ludovick his servant for boots, for belt, for some piece of equipment suddenly mislaid, while she poured out his tea and asked his plans.

"What time tonight?"

"I can't make it before six. Perhaps six-thirty. Don't reckon to dine till then. I may be late. It's going to be another day like yesterday, papers sky-high at the Horse Guards on my desk, besides the stuff that Clinton brings to sign. This recruiting business has set 'em all by the ears, every depot in the kingdom clamouring, and God only knows how many colonels on half-pay wanting to raise levies."

"That's good, isn't it? You need the men?"

"Of course we need the men. Given a free hand, I'd take a leaf out of the Navy's book, and press them into service. No, levies are the devil. It takes us three months or so to fix the terms, and then another six to find recruits, and meanwhile Boney's laughing up his sleeve watching us from Calais. Ludovick!" He bawled to the dressing-room.

"Your Royal Highness?"

"My second pair of boots, not these, I've got a bunion. Another cup of tea, darling, and sugar."

She stretched out from the bed and took his cup, while he sat on the end and struggled with his braces.

"Might have to go to Hythe on Wednesday for three days. They're scratching their heads over the Romney Marsh defences, although they've got my prints in triplicate. I can't spare the time, with all this rush in London, and then a political fracas on top of it all. Addison'll have to resign and Pitt take over, we can't go on like this, it's too damned confusing."

She watched him dress, her hands behind her head. This was the moment that she prized the highest, unguarded phrases slipping from his tongue, as soon forgotten as the tea he drank, while she remembered.

"How's His Majesty?"

"Damned ill, between you and me and the bedpost there. The surgeon, Dundas, was down at Windsor yesterday, and had a consultation with the physician Symonds. They want to get him back to Buck House soon, tomorrow or the next day, but the Queen's against it. Says all this political excitement makes his disorder worse, and once in London he'll want to interfere. Ludovick! My coat."

"I have it here, Your Royal Highness."

He stood fixing it before her mirror. From the half-open window came the sound of horses, as the waiting groom walked them up and down in Gloucester Place.

"No time for more than a cup of tea, my darling. I'll breakfast in Portman Square, and then on to the Horse Guards. If I am late tonight it means I've gone to the Lords—I want to hear what St. Vincent's got to say. I'm all for the Admiralty getting it in the neck, so that we at the War Office can be forgotten for once. It's generally the other way round—the sailors have all the praise, and we the blame. Kneel up in bed and kiss me, I can't bend down."

She laughed and stretched upwards, brushing his chin with her hands.

"You work too hard," she said. "Let me do some of it."

"You've too many fingers in the pie already. Imagine Clinton's face if I took you to the Horse Guards and dressed you up as A.M.S. Though it's true, we might get through the day a little faster. What's the time?"

"It's just gone eight."

"Go back to sleep, and dream it's eleven tonight. Do you love me a little?"

"Sir . . . how you have the face . . . ?"

"I haven't, it's merely a habit. A desire to leave the house with a high morale. Sweet dreams, my precious."

A clanking down the stairs, the front door creaking, the horses trotting off to Portman Square. She lay back on the pillow and closed her eyes. Another hour to doze, then her day began. It was second nature now, this strange, disjointed life. The evenings were his, twelve hours, from seven to seven, but the rest of the time was hers to do as she pleased: and every moment was filled, did he but know it.

Dozing, she thought in retrospect how her life had been building up towards this moment, year in, year out, almost from alley days. That early training, as a cockney child, sharpened her wit and made her seize her chances; the schooling at Ham put on a pseudo polish; marriage with Joseph got the worst over young—so much so, that nothing a man could do, now or in the future, would break her heart. As to the rest . . . all lovers made some mark. She knew how to absorb the benefit and pass it on, be grateful for the teaching. What she had learnt from men, not only lovers, was to the purpose in a man-made world. Therefore, become their equal. Play their game, and add to the game the sense of intuition.

The six months in Park Lane, though heady, violent enough to turn her head and send caution flying, were only a time of trial, to prove her worth. It wasn't enough to laugh and act the wanton. Dozens of others, in Bond Street, waited their turn and were ready to take her place at a moment's notice, if all the Duke needed was a bed companion. But what went on in his mind, in his heart, in his belly? These were the things she set herself to discover. Never by questioning direct, never by probing, but by feeling her way, by looking, by hearing, absorbing.

His wife the Duchess? A foolish, scatterbrained woman,

plain and barren, surrounded by masses of lap dogs. Therefore, unlike James Burton and others she knew, the Duke's married life was empty, savourless, lonely. He wanted a home that smelt like a home, that was living. A place where children scampered on an upstairs floor, without fuss, ceremony, or crowd of flunkeys. A home where he could relax, could yawn—sprawl in. He needed a woman whom he could talk to, laugh with, eat with, love when the mood inclined him, bore, and sleep with. A woman who didn't plague him with woman's gossip, or chatter of frills and laces, gowns and bonnets. A woman who switched her mood to match his temper. A woman whose humour was broad as a barrack-room bruiser. A woman who, swept by anger, probably hit him. A woman who, when moved by passion, undoubtedly bit him. This was what he demanded, and had now discovered. The six months' trial once over, she passed—with honours.

"I'll give you a house in town," he said, "and a place in the country. A thousand a year to run them on, paid monthly. If that isn't enough, you must manage in some other fashion. No one will press you for payment, not when it's known; and I'll see that it is known by everyone, tradesmen included, that you're living in future under my protection. With that tag to your name you'll have all the credit in the world you want. Patronage brings favour, favour patronage. Work it out for yourself and don't bother me. I'm a fool where money's concerned, and I don't understand it."

(This was said in Park Lane at the end of the summer. She thought to herself, "A thousand a year isn't much. Not if he wants to live well." But if she protested the sum was too small she might lose him.)

"Of course," she replied, "I can manage. Where shall we live?"

"I have a house in Portman Square," he told her, "five minutes away. There's another in Gloucester Place; that shall be yours. I'll come to you every evening, dine there and sleep there, and back to my place in the morning. Servants, and furniture, and fittings, I leave all to you."

A thousand a year would about pay the servants' wages and liveries . . . She thrust the thought aside and started to plan. Odd, that the men in her life were so feckless with money, but this time there was no question of pinching. The credit was there.

The tradesmen tumbled over themselves to serve her. The royal patronage was hers to give them. Birkett the silversmith, Parker the jeweller, the one with silver plate from the Duc de Berri smuggled from France, to be paid for at her leisure, the other with diamonds. "A present, ma'am, to the Duke."

Cards at the door, all from prospective tradesmen. "We should esteem it, ma'am, a favour, if . . ." etc. etc. Mortlock of Oxford Street, offering china and glass; Summer & Rose of Bond Street, sending grates; Oakleys of Bond Street, upholstery and curtains. "Mr. Taylor, ma'am, of Number 9, suggested we call."

Tom Taylor, too, produced the ready servants. "My dear, leave it all to me, I know the type. Long service in a house is what you require. These fellows all come to me when they're after a job."

"Why? Do you get a commission on their wages?"

He brushed the suggestion aside and did not reply.

Pierson, the butler, ten years with Lord Chesterfield. McDowell, the footman, five years at Burlington House. The coachman, Parker, warmly recommended, seven years with Mrs. Fitzherbert and wanting a change. Housemaids, laundrymaid, cook, and kitchenmaid . . . all found by Uncle Tom with a whisk of the hand.

"I shall make my personal maid into housekeeper," she insisted.

"Do you think she's quite up to the job, dear?" he demurred.

"Martha knows everything. She is loyal and faithful. Besides, the children love her." No more was said.

Two carriages. Six horses—sometimes eight. Grooms, a postillion (Sam Carter might do for that), a little girl to work with her needle in the morning, a charwoman to scrub at least twice a week.

Linen—how about linen? Tom Taylor obliged. Handmade, a firm in Ireland—personal friends.

"But, Uncle Tom, these people will have to be paid!"

"No hurry, my dear. It's the patronage they want."

If that was so, then banish every scruple, order the best,

136

and damn the consequences. No one would dare to sue a prince of the blood.

The word went round, "Under the Duke's protection," and the effect was magic on the world of trade. As to acquaintances, friends, and even lovers, expressions of delight came flowing in.

James Burton, who might have felt himself cold-shouldered, assured her that her mother could remain at Tavistock Place as long as the house still suited the family plans. "I hear you've found favour with the Duke of York. How splendid! Much the best of the Brunswicks, and the only one who doesn't look German. By the way, put a word in for me and my regiment of artisans. If we have his approval and backing, my scheme can go through."

Cripplegate wrote her from Ireland. "What's this I hear? Rolling around in the hay with Frederick Augustus? Tally-ho-whoops-a-lassie—get cracking, but keep the whip-hand and don't forget your old friends when they ask you a favour. Find out from York what I'd get if I raised some recruits."

Bill Dowler was the only dissentient. Tight-lipped and withdrawn, he called to see her.

"Is it true that you are mistress to the Duke of York?"

"Oh, Bill, don't be stiff, and why that word? I like to say I'm under his protection—it has a fatherly touch which I've never known. I told you when we met that I aimed high, didn't I? And I rather think the arrow has found its mark. But I'll need you in the background all the same."

She took him to see the house in Gloucester Place. James Burton had passed the drains and all the fixtures. So useful, an ex-lover who was also a builder. But Bill could choose the curtains and the carpets.

"You have got a proper agreement with the Duke?"

"Agreement? What do you mean? I've got this house."

"The house is all very well. I mean money to run it. It will cost you three to four thousand a year, at the least."

She thought how exactly like Bill it was to show caution, to move from room to room and shake his head, raising her doubts, damping her ardour.

"He's promised to pay me money every month."

"I see . . . Well, be sure you get that promise in writing soon. Or better still, an agreement with his bank."

"I can't do that. It would look so terribly grasping."

"It's best to have things straight with him from the first."

"Sour grapes," she thought. "Poor Bill, he's hurt, and jealous . . . Still hankering after that cottage at Chalfont St. Peter's. What a far cry from there to Gloucester Place! Protected by the Duke, not Mr. Dowler."

Will Ogilvie gave advice of a different kind. Advice she did not dare repeat to Bill. "Go slow," he said, "don't rush things. Learn the business. I'll let you get settled in, then I'll show you the moves. Now that my office in Saville Row has closed down—they've proclaimed me a bankrupt—no one will connect me with army agency matters. I'll work on my own, as your agent, and take a percentage. I'll pass the fellows to you who want promotion. You pass them to the Duke. And the thing is done. Cash from the fellows who see their names gazetted. The principal to you, the percentage to me. H.R.H. won't ask you any questions. Try him with favours first, where no money's concerned."

The first request was easy. Something for Charley. Charley, whose eyes now shone at the turn of fortune, who saw himself Field Marshal in three years.

"Do you think His Royal Highness . . . could you ask him?"

A family matter, private, quickly fixed.

"Sir, my brother's mad to join the Army. He's played at soldiers since he was six years old. Might I present him to you, perhaps—one evening? He's rather young and shy, but desperately keen."

Charles Farquhar Thompson, therefore, was duly gazetted. Cornet in the 13th Light Dragoons, on the twenty-fifth of February 1804.

Sam Carter, footboy, was jealous at Charley's promotion. If Mr. Thompson joined the Army, why couldn't he? Captain Sutton had always told him a red coat would suit him.

"Ma'am, I've been happy in your service, and you've been so kind. But now Mr. Thompson's gone it's just a bit lonely, and what with the war and all, and everyone busy,

I'd hate you to bother His Royal Highness, but maybe a word . . ."

"Dear Sam . . . of course if you want it, though I can't bear to lose you."

Such fun, though, to give her friends what they most desired. Sam Carter was hardly a friend, but he had served her well, and he looked such a lamb in the pantry, cleaning the knives.

"Sir, you know my Sammy, who waits at table?"

"The youth who bends at the waist like a daffodil?"

"Yes. You'll hardly believe it, he wants a commission. I sent him to school, you know, he's quite educated. A lovable lad, but he's wasting his time as a footman."

"Let me have all the particulars, then, and I'll see."

Samuel Carter was commissioned an ensign, 16th Foot. Gazetted around April 1804. This sort of thing was easy, one name at a time; it was still more or less in the family, and no money changed hands. The test was to come once she started to play with promotions. Each day she made some excuse . . . but Ogilvie waited.

The clock struck nine, and here was Martha with the breakfast tray. The engagement list was brought, and the slate as well.

"Ma'am, that fellow Few is here again."

"Who's he?"

"He had a shop in Bernard Street. You bought a lamp from him for Tavistock Place, nearly a year ago, he says."

"That Grecian thing Lord Barrymore smashed to pieces? I remember. Well, what does he want now? Selling more relics?"

"No, ma'am, he says the lamp was never paid for. It cost him twenty pounds to get it fitted."

"Nonsense! He did it in his own back room. Send him away."

Ridiculous, to pester her at this juncture with a twelve-month-old account from Bloomsbury. Those days belonged to limbo. So did the debts.

"How's Master George's cold?"

"He says it's better, and he doesn't want to go to school today. He wants to watch the Life Guards in the barracks."

"Bless him, so he shall. You take him, Martha."

139

"But what about Miss Mary and Miss Ellen?"

"They don't have colds, so they must do their lessons."

She had a lesson, too—Corri, the music master, at half-past ten. Like Sam, he had been a protégé of Sutton's, but more like a lily than a daffodil, and overblown at that.

"Martha, I have Mr. Corri coming this morning. See that the drawing-room's ready, and my harp uncovered. Mr. Ogilvie at twelve. Miss Taylor said she might call this afternoon. If she does, and I am busy with anyone else, she can go to the children; they'll be home by then. Tell Parker I shan't want the carriage before four. Tell Pierson we shan't be dining until seven, but Cook must have all ready by half-past six, in case His Royal Highness should be on time. We know he can't bear waiting for his dinner. What's on the slate? . . . Roast duck? . . . We had it on Sunday."

"I heard Ludovick mention that the cook at Portman Square had a salmon. If His Royal Highness don't dine there, it will go to waste."

"Not if I know it. Send Pierson there to fetch it. But it must be dressed by the oilman round in George Street—the cook can't do it here, he doesn't know how. Where are my slippers?"

"There, ma'am, under the bed."

"What's in that box?"

"Capes, ma'am, from the dressmaker's. They've sent several for you to try, you can wear them in turn."

"I don't like capes, the gossips will say I'm pregnant. Get Pierson to take them back when he fetches the salmon."

A morning wrapper would do for the music master, hair twisted into a topknot, curls in ribbons. A touch of blue on the eyelid, nothing more.

"Mama . . . Mama . . ."

"George, my love, my angel."

A handkerchief to his nose. "Now run to Martha." The girls aggrieved and prim: "Why is George excused?" "Because, my darling geese, he's only six, and if you're good I'll take you in the carriage. Now disappear, and leave me to get dressed."

Down in the drawing-room Mr. Corri waited, his face round and waxen, on a drooping stem, framed by an aureole of silken hair. He posed by the harp, the door of the drawing-room open, in case the inconceivable should happen and His Royal Highness had not left the house.

No use. The hope was doomed to disappointment. Mrs. Clarke ran down the stairs alone, waving her hand.

"Good morning, Corri. Have I kept you waiting? I'm always late, I never get dressed in time."

"Dear madam, in this house time has no meaning. To breathe the air you breathe is paradise. I passed your fairy children on the stairs."

"I hope George didn't kick you on the shin."

"Dear madam, no. He pursed up his tiny mouth and made the most amusing face at me, for fun."

"I'm glad you thought it funny. When he does that at me I generally beat his bottom. What shall we sing today?"

"A little Mozart?"

"If it will loosen up the voice, we will. But only as an exercise, no more. His Royal Highness doesn't care for Mozart. He likes to hear something with a tune, he says."

"A tune . . . my dearest madam . . ."

"Come on, Corri. You know what I mean. Not tra-la-la, all wind and too much of it, but a song success from Vauxhall, the broader the better."

She flipped the pages of the music while he stood by shrinking, a little pained. "These won't do. I'd sound like a cow in labour. His Royal Highness likes to laugh, not stop his ears."

She threw his music on the floor and found her own. "Here, let's try this, we heard it last Thursday night. 'To London Town I'll Haste Away'—here's something he can beat time to on the floor. And what about this: 'When Sandy Told His Tale of Love'? The third verse is a real shocker."

"If you insist, sweet madam, if you insist."

She rippled the harp. Their voices filled the air. Hers, true and clear; his, throaty, passionate. A knock on the door disturbed the solemn lesson.

"Mr. Ogilvie to see you."

"Tell him to wait."

Just one more song, which Ogilvie should hear through the double drawing-room doors and comprehend: " 'Young William Seeks My Heart To Move.' "

141

She heard the discreet applause at the conclusion. "Now, Mr. Corri, that must be all for now. The same time tomorrow."

He gathered up his things. "Madam, forgive me mentioning it again, but those gentlemen who are so anxious to make your acquaintance, a Colonel French and a Captain Sandon—would it be possible for one or both of them to call this afternoon?"

"What do they want?"

"I cannot say exactly. They are friends of a friend . . . I said I would act as intermediary."

The usual thing, of course. Some favour to be requested. Corri would get a percentage on the deal.

"You mean," she asked, "some military matter?"

"I think so, dearest lady. Your influence is known. A word in the right quarter, you understand."

She understood. It happened every day. Letters, notes, from strangers or from friends. "Dear Mrs. Clarke, if you could see your way to putting forward my name . . . A word from you to His Royal Highness would carry more weight than any application to the War Office . . . and I need hardly say, any recompense you ask I would gladly pay."

She shrugged her shoulders and handed Mr. Corri his sheets of music. "I can't promise anything, Corri. These things are very delicate and difficult. Your friends can call, but they may not find me at home."

"That is for them to risk, dear lady, naturally. But I believe two thousand guineas was the sum they mentioned."

She turned her back and pretended to rearrange flowers. Just as he moved towards the door she said casually: "For whom, two thousand guineas?"

He sighed with a pained expression, his drooping shoulders emphasising that he himself had no concern in the matter.

"Sweet madam, you have direct access to His Royal Highness. Need I say more—but use your own discretion?"

He bowed from the waist, and was gone. Two thousand guineas . . . Double the annual sum the Duke had promised her, which came, at the moment, a dribble month by month, enough to pay the servants and no more.

She opened the double doors and called to Ogilvie, "Well, did you hear me sing?"

He sauntered in with a smile and kissed her hand. No flattery from him, no admiration. He was the only man amongst her male acquaintences who never once presumed, who kept his distance.

"Young William seeks your heart to move? The words intrigued me. I don't seek to move your heart. Only your head."

"Which prefers to think for itself, without your assistance."

She offered him refreshment. He refused. She motioned him to a chair and then sat herself, with her back to the window, watching him.

"You're like an evil shadow in the background. Why can't you leave me alone? I'm perfectly happy."

"Are you?" he said. "I doubt it. No woman's happy unless she has her man under lock and key. Which your prince isn't."

"I keep the cage door open. He's free to fly. But he always comes home to roost, like a faithful bird."

"I'm glad to hear it. Domestic bliss is touching. Providing, of course, the bliss continues to last."

Always the sting, the probe, the innuendo that nothing was permanent.

"Did you ask him about the defences south of London?"

"No, and I'm damned if I'm going to. I'm not a spy."

"A spy is a stupid word for a woman of your intelligence to use. It happens that the information can be useful, not necessarily now, but in the future."

"Useful to whom?"

"To you, to me, to both of us. We're partners, aren't we, in this little game? Or were, when we started out."

The hint, the guarded threat. She was not keeping to the pact agreed.

"You don't understand," she said. "He's honest, direct. The things he tells, he tells in confidence. If I repeated them, I'd call it betrayal."

"How noble you've become, in the last six months. It must be the effect of Gloucester Place. You see yourself established here for good. Perhaps I should remind you of

143

Wolsey's speech. 'Put not your trust in Princes'—or am I a cynic?"

"I think you're a cynic and a traitor too. I shouldn't be surprised if you left this house and went straight to some French agent with all I've said. All right. Go to them. Tell them what we eat and what we drink, what time we go to bed and when we get up. The Paris press can lampoon us if they please; they won't hear any secrets." She pulled a face at him, the self-same face that George had pulled at Corri on the stairs, then stared at him, defiant.

He sighed and shrugged his shoulders. "Don't tell me you've done the one unforgivable thing, fatal to business and fatal to peace of mind—I'd expect it of some other woman, but not of you—don't tell me you've fallen in love with your princely protector?"

"Of course not. Don't be absurd."

She rose and moved about the room. He watched her, thoughtfully.

"I wouldn't be so sure. It's insidious, isn't it? Gives rather a settled feeling, to stick to one man, who isn't ill-looking and holds his exalted position. It must whip up your response in remarkable fashion."

Trust Ogilvie to smear trust and gratitude, and probe a hidden, unadmitted weakness. Love was a thing forgotten. Love was over, but not entirely dead when His Majesty's favourite son was on the pillow.

"I wish to heaven," she said, "you'd go away. You come here day after day. I have nothing to give you."

"A little co-operation is all I require."

"I won't become a spy. Take that as final."

"Nothing is final in this shifting world. Remember that; it may be of use someday. But, for the moment, other things are pressing. I closed my business, you know, to become your agent. When do I start?"

"I tell you, I've nothing for you."

He took a folder from his pocket, opened it, pulled out a piece of paper, and handed it to her.

"Here's a list of names," he said, "a list of officers, in various regiments, all requiring favours. Some of them want promotion, others exchanges. If they go through the ordinary channels, it takes three months."

"Well, can't they wait?"

"Of course they can wait, but it isn't to our advantage to let them do so. You give this list to the Duke, and we'll see what happens. You know what time to choose, what mood, what moment."

"He'll probably refuse."

"Too bad. We think again. But let me make one suggestion, if I may. Before you give him the list, ask for money. Tell him this house is costing much more than you thought; that you don't know what to do; that you're very worried. Then let an hour elapse, and hand it to him."

"Why an hour?"

"The alimentary tract is delicate, the princely organs slow when digesting medicine. By the way, your story is true, so you won't tell a falsehood. The house is costing you money. You *are* very worried."

Useless to protest. He knew too much, knew her basic fear also, the root of the trouble: "If I should fail, what happens to the children?"—that bogey, lurking in the background of her mind.

She stood there, looking at the list of names.

"Will?"

"Yes, Mary Anne?"

"I've had an offer of two thousand guineas. I don't know yet who from or what it's all about. They may be calling here this afternoon."

"See them, have it confirmed, and report to me. Don't look so solemn, my dear. It's all very simple. You've nothing to lose and everything to gain. The easiest game in the world, when you've learnt to play it. Two thousand guineas the richer for playing it well."

"You swear there's no danger?"

"I don't follow you. Danger to whom?"

"To the Duke . . . to me . . . to all of us . . . to the country?"

The sudden panic of a cockney child . . . look out, the beadle's after you, get under the barrow, quick, or up the alley . . . don't you let on to mother where you've been.

He said, "This country has been run on graft since the Norman Conquest. From the highest bishop down to the lowest low-paid clerk, we're all in the same line of business. You needn't worry. Remember your first job with

145

your father's printer? You fooled the dull-witted then, you can fool them today."

"But this is different."

"Oh no, it's not. The game's identical. If you hadn't played it then, you'd have been in the gutter; but you seized your chance and saved your family. If you lack courage now . . ." He paused; the front door banged, a small boy shouted, the sound quickly followed by scrambling on the stairs ". . . If you lack courage now, what happens to him?"

"George is to go to the Chelsea school in the autumn, and on to Marlow in a year or two. His future's quite assured, the Duke has promised."

Will Ogilvie smiled, and gestured with his hands.

"A godfather with a wand? How very delightful. Yet wands have a trick of vanishing, and so do promises. If I were George, I'd rather rely on Mother."

The child burst into the room, excited and noisy. "Martha took me to see the Life Guards doing their drill. You will let me be a soldier, won't you, and ride on a horse after Boney, and cut him to pieces? Hullo, Uncle Will. Tell Mama to make me a soldier."

"I gather from your mother the matter's in hand. Goodbye, you horrible child. Don't touch my breeches. Well, Mary Anne, will you send a report in the morning?"

"I don't know . . . I can't promise."

He left her with the child and she watched him walk away up Gloucester Place. Confidant and friend, or evil counsellor? She couldn't be sure.

"What are you reading, Mama, can I see?"

"It's nothing, darling. Only a list of names."

The children were home from school, May Taylor had come to visit. They all went for a drive in the carriage round the park. Should she confide in May and seek her advice? But that would mean an admission of former lies, destruction of the fable built for her family, and for her friends as well, as to how she met the Duke on the first encounter.

"I'll tell you what happened. I went to an evening party. Someone came up and said, 'His Royal Highness wants to be introduced,' and from that moment . . ." Swallowed by all, accepted and taken for granted. How could she turn

146

to May in the carriage, blurt out the truth, and explain, "Your Uncle's a pimp, and so is Will Ogilvie. They hatched up this business between them, with me for investment, and now they're itching for the dividend"—how could she?

No use. Forget it. Friendship was so easily broken. A family row, the Taylors scandalised, the growing romance between Isobel and one of the Taylor brothers nipped in the bud, and all for nothing.

"Mary Anne, I've never seen you look so preoccupied. Is anything on your mind?"

"Yes, I'm short of money."

"You're joking, surely! You, in your position? You've only got to ask His Royal Highness."

"Have I? I wonder. Never mind it now. Parker, call in at Birkett's the silversmith before we return home. I have some candlesticks ordered that should be ready."

Should be, and were. They had been despatched already to the house, so Birkett told her in person, bending from the waist.

"Can I tempt you with these cupids just come in?"

"Tempt me with nothing. I might run to a sauceboat, coat-of-arms included."

"Madam likes to jest. Have you used the dinner service?"

"Once. His Royal Highness says it tastes of polish."

"Impossible, madam. The Duc de Berri never had silver cleaned. I had it from an *émigré*, who knew his servants."

"Then it must have been mould we tasted, and not polish. Next time we give a party I'll wash every bit of it myself with soap and water."

"Madam is always so gay. Do you need an entrée dish? I have one here that belonged to the Marquis de St. Clair. Lost his head, alas, like so many other noblemen."

"That dish looks big enough to hold it too. But I'm not Salome, begging a boon from Herod. What do I owe you, Birkett?"

The face expressed horror, the hands brushed away the air. Such things were never discussed, but were left to the future.

"Tell me. I want to know."

"If Madam insists . . . about a thousand pounds. Five hundred on account will always suit. But please, don't press His Royal Highness for it." He bowed her from the shop. The children waved. The footman closed the carriage door and climbed to his place, arms folded, beside the coachman. When she got home the candlesticks were waiting. Beside them lay the account, and written across it: "Settlement of the above would greatly oblige."

Patronage was good, but payment better. All the credit she wanted in the world . . . for six months only. Odd that demands for payment were coming in batches now. Could it conceivably be—to the view of a tradesman—that after six months a prince often changed his mind?

She crumpled the bill in her hands and sent the children to Martha.

"Yes, Pierson, what is it?"

"Two gentlemen have arrived and wish to see you, a Captain Sandon and a Colonel French."

"Did they state their business?"

"No, ma'am, but they mentioned Mr. Corri's name."

"Very well. Say I'm at home and bring them to the drawing-room."

A glance in the mirror, a touch to the hair, and she was ready. A thousand pounds for Birkett's silver plate. And these men promised her two thousand guineas. "Settlement of the above would greatly oblige, but five hundred pounds on account would always suit."

Why not use the self-same words and clinch the deal?

FOUR: Dinner was over. The children had been visited and kissed good-night. The drawing-room lamps were lighted, the curtains drawn.

"Pierson."

"Your Royal Highness?"

"Tell Ludovick I'll want him here at six tomorrow morning. I'm driving down to Hythe—away till Saturday."

"Very good, Your Royal Highness."

He settled himself down before the fire, his glass of brandy on the stool beside him, loosened his waistcoat button, sighed, and stretched.

"Sing to me, my sweet."

"What shall I sing?"

"Some jingle from Vauxhall. I'm not particular."

She sang the songs she'd practised in the morning, keeping her eye upon him from the piano. He beat time with his foot and with his hand, and hummed the accompaniment in tuneless fashion. She watched his head loll lower on his chest, then lift itself with an effort to hum once more. "London Town" was spirited and catchy; "Sandy" a mock at love, with raffish words. She passed from them to his favourites of six months past. "Two Strings to Your Bow," a ballad, and mildly salacious; "I'll Do So No More," soporific, conducive to concord.

At last, with the brandy downed and the blue eye glazed, the waistcoat all abroad, and the temper mellow, she gave him the final aphrodisiac:

> "*Love is a Cheat,*
> *Let's be Merry today . . .*"

and, closing the piano lid, came to kneel by his side.

149

"Why did you stop, my darling?" he asked.

"Because I haven't seen you all day. And tomorrow you won't be with me. Do you mind?"

He pulled her across his chair and settled her in his arms with her head on his shoulder.

"If you think I want to jig about the country and sleep on a barrack bed, when I might be with you . . . What's this?"

"An underslip, don't loosen it. Where will you be tomorrow?"

"Hythe, then on to Folkestone, Deal, and Dover. Back, with any luck, by midday Saturday."

She took his hand in hers; played with the fingers; bit each nail in turn; caressed the palm.

"Must you go to Oatlands?"

"The Duchess will turn stuffy if I don't. She always has the house full on a Sunday. Besides, the tongues start wagging when I give church a miss, and the King gets to hear. He has me up on the mat and scolds me like a schoolboy."

"He doesn't do that to the Prince of Wales."

"Of course he doesn't. They're not on speaking terms, so I'm the scapegoat. I tell you what, my sweet . . . go on, I like it . . . there's a house across the park from Oatlands, empty. It used to belong to the steward, but he doesn't use it. Why don't you furnish the place and fix up a staff, and then I can come for the night, after leaving the Duchess?"

"Nothing would please me more. And the wagging tongues?"

"Oh, they won't wag at that. I'd be living at Oatlands. Easiest thing in the world to slip through the park."

"You can't slip anywhere, at six foot two, with all that girth . . . I'd love to go to Weybridge from Saturday to Monday, and get myself country air; but the trouble is, won't it be very dear?"

"The house won't cost you much—it's lying idle."

"It will have to be fitted, furnished, decorated. The trouble is, sir, you're such a child in these matters. It comes from living in palaces all your life. You just don't begin to know how we mortals live."

"I'm learning rapidly."

"You've learnt how to leap into bed without help from a valet. But that's about all. A baby in arms could do better than you in the morning. Ludovick buttons you up like a nursemaid pinning napkins."

"That's mostly your fault. I'm no longer so spry when I wake. Time was when I rode around the park before eating breakfast."

"You're not idle here . . . but the rhythm is not quite the same; one day you'll forget, and put my head in a nose bag. But, sir, I'm in earnest, I'd love to be with you at Weybridge; the thing is, I just can't afford it. To furnish a house, to get a staff, to keep it all going—it's quite out of the question to manage it, on my allowance."

Silence, a moody pause, a restless movement. She changed position, leant more lightly against his arm.

"Don't I give you enough?"

"Enough to maintain a small cottage."

"Well, damn it, I don't know. I'm perpetually bothered. Greenwood and Cox have the handling of all my finances. They and Coutts and the rest of them work through the tangle, and my treasurer, Adam, puts in a word now and then. I'm constantly broke and can't keep my official establishment going, let alone yours. You say I don't know how you live; you, the ordinary mortal. You haven't an earthly idea of *our* total expenses. I and my brother, Clarence, and Kent, and the rest. The Prince of Wales has the capital, he can exist; but the rest of us are up to our necks in debt. The whole thing's mismanaged, I've said it again and again."

Watch out—the subject's tricky, don't pursue it. The seed is sown, let it lie fallow a moment. She slipped off his knee, tended the sinking fire. "I don't want to add to your expenses, ever. Perhaps we were wrong to move to Gloucester Place? And yet . . . it's so handy here for Portman Square, I love it, and so do you . . . but, sir, if it breaks you, let's give the whole thing up. I'll go to rooms, send the children to my mother, sack the servants."

"God damn it, no."

He pulled her back again beside his chair. She knelt between his knees, her arms around him.

"I don't mean I'm a pauper. I'm merely broke." His voice was angry, fretful. "If there's one subject in the world I hate discussing, and always have done, that sub-

151

ject's money. I've told you dozens of times you can live on credit."

"You, sir, perhaps. But not your fancy lady."

She laid her face against his cheek and touched his hair.

"Who bothers you with bills?" he asked.

"Birkett, and others . . . We shouldn't have brought that silver plate; but it was so tempting to think of breast of chicken lying abandoned on the fleur-de-lis, though it tasted no better than it would off chipped enamel."

"If Birkett starts complaining I'll have him arrested."

"Poor little Birkett. How ruthless you are, and hard." Give him a massage behind the ears, a kiss on the eyebrow. "Have you really the power to send a man to prison?"

"Yes, if he gives me cause."

"Is that what it means, 'His Royal Highness used the royal prerogative'?"

"Highnesses don't. You're thinking of His Majesty."

"Archbishops have a prerogative, why not you?"

"Matter of privilege. Must we go into it now?"

"But, sir, I adore information . . . it's the breath of life. Parliament gets prorogued; is that different again?"

"Utterly and completely. Prorogue is another word for discontinue."

"Prerog—prorogue—there must be some connection. Could you prorogue a kiss if I was giving one?"

The matter was put to the test and found impossible. The fire was reduced to embers in the grate. The single armchair proved inadequate to comfort.

"Why are we sitting down here?"

"You're sitting . . . I'm kneeling."

"It must be deuced uncomfortable."

"It is. I was only awaiting the royal command to rise."

They went hand-in-hand upstairs, and from her half-open bedroom door she could hear the sound of clothes flung on the floor. She wondered how the digestive powers were working. Was Ogilvie right or wrong? And did it take an hour to let medicine simmer? She took the list of names and studied it. They were mostly captains wanting majorities—it was impossible to remember all the names. She pinned the list on to the curtained bed, above her pillow, where it would catch his eye.

"Sir?" She called to the dressing-room.

"I'll be with you in a moment."

"Sir, do you know on old boy called Colonel French?"

"Can't say I do, offhand. What's his regiment?"

"I don't think he has one. The thing is, he's retired. Or else half-pay. Not of great importance. But apparently he's been writing to you at the Horse Guards."

"They all do that. Letters pour in every day from half-pay colonels right through the ruddy country."

"He wants to raise recruits."

"Well, he can raise them."

"Yes, but it takes such a time to get his letter of service. I don't know what it means, but I suppose you do."

"He'll get it eventually, if his application is approved. It will go to my M.S., Clinton, or the A.M.S., Loraine, and one or the other will forward it to Hewitt, the Inspector General."

"Then what?"

"Then back to me for comments, and signature, if I agree. These fellows get so impatient, of course it takes time. Do they think we have nothing else to do but sit on our arses reading their ruddy letters?"

"You know, I think they do. They have no vision. But this man, Colonel French, was extremely nice. Apologised for bothering, etc., etc., and said that if I would merely mention his name he'd be infinitely obliged, and rather more."

"What did he mean by that?"

"I hardly know. Perhaps he meant he'd send me a bunch of flowers."

Silence from the dressing-room. Then came the sound of a window opening, the treading of heavy feet on the carpeted floor.

Captain Sandon, in point of fact, had done most of the talking. Five hundred guineas on account, and, the letter of service accepted, another fifteen hundred . . . Then French would go off to Ireland to raise recruits, and for each man raised she'd get a further guinea, to be paid when five hundred men were passed.

"And what do you receive?" she had asked him. The point was interesting.

Sandon, with a face like a ferret, had tried to explain.

153

"The official bounty, ma'am, laid down by government, is that each recruiting party gets thirteen guineas for every man who joins. Some regiments of the line pay nineteen guineas. We want to get it, and we'd find more recruits, but the letters we send to the War Office lie unanswered. A word to the C.-in-C. and the thing would be done. The higher the bounty, the higher your reward."

It sounded too simple. A price upon every head. Each valiant recruit in Ireland a guinea in her pocket.

She got into bed and settled down amongst the pillows; and above her, pinned to the curtains, fluttered the list. An oath rang out from the dressing-room, something crashed to the floor. Digestion was slow in working, or too swift. He padded in. She closed her eyes and waited. She felt him climb into bed on the other side.

"You know," he said, "if you were really clever, you'd never need to pester me for money. That fellow French . . ."

"The bunch of flowers?"

"Bunch of bullocks . . . he'd show his gratitude. You can dandle them all on a string, in your position. And when they don't oblige, just show them the door."

"Won't you make it clear what *is* my exact position?"

"I wasn't certain. Downstairs, we became rather tangled."

An interlude, to thrash the point in question.

"What the devil's that?"

"I wondered when you'd spot it."

"It's the first time I've had occasion to raise my head . . . Whose are all those names?"

"Just names of gentlemen."

"Admirers from your past, who set the standard?"

"No, soldiers of the Crown. It's you they serve. To tell the truth, I've never heard of one of them."

"What's the idea? Am I suddenly lacking in stamina? Is it a gentle hint my strength is ebbing, and these fifteen chaps would put up a better show? If so . . ."

Cessation of the conversation, and another refresher course to win new spurs.

"I only pinned them there to jog your mind."

"I like it jogged at the Horse Guards, not at home."

"The poor men want some grace and favour shown them."

154

"So do I . . . don't throw away the pillow."

"Think how happy they'd be, if they got promoted. Bouquets in either hand, each one for me. The place would look like a hothouse, stiff with roses . . ."

"Are you short of flowers?"

"I'm short of a lot of things."

"Are you asleep?"

"I was. Not any longer . . . If you knew anything of military matters, you'd know I can't promote every Tom, Dick, or Harry. I have to go into each case and read the record, to see if the chap is fit to receive promotion."

"Oh well, forget it. They can all go and join the Marines."

"I'll look them up, but it's impossible to do them all at once. More over . . ."

The digestive juices were apparently working well. The medicine had been absorbed and was coursing through the system. Small doses as prescribed, to be repeated.

"You'll have to shift to Weybridge at weekends, to that house I told you about, across the park. Unless you do I'll cut my throat, mooning around the grotto with the Duchess."

"The lap dogs will keep you busy."

"Mangy brutes. They bite your fingers if you try to stroke 'em."

"Don't waste your talent, then, reserve your patronage for them as likes it. Did the clock strike one?"

"I'm hardly a judge of time. My ears are covered."

"You've got five hours before you ride to Dover."

"I'm told that Boney manages with far less."

"Less what?"

"Less time, and fewer hours in which to sleep."

"He's only five foot four; you've more to carry. Bulk must be housed and rested, soothed and tended."

"I'll warrant that Boney suffers less than I do. If it came to a test of endurance, man to man."

"He'd stand to lose. Winner takes all, plus biscuit."

Silence fell upon Gloucester Place, peace, oblivion. The guttering candles flickered and went out. Darkness, like a mantle, shrouded the room. From one of the pillows came the sound of gentle breathing, and from the other snores more stertorous.

155

"It's six o'clock, Your Royal Highness."

"All right. Get out."

The pallid light of morning through the window, reluctant harbinger of worse to come. Spring rain, a muddied road, a jolting carriage. A camp the other end, at best a barracks. The stink of brass and leather, new equipment. The smell of men *en masse*, of smoke and powder.

"Are you awake?"

She wasn't. Best to leave her, with a kiss on the tumbled hair and on the cheek. She was awake, and, arms lifted, clung to his shoulder.

"Don't go. It isn't morning."

"It is. And Ludovick's here."

"Throw him downstairs."

Regrets and protestations were of no avail. Obligations came first, and dalliance must wait on duty. The bugle called.

"Good-bye, my sweetheart. I'll try and be home by Saturday."

"Don't go to Oatlands. Spend the weekend with me."

Back to the pillows and a vanished dream, to what great depth of slumber heaven knew. Chasing forbidden strangers up the alley, Charley in tow and Eddie on her shoulder. Street sounds, street cries, the smell of onions cooking, cabbages in drains, the sound of water.

When she woke at nine the sun was shining. She felt above her head. The list had gone.

FIVE: Will Ogilvie was right. It was all so simple. And once the word got round that promotion could be obtained through personal channels, requests increased.

"Draw up a regular tariff," said Will, "not too high. I'll put it about that with your influence you can obtain a majority for nine hundred, a company for seven hundred. And say a lieutenancy for four hundred quid, or it's not worth your while; and two hundred quid for an ensign—that's about fair. Make it a point that you'll merely put forward the name, by word of mouth only, with no letters backwards and forwards. Once the names are gazetted, the purchasers pay the cash to you. Don't have it in bills—a bill can be traced, and that's fatal. Insist upon cash, in bank notes, and not in large numbers."

"You'll manage that for me?" she pleaded.

"I'll do what I can, but my name must on no account appear. I'm simply the friend-of-a-friend, who has heard you are generous."

On thinking it over she decided the game was humane. Patriotic and loyal, she was saving the country, flooding the Army with officers, all of them burning to serve. She would get what they asked and charge only a reasonable figure, and of course they would be grateful, and no one would obtain a commission without a good record.

The money they paid was a godsend. Driving to Weybridge that summer, she counted the cost. The house at the end of the park had once been a farm, and no one could live in a farmhouse unless it was gutted first. The stables must be pulled down and rebuilt, a wing for the servants added, new tiles for the roof, and two other rooms turned into one. The staff had to be fed, there would be the grooms and the coachman to house, two men and a boy in the garden—she couldn't have done it but for the patronage business, the game on the side.

The letter of service went through and French sailed for Ireland. But Sandon, his friend, proved an ally, and frequently called. She had to be careful with this—there might be some clashing. He used to bring lists from his pocket as Ogilvie did, and if Ogilvie guessed there was somebody else in the offing who asked a percentage there could be an awkward *débâcle*. As it was, once or twice they produced duplicate lists, with the same names on each of officers wanting promotion. And then, when she'd passed the names on and the men were gazetted, she was forced to give double percentage, at loss to herself.

All went very smoothly, however, and the Duke asked no questions. She would mention a name—Captain So-and-so wants a majority—or jot the particulars down, and let them lie handy. He'd remember the name or pocket the small scrap of paper. The matter was never discussed; discretion was mutual.

Bill was the only dissentient, the fly in the ointment. He called, as ill-luck would have it, at the same time as French, the very morning, in fact, when old French produced the five hundred, the sum on account to facilitate his letter of service.

She was upstairs dressing, and Pierson sent word by Martha, "Mr. Dowler is here, he's gone straight up to the drawing-room," while Colonel French had already arrived and been waiting ten minutes. She hurriedly finished her toilet and ran down the stairs, but one glance at Bill's face was enough to show what had happened. French, voluble, rather excited, had hinted his mission, once Bill had introduced himself as an intimate friend, and the cat—or part of the cat—had leapt out of the bag.

"They must get a move on," she heard as she entered the drawing-room. "How the devil can they expect recruits, if they dilly-dally over letters of service for the people who want to raise them? I've explained this again and again in official letters to Colonel Loraine, the A.M.S. at the War Office. He just ignores them, and the request gets pigeon-holed. Mrs. Clarke says she'll do what she can, and I hope for results."

"Colonel French, I'm delighted to see you. And Bill, what a stranger!"

Small talk to cover the issue, to make a diversion, but the stout little colonel yapped on and wouldn't be muzzled.

"There's so much obstruction high up. General Hewitt's the trouble. He's the Inspector General, and blocks every demand. He has a prejudice against what he calls 'recruiters,' officers on half-pay like myself, whose only desire, you may be sure, is to serve my country. If Mrs. Clarke would but mention to the Commander-in-Chief how Hewitt obstructs us . . ." and so on and so on, while Bill's face got longer and longer.

And then—the final embarrassment—bank notes were produced. "Will your friend Mr. Dowler excuse us? A financial transaction," and French drew her into a corner and chatted in whispers.

It couldn't have been more distressing. She was livid with rage. The only way to surmount the whole situation was by seeming offhand and treating the business as natural. French finally took himself off and Bill, with a face like a parson mounting a pulpit, stared at the ceiling. Attack was the best form of defence, so she rounded upon him.

"Good God, what a face! What's the matter? Have you come from a funeral? I don't seem to have seen you for days, and this is what happens. It wasn't my fault that fat little bore came to call."

Silence. Then Bill, in schoolmaster fashion, "He may be a fat little bore, that doesn't concern me. What does concern me—as someone who happens to love you—is to see you playing a game that you don't understand. Getting yourself mixed up in military matters."

"Oh, don't be absurd. You're always so disapproving. Of course people pester me—I expect it in my position. The Duke told me himself it would happen, and he ought to know. I'm only too glad to help anyone wanting assistance. Genuine people, who show that they're really sincere."

She worked herself up into anger, self-righteous, indignant.

"You don't live in the world," she went on, "stuck down

159

at Uxbridge, pottering about like a rustic from morning to night. I daresay I meet more people, and help them, too, in the course of a morning than you ever do in a week. Not only soldiers like French, but from every profession. I'm applied to for all sorts of jobs, you wouldn't believe it. It isn't my fault, it just happens, and that's all there is to it. If the Duchess showed a little more spirit, and behaved like a wife, they'd suck up to her and then I shouldn't be bothered. But they know she's no one, that she's as helpless as one of her lap dogs, so they all come to me. I get the brunt on my shoulders."

He let her run on, but with Bill it was never much use. He wasn't deceived for a moment, she saw from his eye.

"I may live like a rustic," he said, "but I'm not quite a fool. By all means use your influence to help, but don't take bribes. You'll get yourself into trouble, and him as well."

"I don't take bribes."

"What were those notes just now?"

"Merely a compliment, a sort of present, for furthering matters for him. You heard what he said—obstruction at the War Office, nothing gets passed. I'm simply another channel, and more direct."

"Are you prepared to go to the Horse Guards and say so?"

"I wouldn't mind. It might give them the jerk they need."

"Bravado, and you know it. What you're doing is strictly illegal, and stinks of corruption. For God's sake, give it up and keep your hands clean. Can't you be content to remain his mistress? That's triumph for you enough, without playing with muck."

"How dare you attack me like this . . ."

"I don't attack you. It breaks my heart to see you behave like a fool."

"All right. Well, get out of the house. Go back to the pure air of Uxbridge where you belong. I don't ask for advice, nor for approval. I expect my friends to accept what I do, and keep silent."

"That's not what you said at Hampstead."

"Hampstead was different. The whole world's changed since then."

160

"For you, perhaps."

He went to the door. She let him go, and then, before he reached the stairs, cried, "Bill . . . come back."

He came, and stood in the doorway. She held out her arms.

"Why do you treat me so, what have I done?"

It was useless to argue and plead, to give advice. All she asked for now as approbation, soft words, a kiss of comfort, understanding.

"I have to do it, Bill. I need the money."

"He gives you an allowance, doesn't he?"

"Yes, but it's never enough . . . the expense is appalling. This house alone costs treble what he gives; and now there's the one at Weybridge to add to it all. Horses, carriages, food, furniture, clothes . . . Don't tell me 'cut it down,' it isn't possible. I'm forced to live in this fashion because of him; it's what he's used to, it's how he expects things done. He'd never be content with some backstairs room, a hole-and-corner affair, in slapdash style. This is his second home. He calls it that. His only home, if the truth were told."

"You're fond of him, aren't you?"

"Perhaps . . . that isn't the point. The point is that I can't, and won't ask for more money. He hasn't it to give me, so I'm driven to this." She held up the notes that French had given her. "Corrupt if you like, well, so is every business, and every profession, too: it's a part of life. Politicians, parsons, soldiers, sailors, they're all the same. Have you heard the latest gossip and read the papers? What do you suppose Lord Melville's been up to at the Admiralty? There's going to be a Commission of Enquiry to look into his affairs."

"All the more reason for you to be wary with yours."

"Oh, they'll sit for about a year behind closed doors, and nothing be proven at the end of it, so the Duke says."

"I wonder. I very much doubt it. The Radicals won't let it drop, depend upon that."

"Let us all be convicted of fraud, what on earth does it matter? I'll keep my head above water as long as I can."

He kissed her and went. She sensed the condemnation. The kiss was a kiss of rebuke, of stricture, of blame. Oh well . . . if that's how he felt, no more to be said. He must

161

just keep away from the house and not call any more. He punished himself more than her; she could manage without him. Her life was already so full that there just wasn't time to be bored by displeasure from friends, from ex-lovers like Bill. Sympathy, yes; but no chiding, no passing of censure. That schoolmaster manner jarred, in her present position. He treated her still like the child who had run from her husband, without seeming to realise how she had changed and matured.

The men she knew now were men of the world, of fashion, and beside them poor Bill seemed a stick . . . attractive, but dull. James Fitzgerald, the Irish M.P., was one of her favourites, a great gift of the gab and a lawyer, with a tongue like an asp. He liked to whisper the scandals of Ireland over his brandy, with a skeleton in every Protestant cupboard. William Coxhead-Marsh was another who lurked in the background, a friend of the Duke's, often invited to dinner. He said he adored her, she'd but to command, he'd obey. If she tired of the Duke he'd fit up a mansion in Essex, any day, any night, she had only to murmur the word. This was all said *sotto voce*, knee pressing under the table. Will Boodle, Russell Manners, and others hinted the same. They flattered her, petted her —lighthearted nonsense, of course, received with a smile and five grains of salt, but fun all the same.

It was a pity the royal lover was not more sociable. The lavishly furnished house was so right for receptions. Dinners, and parties, and music—she loved entertaining. He liked a few friends now and then, but never a rabble, and preferred to sit quietly after dinner while she sang to him, or play cards with a handful of cronies, even May Taylor! He put her in mind of Bob Farquhar, his tastes were so humdrum, in a way almost middle-class; it seemed so strange. A raffish joke or song, then a burst of laughter— a servant spilt the soup, and he split his sides. Racing was a topic he found congenial. He was happy to sit a whole evening discussing form with a few horsy friends, a glass of port at his elbow. While the Prince and Mrs. Fitzherbert . . . however, dismiss it. That milieu was different. The Prince had his own special circle, Charley Fox and the rest, the cream of high Whig society, all glitter and show, and assuredly more entertaining. But still, there it was; if

162

he liked to come back from the Horse Guards and get down on his knees with the children, she couldn't prevent him. Better piquet with May Taylor at Gloucester Place than lolling with Lady Hertford at Carlton House.

It gave her a pang, though, that cards were not sent out more often. "Mrs. Clarke, At Home. An evening party. Carriages at eleven," and in small letters, casually scribbled in, "To meet H.R.H. the Duke of York." He used to brush the suggestion aside when she put it to him. "If you'd sat on your arse from nine until seven, running His Majesty's army, you'd want to relax, not fill your belly with food and blab to idiots."

"The Prince of Wales entertains, with Mrs. Fitzherbert . . ."

"He hasn't a job, that's why. He has to kill time."

"You could find out so much if we gave a series of dinners. Politicians and people—not riffraff, but interesting men."

"Politicians are rogues; I prefer to leave them to my brothers. And there's nothing I want to find out; I don't choose to intrigue. What's the matter, my angel? Are you bored, are you sick of my company?"

"Of course not . . . it's only . . ."

"Have them here when I'm out . . . I don't mind. You can do as you please."

But that wasn't the point. She wanted the kudos, the glamour, to stand by his side in the drawing-room, to bow and to smile, with the house filled with guests and all of 'em plastered in diamonds and stinking of titles, not one of them less than an earl. Smirking and grinning and fawning, at *her* invitation, the girl from the alley, who'd hooked the big fish from the stream.

Occasionally, yes, he'd consent. He would give a dinner. Ten people or twelve, but no more, and they'd have to go early. Then there'd be fun and excitement, with two cooks in the kitchen, a man to help Pierson beside the ordinary footman, and four or five courses served, the silver plate gleaming (paid for, thank God, with the notes from Colonel French), and then music to follow, herself at the harp and the whole crowd applauding. This really was living, this truly was heaven, and nothing else mattered. The faces, the smiles and the laughter and clamour of voices, and the Duke overtopping them all, with his hands clasped behind him, winking, indulgent, hearty, and loud in her praises. "I tell you, by God, she's got 'em all beat at Vauxhall!" Throwing a kiss, which they saw—she could see their expressions. This was power and enchantment in one, it was bliss, it was nectar. And when they had gone and she looked at the mess and the débris, the stem of a glass in a chair, the stains on the carpet, they turned into symbols of triumph, reflecting her glory.

"Oh, sir . . . I'm so happy. I do so enjoy it."

"What, playing the hostess?"

"When you are the host. Without you it's nothing."

And lying beside him, nerves strung to high tension, too wrought up to sleep, she looked into the future, wove fantasies, mad ones, of things that might happen, of people who'd die: the Prince of Wales, never said to be strong, Princess Charlotte, so sickly, the Duke heir presumptive and close to the King, and the King always ill, always mad, always something . . . the Duke might so easily reign, in twenty years' time. Then . . . what a blaze! What a future!

Meanwhile the little sips of power were heady and pleasant, the dabble in promotions and exchanges, the boosting up of majors into colonels; small fry, perhaps, but very lucrative. It was exciting to send the notes pinned to Sandon rattled off at breakfast: "Be so good as to look at the *Gazette* tomorrow evening, as I rather expect some of the names to be inserted; I have others, I assure you on my honour. The present for my trouble for the majority is seven hundred guineas, so if you have any more this must be the same. I shall be in town Monday if you have anything to communicate . . ."

Followed by another: "I am thoroughly convinced of the money being too trifling, and I have mentioned it to a person who knows the full value of these things, so you must tell Bacon and Spedding they must give each of them two hundred more, and the captains must each give me fifty more. I am now offered eleven hundred for an older officer. I must have an answer to this, as I am to speak with Him on it. I have mentioned you as being concerned for me . . . I go to the Little Theatre this evening." With an afterthought added later: "Mrs. Clarke's compliments await Captain Sandon, thinks it best for him not to come to her Box this evening, as Greenwood goes with both the Dukes, and of course will watch where your eyes direct now and then; and should he see and know Captain Sandon may make some remark by saying or talking of the Levy business, and it may be hurtful to his and Mrs. Clarke's future interest."

But things did not always go according to plan. The names would be put forward and the bearers botch promotion by their own mistakes.

Again to Sandon: "I am vexed to death, you will know the state of my finances, and I hit upon Spedding for Tuesday, when, behold, the regiment he is in did their exercise so bad that the Duke swore at them very much, and has stopped the promotion of every one in it! He said so much to Colonel Wemyss that if he had been a gentleman he would have given up—but he intends looking over the Memorial to-day, as Spedding has not been long in that regiment, and he is an old officer; so that you see if he gets his promotion how very much he ought to be indebted to my good offices. I must beg hard for him, the Duke is very angry with you, for, when he last saw you, you promised him 300 foreigners and you have not produced one—oh, yes, master Sandon is a pretty fellow to depend on. I told you I believe that things must be done gradually, his clerks are so cunning. Get Spedding to write out a list of his services, and send it to me as a private thing to show him, not addressed to anyone. Adieu."

Sometimes she scribbled, "Burn this," at the top of her notes, but sometimes she forgot; when things went well precaution seemed unnecessary. At the end of July she had a moment's panic. Colonel Clinton, Military Secretary at the War Office, was succeeded by Colonel Gordon, more watchful, more alert. Rumours abounded; the new M.S. was tricky, he intended to look into things, had found his department slack. A hurried note to Sandon went on its way: " 'Ere I leave town I scratch a few lines, begging you to be on your guard in every point; but of my name in particular, for the future never breathe it. I am confident you have a number of enemies, for yesterday the D. was assailed from seven or eight different persons with invective against you. He is a little angry at something, but will not tell it to me."

Angry, she wondered, because Gordon was asking questions, and poking his nose into matters that Clinton had skipped? There had been some yap about the levy business, gossip was rife on that and other things. There were too many go-betweens and whispering tongues. Not Oglivie, of course, he could be trusted; but French, perhaps, in Ireland, or even Corri?

"Have you been talking?"

"Sweet madam, I protest . . ."

"Some rumour's got around, and His Royal Highness knows it. If you've kept any notes about that recruiting affair—you know to what I allude—for God's sake burn them." She sent him flying home with ashen lips.

"Keep calm," said Will. "The wind will die down in time. New brooms are always officious, give Gordon his head."

"You swore there was no danger . . ." she began.

"Nor is there any. We'll let him settle in."

Gordon settled in with a vengeance and seized the reins. One of the first results of the new régime was a letter circularised to all army agents, dated Horse Guards, September twenty-eight, 1804.

Gentlemen, His Royal Highness the Commander-in-Chief, having the strongest reason to believe that an extensive correspondence is carried on with the officers of the army, by persons styling themselves army brokers, to induce them to enter into pecuniary engagements for the purpose of obtaining commissions, contrary to the established regulations, and it being the earnest desire of the Commander-in-Chief to check, as much as possible, a practice so extremely prejudicial to the service; I am commanded to draw your attention to this important point, and to impress upon you the necessity of the utmost vigilance in preventing, as far as may be in your power, any communication whatever with those persons and the officers in your agency. And should it at any time appear that any such commissions should have been negotiated through your office, the Commander-in-Chief will consider it his duty to recommend to the Colonels of the respective regiments to

*notice such irregularity, by withdrawing their regiments
from that agency, and placing it in other hands.*

*I have in further command, to desire that you may be
pleased to convey to the officers commanding regiments in
your agency, the most marked disapprobation of His Royal
Highness of this improper and secret traffic and to assure
them, that if subsequent to the date of this letter any commissions shall be discovered to be so obtained, such commissions will be immediatey cancelled, and the officer be
reported to the King, as having acted in direct disobedience
to the order of the Commander-in-Chief.*

                                    Signed, J. W. GORDON

And how do we laugh that off? wondered Mary Anne,
watching the autumn leaves from her house in Weybridge,
while she awaited the Duke's return from his Duchess at
Oatlands, a grateful scrap from a captain tossed into the
fire and four hundred pounds, in bank notes, in her bosom.

SIX: The game continued, but slowly, with greater stealth. She had gone too far to retract; she was up to her neck. For a time applications cooled—the fish were frightened; but with the turn of the year they nibbled again. There was no other way to live. She was desperate for money. The upkeep of both the houses doubled and trebled, she did not know how to retrench or how to save. Every day Martha would come to her with complaints.

"The butcher's not been paid, ma'am, for three months. He says he won't supply us any more, not unless he's paid part of what's owing."

"Martha, don't tease me, I've got a painting lesson."

Always some lesson, singing, painting, dancing, to keep abreast of the latest craze in town. Painting on velvet was the rage at present.

"If I don't tease you, ma'am, they go for me. The butcher says it's me that keeps the money, and I don't let him have it."

"Here, take this."

There were some notes thrust in a drawer, intended for the jeweller—a pair of earrings fabulous on white, she had to have them—part of this must go to appease the butcher.

"The coal merchant's turning nasty, ma'am, as well. He grumbled last week when he delivered. We're due for another load in a few day's time, what with all the fires in every room."

More notes, found in a box, to feed the coal man. The smaller tradesmen must come first, it was only fair. The jeweller could always wait, or retrieve his earrings. "Martha, it's the kitchen that eats the meat." The kitchen was generally scapegoat at these times. "His Royal Highness and I have the smallest appetites. Great joints go down to the basement. I know, I've seen them."

168

"Well, ma'am, what can you expect? We're ten in the kitchen. The men have appetites and must be fed."

Ten in the kitchen—had it reached those proportions? There was always somebody new, to wait on another. The cooks wouldn't sit down with the scullions, or the maids with the footmen; whoever made the beds wouldn't wash the dishes.

"Oh, Martha, see to it. I haven't time."

Back to the velvet painting and then on to Kensington, the theatre that night, Weybridge the following day—and further demands for cash from the staff in the country. She'd had a whim in the summer to grow vegetables, but instead of a small garden behind the house three fields had been fenced in, the fault of someone—orders mistaken, the job mismanaged—and now she had two draught horses to pay for and feed. This meant, of course, a man for them alone. Her grooms would only touch the carriage horses. "But where's the man to live? He must have a cottage—he's got a wife and four children."

So it went on, a crazy whirligig. The top, once set in motion, never stopped. There were family claims as well, besides the tradesmen and the servants. James Burton, heaven be praised, never asked for rent, but the house in Tavistock Place must be kept for her mother and for Isobel, now engaged to a Taylor brother, with the Taylor circumstances suddenly not so good. May's father was failing on the Stock Exchange, and poor May was in tears. Obliged to leave their house, she and her sister were thinking of setting up school, but it was out of the question unless they had some help.

She must delve in the drawer once more, and somehow find another five hundred to install poor May and her sister in Islington. Then another two hundred to pay for Isobel's wedding. The thing was, money went . . . she could not keep it.

Next Charley decided to turn himself into a problem. He wasn't happy in the 13th Light Dragoons and wanted to exchange. Could his sister fix it? This came at an awkward moment, when things were sticky, but she managed it, however, and had him transferred to the 7th Regiment of Foot, the Fusiliers. Six months later he came running to her again.

"I loathe it in the 7th, I want to exchange."

"But, darling boy, you said that in September!"

"I know. It was all a mistake, I wish now I hadn't. The 7th is absolute hell, I prefer the cavalry. I'm told I can get an exchange into the 14th Dragoons, but of course it will have to be wangled. Can you do it?"

"I'll see . . . but you must understand, you can't play at soldiers."

"I'm more likely to get to the top in the Dragoons."

She felt uncertain of that, but did not say so. The fact that she lived with the Duke had gone to his head, and rumour had reached her ear that he was not liked. "Tell that brother of yours to shut up, or fellows won't stand it. He's far too big for his boots, and doesn't he show it!"

When Charley was fixed, there was a wail from Sammy. Poor Sammy Carter, she'd hoped he was overseas, delighted at being an ensign and dressed to the nines. Not a bit of it—he was stuck in a troopship, lying off Spithead.

Honoured Madam (he wrote from the transport Clarendon), *Impelled by my dreadful situation, and my perfect knowledge of your goodness, I trust you will pardon the liberty of addressing you again. Since my last, the embarkation has taken place, and I am now on board in a situation not to be described. I have no stock for the voyage, neither have I any money to purchase those little things that are absolutely necessary. I have to keep watch four hours every night, and have nothing to eat but salt meat three times a week, and water to drink, the rum being so bad, 'tis impossible to drink it.*

Your goodness to me has ever been such as leaves not the smallest doubt you will not suffer me to starve in the situation you have been pleased to place me, and which is such as will ever tend to make me the most grateful and happy of beings. Should, madam, you be induced to take into consideration my wretched case, and by a little pecuniary aid save me from everything that is horrible, it will be an act worthy of yourself, and that imprint upon my heart which will never be erased.

I am, Madam, your grateful servant,
SAM CARTER

Poor pet of a Sammy, languishing on salt meat. She

sent fifty pounds at once to build up his strength. What a mistake that he had ever left her service—he wasn't cut out for a soldier, she always knew it. He thanked her profusely, enclosing a bill for his clothes. Swords and sashes, belts and feathers, jacket and trimmings, gloves and stockings, even a watch from pledge at two pound ten, the whole thing totting up to another forty. Oh well, it couldn't be helped, poor Sam must be saved. She hoped he would settle down, and not write for a transfer.

"Madam?"

"Martha . . . what now?"

"Dr. Thynne to see you."

Dr. Thynne, at least, did not want money. He had been paid for his services, thank heaven—the children's colds in the winter, her mother's rheumatics, a queasy moment herself lasting forty-eight hours (attended to with skill and discretion, the Duke's hopes dashed), a poultice for Martha, a cupping for Parker the coachman.

"Dear Doctor Thynne, and what can I do for you?"

"Nothing for me, Mrs. Clarke. Just a word for a friend . . ."

The same old racket . . . but Thynne hadn't tried it before. Off with the bedside manner, the patient's smile ("Thank you, I'm better today, I'm doing well"), and on with the business face, the office status.

"What are the particulars?" The routine formula.

"A patient of mine, a lady, has a husband. The husband has a brother, a Colonel Knight."

"In words of three syllables, Knight is the applicant?"

"Yes, Mrs. Clarke. Colonel Knight hopes to make an exchange with a brother officer, a certain Colonel Brook. The matter has been sent up by the regular method, but there is endless delay . . ."

"I know, I know." The usual words, she knew them by heart. "I'll do my best. Did they mention the compliment?"

"Two hundred pounds, I think my patient said."

She had got three hundred fifty for an exchange, but that had been in the past, before Gordon took over. Two hundred was not to be sneezed at, all things considered.

"Two hundred is rather small, but as you're a friend I'll make an exception. Bank notes, of course."

"Whatever you wish, Mrs. Carke. My friend will be grateful."

"The notes to be sent to the house when the names are gazetted. I'll try and get it through by the end of this month."

God, the heat in July. London was stifling. There was hardly a breath of air, even in Weybridge. The sea was what she needed, complete relaxation. If she didn't ease off she'd go mad, as crazy as the King. They'd packed him off to Weymouth to take salt baths. Salt baths were the latest answer to straws in the hair. She would go to Weymouth too, if she had the money. The two hundred pounds from Knight might come in handy. Round and round went the mind, in a dizzy tangle.

War fever had the country again this summer, and invasion was the only topic ever discussed. Would Boney dare? He had the men, he hadn't got the ships, the weather was not right, fog in the channel, one chap can whack ten Frenchmen any day, but if he landed what was the plan for London?

"In your position, you must hear so much. Please tell us, what does the Duke intend to do? And is it really true what Lord Stanhope says, that the French have a secret device to sink our ships?"

As if she knew . . . or, knowing, would have told. So many spiteful tongues awaited the chance to start a smear campaign and discredit the Duke. Those letters in the *Morning Post*, signed "Belisarius"—she tried to track the author, but couldn't find him. Sutton swore it was a man called Donovan, some veteran on half-pay who bore a grudge, but Donovan called and proved his innocence and even undertook to send her clients (getting the usual rake-off on the side).

The greatest surprise of the spring had been Bill's assistance. Since the argument in the drawing room a year before she had barely seen him, for he had chosen to keep his distance. And then the invasion scare had caught him too. He admitted the fact at Isobel's wedding reception, stung to patriotism and rather pompous.

"With the country alarmed as it is, I can't stay idle. I intend to look for a job as soon as possible."

"What sort of a job?"

"It's hardly for me to say. Whatever I can do to most benefit. I'm prepared to offer my services to whichever government branch sees fit to employ me."

She thought of the wedding reception, still to be paid for . . . "Appointments aren't easy to get. The plums are all taken."

"I'm well aware of that," he said. "I'm not out for a plum. Like others, I merely wish to serve my country."

"You may have to pay for the privilege."

"I'm aware of that, too."

"In which case I'll find you a job, and you can pay me."

She said it with a smile. He turned away. But when the bride and groom had left in a shower of rose leaves and the guests had all departed, she caught him, alone—this time without a smile on her face and with tears in her eyes.

"What's the matter?"

"Isobel looked so happy, I'm crying for her. My own wedding, thirteen years back, was very different. No wedding guests for me, and no rose petals. This will have to be paid for somehow, God knows when."

"Finance still difficult?"

"Worse than it's ever been, but I needn't bore you . . . I hope you succeed in finding yourself an appointment."

He knew what she meant. He looked at her, torn in two. Standards, principles, all the things he cherished, swayed in the balance against her necessity.

"Just exactly what do you want?" he ventured to ask her.

"If you'd like it straight from the shoulder—a thousand pounds. Five hundred to pay for this wedding. And the rest? To stop the mouth of a jeweller who's started to press. In return for which I'll find you an appointment, and nobody but ourselves need ever know."

"I'd have to tell my father. I haven't the money."

"Tell your father, then. He knows the world. Appointments don't hang on trees, merely for asking. Someone will have to play the go-between. Why not your closest and your dearest friend? Or aren't I? Is that finished?"

There was no argument, after that, no hope of withdrawal. She had him on a string, hanging and helpless, and before three months had passed he was serving at

Colchester, Assistant Commissioner of Stores to His Majesty's Forces. The wedding expenses were cleared, the jeweller pacified.

"Sir?"

"What is it, my darling?"

"Can I come to Weymouth?"

"Impossible, my angel. The King will be there."

"The King won't be in a lodging at two in the morning . . ."

"Nor shall I be, either. My visit's official. And there's a christening on Sunday, Chesterfield's boy. I'm to be a godfather, a tremendous to-do. If you come to Weymouth I shouldn't so much as glimpse you."

Always that firm line drawn between what was official and what was private, and never by any chance the smallest attempt to bridge the gap; whereas with the Prince of Wales and Mrs. Fitzherbert . . . with the Duke of Clarence and Mrs. Jordan . . . even with Kent and his old French mistress . . . She supposed it was a sense of duty, to spare the Duchess.

"You're not ashamed of me, by any chance?"

He stared at her across the dinner table. "What's troubling you, my sweet, a touch of colic?"

"No . . . thunder in the air; I'm out of sorts."

He wouldn't understand the sudden urge that came on her at times to have more power, to plan, to make decisions, to share his life; not in the way she did, but as an equal. She thought of the fatal breach of tact one Sunday at Weybridge. Careless, not thinking, she had installed herself in a pew, and had preened and smiled as he entered the church with the Duchess. Black as a cloud, he had looked the opposite way, but that night the anger exploded.

"What the devil did you mean by flaunting yourself in church before my household? You dare do that again, and I'll have you whipped." My God . . . and he meant it, too. She hadn't forgotten. And yet her presence in Weybridge was known to all, his visits to her of an evening shrugged at, accepted. The dividing line again. In private it was permissible. But to sing Glory Be with the Duchess

174

brought instant pollution. Not to the Duchess, however, went pleas for preferment.

"Do you know a Doctor O'Meara, sir?"

"Never heard of him."

"He's some sort of deacon in Ireland, and wants to become a bishop. He's begged me several times for an introduction to you."

"Not my department. I don't deal with the Church. Besides, if I did, I don't like the 'O' in his name."

"He's a Protestant . . . Loyal as yourself."

"No Irishman's ever loyal, except to his skin. Tell Master O'Meara from me he can stick to his bogs."

Oh well . . . if that was the form, no rise for the deacon; and no *bilet-doux* of gratitude, smelling of incense. What would be the price of a bishopric? The same as a colonel? Will Ogilvie wouldn't know but Donovan might.

"If you won't let me come to Weymouth, I'll go to Worthing."

"Why Worthing, my precious? Why can't you stay at home?"

"London, the end of July? The place is dead."

Coxhead-Marsh was at Worthing, and so was Willie Fitzgerald, the son of the Irish M.P. and rather amusing. The place was all the rage, and rivalling Brighton. Worthing was the answer to the moment's pique, the children installed at Weybridge with her mother. Even the cash was to hand, and had come that morning: two hundred pounds from Mr. Robert Knight, brother of the colonel who'd got his exchange (per favour of Dr. Thynne) and was prompt in payment.

"Very well, then, go to Worthing. Just as you please. How are you off for money, can you manage?"

Astounding question! A matter so seldom discussed. A prick of the conscience, perhaps, had made him uneasy. And it was not to be wondered at, all things considered. Her allowance had not been paid since the first of May.

"As a matter of fact I'm rolling, thanks to the doctor."

"What doctor?"

"Dr. Thynne, not the Irish deacon. A small matter of exchanges, do you remember? The names were gazetted today. It is beneath your notice. The only trouble—he's sent two notes of a hundred, and it's no use waving them at a lodginghouse keeper."

"Pierson will get 'em changed."

"What, at this hour?"

"Of course. If he says who it's for, any tradesman will do it."

In point of fact, she was thinking, I won't need much money. Coxhead-Marsh and Fitzgerald between them should take care of that. Rooms at the inn on the front, and both dancing attendance.

"Pierson, get change for this, in tens and twenties."

"Yes, ma'am."

The Duke rose from the table and took hold of her hand. "Is my darling going to miss me?"

"You know that I am."

"I'll try not to be away for more than ten days."

"Too long by nine . . . Think of me sitting at Worthing, all alone."

"Ask little May to go with you."

"I might. It depends."

Depended on what? Whether Coxhead-Marsh was amusing, whether Willie Fitzgerald lived up to his Irish eyes.

A long, long kiss. "Take care of your royal person." The head caressed, the ears stroked and fondled.

"Damn it, I'd take you to Weymouth if I could. Blast Chesterfield and his brat."

"I know . . . I know . . ."

Two hours to reassure him, and then the horses. He intended to drive through the night, and couldn't linger. A fond farewell from the window, handkerchief waving.

"Madam, Pierson has brought your change."

"Oh, Martha, thank you."

"And, madam, a Doctor O'Meara has called to see you. He said he had hoped to catch His Royal Highness before he left. He expects to be in Weymouth himself this Sunday."

"Then hope can take him there, and keep him buoyant. If he changes the 'O' to 'Mac' he might do better."

"He asked me to tell you, ma'am, that he's brought a present."

A present! It was a trifle premature. Nor could she receive a deacon clad in negligee and after midnight.

176

"Tell Doctor O'Meara I'll quickly scribble a line to His Royal Highness, which, as he's bound for Weymouth, he can take with him. Tell him, too, that I'm much obliged for the present, and bring it upstairs."

Money without guarantee was rather unusual. Deacons had greater faith than serving soldiers. "The deacon's called," she wrote, "and brings a compliment. I leave the rest to royal grace and favour. Your pillow looks forlorn. I'm very lonely.

"Signed M.A.   Dated the 31st."

Martha appeared once more at the bedroom door, bearing a package wrapped in stout brown paper.

"Unwrap it, Martha, but first take the note to the deacon."

She wrestled with the string, splitting a fingernail, until Martha came to her aid with a pair of scissors. It could be an altar cloth with the money inside it, but felt too hard for that; it must be a stave. She tore off the final wrapping. Martha spoke.

"A set of cricket stumps for Master George."

The deacon's handwriting was across the parcel. "These for your bonny boy. Dolls for the daughters to follow. My humble duties."

It was too late to retrieve the note. The deacon had gone.

"All right, Martha. Cart all this stuff away and take it with you to Weybridge in the morning."

"Kind of the clergyman, wasn't it, ma'am?"

"Very thoughtful."

So much for the church. The deacon could stay a deacon. And how he'd got as far as that would take some guessing. A tennis bat to the Queen? Or a set of croquet? Really, the Protestants! No wonder the Catholics wanted emancipation.

Cricket stumps for George . . . could it have two meanings? A hint, perhaps, that games should be encouraged. Some Irish innuendo, some play upon words? Willie Fitzgerald would know, she'd ask him at Worthing.

Yawning and sleepy, she settled herself on her pillow. It was pleasant to have the space empty for once in a while, with a chance to sleep on until ten without any disturbance. Tomorrow the drive to the sea would blow away cobwebs, blow away boredom, rub up her knowledge of cricket . . . Willie could read her the rules, he was just down from Oxford . . . The Duke was always rushed, always busy, and Willie was amusing—undergraduates out of the egg were as good as a tonic. It was high time for a pat on the crease and a change in the bowling.

SEVEN: The invasion scare was over for the time—
Nelson had seen to that, and lost his life. The glory of
Trafalgar swept the country and the patriotic tempo rose
to fever pitch, only to be damped down by Austerlitz. The
enemy were unbeatable on land, or so it seemed.

The Commander-in-Chief had little time for dalliance.
His hours were nine till seven at the Horse Guards, and
life was a constant battle to get things done. On the one
hand his army was screaming for equipment, priority for
weapons, clothing, guns, the proposed Expeditionary Force
half-trained, not nearly ready; and on the other the politicians were clamouring that a token force should be sent
without further delay and Lord Cathcart packed off to the
Elbe to join General Don—never mind if the business was
skimped, get the men overseas.

The Duke refused to be bullied. His letters to the Prime
Minister were firm and concise. "The Expeditionary Force
is not yet in a fit state to go to war." All very fat and fine
for Pitt to agitate—he'd be the first to explode if the men
were slaughtered, and so would the country too. "Another defeat," fault of the C.-in-C., the job mismanaged.
Let the Ministry shift to the Horse Guards and run the
Army: they'd soon throw in their hands and ask for re-
lease.

The Prime Minister's state of health did not help matters. The judgment of a sick man was seldom sound. If he
should go, there was no one fully capable to take his place
and gain the country's confidence. The breach would have
to be healed between the parties. Fox given a place in
the Cabinet, tempers appeased, and if the King protested
the King must give way. It was still touch and go with

179

him—another problem. One moment as bright as a button, and balmy the next.

"If anyone wants my job, they're welcome to it." The Duke said this one autumn evening when late for his dinner, the edge off his appetite and his temper doubtful. He'd had an interview with Pitt that had got him nowhere; half an hour with the King, who wouldn't sign a paper but pottered about in a dressing-gown playing whist; sneering reports in the papers calling for "action"; a leader in the *Times* that made no sense, with uncomfortable allusions to the Melville business, the scandals of last spring still not forgotten—if the First Lord of the Admiralty had to resign, how about probing into Army methods? And then, to crown all, waiting in the hall at Gloucester Place, a sneering anonymous letter. He brought it out of his pocket after dinner and, back to the fire in the drawing-room, read it aloud:

"Your Royal Highness, and Adulterer. You know the law, no doubt, but if you don't there are professional men who do, and make it their business. It counts as a criminal offence to steal a wife from her husband, and to alienate the affections of the children from their father. You have done both. So await the consequences."

The Duke threw the note on to Mary Anne's lap and laughed. But the laugh was not one of dismissal. It sounded forced. "Some madman, I suppose, from your remote past?"

She recognised the writing instantly and something touched her heart and turned to stone. Joseph . . . The letters smudged, the sentences blurred, but his without any doubt, quite unmistakable. Joseph, who'd been removed, so she'd last heard, to some place in the country near Northhampton, cared for by relations, hopeless, ailing, no questions ever asked, her name not mentioned.

"Either mad or drunk," she answered, "probably both," and tore the note in pieces.

"What does the fellow mean about stealing a wife? A widow can't keep her affections in the grave."

"This man expected me to, that's evident, and has heard

180

our names coupled together. I wouldn't worry. Throw the bits into the fire where they belong."

He did so, his expression baffled, rather gloomy. The note had touched some chord in memory. He'd never listened to the yarn she'd spun him: her husband a rotter, dying of D.T.'s, herself thrown on the world with her four young children, and helped, after a struggle, by the builder Burton.

"Do you ever see any of your husband's relatives?"

"No, never . . . they live in the country. The family's scattered."

He yawned and changed the subject. The matter was closed. She watched the scraps of paper blacken and burn. Was the opportunity missed? Should she confess? Should she say, "The fact of the business is, I'm not a widow. My husband's still alive, but I don't know where. I left him; he couldn't support me or the children." It was a simple sort of admission, amounting to nothing and hardly at variance with the version told him, yet something had held her back, she didn't know why. Was it a fear of seeming foolish, of appearing dishonest, thereby dragging the question from him, "Why bother to lie?" There was still time to say, "That handwriting's my husband's." He sat by the fire and dozed while she played the piano. At half-past nine she thought, "I'll broach the subject . . . I'll say I always believed myself a widow, then heard through some report that the belief was unfounded, that Joseph lived, insane, in an asylum." The clock ticked on and passed to a quarter-to, chimed ten; and then he stretched, and talked of bed. Too late tonight; tomorrow, perhaps, or next day.

A week went by. And then came another letter, this time sent to the Horse Guards, not to the house. "I want my wife and children. Send them back. If you don't choose to return them, I'll take proceedings. A charge in the criminal courts for flagrant adultery would look very well at the moment, with the country in peril." Signed, and no bones about it, Joseph Clarke.

He gave it to her that evening. "How about it?"

One second's hesitation. Tears, or laughter? Tears would be an admission of guilt, so laughter was best. Treat the whole subject lightly, brush it aside.

"Then he *is* alive. I couldn't decide, last week. The

181

writing had altered so, but now I'm certain. They all swore to me he was dead, and I believed them."

"But you told me you sat by his bed and watched him die!"

"Did I? I don't remember, it's so confused. I was nearly out of my mind, my boy was ill." It was impossible to recollect the tale she had told. "His brother, the curate, begged us to go away, the children and myself, or we'd never recover—it took two keepers, you see, to hold him down. Then they wrote to me at Hampstead that I was free."

He was standing in his nightshirt by the bed. The moment was inopportune, ill-timed. She was at the dressing-table, doing her hair in a ribbon.

He said, "Well? What are you going to do? Return to the fellow?"

"Oh! Heavens, what a question! Of course I'm not! Ten pounds will keep him quiet. I'll write in the morning."

There was constraint between them, silence on either pillow.

"As if," he said, "I hadn't enough on my mind without this damn fool business cropping up."

"Darling! Don't worry. I promise you I can deal with him."

"I'll show the letter to Adam."

"Why on earth do that?"

"He's my personal advisor, he'll know what to do. He reads fifty threatening letters every day. He and Greenwood between them will fix the fellow."

Her heart sank. Greenwood . . . Adam . . . The men who handled all his official business, who viewed her with suspicion, dislike, and mistrust. She knew too well, she'd heard it from all his friends. "Watch out," James Fitzgerald had warned her often, "those men are out to get you, especially Adam." She put out her hand to touch him. He was cold, unresponsive.

"Please leave it all to me. I know my Joseph. Ten or twenty pounds will keep him quiet."

"I wonder . . . I don't care for his language. Criminal adultery. I know how these things sound in a court of law. I'd best put Adam on to it."

A fine start to the winter. The luck had turned. Every

182

day brought some pinprick, some new trouble. There were ridiculous rows with servants, disorganization, the staff all complaining of Martha who gave herself airs. "We won't take orders from her. We must have them direct."

"Mrs. Favoury's been my housekeeper now for thirteen years. Of course you'll take orders from her, or you'll have to go."

Martha was sullen, in tears. "I'll go myself rather than cause all this fuss from morning till night. Besides, I want to get married."

"My God, to whom?"

"Walmsley, the coal man. He's courted me now six months."

"But, Martha, I can't do without you!"

"You don't ever say so, and now the young ladies have gone to school at Miss Taylor's and Master George to Chelsea, I don't see that I'm of use to anyone, what with the servants bickering, so spiteful, and all hands turned against me."

"Oh, be quiet! . . . Get out and stop your blabbing. Let me think." More bills, more endless bills, mostly from Weybridge. The stable beams were rotten, the stalls must be renewed, a new set of rooms built over for the coachman. Bills for potatoes enough to feed a regiment. A herd of Jerseys bought that gave no milk, caught some disease and died, so she must buy another. Her own little man of business was called to assistance, Mr. Comrie, an attorney, able and very willing.

"Mr. Comrie, disaster threatens!"

"So it appears." He adjusted his glasses and sorted through her papers, ten, twenty, thirty, tossed on the drawing-room floor. Bills from a hundred sources, all unpaid. "Does His Royal Highness make you no fixed allowance?"

"Eighty a month. What can I do with that?"

She couldn't explain the promotions on the side, dwindling month by month with Gordon in office. "You must plead your coverture. That is your only excuse. Admit you are not a widow to all the tradesmen." Comrie knew—he had done this for her before and settled a case out of court with no one the wiser.

"What happens if I do that?"

"The law can't compel you to pay."

She had heard the words before, an age ago. It was the advice they'd given her mother, when Bob Farquhar left her. Back to the old, old story.

"Will the bills be sent to my husband?"

"If they can find him. Do you know where he lives?"

"No . . . no, I'm not certain."

A hundred bills to Joseph, who could not pay? The bills sent on to the Duke, with a threatening letter? And the bills returned to her. There was no solution.

"I've had another letter from your drunken husband," the Duke would tell her.

She dreaded the words, now sometimes once a week. "I hope you threw them in the litter basket?"

"On the contrary, I've given them all to Adam. He's putting some enquiries into motion."

Enquiries . . . what did he mean, what sort of enquiries? She dared not ask. His mood was strange, preoccupied, his manner evasive, as though the guilt was his. Her nerves were as taut as a fiddle-string, ready to snap. Something was going on, and he did not tell her. He used to send word by his servant: "Don't wait dinner. I'm not sure whether I shall be home tonight."

It was odd, unlike him. He had always been relieved to shake off the dust of the Horse Guards and relax.

There was no one in the house to make a distraction. It had fallen silent, without the children. Mary and Ellen had gone to the Taylor school (largely kept in action by her contributions), and George, now eight, was lording it at Chelsea, a miniature cadet before going to Marlow.

She continued to entertain, but alone, without host or master: the Fitzgeralds, father and son, and Russell Manners, Coxhead-Marsh, the usual crowd of devotees, but the zest had gone out of the game. It was forced, she was acting. Her laugh was a sham, her smile was a façade, the flow of conversation automatic, and always, now, there was a new fear at the back of her mind, "My power isn't what it was . . . it's gone . . . it's slipping."

One morning Mr. Adam called to see her, stating he had been commanded by the Duke of York to make certain enquiries regarding the date of her marriage, the quarter where she had lived prior to marriage, every circumstance, in fact, of her early life.

She showed him the door, with icy courtesy. "My past life concerns nobody but myself. Neither you, nor His Royal Highness, has any right to pry into the matter."

"I put it to you, madam, that you have known perfectly well during these past years that your husband, Joseph Clarke, was alive, and that your statement to His Royal Highness that you believed yourself a widow was incorrect?"

"Not so at all."

"Very well, then. How was it that early in 1804 an action was brought against you, which you kept from His Royal Highness, and which was settled out of court by your attorney, who pleaded your coverture?"

Cornered very smoothly. She shrugged her shoulders. "My attorney and I thought it the best way out. I had no actual proof of my husband's death."

His cold, bland face remained without expression. "Have you any certificates of your children's births?"

"No, I don't think so. And why should you want to see them?"

"It has been suggested to me by persons I need not mention that you gave birth to children prior to your marriage."

Good God! What flaming impudence. She saw it all. He'd sent his spies to Hoxton, ferreted out the neighbours in Charles Square, muddled the husband Joseph with his brother John, planted on her John's brood of older children, now nearly adult, scattered the Lord knew where.

"The initial 'J' has given rise to error," she said. "Go back to Hoxton, and make sure of your facts. My husband has a parson brother with the same initial, but the name is James. If it would make your enquiries any easier, I'll willingly admit I married all three brothers."

"Flippancy won't assist you, madam; I'm sorry. Would you please give me the date and place of your marriage?"

She was damned if she would. He could go and tramp the country. She remembered her mother's wedding to Bob Farquhar. Let him track that down, if he liked, as the past was so vital.

185

"At Berkhamsted," she said. "Go and search the records. You'll find some mention of my family there. And if you wish to go further back, you must travel to Scotland. Dig in the heather for the clan Mackenzie, or go and slit open the cod in Aberdeen."

Livid with rage, that night she forgot discretion. The Duke came home to dine and she attacked him.

"How dare you send that man to question me? Poking his filthy nose into my affairs."

She caught him on the raw. He looked embarrassed. "If you mean Adam, it's nothing to do with me. I merely told him to try and find your husband and give the fellow hell, to be rid of the business."

"Well, tell him the door won't be answered another time. I've never been so insulted in all my life, and God! that's saying something."

She longed for a flaming row to clear the air, to throw a bottle at his head and break it—the head, the bottle, both. It didn't matter. He wouldn't rise. He sat there looking glum, the same expression he had worn now for several weeks, sulky, withdrawn, just like an injured schoolboy.

"I haven't the time to meddle with all this. I've too many things to attend to the livelong day. The pressure at the Horse Guards is nearly killing me, apart from Greenwood nattering, and Adam."

"And yet," she said, "you find time to go to the theatre. I saw it in the paper yesterday. That was the evening you sent word you were kept by His Majesty."

"I was. And by the time I was through at Buck House it was much too late to come back to dinner here."

"The King's theatre. Mrs. Carey . . . Does she dance well?"

"Passably. I didn't really notice."

"Perhaps you noticed her at supper afterwards?"

He reddened, drank his port, and didn't answer. Then Will Ogilvie was right, there was something to it. She clenched her hands to try and keep control. "I understand she's tall. That's an advantage. No danger of falling arches, her reaching up to you. A broken instep's not much use to a dancer."

Before he could answer there came the sound of an up-

186

roar from the basement. A scuffle in the kitchen, the servants fighting? There was no Martha to keep the peace —she had married and left.

"Pierson, for heaven's sake!"

There were whispers in the hall, murmurs and talking. The Duke's complexion was like a turkey cock's. The disturbance served as excuse to evade any issue.

"My Lord! A fine house to return to in the evening. Servants' brawls and shouting. I'd get more peace if I ate my dinner in barracks."

"Or in a theatre dressing-room."

Pierson returned, his manner was apologetic. "I'm very sorry, madam, but it's some woman says she's legal wife to the coal merchant. The man Mrs. Favoury married a month ago. Screaming and shouting, she is, for law and justice."

"Have her removed." The Duke was thin-lipped and frozen.

"They're struggling with her now, Your Royal Highness. Her language won't bear repeating."

"What does she say?"

"She says, madam, you encouraged the husband to leave her, let him come here to Gloucester Place to be with Mrs. Favoury, and that things go on in the basement that would shock the world, not to mention what happens upstairs. She said the house was nothing but a . . ." He stopped and coughed, loyalty overcoming scandal.

"Remove the woman," the Duke repeated; "have her locked up. Get the footman to help you."

"Very good, Your Royal Highness."

The fracas below was renewed. The floors being thin, before the final silence they heard the woman shout, "Your mistress is to blame, the dirty strumpet. Taking a married man into her bed, and him a royal Duke, as should know better."

Once it would have been a matter for giggles and choking laughter, the sort of thing she would imitate and repeat, while, laughing, he would listen in the drawing-room. Not so tonight. They sat like mutes, like strangers, no grain of humour in the situation. Dignity came first.

"Shall we go up?"

187

The piano was left untouched, there was no conversation, each held a book that neither read. The clock in the drawing-room ticked on dragging the hours until eleven. And then, as eleven struck, the finishing touch—a pealing bell, blows on the front door, the sound of altercation on the doorstep. The Duke threw his unread book across the floor. "If that's the woman again I'll call the guard."

Footsteps sounded up the stairs and Pierson entered.

"I'm sorry, Your Royal Highness, to disturb you . . . Madame, it's someone for you, and very insistent. He gives his name as Joseph Clarke."

So . . . here it was. Joseph couldn't have timed it better, not if he'd had the wisdom of the devil. Checkmate, and finish. Seconds, throw in the sponge . . .

"Thank you, Pierson. I'll see him. Show him into the little room below. And stay within call, it's possible I shall need you."

She rose and curtseyed. The Duke did not look at her. The irony was wasted, or maybe he took the gesture as his due. She went downstairs and into the anteroom where visitors waited. Joseph was standing there, or rather his shadow, or worse still not his shadow but his caricature. Shabby, ill-dressed, grey hair touching his shoulders, the shoulders stooping, the body gross and spread, eyes nearly sunken in the flabby face, the chin unshaven, lips swollen and cracked.

This was the man she'd married, loved and cherished, father of her children, father of George.

She said, "What do you want? Be brief, I have guests above."

He did not answer for a moment, but stared at her, the low-cut evening gown, the jewels, the hair dressed high in curls. Then he laughed, the foolish, senseless laugh of a drunken man.

"You look quite ravishing"—slurring, lisping his words—"pink always suited you. Weren't you married in pink? I seem to remember the gown on the end of the bed. Later you wore it on Sundays in Golden Lane. Without those trinkets, though. Diamonds suit you. I couldn't buy you diamonds, hadn't the money. I did my best to save, but you spent it all."

The rambling voice of a man whose mind had wandered, whose senses, soggy with drink, felt no sensation, who twisted the facts of the past to suit his dreams.

"If that's what you came here to tell me you're wasting your time." She had no feeling in her heart save anger. He was only an empty shell without life or substance. She could not even pity him. He was dead.

"I want you back. I want Mary and Ellen. I want my boy."

"You mean you want money. Very well, how much will satisfy you? I have twenty pounds in the house. I can spare you that. It should last you a week or so, till the bottles are empty."

He moved a step towards her. She went to the door. "The house is full of servants. I've only to call, and they'll throw you out of the house, so please don't touch me."

"Is he here?"

"Who?"

"His nibs . . ." He put up his hand to smother a stupid grin, then lowered his voice, jerking his head at the door. "I've frightened him all right, I've seen his lawyer. Keep the case out of court, that's what they say."

"You mean you've seen Adam?"

He grinned again and winked; and then with drunken solemnity waved a finger, choosing his words with care.

"Saw some fellow or other, called himself Treasurer, don't remember his name, but I told him the tale. Oh yes, I managed to give him all the details, how we kissed and cuddled in the alley, and how you first carried on with that printer fellow, not to mention your stepfather on the sly. I told him too how you'd driven my brother to suicide, spent all his fortune and mine and then hoofed it, with the remainder, when I lay dying. The fellow seemed very grateful, very polite. He expressed his deepest sympathy, and said he'd warn his nibs not to be hoodwinked further."

She called for Pierson. "Show this man to the door."

"Not quite so fast," he said; "there's more to tell you."

"I've heard enough."

"Lots of little things come back to me. How you turned your own sister into cook, Bob Farquhar's girl, and dolled her up in an apron. I told him about your mother keeping

189

lodgings, lodgings a good disguise for something else. Oh yes, he was very grateful, he noted it down, put all the details in a little book. 'Thank you, Mr. Clarke, this will come in handy'."

Pierson was there and the footmen, they had heard what was said. They stared at her, round-eyed, waiting for further orders.

"Take him away."

There was no scuffle, no disturbance. He was not carried out like the coal man's wife. He shuffled through the hall with unsteady footsteps, bowing, leering, a crumpled hat in his hands.

"I'll expect you and the children on Saturday. Our wedding anniversary's any day now. We'll hold the usual family celebration. D'you remember how we used to in Golden Lane?"

They bundled him down the steps. The front door closed. Pierson, averting his eyes, led the two footmen back to the kitchen quarters. Turning, she saw the Duke at the head of the stairs.

"I've got rid of him."

"So I see."

"Not only drunk, but mad."

"Lucid enough."

"To those who like to listen . . . Where are you going?"

"I ordered the carriage. I'm not sleeping here tonight."

"Why ever not?"

"I've got an early start. I have to be down at Windsor at half-past ten."

"You never said so before."

"I forgot to tell you."

There was no point of contact between them, only empty, formal politeness. He brushed her hand with his lips before he left and murmured something about dinner on Friday. She heard the carriage leave, and then, with a heart of lead, she walked upstairs. She looked at her face in the mirror in the bedroom. The eyes were anxious, staring, lacking lustre. Two telltale lines ran from nose to mouth. Her birthday in a week, and she would be thirty. She sat before the mirror, smoothing the lines. Nobody to talk to, not even Martha.

On the morning of the eleventh a note was brought to her. It was in the Duke's handwriting, and said, "Adam will call upon you at six o'clock." No more than this. No hint about his business. She did not go out all day. She sat and waited. Then, as the day wore on, she passed through the rooms. The children's first, tidy, because of their absence. Mary's (now nearly thirteen), sombre, religious, with Bibles and pictures of saints—a passing phase. Ellen's (at ten), more childish, a skipping rope, two books of poetry (romantic) and over the bed a large-sized coloured portrait of the Duke, torn from a paper, stuck with drawing-pins. George's, boxes of paints, of marbles. Soldiers with broken heads and broken limbs. The Duke again, seated astride a charger; a picture of George himself as a cadet; the military school at Chelsea, small boys drilling.

The front door pealed. She hurried down the stairs. It wasn't Adam, but Will Ogilvie. They chatted of this and that. She made no allusion to anything that had happened or was likely to happen. She thought he watched her closely, that he was waiting for something, but she made pretence of behaving as though all was as usual. Nothing had happened lately in military matters, business between them had slowed for the past few weeks. He ventured to mention something about promotions. She shrugged her shoulders—nothing had gone through lately. He did not press her, and then, as he kissed her hand, as he took his leave before he went downstairs, he said in a casual way, as though *en passant*, "I see Mrs. Carey the dancer is living at Fulham."

"Oh, really? I don't know much about her. King's theatre, isn't she? I haven't been."

"You're in the minority. Everyone's raving about her. I understand His Royal Highness knows her, and gave a party for her at Fulham Lodge." A happy parting-shot to wish godspeed.

Adam arrived on the stroke of six o'clock. She was waiting in the drawing-room, dressed for dinner, the diamonds round her neck that the Duke had given her.

"I'm afraid," he began, "my mission is not very pleasant. The interview is not of my own choosing."

"Please continue."

191

"I have been commanded by His Royal Highness the Duke of York to inform you, madam, that from today your connection with him must cease. He has no wish to see you, or to communicate with you again. This is quite final."

She felt the colour go from her face. She did not move, only clenched her hands the tighter behind her back.

"Does His Royal Highness give any reason for his decision?"

"No, madam. Only that facts have come to light which show that you have constantly lied to him—about your past, about your family, and many other matters unspecified. His Royal Highness believed you to be a widow, and your husband attempted to bring a suit for adultery into court against him. This is but one detail out of many. Also your extravagance, and the frequent demands upon his purse have so exasperated His Royal Highness that he will submit to it no longer."

"Everything I have spent, I have spent for him. This house, the house at Weybridge, was all his doing." Adam raised a hand to interrupt.

"Forgive me, madam, no explanations, please. His Royal Highness further commands me to say that if you conduct yourself in a proper manner, he is willing to allow you four hundred pounds a year, to be paid quarterly. But he considers himself under no sort of obligation to do this: it is merely an act of generosity on his part, and the amount will be immediately withdrawn should he think fit to do so."

She stared at him, aghast. Four hundred pounds? Her debts were near four thousand . . . Why, at Weybridge alone the improvements he had suggested, insisted, she should do came to at least two thousand. The farm, the gardens . . .

"You must have mistaken your orders," she said. "His Royal Highness knows the financial difficulties. He would never suggest four hundred pounds a year, a quarter of the sum I pay in servants' wages and liveries."

"Four hundred was the sum," Adam repeated. "As to debts incurred, His Royal Highness won't recognise them.

192

You must settle them as best you can by selling up the contents of this house."

She tried to think, to plan, to pierce the future. Where was she to live, what was to happen? And George at the military school, what about George? "My son," she said, "what's to become of my son? His Royal Highness promised to educate him. He's at the school in Chelsea, and in a year or two he's due for the college at Marlow. His name is accepted, I saw the Commandant."

"I regret, madam, I have no instructions regarding your son."

Full realisation began to come upon her. The servants must be told, the wages paid, all of them dismissed. The tradesmen must be settled, curtains dragged down, carpets rolled, the horses and the carriages sent away, and somehow, mixed up in the crazy confusion, her friends and family warned that the whole thing was finished . . . Pitying glances, sympathy forced, not sincere, the mocking smile behind the mocking hand . . .

She said, "I must see His Royal Highness. He can't leave me like this, without a word." Panic swept her now, and chaos, the world disrupted.

"His Royal Highness, madam, declines an interview."

He bowed—he went. She didn't attempt to detain him. She sat by the window, trembling. She thought, "It isn't true. It's all a nightmare. Or Adam's lying, forced him into it. He'll come tonight and explain; he'll be here directly. He told me dinner on Friday, he doesn't break promises. The last thing that he said was dinner on Friday." She went on sitting in the drawing-room, waiting. Seven, eight, no sound of the horses coming. She pulled the bell for Pierson.

"Pierson, there must have been a misunderstanding. Send round to Portman Square and find out if His Royal Highness is coming home to dinner. Tell the cook to keep the dishes hot."

A fumbling pretext, to save her face and theirs. Something was in the wind, they knew it too. Trust servants to smell out a threat or a disaster.

Pierson returned. "Excuse me, ma'am, no one knows anything. The servants at Portman Square thought His

Royal Highness was here. No dinner is ordered at the house, he must be coming. Perhaps His Royal Highness has been detained at the Horse Guards."

Detained? Nonsense! Gone to the theatre, rather. Gone to Fulham Lodge to prepare the bedroom. Slippers laid out, the scent on the dressing-table, pillows side by side behind the curtains.

"Pierson, send someone again, just before nine. It may be that you're right and he's detained."

At half-past nine Pierson was at her side. "His Royal Highness has returned to Portman Square. Mr. Greenwood is with him, and Mr. Adam too. They're sitting down to dinner. His Royal Highness's servant asked me to give you this." He handed her the letter, and she tore it open. It was the Duke's handwriting, but not his composition—stilted, formal, it was a lawyer's letter, couched in legal terms:

You must recollect the occasion which obliged me to employ my solicitor in a suit with which I was then threatened on your account; the result of those enquiries first gave me reason to form an unfavourable opinion of your conduct; you cannot therefore accuse me of rashly or hastily deciding against you; but after the proofs which have at last been brought forward to me and which it is impossible for you to controvert, I owe it to my own character and situation to abide by the resolution which I have taken and from which it is impossible for me to recede. An interview between us must be a painful task for both, and can be of no possible advantage to you; I therefore must decline it.

The panic and the fear went instantly, and in their stead a sort of fury seized her. She ran upstairs, found herself a cloak, threw it around her shoulders, and opened the front door. It was a warm May evening, the sunset gold and gleaming. She ran along Gloucester Place to Portman Square. She didn't care who saw her, who turned their heads. There was only one thought in her mind, to see him, confront him. No use until after Greenwood and Adam left. She stationed herself at the corner of Portman Square in sight of the pillared doorway, watching the fanlight. An hour went by. She didn't care; she waited. Let passing strangers think whatever they chose.

At last dim figures appeared on the doorstep, leaving. It was dusk by now, the whole square was in shadow. Presently his carriage came to the door. That proved it. No single bed at Portman Square tonight, but a ten-foot stretch of thistledown at Fulham. She crossed the square, and as the front door opened, disclosing his servant with his traps and baggage, she mounted the steps and walked into the hall.

"Good evening, Ludovick."

The servant started, stammered, "Good evening, ma'am."

"Where is His Royal Highness?"

"Madam, I hardly know." Shaken and pale, he looked towards the stairway. She gathered up her gown and mounted, calling aloud in clear and ringing terms, "All set for the rough-and-tumble down at Fulham?" A valet she'd never seen appeared from a bedroom. "Get out, and let me pass." She pushed him aside and the man, too surprised to seize her, let her go.

"So this is the bachelor bedroom. I'm glad to see it." She stood in the doorway, smiling, wrapped in her cloak. The Duke was bending down to change his breeches, one leg uplifted, his foot balanced on a chair.

"Caught with your breeches down. I beg your pardon. But it isn't for the first time, after all. That's how the French observed you once in Holland. And Flanders, too, if memory serves me right."

He reached for a dressing-gown, his face dull purple. She slammed the door and leant against it, laughing.

"Oh, God, don't blush for me. I'm used to drawers. I've seen that pair fifty times at Gloucester Place, washed by the laundrymaid and hung to dry. Well, here's to your evening."

She motioned with her hands in gesture of drinking. He pulled on his dressing-gown, restoring dignity.

"I implore you," he said, and his voice was low and hurried. "Leave this house instantly, before my servants throw you out. For the sake of the past, and all that we've been to each other."

"For the sake of the past," she mimicked; "a fine reminder. I'm to remember, and you're to slip off and forget. My God, you've got some recollections coming. At least you've dined, or so your servant said, so you won't have to wolf the food that's waiting at Fulham. Cold soup, if I remember, followed by mutton. Does Mrs. Carey like her lamb with spinach? Pastry hard or puffed? Or daren't she eat it? I'm glad she's up to your weight, it should keep her in training. If she pirouettes in the sheets she'll damage the linen."

"Take her away," he said to the waiting servants.

She'd used the words herself a few nights before. "Take him away," she had said at Gloucester Place. The victim was Joseph. And her staff had obeyed. This time she stood alone at the top of the stairs. Nobody touched her. Smiling, she bowed to the Duke and, for the last time, curtseyed.

"I'm going. But I can tell you one thing first. If you take away your protection from George, from the children—never mind me; I can fend for myself, I'm a woman—you'll suffer for it and regret it always. I'll see that your name goes down to posterity . . . stinking. Remember . . . Well, I wish you luck."

She walked down the stairs, waving her hands to the servants, and crossed the square. Her own house was in darkness, the lights extinguished. She knocked and rang three times; nobody answered. Rats and the sinking ship? She shrugged her shoulders. Presently she heard the sound of horses—it was the carriage driving away from Portman Square. The night was still and warm, and the stars were shining.

EIGHT: Reaction was swift and sudden. It had not happened. Five hours of feverish sleep, and it seemed to her all a dream, Adam an evil spy who had come between them. Everything could be explained: another interview—forget about last night's—would smooth away mistakes and misunderstanding. He had not meant what he said; she'd win him back. Notes were despatched to Portman Square, to Fulham, to Oatlands on the Friday, even to Windsor. Two laconic scraps came in return.

"If it could be of the least advantage to either of us, I should not hesitate in complying with your wish to see me; but as a meeting must, I think, be painful to both of us under the present circumstances, I must decline it." The style was not his own, but Greenwood again. Greenwood and Adam between them, standing behind him.

"I enter fully into your sentiments concerning your children, but cannot undertake what I am not sure of performing. With regard to Weybridge, I think that you had better remove your furniture."

And leave the house stripped and bare for Mrs. Carey? Was it too far to drive from Oatlands to Fulham Lodge?

She sat with the notes in her hands. The bluff was over. It wasn't a dream. She had merely joined the throng of his discarded mistresses, women who'd served their time, and the time was done. He hadn't the courage to tell her so to her face. Therefore, the lame excuse of enquiry into her conduct, and the trumped-up charges of Adam, saved his conscience. A woman who pleased no longer was an encumbrance. Out . . . and the faster the better . . . make way for the next. If you want redress then send for a lawyer, but bid the lawyer beware before he attacks. A prince of the blood royal doesn't submit to blackmail. The lawyer and the client can go to goal. So . . . accept your *congé* with a smiling grace or find yourself in Newgate . . . take your choice.

She put the notes amongst the hundred others, love letters all of them, bound with scarlet ribbon, then sent for her attorney, Mr. Comrie. She told him the truth (she knew him too well to beg for pity), and then she said, "Is there any redress, any claim I can make upon him?"

"None. You have no bond in writing."

"His promises in the past? His frequent vows that nothing and no one would separate us, that if anything happened to me he'd look after the children?"

"Verbal promises only. Nothing is documented."

"I've kept all his letters. I have them here, you can see them."

He shook his head, pursed up his mouth, and declined. "Intimate letters between a man and his mistress, without any promise of settlement, allowance, or annuity, would have no sort of value in a court of law. I'm sorry, Mrs. Clarke, but there's no redress. The only thing I can do is to see Mr. Adam, and make some arrangement for the payment of your annuity. Four hundred a year is small, after all this splendour, but that of course can't be helped: you must live accordingly."

"What about my debts? Who's to pay them? I must owe you a thousand pounds at least."

"His Royal Highness may allow you to sell the house. I would estimate the worth at four thousand pounds. This sum would cover a part of the debts outstanding."

"And these letters?"

"What letters, Mrs. Clarke?"

She pointed to the bundle tied up in ribbon. "These love letters. What are they worth to the world? They aren't all passionate scribbles, you know, Mr. Comrie. His Royal Highness was frequently most indiscreet. There are references here to His Majesty and to the Queen, to the Prince of Wales, the Princess, to the Duke of Kent. I rather think that if the Royal Family saw them . . ."

Mr. Comrie looked very grave. He held up his hand. "My advice to you, then, is to burn them, and burn them at once. Any attempt to threaten His Royal Highness, or

198

any of his family, would be disastrous to you and to your children. That I assure you."

The lawyer mind. All right, she wouldn't press it. She'd pass the matter over but keep the letters.

"Thank you, Mr. Comrie. I rely upon you. Then you'll see Mr. Adam at once?"

"I will see him today. In the meantime, what are your plans? You intend to stay here?"

Her plans? She had no plans. Her world was cracked. There was no need for Mr. Comrie to know it, though. Finance was his affair, not shocked emotions, nor humbled pride, nor outraged sense of justice.

"I expect I shall go out of town, to stay with friends." Which is where, she thought to herself, the pudding gets proven. How many of the flatterers would remain, or were they all in attendance down at Fulham? Less than a week would show, as the word got round. Buzz . . . buzz . . . have you heard? . . . It's true . . . H.R.H. has sacked her . . .serve the slut right, it was time he sent her packing . . . every bitch has its day, and hers was waning.

Roll up the carpets, get out the boards "FOR SALE". But no one must ever know how much it rankled, what it meant to her—the loss of face, position, style, and favour, apart from the loss of a man, and that man a prince. When a pillow was royal, embraces had a pedestal value, but any experience shared, prince or no prince, produced emotion. Shifting, transitory, lasting, what did it matter? All flesh felt the same, for three hours, or for three years; but after three years individuality, the very pigment, had impressed itself. Hands and thighs and shoulders became known, and so did moods, and temperament at breakfast: laughter for no reason after midnight, ease of intimacy, pride of possession, the glow beneath the heart, the knowledge "This man is mine!" Now all that was over. She had been kicked out of bed, like a scullion from a kitchen. Therefore, she must pretend, show the bold front to the world, the careless shrug, tell the blackest lie, if black lies eased the shame.

"H.R.H. is up to his neck in debt. (Pepper a fib with truth, it always paid.) I haven't the heart to be a burden on him, so I'm planning to leave the house in Gloucester

Place, sell most of the furniture and store the rest, and do the same with Weybridge—he can't afford it. It's miserable for us both, but it's really better. I shall move down to the country with the children, and then, if things improve, return to London. Poor darling, he's so involved with this God-damn war, he practically sleeps at the Horse Guards. I never see him."

If she said it often enough she'd really believe it, and so would her friends, or those who mattered most—her family, above all her mother and Charley. And Bill, in case Bill should say, "I told you so. I warned you again and again, I knew this would happen," and then offer her once more that Uxbridge cottage, diffident and shy, but newly confident. "It's all I can do at the moment, but later on . . ."

Bill, in fact, must be the last to know. The closer the friend, the worse the sting of shame. With relief she heard he was due to sail in the expedition to Buenos Aires early in June. It would be time enough to tell him when he returned.

The children—how deal with the children? Mary at thirteen had intuition, and Ellen, at ten, was sharply inquisitive. May Taylor's little boarding school sufficed, but holidays must be thought of, arrangements made, questions fobbed off. "But why must we leave Gloucester Place?" must be answered with, "London is so expensive, darlings, it will do us all good to rusticate." When the moment came, she would borrow somebody's house.

Ireland. What about Ireland, and the Fitzgeralds? Both father and son had sworn friendship again and again. "If ever you want any help just call upon us." She put out a feeler, and found that St. George's Channel made a very effective division when crisis occurred. Protestations came from both, but also excuses: the climate was so damp in Ireland, they knew she would hate it, and Jamie Fitzgerald's wife was inclined to be tricky, and Willie was working very hard, and life was a problem, and so on, and so on, but perhaps they might meet in the autumn?

In other words, Mrs. Clarke, there's nothing doing. Not at the moment, anyhow. Members of Parliament have to watch their step, even an Irish member and a radical, but time may show which way the cat will jump. She thought of the letters Jamie Fitzgerald had written after three glasses of port at Gloucester Place, and of the things he'd whispered during dinner. No wonder his wife was tricky, it didn't surprise her; she'd be even trickier still if she read the letters, which were all in a neat little box, tied up with tape. Who else had vowed fidelity and friendship? Will Ogilvie, but not with his hand on his heart. As man to man, as partners sharing a business. The business had bust, she awaited the curt farewell. She might fool the others, she didn't expect to fool Will.

He called, his usual urbane, casual self, the morning she was trying to decide what furniture to sell and what to store.

"Don't panic," he said coolly; "keep the best. Possessions are an investment, and you'll need them. Throw out the junk, the flashy gimcrack stuff. That'll have a certain notoriety value at the moment, and will sell well."

She looked at him closely. His manner had not changed.

She said. "I didn't think I should be seeing you. I rather imagined you'd have moved to Fulham."

"No business there," he replied; "she's not the type. She won't last long. I give her about six months."

"And then?"

He shrugged his shoulders. "In point of fact, my cards are still on you. I think it's extremely likely you'll get him back."

The turn of the tide. She felt a rush of hope to her heart.

"What makes you think so? Have you heard any rumours?"

"Only that Adam and Greenwood between them cooked your goose. They knew what we've been working at, of course. Our business spoilt their private money market, so you had to go. It's been boiling up for months, ever since Gordon took over as M.S. from Clinton. It was Adam, by the way, who introduced H.R.H. to Mrs. Carey. She hasn't a brain to her head, so she's no danger."

"But the Duke's in love with her, Will?"

"A fillip to a jaded palate. He's working too hard. And he's sensitive as an eel to criticism. There's plenty of it coming, you wait and see. Watch Parliament during the approaching season. The Whigs are out to get somebody's blood, and no one would suit their purpose better than the Commander-in-Chief of an army on the hop."

The turmoil in her mind was suddenly quietened. Will's values were realistic, down to earth, his spades were ruddy shovels, razor-edged, so different from Bill's moral inhibitions. There would be no sympathy from Will, no cottage at Uxbridge, but a brace to the sagging shoulders, a kick on the buttocks.

"All right," she said, "you landed me into this, you and Tom Taylor between you. Now what's the betting?"

He put out a professional hand and touched her face, lifted the contours where the telltale lines, deepened from loss of sleep, betrayed their presence.

"You want it straight?"

"For God's sake, yes. I'm sick of flatterers."

"Lie low, then, for a year and get some rest. Anxiety can play hell with a woman's looks, especially when she relies, like you, on charm and humour. You haven't a decent feature in your head. The expression in your eyes is all that matters."

"What do you suggest, a nunnery?"

"No. Boredom for six months, and a bed to yourself, unless you've some fancy fellow up your sleeve you can whistle along to amuse you now and again. Don't worry about expenses. The game continues."

She looked at him and smiled. "You've missed your vocation. You ought to have been a physician mixing medicines. No pills to a woman past thirty, only champagne. How does the game continue? Where, and when?"

"The split's only gossip so far, and hasn't spread. The small fry all believe you still have influence. Army promotions are out, but there're plenty of government departments I know how to handle, and you can fool the clients you have royal backing. The cash will still come your way, make no mistake. Then, when Mrs. Carey's run her race and you've got back your complexion, we'll see how the land lies. By the way, you kept his letters?"

"Every one."

"Good girl. They may be needed. Lock 'em up. Meantime, if you have any Whigs among your friends cling on to them and let the Tories go. This Coalition won't last another year."

"You don't mean the Whigs would get in? The King wouldn't have them."

"They won't 'get in,' as you put it, but as a strong Opposition, they can make themselves unpleasant, and will nose out any scandal to suit their cause. In which case you and I might find them useful. But never mind that for the moment; one jump at a time. I take it your lawyer Comrie represents you officially, and has squeezed all he can out of Adam and Greenwood and Co.?"

"Four hundred a year and the lease of the house. Nothing more."

"Just about the dirtiest deal a woman could have, and typical, if I may say so, of royal largesse. Incidentally, yours is not the only nose out of joint. The Prince of Wales is living with Lady Hertford, and Maria Fitz has lost a stone in weight."

"He'll go back to her in the end. He always does. She caught him young. I believe that's the only answer."

"Rot. The more pulpy the fruit, the more smashing the fall. If you don't get York back, I'll find you a substitute. Five other brothers, you know, and all very hearty."

"Thank you. Once bitten . . . I'd rather make do with the peerage. I'll remember what you said about the Whigs. Do you know Lord Folkestone?"

"William Pleydell-Bouverie, His Radical Lordship? Spent his early days in France and talks revolution? I've seen him two or three times. Intense, but engaging."

"He came to my box at the theatre a few weeks ago, before all this happened. I haven't thought of him since, but we did rather well in the time . . . he was very attentive."

"Keep him hooked if you can, then; he might prove a valuable ally. What other admirers are likely to spring to assistance? The worthy Dowler can't be far afield."

"Bill's going to Buenos Aires, he's out of the running. There's Coxhead-Marsh in Essex, but hampered as all the chaps are, with a wife. He's stiff with property, though, and could be helpful; I might moulder away six months or

203

so with him. My Irish contingent have rather let me down, otherwise Dublin would have been amusing. Immediate response, of course, is easy. General Manner's son, Russell Manners, another M.P., is dying to put himself at my disposal. His house in Old Burlington Street is mine for the asking."

"Seize hold of it, dear, if it's empty."

"It's not. That's the trouble. He'd expect to be there in attendance, and have his reward."

"You could always plead nerves."

"For three nights, yes, but not for a fortnight. I'd rather go through the performance, his snuffles and all, than think up a different excuse for fourteen days . . . Yes, Burlington Street could be my *pied-à-terre*. And he's got a rich brother-in-law called Rowland Maltby, who backs all his bills and is a City merchant at Fishmongers Hall. We might make some money through them—they know lots of people, all with their noses rammed to the right hindquarters."

"Press on, press on. The temperature's steadily rising."

"My God, I've forgotten Lord Moira . . . he's clay in my hands, or was, when I saw him in April; two months make a difference. But all aboveboard and correct, no rough-and-tumble. He took a great interest in George, and played with his soldiers. Sob stuff would get him, I fancy, a woman distressed."

"Keep that in reserve, Mary Anne. The last card in the pack."

"When all else has failed?"

"When the ultimate pip has been squeezed. Now, take my advice and relax, and get out of London. Forget H.R.H. for six months. That's all I demand."

It was strange how morale rose to heaven because of his visit. Before, she'd felt senseless and numb, and there wasn't an answer. Her spirits were at zero, she hadn't a hope in the world. Now, because of his chat, she was singing again. Despondency vanished, gloom was flung out of the window. Ill-luck was an imp to be spat at, fought with and vanquished; fortune a sprite to be seized, held on to, and guarded; life an adventure, an ally, and not an antagonist. She moved amongst her possessions, cool and clearheaded, wasting no sentiment, sorting the good from the trash.

"Those can go, and that, and these as well."

Chandeliers and lamps and fitted curtains—a better price for the house with the fittings thrown in. "But that I'll keep, and this, and the dozen chairs." It might have been six years back in Golden Lane, the bailiffs in and Joseph in a stupor. Only six years ago? An age. Eternity. And Joseph to blame for this, as in Golden Lane, Joseph and Adam between them, with lies and cunning. "Yes, sell the curtained bed. It will fetch a price, especially when it's known who slept in it. The mattress, too, it's seen a bit of service. But not the sheets. I'll keep the monogram."

Sentiment? No . . . a business proposition. They might suit the Duchess at Oaklands, when closets were bare. An offer to sell would have to bring an answer. "May it please Your Royal Highness, I have some sheets. Part worn, but in good order and monogrammed. If the purchase is refused, then they will be publicly offered at Christie's, with full details of when last used and by whom. The motive for giving Your Royal Highness the first refusal is sheer delicacy, thus avoiding any offence to taste." Good for a hundred guineas? The Duchess could spare it. She might buy the sheets, and hem them short for the lap dogs.

"What price a stout commode?" No, not for auction. Another private deal, with Colonel Gordon. "Knowing the shortage of fittings at the Horse Guards, the scarcity of materials due to war, Mrs. Clarke is pleased to offer, item —one large commode, solidity guaranteed. For use of Colonel Gordon, Military Secretary. Lately installed at 18 Gloucester Place, and tested by the Commander-in-Chief himself. If private sale is refused, then to be offered at Christie's, or at the Royal Exchange for double value."

Gordon wouldn't dare to let it go. He'd have to stump up the cash to squash the story. What other souvenirs would pay their way, lift pious hands, and shock the eager eye? A nightshirt back from the laundry girl, and torn? Despatched to Mrs. Carey, along with a cake of soap and a reel of cotton.

A pair of underdrawers, perhaps, to the Queen? "Being aware of Your Majesty's deep affection for Prince Frederick Augustus, Duke of York and Albany, I, Mary Anne Clarke, most devoted of your servants, do humbly dare to send you this touching token, that clothed the nether limbs of your second son, just found, to my great surprise, on the drawing-room divan." That ought to cause a flutter down at Windsor, and a *frisson* amongst the ladies of the bedchamber.

Will Ogilvie was right. The game continued. There were fools still willing to pay for place and position, believing she pulled the strings in the right direction. The friend-of-a-friend-of-a-friend—and money changed hands. Burlington Street was the centre of operations, once Gloucester Place was sold and the furniture stored, and Russell Manners, M.P. (with a sweet young wife in the country, somewhere in Wales), was her host in spite of his snuffles. When Parliament dissolved for the summer recess and husbands were claimed by wives, he changed headquarters. Cash was getting short and rest was imperative. The snuffles had been endured, but nerves were fraying. In a moment of madness she scribbled a note to the Duke, "I must have a hundred pounds to get out of town. My debts are still unpaid, and my creditors are after me. Everything I got for the house has gone in paying off the poorer tradespeople. If you fail me with this, I'll come and camp on your doorstep."

She received a reply by return, and bank notes for two hundred. The letter was brought by a servant from Portman Square, who said His Royal Highness had been alone, and that neither Mr. Adam nor Greenwood was with him. So . . . when the spies were absent, conscience pricked. The letter said he hoped she was well, and that her children were with her. She need have no fear for George: his schooling was settled, his future was well assured, he gave his promise. As to herself and the very immediate future, a grace-and-favour house was at her disposal, standing empty at present while awaiting a suitable tenant, and she might use it until the tenant appeared. The house was rather far from London, at Exmouth, but doubtless sea air would benefit her and the children, and he hoped that her stay would prolong itself through the winter. He was hers, in all sincerity, Frederick P.

Had Fulham begun to pall? Not yet, she decided. If it had been so he would never have sent her to Devon. Two hundred miles from town gave him breadth and freedom. What a contrast to his letters a year ago! She took one from the packet, written from Weymouth. "How can I sufficiently express to my sweetest, my darling love, the delight which her dear pretty letter gave me, or how much I feel all the kind things she says to me in it? Millions and millions of thanks for it, my angel, and be assured that my heart is fully sensible of your affection, and that upon it alone its whole happiness depends." Etcetera . . . etcetera . . . and finishing with, "God bless you, my own dear, dear love. I shall miss the post if I add more; oh, believe me ever, to my last hour, yours and yours alone . . ."

Back to the ribboned pile and the black tin box, placed in the depths of her trunk for full security. And so to Exmouth, sand-in-the toes, and freckles, with the children, her mother, Isobel, Isobel's husband; with Charley, on sick leave again from another new regiment, having left the Dragoons and exchanged to the 59th Foot; May Taylor and her sister, term over and nowhere to go; poor Mr. Corri, ordered sea air by his doctor and nobody asking for music lessons in London; and Martha—thank God for Martha, fed up with the coal man and bigamy in a bed-sitting-room at Woolwich, eager to housekeep once more for a dozen-odd people. The whole world was welcome to grace and favour at Exmouth. Manchester House was enormous; it could shelter the lot, and the bill for the food could be sent to the Duchess at Oatlands . . . Repose, then, relax, forget the past and the future. Lie in the sun all day long and play with the children.

And what of the winter, when everyone scurried for shelter, and the mist and the rain in the west drove spirits to zero? Back to Old Burlington Street or eastwards to Essex, the loan of that house at Loughton and Coxhead-Marsh?

At least one of the chaps could afford to turn out his pockets, considering what she had done for them all in the past: places, promotions, jobs on the side. In other words, pick up a flat and keep the ball spinning.

NINE: "I tell you it's true."

"But darling boy, it's quite incredible."

"Incredible perhaps, but you don't know Fane. He hated me from the first, and so did the others. As soon as I joined the regiment I knew I had blundered; they made life as damned unpleasant as they could. Their orders came from higher up, that's obvious—I heard as much from a rumour in the mess. 'Watch out, Thompson, the C.O.'s out to break you!' I said, 'What's the reason?' At first they wouldn't answer, but after I'd pressed the point they let me have it. 'It's too bad your sister split with the C.-in-C. Her name's mud at G.H.Q. and everyone knows it. Anyone connected is going to be booted. Some fellow saw it in Orders, I can't tell you who.' Then I got sick, you know how ill I've been . . . three doctors told me I was unfit for duty. I applied for sick leave. The C.O., Colonel Fane, wrote it was out of his power to grant it, that I had to apply to the Inspecting Field Officer, sending a doctor's chit. The I.F.O. was at Newark, I was up at Leeds. I was distraught with pain, I couldn't delay, I simply had to get to London for the best medical advice. So while I was being nursed by you at Loughton, with double mastoid, practically off my head, they plotted this." The *Gazette* was thrown at her feet—"Captain Charles Farquhar Thompson, 59th Regiment of Foot, superseded."

She looked at his blazing eyes and his trembling hands. He was no longer a man, but a little boy in the alley, saying, "It isn't fair. The big fellow hit me. He's stronger than me, he kicked me into the gutter," and she was wiping his nose and drying his tears, saying, "I'll look after you, don't be afraid," raging, boiling, seizing the nearest implement to hand—a broken saucepan, a poker,

208

a headless broom—and running down the alley after the bully. She took the *Gazette* and read the statement again.

"Don't worry, Charley, I'll have you reinstated."

"How can you? You haven't the influence any more. You've lost your job and so have I. We're finished."

He threw himself on a chair, his hair dishevelled, his tunic soiled, unbrushed, the buttons unpolished. "I tell you I haven't a chance. I've known it for months. You've known it too, but you've tried to fool yourself. Those weeks at Exmouth, pretending all was well, that H.R.H. had lent you the house for the summer and couldn't wait for the autumn to see you again. What happened when autumn came? You flitted to Loughton, saying you'd got yourself used to country air, and that Coxhead-Marsh had been asked by the Duke to look after you, that Rowland Maltby and Manners were paying the bills. Have you seen H.R.H.? Not a glimpse. Not even a letter. He's broken with you for good, and the whole world knows it. Not content with that, he's put his spies on me, and I'm to be broken, too, kicked out of the service. And as for George, he's for the boot as well. No new cadets at Marlow, the lists are closed. I had it from some fellow on the staff."

He laughed, and all the past was in the sound. The heat of the alley, the stench of the running drain, the cries of children, the taste of flyblown food, their mother's weary call from the back kitchen, Bob Farquhar's jug of ale spilt on the table.

"For God's sake hold your tongue . . ."

"Why should I hold it? You've brought me up. I've followed you all my life. You taught me what to expect, and what to look for. 'Aim high,' you said, 'and if you don't get what you want, I'll get it for you.' That's been your talk from the start. My first commission, my first exchange, promotion; everything coming easy, I was bound to succeed. And then, because of some footling God damn quarrel, you muck things up with the Duke and mess my life. I have to suffer through your stupidity. Not only me, but George, the girls, and all of us."

He started to sob, hysterically, like a child, reverting to the days when tears brought kisses, comfort and a box on the ear, a slap and a toffee apple, tales of the silver button, the clan Mackenzie. Now they brought silence, eyes that were suddenly stricken, a hand that touched his hair in a known caress, a voice that sounded distant, strangely frightened. "I never knew it meant so much to you, my living with H.R.H., and Gloucester Place. I thought you looked upon it as a business, a place where you could stay when you came on leave."

"A business? What sort of business? It was my world. The world you'd promised me when we were children. Remember my hero worship for Prince Charlie? You made it all come true, or so I thought. He used to smile and chat to me after dinner, those times I stayed in the house—you wouldn't remember—and I'd go back to duty as proud as a king, feeling I'd talked to God . . . You don't understand. You were only a woman, his mistress, but we were men; we spoke the same language; he asked me about the regiment. I honoured him more than anyone I knew. He stood for something that I can't explain, a dream at the back of my mind that came to life. And now it's all over. There isn't anything left."

She watched him tear the *Gazette* into tiny strips and throw it in the fire where it blackened and smouldered.

She said, "Do you think that George feels the same as you do?"

He shrugged. "How should I know? He's still a child. At nine years old he might think anything. I only know he believes the Duke's his father."

She turned and stared at him, her eyes bewildered. "Who told you so?"

"George did himself. Ellen believes it too. Some tale of Martha's. Mary knows better, she remembers Joseph, but he's rather dim in her mind and will soon be forgotten. They won't forget H.R.H.—he's implanted for life. And the rooms at Gloucester Place, and all the splendour. Nothing will equal that in the whole of their lives. You've spoilt the future for them, and you might as well know it."

Every word he said disclosed her hidden feelings. The past eighteen months, tedious and trivial, spent between Exmouth and London and Loughton Lodge, with any friend who offered to pay a bill—Russell Manners, Cox-head-Marsh, Jamie Fitzgerald—a means of marking time, to postpone decision, now rolled away as though they had never been; and she was standing once more in Gloucester Place, stacking the furniture, this to be sold, this to be kept, Will Ogilvie at her side saying, "The game continues."

The game in the lower brackets, fiddling, foolish, never worth the candle—that was a game for amateurs. A game for office clerks in a third-rate store, who counted a ten-pound bill as the height of ambition; no pride, no power, no juggling with high names. "Mr. Rowland Maltby can get you a place as a waiter," no longer "His Royal Highness will recommend . . ." Lolling about at Loughton with Coxhead-Marsh, yawning at tales of woodcock, partridge, pigeon, telling herself the autumn was pleasant in Essex, and all the while the fever under the skin: "I want him back. I want the power, the position." The well-remembered whisper round Vauxhall: "Look! There's Mrs. Clarke . . . watch for the Duke"—a bustle, smiles and nods, and a sea of faces.

It was all gone, a bubble burst, the running stream a patch of stagnant water.

"What's beaten me," said Charley, "is the way you've taken the whole thing lying down. No sort of fight. Is it that you're getting old and just don't care?"

This time he might have got a box on the ears or a strangle-grip on the throat—two children punching noses in the gutter, tearing each other's hair, shouting, "Stop, or I'll kill you!" Instead, she went and looked out of the window at the neat box garden, the gravel drive, the trim, smug Essex landscape.

She said, "Go and pack your things. We're going to London."

"Why? What for?"

"Don't ask questions. You trusted me as a child, you can trust me now."

"You'll get me reinstated?"

"Yes. And then you'll report for duty. On your C.O.'s reaction to that depends your future. If he's really out to break you, he'll show his hand."

Here was action at last, something to bite and tear. Her fury was projected on to Colonel Fane, a stuffed dummy representing law and order, emissary of Adam, of

211

Gordon, the War Office, hatred begetting hatred, a world in arms. One woman alone against a race of men, antagonistic because they knew her worth. Keep out of our ranks, don't poach on our preserves. That was why they hated her—she'd proved equality. They didn't hate Mrs. Carey down at Fulham, or standing tiptoe on the theatre boards—art was accepted, artists didn't meddle. But once a woman stole the initiative, plundered the perquisites, and took the lead, what happened to the globe? The fabric cracked.

Charley said to her in the post-chaise, driving to London, "What are you thinking about? You look so stern."

She laughed. "I was miles away, in point of fact. It was nothing to do with you or me or the present. I had a picture of Mother washing the dishes, bending over the tub in the small back kitchen—you know how dark it was, with no window—and the boys crawling under her feet, clinging to her ankles, so that she couldn't move. Father came in and shouted, wanting his supper . . . I remember I went and hit him. I've never forgotten."

"What made you think of that, after all these years?"

"God knows . . ." The post-chaise bumped along the lanes, swaying from side to side. She clung to the strap, and with her other hand held on to Charley. Something had cleared in her mind. She was confident, happy. Burlington Street as a *pied-à-terre* was finished. Russell Manners had gone to India—just as well, she did not want to be bothered with complications at the moment, nor advertise her presence to stray creditors.

Two days at a hotel, then lodgings at Hampstead. She put flowers on Edward's grave, planted bulbs for the spring, not consciously thinking of Edward, only of George. Hampstead was nostalgic, familiar, full of memories, not of the honeymoon with Joseph, but of Bill. Mrs. Andrews at the Yellow Cottage was warm and welcoming, but alas, she had no rooms to let for at least six months; the whole of the upper floor was let to a publisher, Sir Richard Philips. Did Mrs. Clarke know the name? She did . . . and made a note for future reference. A publisher might be useful, depending on plans. Meanwhile, would Mrs. Andrews recommend lodgings for herself and Captain Thompson, and later the children? She could certainly try Mr. Nicols, Flask Walk, New End. He was a very respectable man, by profession a baker. The lodgings were taken.

Round one of the contest was staged.

A note to Portman Square produced no answer, but ... on the twentieth of November Captain Charles Farquhar Thompson, 59th Regiment of Foot, was reinstated. She showed Charley the *Gazette* with a smile of triumph.

"I promised, didn't I?"

"Yes, but what happens next?"

"Go and rejoin the regiment down at Colchester. If Colonel Fane is aggressive, write me at once."

George was still secure at Chelsea, but Charley was right, his name had been erased from the lists for Marlow. Adam was one of the governors, so was Gordon— it was easy enough to see where the influence lay. For the moment Charley came first. George must be second. There was room for them all at Hampstead, at Mr. Nicols', for the French governess, too (she must forget about school), and for Martha. Her mother could stay down at Loughton for the present; she was getting old and shaky, always complaining and asking why H.R.H. didn't come to see her. At the end of the week Charley returned from Colchester. One glance at his face told her of further trouble.

"What now?"

"I've got to exchange. Colonel Fane says he won't have me in the regiment."

"Does he give his reasons?"

"The same as before—absent without leave. And another thing too. You remember those bills drawn on Russell Manners that Mother signed and you sent me back in the summer? They were payable through Rowland Maltby at Fishmongers Hall, and I got the paymaster up at Leeds to cash them, just before I was ill and came on leave. The bills were refused, and we've got no proof that I believed they would be honoured. The C.O. says a charge of fraud can be brought against me."

"But that's ridiculous. Rowland Maltby always honours Russell's bills."

"That's where you're wrong—Maltby refused to honour these particular ones. Wasn't there some brush between

213

you and Manners and Maltby at Burlington Street, before you went down to Loughton? Both knocking at your door, and you wouldn't admit 'em?"

"Oh, good God! They were both as drunk as owls, and I was dead."

"Well . . . there's his answer. But the paymaster had given me the money, and the bills were returned. If the matter gets to court it will be my finish."

"Did Colonel Fane say a charge would be brought against you?"

"He told me the matter would close, if I'd get an exchange."

"Very well. You shall get an exchange. You shall have it by Christmas."

This time nothing happened. The notes sent to Portman Square were returned, unopened. Charlie wrote for an interview. The request was refused. Martha, who used to hobnob with the Portman Square staff, went down to pay a call on old friends in the kitchen. She found new faces, who firmly closed the door. Mr. Adam, it seemed, had given her old friends notice. Mary and Ellen, walking up Heath Street, were followed. The French governess had hysterics and asked to leave. A man had touched her arm and tried to question her. "Is Mrs. Clarke in Hampstead? What's the address?"

It could be creditors, or even Joseph, but more likely spies of Adam on the prowl. Charley paced up and down in the small front parlour, biting his nails and peering out of the window.

"Any word of my exchange?"

"Not yet. I've written."

No need to tell him his career was blocked. She'd written to fifty regiments and they'd all refused him. No agency would take him on their books. Word from G.H.Q. must have gone round, "Black-listed: C. F. Thompson." Friends who two years back would have done her favours were suddenly out of town, or ill, or busy. She went to Will Ogilvie. At least she would get the truth from him.

"What's happened, Will?"

"Haven't you read the papers?"

"You know I've been down at Loughton all the summer, and through the autumn too, until last month."

"I told you to watch events. They're illuminating. Instead of which you've let your mind go rusty, gazing at Coxhead-Marsh in a blaze of pheasants."

"If you think I enjoyed it . . . What about the papers?"

"Attacks against H.R.H. almost every day. Pamphlets spitting abuse, very near the knuckle."

"What's the got to do with me?"

"Officially, nothing. But everyone at the War Office thinks you write them."

"My God! I wish I did."

"They've just worked around to probing into your past. Or rather Adam has, and Greenwood too. Not your marriage, dear—your fun with the Grub Street boys, that money you made on the side when you lived in Holborn."

"Is that why they're trying to throw Charley out of the regiment?"

"Of course. As your brother, he's in it up to the neck."

"But Will, it isn't true . . ."

"That doesn't matter. You're smeared with the dirt, and it all fits in very well. The point is this—the people read the pamphlets and say to themselves, 'No smoke without a fire, a fish stinks at the head,' and all the rest. Our friend, dear H.R.H., begins to lose favour. Popularity wanes, and so do the things he stands for: the Army, the Church, the Tory Government, the war with France, the British Constitution. Let a few more months roll on, we can start doing business in rather a bolder way than we did before. You don't play chess, so why should I explain? You're an excellent pawn, Mary Anne, in a certain game that I've been playing now for fourteen years, since France disencumbered herself in '93."

She shrugged her shoulders in exasperation. "Still harping on republics? Well, play it alone. I've told you before, security comes first. My family's, and my own. What concerns me at the moment is my brother Charley. They're trying to boot him from the 59th."

"Let him be booted, then. It doesn't matter."

"It matters to him. It matters to me as well. I'm damned if I'll see him booted without a reason. Can't you get him an exchange?"

215

"He's on the black list. I can't do a thing, nor can anyone else. Take the long view, dear, and don't get so excited. In a year from now the government will fall, H.R.H. will lose his command . . . why can't you be patient?"

"I love my brother, and his heart is breaking, and my only hope is to get the Duke to see reason. Is he still visiting Mrs. Carey down at Fulham?"

"You're out of date, he's toying with a peeress . . . Now, listen to me, the tactics have changed entirely. You are *not* going to get him back. You are going to smash him."

The urbane mask had dropped. The dark eyes glittered. This was another Ogilvie, hard and ruthless. "Behave like a fool for your brother—you're wasting your time. But when he's had the sack, and sacked he will be, come back to me: I'll tell you what to do. It's been rather dull at Loughton, hasn't it? Duller still in Devon, amongst the seaweed."

She loathed him, liked him, feared him, trusted him.

"Why," she asked, "should I always do what you tell me?"

"Because," he said, "you can live no other way."

He escorted her down to the carriage and closed the door. She went back to Hampstead and found Charley waiting, the children with him, all with anxious faces.

"A man's been watching from the doorway opposite. He asked Mrs. Nicols if you wrote letters to Fleet Street."

"Nonsense. Don't take any notice. Some drunkard or other."

She made one last request to Portman Square, and a letter from Charley was sent direct to the Horse Guards.

Hers had a scribble in answer, penned at midnight. "I do not know what you mean. I have never authorized anybody to plague you or disturb you, and therefore you may be perfectly at ease on my account."

The letter to Charley was terse and official, with instructions to report at once to Colchester.

"Then everything's all right? I don't have to exchange?"

Charley waved the printed form. His eyes were shining. All his self-confidence was back again. "Why, yes . . . It

216

must mean just that," she smiled, and kissed him. So Ogilvie was wrong. There was no vendetta.

He rushed to get his equipment and start immediately.

George was the next to be planned for. Marlow or Woolwich—it would be easy enough to arrange now Charley was fixed. Everything seemed simple. The children were happy. No one was being a nuisance and spirits were high. There was only one thing lacking, of course, with Charley gone; a man about the house who knew her moods, not anyone fresh, requiring poise and effort, but a man who did not matter, who understood. But nobody fitted the bill . . . She seized the paper. "Is the expedition back from Buenos Aires?"

The South American war had been a fiasco. It was a dispersal of effort, just what the enemy wanted. A mistake by Supreme Command or the politicians? Never mind about that, the point was, Bill might be home. She hadn't thought of him for eighteen months, but now he was the answer to her mood.

"I'll write at once to Uxbridge. He must be home."

She'd forgotten how she had wanted him out of the way, because of pride, when Gloucester Place was sold, glad to think he was out of sight and hearing, thousands of miles away in Buenos Aires.

Now, like a weather vane, the mood had shifted. Hampstead . . . association . . . Bill was the man. Heavens! So much to tell him. All the upheavals, the diabolical plotting of Adam and Greenwood, with poor H.R.H. a helpless tool in their hands, obliged to give her up because of their pressure (no need to mention the advent of Mrs. Carey). Disaster upon disaster, but she had survived, all through her own unaided, determined efforts. Russell Manners, Rowland Maltby, and Coxhead-Marsh? Just dull old friends in the country, being obliging.

Charley was packed off to Colchester and Bill was summoned. He tried to tell her some of the hell endured in Buenos Aires, the privation, sickness, climate. She listened five minutes, shaking her head in distress, then interrupted; he was back in the well-accustomed role of listener. The months and the years slid away, he was here again, quiet, dependable, solid, faithful, adoring. It was happy, relaxing, the touch of someone familiar, like wearing comfortable shoes, or a three-year-old gown found at the back of a closet and quite forgotten, the colour somehow becoming, enhancing the eyes.

"You'll stay with me, won't you?" She kissed him behind the ear.

"Won't it look odd? The children are so much older."

"I'll send them back to Loughton. Mother's there."

Back to the known routine, and very pleasant. Adoration was soothing to the nerves, especially when the palate was rather jaded and interest in exploration was completely lacking. Bill could stay until his next assignment, whenever that should be. No orders had come. Half-pay at the moment should cover their expenses.

The annuity from the Duke had not been paid, but that had not worried her, living at Loughton Lodge. Adam's doing again, of course, he was stopping the payment. Another small matter she'd fix before very long.

"Bill, it's rather strange. Not a word from Charley."

"He's probably waiting for orders, the same as I am. His regiment may be going on foreign service. The rumour is all over London that we're off to Spain, with Wellesley in command, on a new expedition."

"I'm afraid Charley may be ill. He isn't strong."

"It would do him a power of good to see some fighting."

"It's exactly what he wants," she answered swiftly, "to show what he's worth, and prove it to the regiment. He hasn't been given a chance up to the present."

The silence from Charley was the first cloud in the blue, the gathering of the storm. And then, after twenty-four hours, she had the truth direct. Seen in the London *Gazette*, in black and white: "Captain Charles Farquhar Thompson, 59th Regiment of Foot, is now under close arrest, pending Court Martial."

Will Ogilvie, god or devil, had been prophetic. The Hampstead idyll was over. The fight was on.

TEN: Mary Anne sat in the inn at Weeleigh, Colchester, with a copy of the charges in her hand, and by her side the lawyer recommended by Comrie, a man called Smithies, who took notes at her direction.

At the opposite side of the table sat Rowland Maltby, a reluctant witness, sulky and ill at ease, dragged from his home in Hertfordshire to give testimony. She had fetched him herself by coach the day before, threatening that, unless he admitted that the bills which were mentioned in the charges had been backed by him, she would summon his wife downstairs and make a disclosure, a disclosure unpleasant for him and for Russell Manners, out of the way, lucky devil, somewhere in India.

"What am I going to say?"

"You can say what you please, as long as you clear my brother of fraudulent charges."

"I've no desire to get mixed up in the business. A court martial's a matter for soldiers, not civilians."

"You helped to bring it about, and now you can speak for him. Or shall I get out of the coach and ask for your wife?"

She had had the door wide open, about to descend. He handed her hurriedly back, his eye on the window. "Very well, I'll travel with you. Give me time to make excuses. I'll be with you at the crossroads in an hour."

He had sulked all the way to Colchester, hoping to taunt her, and she hadn't bothered so much as to turn her head, but scribbled right through the night on a piece of foolscap, notes for her blasted brother, he supposed, and then, when they reached Weeleigh at 2 A.M., all he had got was sandwiches in the bar and a brief good-night. A fine sort of a fool he must seem in front of the landlord.

She was reading the charges and the lawyer was taking them down.

" 'Charge One. For scandalous and infamous conduct unbecoming the character of an officer and a gentleman in absenting himself on or about the 21st of July 1807, without leave from his Commanding Officer.'

" 'Charge Two. For scandalous and infamous conduct unbecoming,' etc., etc., 'in defrauding Mr. Milbanke the Paymaster of the Leeds Recruiting District of one hundred pounds, by prevailing upon him to cash two bills, neither of which was paid when presented for payment.' "

She paused and ticked the charges with her pencil. "Now, Mr. Smithies, I want you to understand that my brother's unable to speak on his own behalf. You will represent him and cross-examine witnesses. I shall be one, and so will Mr. Maltby. My brother pleads not guilty to both charges."

"I understand, Mrs. Clarke."

She tore off a sheet of paper and handed it to him. "The first charge, this business of leave. Here are the questions I want you to put to the Prosecution, as coming from my brother. Question One: 'Do you know that at the time of my absenting myself and going to London I was crazy with pain, and was stated by three doctors to be unfit for service?' You must realise, Mr. Smithies, that this court martial is what in cockney language we call a 'frame.' They want to kick my brother out of the Army, and any stick will do to beat the dog.

"Question Two: 'Do you know that as soon as I got to London I sent a doctor's chit certifying my unfitness?' Have you got that clear?"

"Yes, Mrs. Clarke."

"Right. To the second charge. What the Prosecution will ask me we can't foresee. It will relate, of course, to the bills I gave my brother, signed with my mother's name, Elizabeth Mackenzie Farquhar. The fact is that she's crippled with rheumatism and can't write herself, so I write all her letters for her, guiding her hand. The reason I used her name and not my own was that I didn't want my name connected with Russell Manners—brother-in-law to Mr. Maltby here. What I shall want you to ask me in Court is this: 'Did you ever receive information from Mr. Rowland Maltby that he would not honour any bill drawn on Russell Manners and payable through him at Fishmongers Hall?' To which, Mr. Smithies, I shall answer, 'Never.' "

She looked across at her gloomy, silent witness. He sipped a glass of ale and did not speak. The lawyer scratched at the foolscap paper in front of him.

"After which, Mr. Smithies, I want you to say to me: 'From your knowledge of the transaction relative to the bills in question, can you state whether it was possible for Captain Thompson to have any fraudulent interest when he induced the paymaster to discount the bills?' To which you will hear me answer, 'Certainly not. Captain Thompson was aware that Mr. Manners was indebted to me.' "

Rowland Maltby moved uneasily in his chair. "Look here, you can't bring that up in open court!"

"Bring what up?"

"The goings-on at 9 Old Burlington Street, the two of us there with you, when our wives were in Wales."

"I don't know what you refer to . . . my mind is a blank. By indebted, I mean a reference to money. I sold a bracelet, for which I got three hundred, and gave a hundred to Russell, who was short of cash. Therefore he was indebted. Don't you agree?"

Rowland Maltby shrugged his shoulders and glanced at the lawyer.

"Indebted, Mrs. Clarke. I have that down."

"Thank you, Mr. Smithies. That's all that concerns me now. Let's have some coffee."

She rose and stretched her arms above her head. God! It was fun to fight, and to fight alone, to carry the weight herself, without interference. Bill would have begged for caution, safety, prudence. The very last words he said to her had been, "Be careful. You'll do more harm than good by intervention." As if poor Charley could face this charge alone . . . Three months the brutes had kept him under arrest, the charges not disclosed until last week; and now as she read the names she saw the reason—every man at the Court hand-picked and connected with Adam and Greenwood and Colonel Gordon.

The dice were loaded against her but she did not care. She would clear Charley's name from fraud; nothing else mattered.

"And the defence?" asked Mr. Smithies. "Mr. Comrie suggested that I should call in a colleague from Lincoln's Inn. We could prepare the statement together for your brother's approval."

She looked at him and smiled. "No need for that."

"You have someone else in mind?"

"I shall write it myself."

"But, madam . . ."

"Oh! Please don't argue. I know what to say."

"The legal language . . ."

"The longer the word the better! They shall have their bellyful. I corrected copy, Mr. Smithies, when you were in petticoats. Smudged lawyers' briefs were part of my earliest reading, sitting cross-legged on a doorstep in Bowling Inn Alley. You can rest assured the defence will be laced with learning."

She kissed her hand to them both and went upstairs. Mr. Smithies coughed and glanced at Rowland Maltby.

"You'll lose, of course?" said the latter.

"I rather fear so."

The proceedings were brief. Witnesses in plenty testified in support of Charge One. Charge Two required more time, and the Prosecution, unable to spike the guns of the prisoner's sister, wasted a lengthy morning with Mr. Maltby, who contradicted himself a dozen times, and was closely questioned, not about bills or money, but about how often he'd stayed with Mrs. Clarke at Loughton, and whether she owned the house, and who was there. There was a pause for adjournment, requested by the prisoner. The weekend was spent by the prisoner's sister at Weeleigh, shut up in her bedroom, covering sheets of foolscap. When the Court sat again, upon the Tuesday, the defence of Captain Thompson was read to the Court:

"Mr. President, and Gentlemen of the Court Martial,
"Having been little more than four years in the Army, a very young man and not possessing the advantages of extensive experience, I feel most strongly the necessity of

throwing myself upon your protection, and seeking pardon for any irregularities I may have unintentionally committed.

"If I did not feel confident that I should most satisfactorily discharge myself, before this honourable Court, of the remotest imputation of guilt in the charges which have been preferred against me for the purpose of steeping my reputation in infamy, I would rather have withdrawn from the society of men, have hidden myself from the face of day and shrunk into obscurity, though unaccompanied, uncheered by one consoling reflection.

"But, Gentlemen, I can boldly assert and with confidence, though in all humility, that the envenomed shafts which have been levelled at my private peace and public reputation, by the accumulated force of pique and military rank, will be repelled by the shield of honour, innocence, and integrity.

"Gentlemen, when first I had the honour of joining the 59th Regiment, I had very early the misfortune to discover that I possessed not the countenance, and was indulged not with the friendly attention, of Colonel Fane. In justice to my own character I must admit that my youth and inexperience might have permitted little irregularities against which more extensive experience and knowledge of the world might have protected me. Colonel Fane was unwilling no doubt to trouble himself with the task of becoming my friendly mentor, and I was suddenly, and without preparation, commanded to quit Newark and to report to Leeds upon the Recruiting Service.

"I exerted myself in the execution of my duty with a zeal and attention which would not have disgraced a more able and experienced officer, until about the month of July 1807, when I was attacked with a most serious illness. In this situation, attended by the most skilful of the Medical Gentlemen of the neighbourhood till they pronounced they could suggest nothing further for the relief of my unremoving malady, I wrote to Colonel Fane stating my extreme ill-health and requesting leave of absence. In reply to that application I received a letter from Colonel Fane stating that it was not in his power to give me any leave, and that if my health absolutely required it,

223

I must send a doctor's certificate to that purport to the Inspecting Field Officer. I did so, but after proceeding first to London. I will admit that this was an error of judgment on my part; but let me appeal to this honourable Court whether it should have induced a Commanding Officer to bring me, a very young man, to a Court Martial for the purpose of destroying my life (for character is life, to an honourable man) and of the blasting of every future prospect?

"I now proceed to trespass upon your attention for a few remarks upon the second charge. I had applied to a near relation of mine for some pecuniary assistance. She supplied me with the two bills in question, drawn by her on Mr. Russell Manners, Esq., payable at Mr. Maltby's Fishmongers Hall. That the Bills were good, and would be paid when they became due, I had not the slightest doubt, and therefore requested Mr. Milbanke, the Paymaster of the District, to discount the Bills, which he consented to do. I have since learnt that the Bills have not been paid. I will not occupy your time with a recapitulation of the evidence, because every word of it exculpates me and asserts my innocence.

"Gentlemen, I am much distressed that I should have trespassed thus long upon your time, but my anxiety to explain every circumstance with the utmost truth and accuracy has lengthened the detail. I feel no disposition to supplicate the honourable Court for any unbecoming favour. I feel no apprehension for the result, because your decision will be founded on liberal and enlightened understanding. To that decision I shall bow with humility and submission, and I entreat the Honourable President and Deputy Judge Advocate to believe that, whatever my fate, I shall retain a grateful remembrance of the attentions I have received."

Mr. Smithies sat down, a small, bespectacled man, grey-haired, with stooping shoulders. His voice was flat. He had read the defence like a curate reading the Lesson. Not once had he paused to make a point or produce an impression. The words that had sounded clear in the hotel bedroom, vivid, engaging, innocent, were lost. The prisoner sat rigidly to attention. His eyes never wavered once from his sister's face. She was watching Colonel Fane as he rose to his feet. At once the President of the Court relaxed, the gentlemen crossed their legs, shifted position. A wave of agreement, of sympathy, drifted towards him. He cleared his throat, smiled, and began to speak.

"Mr. President, and Gentlemen of the Court Martial. I should not have thought it necessary to detain you by making any answer to the prisoner's defence had he not thought it proper to make some severe observations on my personal motives and conduct upon this occasion.

"If the prisoner is innocent of the charges he ought to be grateful to me for giving him an opportunity to justify himself. That there were grounds for the charges is evident, and he must well know that under such implications the officers of the regiment could not have associated with him till he had justified his conduct before a Court Martial.

"The prisoner had also thought proper to assert that he had not so much of my attention at Newark as other officers and thence infer an improper motive on my part. I defy him to prove it by the slightest evidence. On the contrary, I showed him more favour than I have since thought I was justified in doing. He has also attacked me for sending him on the Recruiting Service: that I had a right to select what officers I thought proper at a moment's notice to send on that duty is undoubted, but I will state to the Court my reason for fixing upon Captain Thompson.

"A Mr. Lawton, a most respectable innkeeper at Newark, came to me and told me that Captain Thompson's conduct in his quarters was unbearable, that the evening before he had grossly insulted him, that it was with difficulty he had prevented him fighting with the waiter, and that unless I took steps to prevent it in future, he should be under the necessity of sending a memorial to the Commander-in-Chief.

"Conceiving such conduct extremely prejudicial to the standard of the regiment, whose officers were most of them very young men, I thought it right to send him where his example could do no harm.

225

"Upon the first charge the Court will recollect that my letter gave the prisoner no leave of absence, but only explained, if he were really ill, how he should apply for it. He failed to follow my instructions.

"Upon the second charge I have already stated to the Court I know nothing. The charge of having passed the bills has been proved, but it remains for the Court to determine whether there was any fraud in the transaction.

"I shall not detain you, gentlemen, any further, but declare that it is my wish, as it must be Captain Thompson's, that he has convinced the Court that he is not guilty."

Colonel Fane sat down and the Court withdrew to consider their verdict. It did not take them long. The judgment was delivered by the President, who, after vindicating Colonel Fane and absolving him from all accusations of unfair treatment, went on to a severe indictment of the prisoner, whose attack on his commanding officer had been unjustified and most improper.

Captain Thompson was found guilty of the first charge, but honourably acquitted on the second. Sentence, to be cashiered, which sentence must be confirmed by the Commander-in-Chief.

On the twenty-fourth of May, 1808, the sentence was confirmed in a letter from the Duke of York to Lieutenant General Lord Chatham, the officer commanding the Eastern Division. And from this day, Mary Anne, the prisoner's sister, determined upon revenge, no matter how.

ELEVEN: "You still intend to handle this matter yourself?"

"I hope so."

"In spite of the fact that the Court Martial went against you?"

"That was a foregone conclusion. I saw their faces. But at least I was able to clear the second charge."

"Have you any money?"

"Not a single guinea. We've left the lodgings in Hampstead without paying the bill. The Nicols have got my harp and some books in exchange."

"And Mr. Dowler?"

"Recalled to duty over a month ago. He sailed with the first expeditionary force to Portugal. I'm entirely alone at the moment but for Charley, who's had a breakdown—he won't let me out of his sight."

"The obliging Coxhead-Marsh?"

"Become rather chary. The Court Martial figured largely in the Essex papers, and the name Loughton Lodge was rather too much *en évidence.*"

"To call a spade a spade, you're without a protector?"

"Except yourself. And my own indomitable wits."

Will Ogilvie laughed. "Once more in double harness? The world's our footstool—I am delighted. The first necessity, then, is a roof for your head. Do you know an upholster called Francis Wright?"

"Only that he stores my furniture, the stuff I didn't sell at Gloucester Place."

"Of course, I sent you to him, I remember. He works for me on the side, in various ways. He'll find you lodgings, and then see about a house. I advise you, wherever you go, to call yourself Farquhar. The name of Clarke is

227

suspect in certain quarters. Not so, though, amongst the people you'll meet in the future. Folkstone you know, likewise Burdett and Cobbett: they're the idealists of the Radical group. The opportunists are the boys we're after. Wardle, M.P. for Okehampton, is your chap, determined to reach the top by fair means or foul, the fouler the better if only he feathers his nest."

"I'm not going to get myself mixed up in politics."

"Oh yes, you are . . . if you don't want your children to starve. Any means to an end, I thought you'd learnt that already. Have you had a chat with the publisher, Richard Phillips?"

"I called on him at Hampstead before I left. Unpleasant, I thought, puffed up with self-importance."

"So are they all. You want to add to it. He'd like the job of printing the Army lists, but won't get it unless there's a change of government, including a new Commander-in-Chief at the Horse Guards. Have you met McCullum?"

"The pamphleteer? No, he's a third-rate scribbler."

"He's producing a kick in the pants in the very near future, an Enquiry into the Abuses of the R.M.C., proving that seminary to be an imposition on the public, the cadets all riddled with venereal disease. He finishes with some remarks about British generals which made me crack my ribs . . . I think you'll like him."

"And why do you intend that the pamphleteers and I should become acquainted?"

"Because, my sweet blind bat, you know more than all of them. They want the truth. You can supply it—and then live like a queen to the end of your days. Now go and see Francis Wright about a house."

Number Eleven Holles Street, in Cavendish Square, provided temporary lodgings for a Mrs. Farquhar, accompanied by her brother, Captain Thompson. A most respectable lady from the country, vouched for by Francis Wright of Rathbone Place. The lodgings were required for the month of June, after which Mrs. Farquhar hoped to remove to Bedford Place.

On Monday June the twentieth Mr. Adam, who lived in Bloomsbury Square, received a letter.

Sir,

On the 11th of May, 1806, you waited on me, by the desire of His Royal Highness the Duke of York, to state H.R.H.'s intention of allowing me an annuity of four hundred pounds per annum.

H.R.H. by his promise is now indebted to me five hundred pounds. I have written repeatedly, but to no avail. His Royal Highness's conduct towards me has been utterly devoid of principle, feeling and honour, and as his promises are not to be depended upon, though even given by you, I have come to the determination of making my intentions known to you, for the consideration of H.R.H. and thus it is: I solict His Royal Highness to make the annuity secure for my life, and to pay me the arrears immediately, as my necessaries are very pressing (this he knows). If H.R.H. refuses to do this, I have no other mode for my immediate wants than to publish every circumstance ever communicated to me by H.R.H. and everything which has come under my knowledge during our intimacy, with all his letters. Those things amount to something serious. He is more within my power than he imagines.

Yet I wish for H.R.H.'s sake and my own that he will make my request good, as I know full well I should suffer much in exposing him in my own mind. Before I do anything publicly, I will send to every one of His Royal Highness's family a copy of what I mean to publish. Had H.R.H. only been a little more punctual, this request had never been made.

One thing more: should H.R.H. throw up his protection to my boy (and I thank him much for the past), I hope he will place him on the foundation of the Charterhouse, or any other public school; the child is not accountable for my conduct.

You will please, sir, to state this communication to the Duke of York, and on Wednesday I will send to your house, to know what may be H.R.H.'s intention, which you will please to signify by a letter to

Your most obedient, humble servant,
M. A. Clarke

P.S. H.R.H. must feel that his conduct on a late affair deserves all this, and more.

Mr. Adam sent no reply to this letter. The following Saturday he received a second:

Sir,
    On Wednesday, finding there was not any answer to my letter, I am led to enquire whether H.R.H the Duke of York thinks proper not to make good his promise, given by you, and that you encourage him in it.
    I have employed myself since in committing to paper every circumstance within my recollection during the intimacy of H.R.H. and myself.
    The fifty or sixty letters of H.R.H. will give weight and truth to the whole. On Tuesday I have promised to give these up, if I hear nothing further after this last notice; and when once given out of my possession they will be impossible to recall.
    It is to gentlemen, and not to any publisher, that they will be committed, and these gentlemen are just as obstinate as His Royal Highness, and more independent. They are acquaintances of yours, and to relieve my wants, in pique to others, will do what the Duke will not.
    However, he has all within his own power, and so he may act as he pleases.

                    I am, sir, your most obedient
                         M. A. Clarke

On the Tuesday morning a sheriff's officer, armed with a writ, arrived in Holles Street. He denied all knowledge of anyone called Adam, but said he had come to arrest a Mrs. Clarke, who owed a sum of money to a tradesman, a Mr. Allen, who lived near Gloucester Place. Repeated requests for payment had not been acknowledged.

Mrs. Clarke was removed by the officer to custody and released, on bail, the following afternoon. The bail was paid by Francis Wright, upholsterer. In the action Clarke versus Allen, Clarke was successful: she declared herself a married woman, husband's address unknown. The rent for the month of June in Holles Street was settled also by

Francis Wright, the same upholsterer, acting, so it would seem, from motives of chivalry, motives which led him to place at her disposal the house of a friend-of-a-friend, in Bedford Place.

Rounds three and four of the contest—roughly equal. Advantage to neither side and no losses sustained.

Towards the end of July or at the beginning of August, the Prince of Wales, before proceeding to Brighton, received a scented note at Carlton House. The sentences were few and the note unsigned. The address was given as 14 Bedford Place. The scent intrigued him, also the allusion to his younger brother, the Duke of York. The thing that caught his eye was the seal at the bottom. Cupid riding an ass . . . the humour pleased him. He tossed the note to McMahon, his private secretary. "Go and see what she wants, but don't go upstairs. If it's who I think it is, she'll tear off your breeches."

Colonel McMahon, used to such encounters, saddled with many before of a similar nature, called at Bedford Place with a certain assurance. The servant who opened the door was round and stolid.

"Yes, sir?"

"Excuse me. Whom does this house belong to?"

"Mrs. Farquhar, sir."

The name was unfamilar. His master had made a mistake. The house was respectable.

"I should like to see Mrs. Farquhar."

"Please to come in, sir."

The parlour was rather untidy and not very clean, the chairs still round the table from last night's supper.

"What name, sir?"

"I prefer to give no name." He produced the note from his pocket. "I have called in answer to this, your mistress may know."

The round-faced servant stared at the scented note.

"That's right, sir. I put it in the post myself. I'll go and tell the mistress you want to see her."

She spoke in a familiar tone, with no respect—she must be a servant of long standing in the family. He waited with some impatience in the parlour and finally, after nearly twenty minutes, was shown up to a drawing-room.

The sofa was à la Récamier, with a figure reclining, her hair in a Grecian knot, slim feet in sandals. The room was well screened . . . and no one within earshot. She rose with a brilliant smile to drop a curtesy, then saw it was not his master . . . and relaxed.

"How do you do? I don't think I have the pleasure?"

"My name is McMahon. I have the honour to be the private secretary to the Prince of Wales. You are Mrs. Farquhar?"

"I call myself Mrs. Farquhar from time to time."

"You are, I take it, a friend of Mrs. Clarke's?"

"Her closest friend. Nobody knows her so well. I may say, with perfect frankness, that nobody living has such a regard for Mrs. Clarke as I have. You don't know her?"

"No, ma'am. Her reputation, but not her person."

"Which speaks for itself, or doesn't it? Please inform me."

"I am sorry, Mrs. Farquhar, if the lady's your friend, but nothing I've ever heard is to her advantage. Her gross ingratitude to the Duke of York after extreme generosity is common knowledge."

"Is it gross ingratitude to give up your life to a prince, and after three years to be scuttled away to the country, on promise of a pension that isn't paid?"

"As to that, ma'am, I know nothing."

"Harassed by spies and creditors, threatened with prison, her brother disgraced from the Army—is that generous? Would the Prince of Wales treat Mrs. Fitzherbert so?"

"I regret, I cannot discuss my illustrious master."

"I could—I think he's delightful, and always have, but that's beside the point. Colonel McMahon, Mrs. Clarke cannot possibly communicate what she has to say to a third person, but only to the Prince of Wales himself."

"Mrs. Clarke must be disappointed, then. His Royal Highness left this morning for Brighton. He told me to receive any message and pass it on."

"If I'd known he was going to Brighton I'd have gone there."

Colonel McMahon twisted his grey moustache. "His Royal Highness will regret the missed occasion. In the circumstances, please make do with me. Am I guessing correctly—you are Mrs. Clarke?"

She smiled and held out her hands. "Of course I am."

"A thousand pardons, then, for all I've said. Hearsay, please understand, and I'm not the painter. The picture in front of me now is very different from the portrait drawn by others."

"Drawn by Adam? And probably Greenwood, too? You shouldn't have listened. Come and sit down beside me on the sofa."

It was rather a pleasant morning, by no means misspent. Biscuits and wine were brought at eleven, and then the session continued with this and that and the other till nearly twelve.

"The thing I like most, of course, and so did the Prince, was the seal at the foot of the letter."

"I'll give you one."

"Ah! But how many others have that promise . . . ?"

He dragged himself away at last, with an undertaking to act as intermediary. "You must understand, of course, that the Prince of Wales can't possibly interfere between you and his brother, but anything I can do, any message I can send, I will gladly, next time I see the Duke—possibly at Windsor. As to the other matter, the letters you mentioned, far better burn them, my dear, they'd make bad blood. Any coolness between the princes is past and done with." He patted her hand. "There, there, dear lady. All will come right in the end."

All right for whom, you fool? She smoothed her hair and tidied the cushions when he'd left the house. Round five had been attempted, and not much accomplished. Honours were still even. The world went out of town until October. Nothing more could be set in motion until the autumn, when Members returned and Parliament reassembled, by which time Will's Radical friends would have laid their plans.

"I suggest," said Will, "that you move away from Bloomsbury. Proximity to Adam might have its drawbacks. Wright can easily find a house in another district, but don't forget to use the name of Farquhar."

"And who," she asked, "is going to pay for the house?"

233

"Wright will continue to advance you money. He knows you're a good investment; he'll get it back."

She searched the papers for advertisements and saw a house to let in Westbourne Place, five minutes' distance from the Chelsea school—George was still a pupil, not yet removed. The Duke when he drove to inspection would pass her window. The thought was tempting; herself in an open carriage, the Duke in his, a smile, and a wave of her sunshade. Too good to miss. And May Taylor was round the corner, in Cheyne Row, after many vicissitudes. The girls could walk to school. They would all be together. She signed the lease, once again in her mother's name, and if anyone asked any questions she'd plead her coverture. It was really the only service Joseph had done her, to stay alive, and so remain legally liable for any bill she hadn't the cash to pay. The lease was signed on the eleventh of November, and during the move—a matter of two or three days—Will Ogilvie set a certain ball in motion, the result of which was a call from Colonel Wardle, at one o'clock on November seventeenth.

She received him in the partly furnished drawing-room, apologising for the great disorder.

"I've only just moved in, as you can see. The whole house is upside-down, a fearful upheaval."

She watched him closely as he kissed her hand. Long-nosed and sallow, most unprepossessing, brown hair curled by tongs, eyes close together.

"Dear madam, I've wanted to meet you for six months, but you're such an elusive lady, there was no getting at you. You know, of course, I am Member for Okehampton. No doubt you followed my speeches during last session?"

"I know who you are. I can't say I've read your speeches."

"I'll send you copies, I think they'd interest you. The truth is, Mrs. Clarke, I am a patriot. My only aim in life is to set my country free from abuse and corruption." He paused to watch the effect.

She asked him to sit down on a packing-case, which he dusted first, gingerly lifting his coattails.

"Corruption continues with us beyond the grave," she said, "and then plays merry hell with all ideals. Do you want some coffee? The saucepans have been unpacked, and a box of china."

"I want nothing but your attention, Mrs. Clarke. When this great country of ours, yearning for freedom, trammelled with outworn bonds . . ."

"Suppose we cut that out, and get to business?"

He paused. The narrow eyes came closer together. "Forgive me—I made the mistake of talking as I would to a constituent. I gather from a journalist friend of mine, McCullum, that you're not prepared to assist him with his pamphlets, which have as principal target the Duke of York?"

"You've gathered correctly."

"And yet, Mrs. Clarke, you've been very badly treated. I should have thought any woman of spirit would want revenge?"

"Revenge, Colonel Wardle, is useless without security. Five pounds on the side for a pamphlet doesn't guarantee the future for myself or for my children."

"I understand. You'd play for a higher reward? In which case I'll place the relevant cards on the table. My friends —Members of our side of the House—and I are determined to expose Army abuses during the coming session, with the ultimate object of turning the Duke out of office."

"Why? What's he done?"

"He represents a system we want abolished. By starting with him we may tumble a pack of cards and ourselves take over, using, as figurehead, a far more amenable person who will do what we tell him."

"How highly patriotic . . . Who is this person?"

Colonel Wardle glanced over his shoulder. The door was closed. "The Duke of Kent," he whispered.

She laughed and stifled a yawn. "I'm disappointed. I'd hoped you'd promote a corporal from the ranks. That method proved so successful in France. You're merely exchanging Peter for Pompous Paul."

"The people in this country are used to tradition. Not too many changes at once—they must be gradual. His Royal Highness the Duke of Kent is highly ambitious."

She noticed the covert sneer, the tone of voice. All this from the man who put his country first.

"Perhaps you'd explain," she said, "where I come in?"

"You know, of course, the ill-will between the brothers, the jealousy one of the other? We hope to fan it. McCullum's pamphlet brings out some of the highlights—that's where we wanted your help, you would know the details. Since you refuse, you can help in another direction, by giving me particulars of promotion traffic, which I understand was your only method of living when under the Duke's protection, and which had his permission."

"And how did you hear it?"

"The proverbial little bird . . . If I had the proof to lay before the House, he'd be kicked out of office."

"What good would that do me?"

"Wrongs would be righted. The Duke of Kent would become Commander-in-Chief. He's been known to say, to a personal friend of mine, that anyone who helped him to this position would have full recompense and more besides. Incidentally, he's much appalled at your shocking treatment; not only yours, but the affair of the Court Martial. I understand he would make it his personal business to reinstate your brother and give you a pension; no beggarly three or four hundred, but several thousand."

She said, "I'm rather tired of promises, especially from princes. I've heard them too often."

"If you need further assurances, I can give them. The personal friend I spoke of is Major Dodd."

"The Duke of Kent's private secretary?"

"Exactly. He is extremely anxious to meet you, and the sooner the better. If you want to know what he says, you can read his letter." He took a sheet of note paper from his wallet and gave it her to read.

My dear Wardle,

The more I reflect on the conversation we had this morning, and which had for its object the pure honour and interest of our country, the more I feel convinced that every individual who is assisting in the great cause is entitled, not only to our private, but to public protection. If this assurance from me can be of any service, you have my authority to use it as you please. From what you mentioned of a certain female, I have no hesitation in believ-

236

*ing that her co-operation will be more material than that
of any other human being. God knows she has been in-
famously and barbarously treated by an illustrious great
beast; but she may now have an opportunity of redressing
her wrongs; and by serving a generous Public, most essent-
ially to benefit herself.*

> *I remain, my dear Wardle, ever,*
> *Thomas Dodd*

"Plausible," she said, "but it's only paper."

"Then I beg your consent to meet him, and hear for
yourself. I need hardly say that whatever you care to ask
for he will pass on, in confidence, to his master; the Duke
of Kent is most liberal in every way."

"He wasn't very liberal at Gibraltar, putting the troops
on rations and closing the wineshops."

"Discipline, Mrs. Clarke, the iron hand. Just what his
country needs at the present time."

"Does he take an iron hand to his old French mistress?
Perhaps he wears velvet mittens down at Ealing. I hear he
waters the plants and keeps canaries. You can tell Major
Dodd from me that my tastes are extravagant. I shall require, besides a pension, a coach-and-four, a turreted mansion, and two or three lakes in the garden."

"I'll pass the message on."

Good God, he believed her! He was more of a fool than
he looked, which was saying something. "Tell me, Colonel
Wardle, when the government falls and all your designs
are accomplished, that is to say, when the people of England are freed from taint and corruption, what post do
you hope for yourself, what final reward?"

He answered, without flinching, "Secretary for War. At
least, that is what the Duke of Kent suggested."

"How noble, a drop in the ocean. I can't wait to meet
your friends, especially Dodd. When shall the meeting take
place?"

He consulted a notebook. "In a few days' time I intend
going down to Kent. Dodd will be coming with me, and
Major Glennie, who is writing a memorandum on fortifications. He intends to discredit the present coast defences

237

and we have a pass to visit the Martello Towers. How about joining the party?"

"Delighted. We can picnic on Romney Marsh, and decide upon the best place for invasion."

"You're not suggesting . . ."

"That your sympathies lie the other side of the Channel? Dear Colonel Wardle, the thought never entered my head. I realise only too well how you love your country."

It proved a most amusing, instructive expedition. First stop at Maidstone, the second night at Hythe. One lady with three embittered, ex-military gentlemen, all of them proven failures in their careers and talking as if they had led the Guards into action. She hadn't enjoyed herself so much for years.

They drove along the coast for twenty miles, the weather fine and frosty, while Major Glennie, the fortification expert, jotted notes, and Major Dodd (ex-artillery captain, but his knowledge of gunfire mainly salutes ceremonial) extrolled the virtues of his royal master: capable and brave and uncomplaining, a pattern of what a commander ought to be.

"So odd, then, if that's the case," murmured the lady, "that he's had no administrative job for over five years?"

"Jealousy, Mrs. Clarke, on the part of his brother."

"I see. Of course. What a pity! Such wasted talent—Kent's vast experience of battle thrown away. All those tiring field days down at Salisbury, with Irish stew for dinner and clouded ale."

Colonel Wardle watched her, extremely puzzled. For a woman who ought to be burning with revenge, she handled this meeting with Dodd in extraordinary fashion. As for himself, he wasn't a mathematician and needed all his powers of concentration to understand the figures Glennie gave him and why the Martello Towers made poor defences. He'd muff his speech to the House unless he knew.

Over dinner, at Hythe, the others drew diagrams and the lady of the party sipped her wine.

"My son George has a little book at home. He'd be delighted to lend it to you, Colonel Wardle. It shows the difference—on I think Page Three—between an octagon and

238

a triangle, first step for beginners . . . Do tell me more, Major Dodd, about Madame de Laurent and her devotion to the Duke of Kent."

"She knows she is in safe keeping, Mrs. Clarke. The only prince with a loyal, with a faithful heart, tender towards her, grateful for what she gives him."

"He sounds a dream . . . except for the bushy eyebrows. Have you told him what I expect, if I help your cause?"

"Five thousand down, an annuity for life, debts all discharged, a settlement on your daughters. All that I can promise, and more; and in the meantime, Colonel Wardle no doubt will furnish you with assistance. What we need from you are letters and proof of corruption, the names of officers promoted through your influence, the names of friends you can produce as witnesses. Then Wardle can quote them in the House without contradiction."

"And have us all put in the bughouse?"

"The law can't touch you. By exposing the Duke of York, you'll have the country behind you. Public opinion will rally to our cause and you, Mrs. Clarke, will be the heroine of the day. Another Joan of Arc, the people's champion."

"You have your history muddled; Boadicea—riding a chariot over dead men's bodies. I'll think the matter over, Major Dodd."

Back to London and to Westbourne Place, with one or the other calling every day and notes on the side from Will. "What other hope have you? What happens to your children if you refuse? At least it's worth a gamble, a final fling. There's no danger to yourself, Dodd is perfectly right. They can't put you in prison, or prosecute you. If the whole shoot misses fire you don't stand to lose."

All right, then, she would go ahead, sort through the letters, reawaken the memories of the past few years. So many letters had been burnt, and those remaining were better for personal reasons than for official ones. Where were the various chaps who'd paid the cash? Most of them overseas, or lost, or forgotten. Colonel French . . . Captain Sandon . . . Sandon was somewhere in England. Donovan might remember other names. Corri, the music master, he might come forward, and somebody called Mr. Knight,

Doctor Thynne's patient. It had never entered her head to keep this information: love letters were tied in the ribbons, not military business.

"Have you been through all your trunks?" asked Colonel Wardle. The thin, inquisitive fingers were probing, peering.

"I've moved half a dozen times since 1806. It will take me weeks to sort through the stuff in store."

"Where is it stored?"

"With Wright, in Rathbone Place."

"Can I go there with you?"

She looked at the close-set eyes, the twitching hands.

"I owe Francis Wright a fair amount of money. This house isn't furnished fully, as you can see. He'll hold on to what he has unless I pay him."

"Then you'd better explain what hopes you have for the future."

"Guaranteed by you?"

"Why, naturally."

She took him to Rathbone Place, where they discovered that Francis Wright was in bed, with an injured leg. The brother Daniel received them, apologising. Was there anything he could do, anything he could show them?

"Yes, Daniel. Show Colonel Wardle some of my stuff, the curtains and carpets and chairs that I want out of store for the new house in Westbourne Place. What do you think of that mirror, Colonel Wardle?"

"Very handsome indeed."

"And those dining-room chairs? Hand-painted, you know, by me, at Gloucester Place. Take the Colonel through to the warehouse, Daniel, and show him the rest. He is anxious that I should have everything moved out of store and taken to Chelsea, with anything else I may order. I'll go and enquire for your brother and leave you together."

Protestation out of the question—Wardle was floored. It was a pistol-shot to the head. Have the furniture moved, en bloc, to Westbourne Place and damn the cost, or lose the chance of letters and valuable testimony? He wandered through the warehouse, trapped and angry, with the upholsterer making items on a list. "Do you mean she had

240

all this at Gloucester Place?" he asked, prodding the lavish carpets with his stick.

"Oh no, sir; these are new; they've taken her fancy."

"Well, sir, you know how it is with Mrs. Clarke. She's gay, likes living well and in good style. I hear she has influential friends behind her."

"Oh, do you?" Damn the woman, she'd been talking.

She came down the stairs behind them, wreathed in smiles.

"Poor Francis Wright, I've advised an embrocation. So everything is settled? You approve my choice?"

"We'll talk about that later."

She turned to Daniel. "Colonel Wardle means he approves. Have everything shifted. And don't forget the Duc de Berri's service . . ."

Silence outside in the carriage, at least from the colonel. She prattled gaily on without discomfort. "It will be so lovely to live in luxury once again. I can't thank you enough for your kindness, so very generous. As soon as they bring my desk I'll look for those letters."

"Desk be damned!" she thought. "The letters are at home." What rapture, though, to twist the patriot's tail, and sting him for all the furniture, carpets included! No wriggling out of the business, she had him nailed. The stuff was all delivered the next afternoon, and a fortnight later Francis Wright, recovered, called to see Colonel Wardle at Westbourne Place. "I believe, sir, you're the influential gentleman who has made so many promises to this lady. She gave me to understand you were one of her backers. That being so, I'd be very much obliged for five hundred pounds on account of a sum outstanding."

The lady in question smiled and looked innocent, murmured something about the House of Commons and a brave new world for all, Wardle included. The right honourable Member for Okehampton tried to bluster. "I haven't the money," he said. "I can't sign a cheque. I gave Mrs. Clarke a hundred the other day."

"But that," she said, "only covered the tradesmen in Bloomsbury. Poor Mr. Wright has to live, the same as the rest of us. Besides, it won't have to come from your own

241

worn pocket, those friends of yours in Ealing . . ." she didn't finish, seeing his look of alarm, of apprehension.

"I'll see that you're paid," Wardle stammered to the upholsterer; "but please understand that my name mustn't appear. With this delicate business ahead of me in the Commons, revelation would be disastrous to my plans. I'll endeavour to arrange things through a tradesman."

She winked at her upholsterer through the looking-glass. "I'm sure Mr. Wright has no wish to be difficult, as long as he has some sort of guarantee."

The guarantee was produced, just after Christmas, by Illingworth, wine merchant, 10 Pall Mall (wine merchant to His Royal Highness the Duke of Kent), in the shape of a promise to accommodate Francis Wright with the sum of five hundred pounds in three months' time. A case of wine was delivered to Mrs. Clarke, with Mr. Illingworth's compliments, and a wish that he might be able to serve her in the future, with a copy of Wright's receipt concealed in the straw: "Received of of R. S. Illingworth, January 2nd, 1809, a Bill of Acceptance, this date at three months, value five hundred pounds which, when paid, will be on account of household furniture delivered to Mrs. Clarke, 2 Westbourne Place."

The wine came in very useful for a party which she gave on Twelfth-night to a group of friends, a mixed bag—rather amusing, as it happened—ranging from Mr. Corri and some boys, Charley, of course, May Taylor and Uncle Tom to McCullum the pamphleteer, Dodd, and Wardle. All were introduced by pseudonyms and handed a glass of brandy on arrival, which set the party going with a roar, and while the singing boys made eyes at Charley, and Dodd sat down to draughts with Uncle Tom, Corri the music master, in seventh heaven, was pumped by Colonel Wardle about the levy raised by Colonel French in 1806.

Tongues babbled on . . . heads swam . . . nobody minded . . . the cake was brrought in, McCullum had the bean

"Who *are* these other gentlemen?" whispered Corri, his mind on fire with brandy and excitement "I fear I've let things slip, been slightly indiscreet."

"Don't worry, they're sworn to secrecy," murmured his hostess. "They are all men of great integrity and principle.

The one standing there, with the bean, writes newspaper articles, but all for church magazines and diocesan papers. The gentleman on your left is a Member of Parliament. Name of Mellish, sits for tht county of Middlesex, the most highly respected member in the Commons."

She wiped the tears of laughter from her eyes, and thought of the real Mr. Mellish—she'd seen him once, red-faced and pompous, stalking down St. James's. The music master gaped, his eyes on sticks.

"So kind of you to ask me . . . so very exclusive."

She moved to see how the game of draughts was progressing. Uncle Tom, having beaten Dodd twice, was proving loquacious and giving away royal secrets by the dozen. She filled their glasses and watched them, inwardly choking. "I've fitted 'em all for years," Uncle Tom was saying, "not only with boots and shoes, I can promise you that. Each one of the princes came to me in turn."

"Except," said Dodd stiffly, "the Duke of Kent."

"Prince Edward?" spluttered Taylor. "Why, he was the worst, before he got caught up in this French affair. So afraid he'd be found out that he came disguised, wearing a borrowed wig and a coachman's hat. His brothers used to nickname him Simon Pure."

Dodd pushed aside the draughtboard and made his excuses. Uncle Tom, eyes squinting, saw his coat. Jesus! The man was wearing Household buttons. Had the world gone topsy-turvy or was he mad? He pulled the hostess's gown. Who *is* that fellow?"

"Don't worry, a secondhand clothesman, deals in apparel." Uncle Tom heaved a sigh of relief and finished his brandy.

"Did you give my message to the Duke of York?" she asked him.

"I did, my dear, and I'm sorry, there's nothing doing. If you dare write a word against him, he'll put you in in prison."

The last effort for a settlement had failed. On, then, to battle and to victory. The method didn't matter, as long as she won. Witnesses must be found for corroboration: Dr. Thynne, Mr. Knight, even Bill—Bill on his way back home again from Portugal. All must be begged, or induced, or even subpoenaed, so that Wardle could present his case at the end of the month. Some of them would protest and deny all knowledge, but certainly not friends like Bill. Wardle would have to take his chance with the others: if they lied and protested innocence, so much the worse.

"Must I appear in the House as well?" she asked him.

"But of course," he replied; "you'll be the leading witness."

A sudden pang filled her heart, and apprehension. It was too late now to turn back, the ball was in motion.

"What questions will you ask me?"

"Nothing alarming. We'll rehearse them here at home in your drawing-room before you're called. You merely tell the truth about the transactions."

"But you won't be the only one to question me. What about Government members, protecting the Duke? Won't they try to trip me up and discredit my story?"

"They may. But you have wit enough to handle them."

She did not trust him. She trusted no one, with the exception, perhaps, of Will, the mastermind. The night before the motion was put to the House he came alone to dinner, to wish her courage.

"You mean," she said, "I shall need it?"

"Every ounce."

Here was the truth at last. He looked at her steadily. She felt her hands grow cold as she touched her glass.

"If you keep your head you'll survive. Here's the position. There'll roughly be three parties in the House. First the Government, practically solid behind the Duke, though some are bound to waver during proceedings, especially when the facts are brought to light. The Opposition will support the charges and do everything they can to help you out. If Wardle goes back on us, as well he might, Francis Burdett and Folkestone will stand by you. The sobersides will compose the third and remaining party the moralists and the rest, led by Wilberforce. The fact that the Duke had a mistress is all that concerns them; they'll side with the Opposition to have him removed. The chaps you want to watch for are Spencer Perceval, Leader of the House, and Vicary Gibbs. Vicary Gibbs is the Attorney-General. They'll try to tear your evidence to shreds, not so much by disproving the actual transactions as by raking every bit of mud they can from your own personal past, in order to discredit you. In other words, 'This woman is a whore, a liar from start to finish, and we can prove it.' They'll do the same to William Dowler, though he won't be so easy. They'll bring witnesses to speak against both of you, all of 'em bribed by Adam. So now you know. Chin up, my dear, and smile . . . We're going to win."

Win what? The doubtful pleasure of revenge? Kicking a man once honoured, loved, and respected? A sop to damaged pride, to lost position?

"Remember," murmured Will, "your children's future. Your brother too," he added. "He stands to gain. Once the Duke has lost command, the Court Martial verdict will probably be squashed and Charles reinstated. I've never seen a boy with such altered looks. He knows he has nothing to live for unless you help him."

Gently he took the wine and filled her glass, watching her look of doubt, of indecision. Where was she now, he wondered, past or future? Hiding beneath a fruit barrow in the alley, stealing the apples one by one for Charley? Or standing before the bar of the House of Commons, the only woman in a world of men?

Suddenly she smiled and raised her glass, then snapped it over her shoulder. It fell in pieces.

"I did that once before," she said, "in Fulham. Here's to the clan Mackenzie. The game continues."

PART THREE

O N E : On the twenty-seventh of January 1809, Colonel Wardle, Radical Member for Okehampton, rose in the House of Commons to submit a motion enquiring into the conduct of His Royal Highness the Duke of York, Commander-in-Chief of the Army, respecting promotions, the disposal of commissions, and the raising of new levies for the Army.

"To stand forth the public accuser of a man of such high rank as the Commander-in-Chief," he said, "may be deemed an arduous and presumptuous undertaking. However arduous and presumptuous it may be, nothing shall divert me from the performance of my duty; and I trust he will feel that, however high he may stand in point of rank and influence, the voice of the people, stated through their representatives, will prevail over corruption, and that justice will be done to a suffering nation. Unless corruption be attacked, and attacked strongly too, this country will fall an easy prey to an inveterate enemy.

"I hope that no man will think that I have taken up this matter lightly. I have pressed it upon sure grounds, and am prepared to prove these assertions; and in order that they may be investigated, I beg to move that a committee be appointed to investigate the conduct of His Royal Highness the Duke of York."

Spokesman for the Government rose to protest vehemently that the illustrious Commander was ready to go into a full investigation of the charges brought against him. They begged the House to consider whether the manner in which the Army had been fitted out that was lately sent to Portugal was not a striking mark of the superior military talents of the Duke of York, totally refuting the Opposition's accusations; and gave it as their opinion that the stream of scurrility which had recently been poured forth against the various branches of the Royal Family could be viewed only as a vile conspiracy against the illustrious House of Brunswick. (Loud cries of "Hear! Hear!" from all parts of the House.)

The debate wound up with a suggestion by Mr. Spencer Perceval, Chancellor of the Exchequer and Leader of the House, that the committee to investigate the matter should be a committee of the whole House—a motion which was carried without a division. It was ordered that the committee should sit in five days' time, on February first.

The few days' grace allowed the news to spread—the front page of every newspaper told the tale—and when the day came the House was crowded. Members from the country who let a session pass without attendance jostled for places on unaccustomed benches, the galleries were crammed, the lobbies swollen.

Colonel Wardle began the proceedings by announcing that he would bring evidence to support his opening charge, relating to an exchange effected between Lieutenant Colonel Brook and Lieutenant Colonel Knight, and he called his first witness, Dr. Thynne. A tall, grey-haired, elderly man stood before the House and testified that in 1805 he had applied to Mrs. Mary Anne Clarke (whom he had attended professionally for the previous seven years) on behalf of an old friend of his, Mr. Robert Knight, brother of one of the two gentlemen concerned. He had been authorized to tell Mrs. Clarke, he said, that if she would use her interest to expedite the exchange she would receive compensation to the sum of two hundred pounds. He agreed, in reply to Colonel Wardle's questions, that the application was made to her solely because she was under the protection of the Duke of York. Dr. Thynne's evidence was confirmed by Mr. Rober Knight himself, who added that after the exchange had been gazetted he had sent Mrs. Clarke, by his servant, two hundred pounds in bank notes.

Now came the witness for whom the House was waiting —Mrs. Mary Anne Clarke. "Dressed as if she was going out to an evening party," the *Morning Post* reported the next day, "in a light blue silk gown edged with whit fur, white muff, whie cap and veil, her dazzling smile, slightly retroussé nose and lively blue eyes entirely capitvated the House."

Colonel Wardle put the following questions to her:

"Did you reside in a house of His Royal Highness the Duke of York in Gloucester Place in the year 1805?"

"I did."

"Did you then live under his protection?"

"I did."

"Was an application made to you respecting Colonels Knight and Brook?"

"There was."

"Did you speak to the Commander-in-Chief on the subject?"

"I did."

"How did you mention the business?"

"I told him of the matter, and gave him the slip of paper which Doctor Thynne gave me."

"How much pecuniary compensation did you receive?"

"Two hundred pounds."

"Did the Commander-in-Chief know the amount?"

"Yes, I showed him the two notes for a hundred each. I think I got one of the servants to get me the change of them."

Mr. Beresford, for the Government, rose to question her.

"Where were you immediately before you came to the bar of this House?"

The witness turned and stared. A titter ran round the House. Mr. Beresford reddened. Slightly raising his voice, he repeated his question.

"Where were you before you came to the bar of this House?"

"In some room adjoining."

"Who was with you?"

"Captain Thompson, Miss Clifford, Mrs. Metcalfe, Colonel Wardle."

"Had you any conversation with Doctor Thynne?"

"Yes, he was sitting beside me."

"What was the purport of his conversation?"

"It was addressed to the ladies that were with me."

"What was that conversation?"

"I can't repeat it. The subject was indelicate."

Loud laughter rang through the house. Mr. Beresford sat down. Sir Vicary Gibbs, the Attorney-General, rose to his feet, and folding his arms in front of him, eyes on the ceiling, began to question the witness. His manner was diffident, gentle, the House knew it well, and settled down to listen, respectfully silent.

"At what time of the year was the application about Colonel Knight gazetted?"

"I think it was the latter end of July, or beginning of August. His Royal Highness was setting off for Weymouth for the purpose of standing godfather to Lord Chesterfield's child."

"When did you first mention the matter to Colonel Wardle?"

"Very lately. Within a month."

"To whom else did you speak of it?"

"I don't recollect. Possibly to some of my friends."

"Had you any end to accomplish by making the affair known?"

"Certainly not."

"Did you ever state you had grounds of complaint against His Royal Highness the Duke of York?"

"My friends know I have."

"Have you not stated that if His Royal Highness did not comply with your demands you would expose him?"

"No. I wrote two letters to Mr. Adam. Perhaps he will produce them."

"Were there threats in both?"

"They were not threats. They were solicitations."

"Did you accompany these solicitations by saying, if they were not complied with, you would expose His Royal Highness?"

"I don't remember. You had better ask for the letters. The Duke sent me word once that if I should speak or write against him, he'd put me in the pillory or the bastille."

"Who brought that message to you?"

"A particular friend of the Duke of York's. One Taylor, a shoemaker in Bond Street."

"Had you sent His Royal Highness a letter?"

"I had."

"By whom did you send that letter?"

"By that same ambassador of Morocco."

A shout of laughter went up from all sides of the House. The Attorney-General lifted his hand for silence.

"What is your husband's name?"

"Clarke."

"What is his Christian name?"

"Joseph, I believe."

"Where were you married?"

"At Pancras, Mr. Adam can tell you."

The witness was admonished from the Chair, and warned that if she persisted in giving her answers in that pert manner she would expose herself to the censure of the House.

"Did you make Mr. Adam believe you were married at Berkhamsted?"

"I don't know what I made him believe. I was merely laughing at him."

"Did you represent your husband as being a nephew of Mr. Alderman Clarke?"

"He told me he was. I have never taken any pains to ask anything concerning him. He is nothing to me, or I to him, nor have I seen him these three years, nor heard of him, since he threatened to bring an action against the Duke."

"What is your husband?"

"He is nothing but a man."

"What business?"

"No business. He lives with his younger brother and his brother's wife, that's all I know of him."

"Were you ever in Tavistock Place?"

"I was."

"Whereabouts in Tavistock Place?"

"I don't remember."

"Did you live anywhere else between living in Tavistock Place and living in Park Lane?"

"I don't know. The Duke knows. I might have gone to some of his houses."

"When did you first become acquainted with the Duke?"

"I do not consider that a fair question to put to me. I have a family of children to bring up."

"Were you under the Duke of York's protection when you first lived at Tavistock Place?"

"No, I was under the protection of my mother."

"Do you know a Major Hogan who wrote a pamphlet against the Duke?"

"No, I don't know him, and I never saw him. Taylor the shoemaker told me Mr. Greenwood said I was connected with pamphlet writers, which I then denied, as I do now."

"Did you ever say to Mr. Robert Knight you were anxious to conceal the transaction of the two hundred pounds from the Duke of York?"

"No."

"If anyone represented you as having said so, do you declare him to have spoken falsehood?"

"Certainly."

"Had you any reason for wishing to conceal Dr. Thynne's visit about Mr. Knight from the Commander-in-Chief?"

"I never was desirous to conceal his visits, or those of any other gentlemen, from His Royal Highness."

The Attorney-General shrugged his shoulders, and making a deprecating gesture with his hands, gave place to the Leaders of the House.

"How soon after the exchange did Mr. Knight fulfil his promise?"

"Immediately, the same day."

"And do you allege that it was on the same day that you asked the Duke of York for change?"

"I did not ask the Duke of York for change, the servant went for the change."

"Have you received money upon any other occasion for applying to the Duke of York on behalf of officers seeking promotion?"

The witness sighed, looked to the Chair, and said, "I thought that when I had spoken as to the Knight's business, I should be let away."

She was at last permitted to withdraw, and the Leader of the House asked that Mr. Adam might be allowed to make a statement. In a speech lasting twenty minutes this gentleman told the House that late in 1805 it had come to his knowledge that Joseph Clarke was threatening an action for adultery against the Duke of York, and it fell to his lot to direct enquiries, he having been for more than twenty years in the service of His Royal Highness. In the course of these enquiries he found reason to believe that Mrs. Clarke's conduct had not been correct, that she had taken bribes, and he felt it his duty to inform the Duke of York of this. It was an unpleasant task, His Royal Highness not being inclined to believe that anything was wrong in that quarter. But the evidence was irrefutable, and soon after, His Royal Highness's mind being finally made up to separate from Mrs. Clarke, Mr. Adam was asked to announce the royal decision to her. His conversation with her on this occasion was brief, and he had not seen her from that day to the present time.

A Member now rose to protest vehemently against a witness of Mrs. Clarke's character being examined in the House about the conduct of the Royal Family. Mr. Perceval replied that, distasteful though the matter was, he felt that the enquiry should nevertheless take its full course. "The question the House has to consider," he went on, "is whether His Royal Highness was acquainted with the circumstances that money was given in the way she described. The entire case will be defective if the credit of Mrs. Clarke can be shown unworthy. She stated that she was a widow, when her husband was and is alive, she said to Mr. Adam she was married at Berkhamsted, when in fact she was married at Pancras. I am confident that the charges will be disproved through her false testimony." The proceedings were then adjourned.

Mary Anne left the House of Commons attended by her brother, Captain Thompson, and the two ladies who had arrived with her. She was handed into her carriage by Lord Folkestone, who was most solicitous and expressed the utmost concern for her health. Crowds gathered round them, inquisitive faces peered through the windows, and it was some time before a way could be cleared for the horses to move forward.

Once back at Westbourne Place she accepted a sleeping draught from Doctor Metcalfe, her physician, and went upstairs to her room, followed by her brother and her sister Isobel.

"The brutes," exploded Charley, "putting you through the mill like a common criminal. What has it to do with this present investigation when you were married, and in what church, and where you lived? Why didn't you send the Attorney-General to hell?"

She had flung herself on her bed and closed her eyes.

"I did," she said, "as courteously as I could. Don't worry, I know now what I'm up against. Will Ogilvie warned me. It was rather worse than I thought, but that can't be helped. Isobel, fetch me a drink of water, will you?"

Isobel gave her water, took off her shoes, and knelt down to fan the fire and cheer the room.

"Don't worry with me, dears. Get off to bed. You must be as tired as I am—possibly worse. You might see if there are any letters for me, Charley."

"There was only one. I have it here."

He gave her a letter with a Tilbury postmark. It had been sent to Bedford Place and forwarded. Bill's handwriting. She crumpled it up in her hand.

"I'll be all right. Tell Martha not to disturb me."

They left the room and she opened the letter.

"Dearest, where are you, and what in the world is happening? I got your note in Lisbon before Christmas about exposing the D . . . Have you gone quite mad? I beg of you not to listen to unwise counsel. I shall be in London on Thursday, at Reid's Hotel."

Thursday. Today. She glanced at the clock on the mantel-piece. She must go to him at once and break the news. Tomorrow would be too late—he would see the papers and form his own opinion of the business, perhaps condemn her and refuse to be mixed up in it.

She rose from her bed and seized a cloak, tiptoed to the door, and opened it. Everything was quiet, the house in darkness. Isobel and Charley had gone to their rooms. She left a note for Martha on her pillow and crept downstairs.

She called a hackney carriage on the corner and told

the driver to take her to Reid's Hotel. It was nearly midnight when they reached St. Martin's Lane. The quarter was almost deserted; only a few late stragglers were standing about in the court.

The proprietor of the hotel, Mr. Reid, was talking to some customers in the saloon. He recognized her at once and came forward smiling. Thank heaven he did not connect her with the gossip obviously being discussed amongst his clients—she caught the words "the Duke" and "lying strumpet." Mr. Reid knew her only as "Mr. Dowler's lady."

"Come for your gentleman?" he said. "He's gone upstairs—finished his supper about two hours ago. He was glad to get a bit of English food inside him. He's looking well. Sam, take Madam up to Number 5."

The waiter led the way to the first-floor passage and tapped on the door. She opened it and went inside.

He was kneeling on the floor beside his trunk, shirtsleeves rolled to the elbows, and at sight of him, known, familiar, dependable, anxiety went from her. She shut the door behind her and called his name.

"Bill . . ."

"Why . . . Mary Anne!"

So much to disentangle, so much to explain—the whole long story of the past nine months. He knew the Court Martial verdict, but not the sequel—not the letters to Mr. Adam, the night of the arrest, the nowhere-to-turn-for-money, the weeks of worry, the November encounter with Wardle and Major Dodd; and the final decision to throw in her lot with theirs.

"You were wrong, you were terribly wrong."

But she interrupted. "What else in the world could I do? You weren't here to advise me. I've never been more alone, more utterly stranded."

"I warned you four years ago . . ."

"I know . . . I know . . . What's the use of raking up that? The damage is done. If the Duke had only made some proper settlement none of this would have happened, but since he didn't my only redress was to do what I've done today—bear witness for the charges brought against

257

him. It's torture, it's hell and damnation, but there's no other way."

"You expect me to help you?"

"You must. Without you I'm lost. We can't rely on any other witness. Wardle told me this evening, before we left the House, that most of the people concerned will deny everything—they're all too terrified of getting into trouble. You remember Sandon, Colonel French's friend? He's supposed to be a witness for us, but he's likely to turn. So is an agent called Donovan, whom I thought I could count on, after the money he's had from me in the past. Bill darling, you will . . . you must, stand by me."

There was anguish in her voice and tears in her eyes. He took her in his arms and held her close.

"We'll talk about it tomorrow."

"No, tonight."

"But it's late. I must call a carriage to take you home."

"I'm not going home. I'm staying here with you."

"It isn't wise . . ."

"Oh, God, don't talk of wisdom . . . Don't you want me?"

The porter received a message which he handed on to Samuel Wells the waiter: "On no account disturb No. 5 before the morning. Breakfast for two at eight."

The following day Colonel Wardle had information that Mr. William Dowler, late of Lisbon, was prepared to act as witness in support of the charges, and hoped to meet him on Sunday at Westbourne Place. . . .

What would they say to Bill? wondered Mary Anne, and why was it that answering questions tortured the mind, driving it instantly to subterfuge? She had nothing to fear in the evidence brought for the charges. She had taken the bribes—it was known, and the fault was admitted. She did not mind how much she was questioned on this; but when the Attorney-General had touched on her past, a feeling of being trapped had at once engulfed her, a sensation that she was cornered, with no escape. She was afraid she would be forced into some admission about her former life, about her lovers, and it would all come into the papers in printed headlines, finding their way to the country, to the children.

Poor Bill, possibly he would feel guilty too, remembering his father down at Uxbridge, always so ashamed of the bribe and appointment, which now must be disclosed to support the charges. In sudden horror she felt she could not face it, and when Will Ogilvie called on the Monday evening she told him he must get her out of town.

"I've lost my nerve. I can't go through with it."

For a moment he did not answer. Then he walked across the room and stood in front of her.

"You bloody coward," he said, and slapped her face.

Rage filled her instantly. She hit him back. He laughed and folded his arms. She started crying.

"All right, then, whine," he said, "get back to the gutter. Crawl like a rat to a sewer, and hide yourself. I thought you were a cockney and had some pride."

"How dare you call me a coward!"

"You are a coward. You were born in an alley and bred on the streets of London, and yet you haven't the guts to stand up for your class. You're afraid, because the King's Attorney-General, whose job it is to be unpleasant, asks you questions. You're afraid, because the Tories call you a strumpet. You're afraid, because it's safer to blub than to battle, and the House is composed of men and you're a woman. Rat, then, if you like—you can do as you please. It may interest you to know that you'll be in good company. The Duke of Kent has just made a speech in the Lords. I suggest you go and join him down at Ealing."

He threw a piece of copy on the floor and left the room. She heard the front door slam. She picked up the paper and read the notes, intended for the press the following morning.

House of Lords, February 6th, 1809. "The Duke of Kent thought it proper to remark that it had been supposed by many that he had been at variance with his Royal Brother, from which an inference had been drawn that he countenanced the charges brought forward against the Commander-in-Chief. Whatever professional differences there had been between them, he entertained the highest respect for his Royal Brother, and believed that he was wholly incapable of acting in the manner imputed to him. Instead, therefore, of countenancing such charges, he would do everything in his power to repel them. On this subject there was no difference of opinion in his family, all the members of which concurred in the statement he had expressed."

She threw down the paper and went to the window, but Will Ogilvie had gone. She called for Martha.

"If Colonel Wardle comes, I've gone to bed. But tell him I'll be at the House of Commons tomorrow, at whatever hour of the day he likes to call me."

Simon Pure might recant. Not Mary Anne.

TWO: On the following Tuesday, when the investigation was resumed, Colonel Wardle stated that he would proceed to his second charge, regarding Colonel French's levy, and he called Captain Sandon. As he had feared, the witness denied any recollection of having spoken in the matter to Mrs. Clarke: the levy, he declared, had been entirely settled between that lady and Colonel French, and he thought he had nothing at all to do to interfere in it. Pressed by Colonel Wardle, however, he admitted that he had at various times paid her eight hundred pounds, or perhaps eight hundred fifty, in addition to the original payments which Colonel French had made to her and to her agent, Mr. Corri.

He had not, he went on to say, believed Mrs. Clarke to have much influence with the Commander-in-Chief, and had never supposed that the application to raise the levy would have been refused through the ordinary channels, but Colonel French had thought the matter would be hastened by giving money to Mrs. Clarke. Mrs. Clarke had been most secretive about the whole business, and whenever he saw her had urged on him the greatest caution, lest the passing of money should reach official ears, and most particularly the Duke of York's.

Captain Sandon was then permitted to withdraw, and Mr. Domengo Corri was summoned. The music master, smiling and full of confidence, hair frizzed for the great occasion, glanced about the chamber in the hope of seeing famous faces; he was then called to attention, and examined by Colonel Wardle.

"Do you recollect introducing Captain Sandon to Mrs. Clarke?"

"I never introduced him; he introduced himself."

"Do you know anything of the bargain between them?"

"They settled it all between them, and in the month of June I was sent a bill for two hundred pounds, at the Cannon coffeehouse."

"You know nothing further?"

"Several people came applying to me for places, and I told Mrs. Clarke, but I never heard any more and no business passed between us except the music."

"Have you, since this matter came before the House, destroyed any papers?"

"I destroyed a paper in the month of July, that same year, after Captain Sandon's business. One day I went to Mrs. Clarke's house, and she told me there was a terrible noise, the Duke was angry, and desired I would burn all papers and letters that I had."

"Did she explain why the Duke was angry?"

"Yes; she told me that the Duke was watched very closely by Colonel Gordon, and that Mr. Greenwood also watched her movements; therefore, she was so situated she could get nothing through, almost. She was just going to Kensington Gardens at the time, the carriage was at the door, and she said, 'For God's sake go home and burn those papers,' and there was very little more that passed, in the hurry."

Mr. Sheridan, Irish Member, rose to question the witness.

"Have you had letters from Mrs. Clarke since that time?"

"Yes, this year I had an invitation on the sixth day of the month to go and see her. She desired me to dine, which I did."

"Was there any conversation respecting the transaction of 1804?"

"Yes, I was a little surprised, because soon after dinner she sent for the Twelfth cake, and some gentlemen came in, and as soon as they came the conversation of this affair of Captain Sandon was introduced, and I repeated every word, just as I have here."

"Did Mrs. Clarke allude to any other transaction of a similar nature?"

"No, the rest of the evening was spent in convivial conversation and merriment, and I left the gentlemen at a little after twelve, drinking there."

"Do you know who the gentlemen were?"

"I am not altogether certain. There was a long-nosed one, a friend of Mrs. Clarke's, and a writer of some paper, they mentioned the paper but I forget what it was—she said she was obliged to have him with her to take care of her—and another gentleman who appeared like a lawyer, he laughed very much, this gentleman did, when I said he appeared like a lawyer."

"Who was the gentleman who was a friend of Mrs. Clarke's?"

"Must I tell, for she told me in secret?"

The witness was directed to answer the question, it escaping the attention of the House that Colonel Wardle, who had first examined the witness and appeared to be suffering from toothache while he did so, holding a handkerchief before his face, was now sitting down, screened from view, perhaps in pain.

Mr. Corri replied, "Well, she told me it was Mr. Mellish, the Member of Middlesex, who is, I suppose, in this House."

A gasp of amazement rose from all sides of the House, quickly followed by loud laughter and jeering from the Opposition. A stout gentleman, sitting on the Government benches, was seen to turn purple in the face and shake his head vigorously. The witness was directed to stand down. Mr. Mellish, the stout gentleman, then rose to his feet, and said that he was apprehensive that it might not be in order, but he wished some gentleman would interrogate him.

He was then asked if he had been present at Mrs. Clarke's in January. He replied: "I never was at Mrs. Clarke's in my life, nor did I ever see her until I saw her in this House."

At the request of Mr. Mellish Mr. Corri was again called, and the honourable Member went close up to the bar to enable the witness to have a complete view of his person.

Mellish said to the witness: "Did you ever see me at Mrs. Clarke's?"

Mr. Corri replied, "No, it is not you, but I only said what she said to me; the person I saw was of darker complexion than you. If she told me a lie I can't help it."

There was loud laughter and applause as the honourable Member for Middlesex, his reputation cleared, once more took his seat on the Government benches.

Colonel Wardle, having recovered from his toothache, now rose to call Mr. William Dowler to the bar and the witness entered, his expression grave but composed. He stated that he was just returned from Lisbon with despatches, that he had known Mrs. Clarke for several years, and that he recollected having seen Colonel French and Captain Sandon at Gloucester Place while she was under the protection of the Duke of York.

Asked whether he recollected any conversation with Colonel French on the subject of the levy, he replied, "I once saw him at Mrs. Clarke's house and was informed he was there on the subject of the letter of service. I questioned Mrs. Clarke regarding the nature of the business, and I recollect perfectly that I took the liberty of saying that I disapproved, or thought it exceedingly wrong. That was after Colonel French had left the house. He had paid Mrs. Clarke five hundred guineas of the total sum promised."

"What answer did Mrs. Clarke make to your remonstrance?"

"She replied that the Duke of York was so distressed for money that she could not bear to ask him, and that it was the only way in which her establishment could be supported. She was offended with my freedom, and I ceased to see or hear from her for I cannot tell how long."

"In what situation are you now?"

"I have lately been in charge of the Accounts Department of the Commissariat at Lisbon."

"How did you obtain your situation?"

"I purchased it of Mrs. Clarke."

A whistle sounded from some part of the house. Mr. Dowler coloured.

"Did you pay any money to Mrs. Clarke for the benefit you received?"

"I gave her a thousand pounds."

"Did you make any application for the situation to anyone but Mrs. Clarke?"

"To no one."

"Did you understand Mrs. Clarke obtained the appointment from the Duke of York?"

"Certainly."

Cross-examined by the Attorney-General, Mr. Dowler said that Mrs. Clarke had herself suggested that she might procure the office for him—the proposal did not come from him; and that his father would not at first give his assent, but later agreed, as his son seemed confident that the matter would not become public. He denied repeatedly that his father could have made application through friends: it was his firm and unshakeable conviction that Mrs. Clarke had obtained the appointment through the Duke of York himself.

Mr. Sheridan, Irish Member, rose finally to question the witness.

"If, from respect to Mrs. Clarke, you thought it right to remonstrate against the transaction with Colonel French in 1804, why did you yourself, in 1805, bribe her with a thousand pounds to get an office for you?"

"Because she was peculiarly distressed for money at that moment, and because the appointment would remain a secret in my breast, and nothing but such an enquiry as this would have drawn it from me. The Duke of York's character and Mrs. Clarke's would never have suffered from that which unfortunately I am now obliged to communicate before this House."

"Then the committee is to understand that your only reason for remonstrating with Mrs. Clarke was not against the impropriety of the act, but on account of the risk of discovery?"

"For both reasons. I stated that the transactions seemed to give her nothing but worry and anxiety, and I advised her to have a regular payment from the Duke of York, instead of meddling with such matters. She told me he really had not the money."

"Do you recollect the first time you ever gave money to Mrs. Clarke?"

"I have lent her various sums of money at different times."

"Had you any security for those sums of money?"

"None."

"Were they loans to Mrs. Clarke?"

"Yes."

"You took no memorandum for those sums?"

"No."

"Have you seen Mrs. Clarke since your return from Portugal?"

"Yes."

"When did you see her?"

"I saw her on Sunday."

"Have you seen her since?"

"I saw her just now in the witness's room."

"Was anybody with her?"

"Nobody but a young lady or two."

"What passed between you when you called on Sunday?"

"I lamented the situation in which I found her placed, and she said the Duke of York had driven her to it by not paying her annuity."

"Did you see Mrs. Clarke before you went to Portugal, during the course of last year?"

"Yes."

"Frequently?"

"I cannot positively say how frequently."

"Do you recollect what was the last time you gave her money?"

"No, indeed."

"Have you given her money since the time of your appointment?"

"Upon my word, I cannot recollect; if I have, it must be very trifling."

At last William Dowler was allowed to leave, having stood at the bar for over an hour.

Mr. Huskisson, who had been Secretary of the Treasury in 1805, thereupon stated that he had no recollection of Mr. Dowler's appointment, and did not think even the most diligent search into the records of the Treasury would afford any trace of the quarter from which the appointment was made. He sat down, amidst murmurs and catcalls from the Opposition.

Upon Mr. Perceval, Leader of the House, contending that it was essential that Mrs. Clarke should be examined that night, and that they should proceed to it without delay, she was accordingly called to the bar. After some interval the Chairman stated he had received a message from Mrs. Clarke—she was so much indisposed and exhausted with waiting, she said, that she wished to be excused from attending. There was a general cry of "Call her in, and order a chair for her." A considerable delay followed before she appeared at the bar. When she did, she said, "I am so exhausted by waiting for upwards of over eight hours, that I am not able to be examined tonight." There were loud Government cries of "Go on . . . Go on . . ." The Chairman said, "There is a chair for you, Mrs. Clarke." She answered, "That will not take away the fatigue I have suffered in body and in mind."

She was then allowed to go, amid much uproar, Government members saying she should be examined forthwith, and members of the Opposition suggesting it would be more humane to defer the discussion with a suggestion that Mr. Dowler might be interrogated as to whether he had had any communication with Mrs. Clarke since the examination. Mr. Dowler was accordingly called in again and examined.

"Since you quitted this bar, have you had any communication with Mrs. Clarke?"

"Only to offer her refreshment, as she was very unwell. I procured a glass of wine and water for her, which I put beside her."

"Have you communicated to her what passed here during your examination?"

"No."

"How long were you in the room with Mrs. Clarke?"

"Five or ten minutes. She was unwell, and there were several gentlemen gathered round her, and asking whether she would take refreshment."

"Were you apprised that you ought not to have any communication with Mrs. Clarke?"

"I felt so."

"And acted entirely from your own feelings on the subject?"

"Yes."

The House then rose, and the committee was ordered to sit again on Thursday.

No Reid's Hotel for Mrs. Clarke that night, no hackney carriage to St. Martin's Lane, but bed at Westbourne Place and black exhaustion. Ready and primed at three to face the ordeal, she had expected to be called at once, but the hours dragged on from afternoon to evening. Nor did it help to catch a glimpse of Few, the auctioneer, who used to live in Bloomsbury; and then of Bill. Bill had been absent an eternity, and when she begged a member in attendance to find out what was happening, he said, "They're raking up the dirt. Whom he first met you with, and where, and when."

French and the levy seemed to have been forgotten. The only thing that interested the questioners was probing into the past, disclosing secrets, and Bill, who had bought his appointment for her sake, hating his action, seeing it as shameful, was now, for her sake again, forced to disclose it.

When he came out of the chamber his face was haggard, and he looked years older as he said to her, "I'd rather give every guinea I have in the world than be brought to this place again."

She was told that night, before she left the House, that until proceedings were closed she must not see or talk to witnesses. Bill must not come to her house, she could not see him, no sort of communication would be allowed between them. Thank God for the day's respite before the Thursday, thank God she could lie in bed with the curtains closed, with bandaged eyes, with a pillow under her cheek, a cup of broth on a tray brought in by Martha. No Dodd, no Colonel Wardle, no one to worry her. Even Charley had sense enough to stay away.

God! How she hated this world, suddenly turned hostile, smirching her name in the papers, pointing and jeering. Already the street boys had thrown a brick and broken a window.

"It's ignorance, ma'am," said Martha. "They little know that you're saving their bread and butter by what you're doing, and trying to free the country from vicious tyrants."

What in the name of heaven had Martha been reading? *The People's Globe?* Or *Truth for the Underdog?* She closed her eyes and buried her face in the pillow.

No way of escape. On Thursday again, at three.

THREE: On Thursday, after preliminary business, Colonel Wardle moved "that Mrs. Mary Anne Clarke be brought before the bar."

Orders were accordingly given to the Serjeant-at-Arms to call her in, but there was some delay before she appeared. When she did so she seemed distressed and there was a general cry of "A chair, a chair," the members assuming that she was not well. She did not sit down, however, but, looking toward the Government benches, said, "I have been very much insulted coming to this House. It was impossible to get out of my carriage for the crowd pressing against the windows, and the messenger couldn't protect me. I sent for the Serjeant-at-Arms to bring me into the lobby, hence the delay."

She was given a few minutes to recover, and then Colonel Wardle began to interrogate her about the affair of Colonel French's levy. She replied that both he and Captain Sandon had continually teased her with applications, and that she had always passed on Colonel French's notes to the Duke without bothering to read them—His Royal Highness understood them, she believed. Seeing that she was still ruffled from her ordeal in Palace Yard, Colonel Wardle paused, intending to spare her, but Mr. Croker, for the Government, rose and asked her, "How long have you been acquainted with Mr. Dowler?"

"Nine or ten years. I don't know exactly."

"Do you owe him any money?"

"I never recollect my debts to gentlemen."

"State the names of all the men who met Mr. Corri at your house in January."

270

"If I did so I should never have a decent man call on me again."

The burst of laughter from the House appeared to steady the witness, for she lifted her head and stared at Mr. Croker.

Various members now rose in turn to question her about the establishment at Gloucester Place, who paid for it, when she first made application to the Duke for anything connected with army promotions, whether she had trusted to her memory on such occasions or recorded the applications on paper.

"If it was a single application I trusted to my memory or that of His Royal Highness, who has a very good memory, but if there were many I gave him a list, not in my own writing. I remember a very long one once."

"Is that list in existence now?"

"No. I had it pinned to the head of the bed and His Royal Highness took it away in the morning. I saw it some time after, in his private pocketbook."

Loud laughter rose from the Opposition benches.

"Do you recollect from whom you received that particular list?"

"I think either from Captain Sandon or Mr. Donovan, but both are quite prepared to deny it."

"You received many letters from other applicants?"

"Hundreds and hundreds."

"And you showed these letters, containing promises of money to you, to His Royal Highness?"

"He was aware of everything I did."

The government being momentarily nonplussed, Colonel Wardle called his next witness, Miss Taylor, who, shy, flushed, and exceedingly nervous, appeared at the bar in place of Mrs. Clarke.

Colonel Wardle asked her: "Were you in the habit of visiting Gloucester Place when Mrs. Clarke was under the protection of the Duke?"

"Very frequently."

"Did you ever hear the Duke of York speak to Mrs. Clarke regarding Colonel French's levy?"

"Once only."

"Relate what passed at that time, please."

271

"The Duke's words were, as nearly as I can recollect, 'I am continually worried by Colonel French. He is always wanting something more in his own favour.' And then, turning to Mrs. Clarke, he said, 'How does he behave to you, darling?' or some such kind words as he used to use, and she replied, 'Middling, not very well.' That was all she said."

"Was that the whole of the conversation?"

"The Duke then said, 'Master French must mind what he's about, or I'll cut him up, and his levy too.' That was the expression he used."

Colonel Wardle then stated he had no further questions to put to the witness. She turned as though to go, but the Attorney-General rose to his feet. A murmur of sympathy for the young witness came from the Opposition benches.

The voice that had been so soft and suave with Mrs. Clarke was harsh and abrupt to Miss Taylor.

"How long have you known Mrs. Clarke?"

"About ten years; it may be something more."

"Where did you first become acquainted with her?"

"At a house in Bayswater?"

"With whom did you live in Bayswater?"

"With my parents."

"What are your parents?"

"My father was a gentleman."

"With whom do you live now?"

"With my sister."

"Where do you live?"

"In Chelsea."

"In lodgings or as housekeepers?"

"Housekeepers."

"Any profession?"

"If a boarding school be a profession."

"Who lived with Mrs. Clarke at Craven Place?"

"Her husband, when I first knew her."

"Who lived with her afterwards?"

"His Royal Highness the Duke of York."

"Have you known any other man to live with her?"

"Not to my knowledge."

"Are you related to her?"

"My brother is married to her sister."

272

"What was her husband?"

"I always understood he was a man of fortune."

"Did you live with her at Tavistock Place?"

"I never lived with her at all."

"Did you never sleep in the house?"

"Yes, occasionally."

"You took her to be a modest, decent woman, whilst she lived in Tavistock Place?"

"She lived with her mother, I knew nothing to the contrary."

The witness was now in tears. Murmurs of indignation rose from the Opposition benches. The Attorney-General took no notice.

"At whose request do you attend here tonight?"

"At the request of Mrs. Clarke."

"Do you know Mr. Dowler?"

"Yes."

"Did Mrs. Clarke tell you she represented Mr. Dowler to the Duke of York as her brother?"

"No, never."

"How long is it since you heard the conversation you spoke about between Mrs. Clarke and His Royal Highness respecting Colonel French?"

"I can't exactly say. It was when she was at Gloucester Place."

"Did you ever see Colonel French in Gloucester Place?"

"I have heard him announced. I cannot say I was ever introduced to him."

"And after an interval of five years you recollect a particular expression without any intervening circumstance calling it to your remembrance?"

"I thought of it since, but I did not mention it."

"What brought it into your thoughts?"

"I was curious about a man I was not allowed to see."

"What time of year was it?"

"I don't recollect."

"Winter or summer?"

"I don't recollect that either."

"Yet your memory is not defective about the expressions used?"

"No."

273

"Doesn't that seem to you extraordinary?"

"No."

"Are your father's affairs in a state of embarrassment?"

There was a moment's hesitation, and then the witness replied, in a low voice, "Yes."

"How many scholars have you?"

"Twelve."

"What is the age of your youngest scholar?"

"Seven."

Loud cries of "No. No . . ." rang through the House, as Miss Taylor was seen to be in deep distress. The Attorney-General shrugged his shoulders and sat down. Miss Taylor was told she could go.

Mrs. Mary Anne Clarke was next recalled for further examination by Mr. Croker. For over an hour he questioned her on the establishment at Gloucester Place, the number of menservants employed, whether they slept in the house, who paid their wages, how many carriages had been in her possession, how many horses, what jewels had she worn, had she pawned her diamonds. Then, glancing at a note passed to him by the Attorney-General, Mr. Croker enquired: "Did you at any time live at Hampstead?"

There was a pause on the part of the exhausted witness, and then she answered, "I did."

"In what year?"

"Part of the year 1808, and the end of the year 1807."

"In whose house did you live?"

"A Mr. Nicols'."

"During the whole of that time did you pass under your own name?"

"Yes."

"Did you ever assume the name of Dowler?"

"No, I did not."

"How many times have you seen Mr. Dowler since his return from Portugal?"

"I saw him that Sunday in my house, and I have seen him here in the witness's room."

"That is the whole number of times you have seen him since his arrival in England?"

"I believe that the honourable gentleman can tell quite

274

well, for his garret window is very convenient for his prying disposition, as it overlooks my house."

There were whistles and loud applause from the Opposition benches.

"You are certain those are the only number of times you have seen Mr. Dowler?"

"If the honourable gentleman wishes it, I will say I have seen him oftener, if it will tend to anything, I have no wish to conceal that Mr. Dowler is a very particular friend of mine."

"At what other places have you seen Mr. Dowler since his arrival?"

"I have seen him at his own hotel."

"When?"

"The first night he came home, but which was to have been a perfect secret, as I did not want my own family or anyone to know that I saw him that night."

"Were you in company with Mr. Dowler for a considerable time on that occasion?"

"I have stated that I was in company with Mr. Dowler; and I beg leave to ask the Chair whether this is a proper question, whether it is not unbecoming to the dignity of this House?"

Mr. Wilberforce rose, protesting that it was perfectly incorrect and immoral for the committee to enter into a detail of the private concerns of the witness. But he was shouted down, and Mr. Croker repeated his question.

"Did you visit through Thursday after midnight?"

"My visit continued until the Friday morning."

To the disappointment of all sides of the House, Mr. Croker had no further questions, and the day's proceedings were declared over.

As Mrs. Mary Anne Clarke went to her carriage in Old Palace Yard, a messenger touched her shoulder and handed her a note. She read it, and said to the messenger, "No answer." When she arrived home at Westbourne Place she stuck the note in her mirror, beside the many valentines that had already come her way. It was signed with the well-known initials of a prominent Tory Member: "How about three hundred guineas and supper tonight?"

FOUR: The Investigation in the House of Commons now had the entire country fascinated. The Peninsular War was forgotten and thrust aside, and day after day the leading newspapers quoted the full proceedings in their columns. Napoleon and Spain had secondary importance. Pamphleteers ran riot, cartoonists and lampooners cashed in on the Great Discussion, and trade was brisk. Articles of china appeared by magic—Staffordshire jugs with Mrs. Clarke adorned in widow's weeds, in her hand a list of officers' names; gross, coloured portraits of the Duke of York, clad in a nightshirt, climbing out of bed; caricatures of Dowler and other witnesses. Lives of all of them, smudged and hastily printed, calling themselves "authentic," were sold at street corners. Comic songs by the dozen were whistled in theatres. And finally, as a gesture to the fashion, when a coin was tossed in the air on sporting occasions the call was not "Heads or Tails" but "Duke or Darling."

At London parties no other subject was mentioned. At coffeehouses and taverns there was one single topic of conversation. Mrs. Clarke had taken the bribes, but had the Duke known? Opinion was evenly divided, but in between the two opposing sides—the parties who said he had pocketed bribes himself and the other faction declaring him pure and unsullied—stood a stolid middle brigade, who shook their heads and said the liaison itself was what really mattered. A Prince of the Blood, who was married, had kept a mistress, given her houses and diamonds—while people starved. Men and women toiled in factories, soldiers fought, the mass of the British people led decent lives; but the Commander-in-Chief, the King's own son, kept a whore. Here was the point that rankled. This was the rub. Tub-thumpers and street-corner orators let themselves go, and so did plain John Citizen at home. "We're supposed to look up to the Brunswicks. They set the example. If that was the way the Bourbons behaved in France small wonder the Frogs chopped their heads off . . ." The mood was infectious and fanned by those it most suited—the stirrers of trouble.

Will Ogilvie, sitting alone at the desk in his office, smiled as the match lit the straw, as the straw burst to flame, as the flame caught the gust of the monster—public opinion. This was what he had planned from the beginning, and the straws that were burnt in the blaze had served a purpose. May Taylor was one of the straws. The parents of all her pupils removed their children, and her landlord in Cheyne Row told her to quit. He gave her three days to get out; half an hour in the House of Commons had ruined her life. She did not run a boarding school, so Government pamphlets sneered, but a bawdyhouse where street girls learnt their trade.

Do we win? Do we lose? Every day Mary Anne asked this question. She did not know of the notes despatched to Windsor by the Leader of the Commons, who sensed, as she could not, the mood of the House. He knew the doubts amongst his own supporters, he felt the growing coolness towards the Duke. So, from the House of Commons to Windsor Castle: "I think it only right to warn Your Majesty that the situation is becoming serious . . ." "The Duke knew what she was doing, and shut his eyes" —this was the murmur heard on all sides of the House. Government spokesmen made a poor impression. Adam, Greenwood—of Greenwood and Cox, army agents—Colonel Gordon, Military Secretary, and his assistant produced papers, documents, files, all proving nothing but that promotions had taken place and had been gazetted. And still the single weapon the Government used was that of disparaging the chief witness, Mrs. Clarke, so that her character, by being smirched, should throw doubt on her testimony. Amongst the witnesses who were called to discredit her, in the second week of the Investigation, were Mr. John Reid, proprietor of the hotel in St. Martin's Lane, and Samuel Wells, waiter. Both declared that the

277

lady who was with Mr. William Dowler on Friday night had always called herself Mrs. Dowler—until now, they swore, they had been totally ignorant that she had no right to the name. Next came Mr. Nicols, baker, to testify to the same effect. Mr. Dowler was frequently in his house while Mrs. Clarke lived there. She had first represented herself as a widow, but later told him that she had married Mr. Dowler. She had never paid him any rent, but he had in his possession some musical instruments belonging to her, and also some letters, which had once been sent down to be burnt but had been forgotten in a cupboard. These, however, he would not wish to produce unless by request of the House.

He was directed to withdraw while the House discussed whether the letters should be read or not. Some rapid thinking had to be done by the Leader of the House. If the letters should discredit Mrs. Clarke the cause of the righteous would triumph and all would be well. If the letters concerned the Duke, the matter was different. They might be damaging evidence, backing the charges. Mr. Perceval, after consideration, decided the risk was too great, and announced that there was no reason to examine letters merely because they belonged to Mrs. Clarke. Colonel Wardle suspected that these letters might in fact contain matter valuable to the Opposition, and he vigorously disputed the Leader's decision. After much wrangling the letters were procured and read from the Chair.

The first turned out to be from Samuel Carter. Poor Sammy, in the West Indies, happily ignorant that his letter, written from Portsmouth in 1804 asking for leave of absence to buy his tunic, would ever be read aloud in the House of Commons. A second letter from Sammy, and then a third. The House sat stunned and shocked at the new information, disclosed merely by chance, that Mrs. Clarke's footman had been commissioned an ensign.

Two letters from the Baroness Nollekens—a name well known in diplomatic circles—thanking Mrs. Clarke for favours received and asking for thanks to be passed to His Royal Highness.

Three letters from General Clavering asking for interviews and begging Mrs. Clarke to intercede with the

C.-in-C. about raising some new battalions. The Government benches looked glum, the Opposition jubilant. The letters, saved from destruction by the merest hazard, though not bearing specifically on the charges, helped to establish the fact that favour was given. They were read in silence. Then Colonel Wardle called Mrs. Clarke to identify handwriting, which she did with every one, having long forgotten the contents of all the letters, believing them burnt.

Colonel Wardle seized his advantage to question her at length about the occasion of the letters. Did she get Samuel Carter his commission? Did she apply for it to the Duke? Was His Royal Highness aware that it was the same person who waited at table at Gloucester Place? Did the Duke see him after he had been commissioned? Had she applied to the Duke in respect of the Baroness Nollekens? Her answers were in the greatest degree satisfactory to him.

"Do you," he continued, "recognise the handwriting of General Clavering?"

"Yes, and in a letter from the Duke I found this morning there is mention of Colonel Clavering and his battalions."

The letter was handed over and read to the House, the reading interrupted by bursts of laughter.

"Oh, my angel, do me justice and be convinced that never was a woman adored as you are. Every day, every hour convinces me more and more that my whole happiness depends on you alone. With what impatience do I look forward to the day after to-morrow. There are still however two nights before I shall clasp my darling in my arms. Clavering is mistaken, my angel, in thinking that any new regiments are to be raised; it is not intended. Only second battalions to the existing corps; you had better therefore tell him so, and that you are sure there would be no use applying for them.

"Ten thousand thanks, my love, for the handkerchiefs, and I need not assure you of the pleasure I feel in wearing them, and thinking of the dear hands that made them for me.

"Nothing could be more satisfactory than the tour I

279

have made and the state in which I have found everything. The whole of yesterday was employed in visiting the works at Dover, reviewing the troops there, and examining the coast as far as Sandgate. I am now setting off immediately to ride along the coast to Hastings, reviewing the different corps as I pass. Adieu, therefore, my sweetest, dearest love."

The letter was addressed, rather oddly, to George Farquhar, Esq., and not to Mrs. Clarke—a fact which escaped the attention of Members.

The revelations in the Hampstead letters considerably shook the confidence of Government supporters, and on the sixteenth of February the Leader of the House, hoping to reestablish faith in the Duke of York, rose to make an important announcement regarding the appointment of a Major Tonyn. Mrs. Clarke had testified in her evidence some days ago that the agent who gave her Tonyn's name was Captain Sandon. Captain Sandon had admitted this, but had suppressed in his evidence a certain vital fact that had since come to light outside the House of Commons. The fact was this—and discovered by Mr. Adam— that Captain Sandon had in his possession, amongst his baggage, letters from Mrs. Clarke; and one note in particular had been mentioned, alluding to Major Tonyn and his promotion, this note purporting to be from the Duke himself. Mr. Adam had spoken of this to His Royal Highness, who declared at once the note was a forgery.

"My point is this," said the Leader of the House. "If this note can be produced and proved a forgery, it will show that Mrs. Clarke knew how to impose, not only by word, but by falsification of signature. If, on the contrary, the note is authentic, it will tend to countenance the charges before us. I find myself so convinced in believing the former that I have no hesitation in bringing the matter before the House tonight to be discussed, and suggest that Captain Sandon be brought to the bar."

Colonel Wardle agreed. He had never heard of a note, nor of any other letters in Sandon's possession. But let them be shown—he was sure they would back the charges, and could certainly do no harm to Mrs. Clarke.

Captain Sandon appeared; and, greatly to the astonishment of the Leader of the House and the whole committee, denied all knowledge of the note in question. There may have been a note. He did not remember. The note did not now exist. It had been destroyed. He did recollect a note but it had vanished. He could not remember the contents. The note had gone. His state of abject guilt was so apparent, not only to Mr. Perceval but to the House, that after a tense half hour of examination he was ordered to withdraw in custody, and the House agreed without a single dissenting voice that he should be conducted to his lodging by the Serjeant, and a search made for the missing note. While the House awaited his reappearance Mrs. Clarke was once more called, and examined by Mr. Perceval.

"Do you recollect Captain Sandon's coming to you upon the subject of Major Tonyn in 1804?"

"I recollect that Captain Sandon was employed by Major Tonyn; I am confident as to that."

"Do you recollect ever having sent any message to Major Tonyn by Captain Sandon?"

"I cannot recollect that I did; perhaps it is likely, but it's a long while since."

"Do you recollect ever having sent any *paper* to Major Tonyn by Captain Sandon?"

"What sort of paper?"

"Any written paper, either by you or someone else?"

"I don't think I did. I was always very cautious of giving any written paper out of my hands."

"If you had sent such a paper by Captain Sandon to Major Tonyn, is it possible that you could have forgotten it?"

"No, I'm sure I should not have forgotten anything of that sort belonging to the Duke of York."

"Was Captain Sandon to have any percentage of the profit arising from the success of Major Tonyn's application?"

"I believe he was, for I understood Major Tonyn was a generous sort of man, and Captain Sandon would not have interested himself so much as he did for him without a reward."

"Before you came to the bar just now, had you any information of the substance of the examination of Captain Sandon before the committee here tonight?"

"Not the least."

The witness's manner had been frank and natural throughout. Had there really been such a note it was obvious that she had forgotten it. The House waited in impatience for the return of Captain Sandon and the Serjeant-at-Arms. After more than an hour had passed he was brought once more to the bar, and immediately examined by the Leader of the House.

"Have you found the paper?"

"I have."

"Have you got it with you?"

"The messenger has it, and every other paper that I had connected with it."

The messenger was directed to give up the papers, which consisted of a bundle of letters, and on top was the missing note. In complete silence Mr. Perceval handed the note to the Chairman, who read it aloud to the House: "I have just received your note, and Tonyn's business shall remain as it is. God Bless You." The note was unsigned, but it was addressed to George Farquhar, Esq., 18 Gloucester Place.

A murmur rose from the benches. What was the significance? Was the note then indeed from the Duke? But who was George Farquhar?

Mr. Perceval at once examined Captain Sandon.

"What motive had you for concealing this note?"

"I had no motive whatever, I am ashamed of myself."

"Were you directed by any person to conceal it?"

"No."

"When Mrs. Clarke gave you the note did she tell you it was written by the Duke of York?"

"I do not recollect her exact words, but she said that it came from him."

"Do you know the Duke of York's handwriting?"

"I never saw it in my life."

"Does the writing on this note appear to you to be the writing of Mrs. Clarke?"

"No, it does not."

"Who is George Farquhar, Esq., to whom the letter is directed?"

"I have not the slightest idea."

Captain Sandon then withdrew, and Mrs. Clarke was summoned to the bar, and questioned by the Attorney-General.

"Do you recollect ever seeing this paper before?"

"I suppose I must have seen it, for it is His Royal Highness's handwriting. I do not know how it could have got into that man's possession unless I gave it to him."

"Look at the seal of the note. Do you know it?"

"It is the Duke of York's private seal. I dare say I have many like it at home. The inscription upon it is 'Never Absent.'"

"Who is George Farquhar?"

"There is no such person in existence now. It was one of my brothers. I lost two in the Navy, and that was one of them. It was a name that the Duke always called me by when sending me letters."

"Have you ever imitated anyone's handwriting?"

"No, not to make any use of it. I might, with two or three women, laughing, imitate a hand. There is a game one plays—it's rather ridiculous to mention it here—one puts down a man's name, and then a woman's, and where they are, and what they are doing, and then makes a long roll of it, and then one says, 'Isn't that like the way So-and-So writes himself?' if they should be friends whom one names."

"Can you imitate the handwriting of the Duke of York?"

"I don't know. He is the best judge of that. I sometimes tried to write like him, when he was by. He fancied I could write his name a good deal like his signature Frederick, but I never made use of it. Had I ever tried to, it would have been brought up against me long before this."

"Do you always write the same kind of hand?"

"I can't say exactly how I write. I generally write in a great hurry."

"You guided your mother's hand on the bills that were produced at the Court Martial of your brother. Is not that then a different sort of hand again?"

"I don't write so quick when I guide her hand. I suppose it is my writing really, and not hers, as she has so very little use in her hand."

"In point of fact, then, you can write in two different hands?"

"I don't see much difference between them."

"You see no difference between your own handwriting, and the writing on the bills produced at the Court Martial?"

"It doesn't strike me there is a great deal of difference . . . Are you trying to insinuate that the writing on the bills was a forgery?"

"I do not insinuate any such thing. You hold your mother's hand and then guide it?"

"She takes the pen, I perhaps hold it lower down, and so guide her hand. You can see us write any time you like."

"Then both the bills are entirely your handwriting?"

"If you please to understand that, you may. I had the use of my mother's hand and they are my writing, I suppose."

The House now adjourned, having previously agreed that a select committee be appointed to examine the other letters from Mrs. Clarke that had been found in Captain Sandon's lodging with the missing note, and to report upon them the following day. Accordingly, on February seventeenth, the letters having first been identified by Mrs. Clarke as in her handwriting—although she was only permitted to read the envelope and not the contents—a number of them were read to the assembled House. They were not in any sort of order, and most were dated in the summer of 1804.

In every one there was some linking, openly or by implication, of the Duke of York with the promotion of various gentlemen—including Major Tonyn. "Tell Spedding to write in for what he wants, the D. says this is much the best . . . Will you ask again about an Indian lieutenancy? The D. assures me there are two for sale . . . I have mentioned the majority to the D. He is very agreeable. Do you think you could oblige me with one hundred? . . . Most unfortunately, Lord Bridgewater has asked for the vacancy, ere indeed it was one, but H.R.H. will let me know what he can do . . . I am thoroughly convinced of the money being too trifling and you may tell Bacon and Spedding they must each of them give two hundred. I must have an answer to this, as I am to speak with Him on it and I have mentioned your being concerned for me . . . The Duke has ordered Tonyn to be gazetted . . ."

The reading of the letters produced a profound effect upon the House. It was realised by all Members that the letters had been discovered by chance, that Mrs. Clarke had not known they were in the possession of Captain Sandon, neither had Colonel Wardle. If they had known, the letters would have been offered long before as evidence.

Mr. Perceval now asked Colonel Gordon, Military Secretary, whether, in his opinion, the handwriting of the note which had started the whole matter—"I have just received your note, and Tonyn's business shall remain as it is. God Bless You"—was that of the Duke.

"The utmost I can say is that it bears a very strong resemblance to His Royal Highness's handwriting, but whether it is or not, I cannot take it upon myself to say."

"Have you had any conversation with the Duke of York upon this subject?"

"Yes, I have."

"What passed in conversation?"

"The last conversation took place at half-past ten this morning, when I went to the Duke of York at my usual hour of business. The first word he said to me was, 'As you are to be called upon to answer certain questions in the House tonight I won't speak to you on the matter, but I can only state what I have stated before, that I've no knowledge of the thing, and I believe it to be a forgery.'"

Further witnesses were questioned, but none of them could positively state whether the note was in the Duke's hand or not. Amongst them was a clerk at the bank of Messrs. Coutts who declared that the writing was similar to the Duke's, but without a signature he could not swear to its authenticity.

In a final attempt to accuse Mrs. Clarke of forgery, the Leader of the House called a Mr. Benjamin Towan.

"In what line of business are you?"

"I am a velvet painter."

"Were you acquainted with Mrs. Clarke in Gloucester Place?"

"I was."

"Do you ever recollect her saying anything respecting handwriting?"

"Yes. In the course of conversation she observed she could forge the Duke's name, and she showed it to me upon a piece of blank paper, and I could not tell the difference between the Duke's and her own."

"Do you mean she introduced the subject, and immediately imitated the handwriting in your presence?"

"Yes."

"She showed you a signature of the Duke's?"

"Yes. On a piece of paper. It was either Frederick, or York, or Albany, I don't know which."

"Did you make any observation on the matter?"

"I said it was serious."

"What did she say?"

"She laughed."

Lord Folkestone rose at once to question the witness.

"What branch of painting do you profess to teach?"

"Flowers, landscapes, figures, and fruit."

"Do you teach your pupils to draw letters in any particular way? With flourishes and so on?"

"Yes, I do."

"Did Mrs. Clarke state that she could imitate the Duke of York's signature only, or his handwriting in general?"

"She only mentioned his signature."

"Were you much in the confidence of Mrs. Clarke?"

"No."

"How long is it since you gave any lesson to her?"

"I can't say, without reference to my books."

"Did you and she part on good terms?"

"She is in my debt."

"Has she paid you all that is due to you?"

"No."

The witness withdrew in some confusion, and the House then adjourned, after it had been decided to submit the Tonyn note to some person acquainted with the differences of hands, in order that his opinion might help the House in forming their own judgement in the matter at the next sitting.

FIVE: Whenever Mary Anne closed her eyes she saw the two bills in front of her and heard her mother's voice, peevishly saying, "Why do I sign my name, what does it mean?" and she, losing all patience, answering, "For heaven's sake, do what I tell you. Charley's in need of money, and he can cash these bills drawn on Russell Manners. It looks better for you to sign them than for me." Then, seizing her mother's hand, she had guided her signature.

"Does it mean they'll come to me for the money? I can't send Charley any money."

"No, of course not. Don't be so stupid."

The wretched bills had been sent off to Charley, cashed, and then returned; brought up and discussed in detail at the Court Martial; forgotten, because he was acquitted on that charge; and then dragged out again in the House of Commons. There was some fate, some devil's curse upon the bills. Had she done wrong? Wasn't the process legal? Was it forging when you guided a person's hand? It was impossible to swear, with the Bible in front of her, that her mother really knew what she was signing. She was far too feeble and shaky to understand the intricacies of bills, of cheques, of money, nor did she know what her daughter had been doing at 9 Old Burlington Street with Russell Manners.

What if they brought her mother to the House, put her before the bar and questioned her? The thought was sickening . . . agony—her mother, shaking in a chair, bullied and badgered by the Attorney-General. Mary Anne tossed and turned, her hands pressed to her eyes. How long would the torture go on? When would it finish?

No good had come of any of it, only slander. Dishonour, abuse, lies, and sordid exposure. She drank the powder prescribed for her and shuddered. Two days in bed. No visits from friends or relatives. That was the doctor's order, and she'd obeyed it. But she could not rest, with the new accusation of forgery flung upon her.

A tap on the door. Martha again, she supposed, to smooth the pillow.

"What is it, Martha? Can't you let me sleep?"

"Lord Folkestone's brought some flowers."

"Well, put them in water."

"He hopes you're better, ma'am, and sends his love."

"Did he say he wanted to see me?"

"He didn't presume."

She yawned and glanced at her clock. Only half-past nine. Hours to be gone through yet, and she'd never sleep. It might distract her to have a word with Folkestone. He was really very attentive, and rather attractive, and obviously *épris*, like a wide-eyed calf—he had lost his wife, it seemed, and hadn't recovered, but bereavement could ripen the senses, she'd struck it before. She sat up and reached for a shawl to put around her shoulders, touched up her face, and dabbed some scent on the pillow. "Tell his lordship to come upstairs."

Martha departed.

She leant back on her pillow, pale and languid. The lamp by her side was turned low, which was always becoming. The tap on the door was assertive, slightly intriguing—it was months since a man had done that, she could hardly remember it. "Come in," she said, and her voice was no longer bored, but melting, inviting, conducive to cosy intrigue.

"How sweet of you to call. I've been so lonely."

"I'll only stay a moment. Swear that you're better."

"Of course I'm better. Why are you so concerned?"

"When Doctor Metcalfe came to the House and said you were ill and couldn't attend today, I nearly left. It was as much as I could do to sit through the proceedings. I called him to the bar to be examined and he satisfied the House that you were really ill, but it only made me all the more anxious to see you. Is there anything you need? Anything

288

I can bring you? Are you sure your doctor's opinion can be trusted, or would you like me to send for my own physician?"

"I'm perfectly all right—merely exhausted. I thought the weekend would rest me, but it didn't. Well, tell me. How is it going?"

"Splendidly. The day's been spent in examining writing experts. Two fellows from the General Post Office, inspectors of francs, who came with microscopes, a second chap from Coutts Bank, and three from the Bank of England. Every one of them gave much the same sort of answer, though Perceval did his best to twist it about."

"What was the answer?"

"Resemblance strong, but they couldn't swear that the writing was identical. They thought it was the same, but that was all. What made them look rather foolish was when I asked them if they'd read the argument in the newspapers as to whether the note was a forgery or not. Of course they admitted they had, which meant, in practise, that all of them had arrived to examine the note with a certain prejudice, believing it mightn't be genuine."

"So the Government aren't any further?"

"Certainly not. We're just where we were before, and it won't be settled now before division. After the experts went we had the general—old Clavering, who hoped to deny he knew you. Useless, though, when he saw your various letters. We had some fun with him. Sam Whitbread questioned him, and tied the old fellow in knots until he was glad to get out. His evidence did not really affect the charges, but the House could tell, by the way he muffed his answers, that he'd been in touch with you about promotions. Then Greenwood and Gordon were called. Nothing material. They produced a heap of papers without significance. The House was very bored. In fact, everyone lost interest as soon as they learnt you weren't coming, so there you are."

"How brutal of them to want to see me tortured. A victim thrown to the lions."

"But not at all. You never give the appearance of a victim. You look as though you revel in every moment. The Attorney-General's the bear, and you are the baiter. The

289

whole House raves about you, including the Government. Even Wilberforce has forgotten his Negro slaves and talks of nothing else. I heard him sigh to one of his chapel friends, 'She's good underneath.' "

"Underneath what?"

"Underneath the surface. You've been in evil hands, or so he says."

"He's probably right. I've been in so many hands, according to the pamphlets, there can't be very much left of me. Have you read them?"

"I'd scorn to read the filth. Look, am I tiring you?"

"Not a bit. I find you restful."

"The business of the note is extremely odd. I can tell you what they're saying in the lobbies—that Sandon realised the note was written by the Duke and would support the charges, and so he pretended he'd lost it, never dreaming that Adam would bring it before the House."

"Why did Adam bring it up? It could only damage them."

"Because, don't you see, he clearly had no idea that the note *was* really genuine; he thought it was faked. And now, because Sandon made such a hopeless bungle, they've not only had the note read out in evidence, but all those other letters as well—and *they* produced them! That's where the note's such a triumph for our cause. Perceval's kicking himself, and so are the others. I bet H.R.H. gives Adam hell tomorrow."

"He's much too scared of him to give him hell. He's entirely in Adam's clutches, I always said so."

"You really bear no resentment. I think it's wonderful."

"What's the use of resentment now? It's all too late."

"There's still a confounded rumour going around—which nobody believes in, by the way—that Kent is somehow at the back of us. I know how it arose—from your mentioning one day in your evidence that you knew Dodd, Kent's private secretary. But everyone knows Dodd."

She did not answer. She knew she had to be wary. Folkestone, the idealist, had no idea of the plot behind the Investigation.

"Do you know him well?" asked Lord Folkestone.

"Who, Dodd? Good heavens, no. He's a fearful bore,

but happens to be a neighbour. He lives in Sloane Street, and likes to come here and call if he gets the chance."

"I'd keep him at a distance, if I were you. All courtiers gossip madly, it's part of their business. That's what I found so fresh when I lived in France—before the Terror, of course, when ideals were strong. They really felt reborn, a lot of those fellows, with tyranny overthrown and a future to live for."

Thank God, he was off and away on his favourite subject. The danger was over, at any rate for the present. Brandy, perhaps, in ten minutes to make distraction; then, if she felt in the mood, he could sit on the bed.

Distraction came, but not in the form of brandy. Martha appeared again with news of the front-door bell. "Colonel Wardle and Major Dodd have asked to see you."

Silence. A horrible moment, then great surprise. "How strange! Have they come together? I wonder what for?"

"Colonel Wardle hopes he can see you."

"He hopes in vain."

Lord Folkestone rose from his chair. "Won't he think it odd if you choose to see me and don't say good evening to him?"

"He must think it odd. I can see what friends I please."

"I find myself embarrassed. Please receive him. If he knows I'm here there might be some foolish gossip."

His lordship was afraid to be compromised? Her opinion of him fell. His attraction withered. "All right. We'll have him up." His lordship relaxed. Colonel Wardle was then shown into the bedroom.

Instead of the smirk that might have been expected, the dig in the ribs, the remark, "You've beaten me to it," with other sly allusions to bedside company, the Member for Okehampton looked uneasy. He murmured a word or two, then sat in silence. Something was wrong. She sensed the change of atmosphere. She said, "Lord Folkestone's told me about today. I gathered things went well, but nothing was settled."

"Yes. The mood of the House was good, and in our favour. That's partly why I've come to see you tonight. I think it would be best if you seized advantage of the fact

291

that you're rather unwell, and let it excuse you from any further attendance in the House."

"I couldn't be more pleased or more relieved."

Lord Folkestone stared at Wardle in disbelief. "You must be mad! Why, Mrs. Clarke's our ace. Her presence alone is enough to win the House."

"I disagree."

"You mean to say that the evidence she has given has been harmful rather than valuable to our cause? The suggestion's monstrous. Without her we hadn't a chance."

"Don't mistake me, Folkestone. Of course Mrs. Clarke has been helpful. My point is that she has said all she has to say. If she comes to the House again she'll be cross-examined on all sorts of other subjects that might be damaging."

So Wardle had heard that rumours were circulating about the Duke of Kent's part in the affair. That's why he called with Dodd. She shrugged her shoulders. They must fight it out together, she didn't care.

"Look here," said Folkestone, "what's at the back of this? Is something going on that you haven't explained? Is there any truth in this rumour about Kent?"

"I assure you, no."

"Then what's it all about?"

"My apprehension lest Mrs. Clarke should be worried."

"They can't do worse to her than they have done already, you know that well, and she handled them with ease. What further subjects are there that could be damaging?"

Colonel Wardle looked for help to his Number One witness. She took no notice, closed her eyes, and yawned. He turned once more to Lord Folkestone in desperation.

"Very well, I'll be frank. This is a personal matter, something to do with myself and Mrs. Clarke. I'd be most obliged if you'd leave us for five minutes."

Lord Folkestone rose stiffly to his feet. "Of course, if you put it that way I have no alternative."

He went from the bedroom, leaving them together. Colonel Wardle began at once in agitation, "You've said nothing to Folkestone about the Duke of Kent?"

"Of course not."

"He's suspicious. That's why he called to see you, naturally."

"Nonsense, he brought me flowers."

"Just an excuse. I warn you, we must be careful. Rumours abound. If the Government smells a rat, our cause is lost and the whole of the charges will fall into disrepute."

"Folkestone isn't a member of the Government."

"That makes no odds. He'd throw in his hand if he knew."

"You're ashamed, then, of the plot behind the charges?"

"It's not a question of shame, nor is it a plot. It's all a matter of policy, very involved."

"Involved's the word. And you've landed me in the muddle. Not only must I be wary of the Government, but of Folkestone too, the man who's done most to help me."

"I'm sorry. It's very unfortunate. But in politics, our dearest friends are sometimes those who betray us inadvertently."

"Well, what do you want me to do?"

"Reassure Folkestone that Kent is *not* behind us. Say, if you like, that you and I are *intimes,* and that I'm alarmed the scandal may be discovered."

"Thanks very much!"

"The suggestion may keep him at bay and put him off from further questioning."

"Why should I keep him at bay? I find him pleasant."

"Then tell any lie you please, but don't tell the truth."

She sat up in bed and pummelled the pillows behind her, took another peep in the glass, and arranged her shawl.

"For a patriot, Colonel Wardle, you're very impressive. What a shame the Attorney-General can't hear you now."

"Dear lady, political measures . . ."

"Political balderdash. Don't talk to me of politics, they stink. All right, I'll fool his lordship, you needn't worry; and if I'm called to the House I shall appear. I'm not going to blow the gaff, so keep your head . . . Now, hadn't you better go and find his lordship and tell him our tête-à-tête is over and done with?"

Anxiety dropped from Wardle's shoulders. The haggard expression, the frown, all disappeared. He went, and she could hear them talking in the drawing-room. She pictured the scene: Folkestone inquisitive, Dodd and Wardle cagey, and heaven knew what gossip smeared at herself. Presently there was a slamming of doors and steps in the street. They'd gone, and she could relax and go to sleep. She was about to throw off her shawl and turn out the lamp when she heard another knock at the bedroom door.

"Come in!" What did Martha want now? But it wasn't Martha—it was his lordship again, with a feverish, furtive air.

"They've gone. I've got rid of them both," he said, and tiptoed towards the bed and took her hand.

Oh, Lord . . . her heart sank within her. Must she face this? Her mood of half an hour back had entirely changed. The moment had passed, all she wanted to do was to sleep. She stifled a yawn and tried to summon a smile.

"I thought you'd gone too?"

"I came to wish you good-night."

She knew what that meant—she'd been through it dozens of times. Not with his Radical lordship, but with others. All aboveboard for five minutes, a stroking of hands, murmurs and whispers; and then a hurried request. Best get it over and done with, then pack him off home. Pretend an ecstatic fatigue—it generally worked. He'd slip off to bed believing he'd conquered the world.

"Shall I turn down the light?" he whispered.

"If you prefer it."

She glanced at the clock. A quarter to eleven. If he went at a quarter-past, which was optimistic, she'd have eight hours before her tea at seven . . . But if, as instinct warned her was highly probable, his Francophilian lordship lacked instruction—all promise and no performance—then time was pressing—a case of *faites vos jeux* and *allons y*.

SIX: Wednesday the twenty-second of February was the final day on which evidence was to be taken, and Colonel Wardle, having declared he had no wish to bring forward further witnesses in support of his charges—the letters found in Captain Sandon's possession being proof enough of the Duke of York's complicity in promotion traffic—then gave place to the Leader of the House.

Mr. Perceval began by stating that he desired to allay any misapprehension there might be on the part of the House regarding the delay in bringing forward the evidence of Captain Sandon and producing the note about Major Tonyn. There had been rumours on the opposite side of the House that Captain Sandon had been told to destroy the note by persons who were friendly to the Duke of York. This was entirely untrue.

The Opposition received his statement in silence. They noticed, and so did members of the Government, that no more was said about the note being a forgery, and no further handwriting experts were summoned to the bar.

In a last attempt to discredit Mrs. Clarke the Leader of the House called upon Mrs. Favoury, housekeeper, to give evidence, trusting that she would bring contempt upon her mistress; and Martha, round-eyed with wonder and surprise, was delivered over to the Attorney-General.

"Were you housekeeper to Mrs. Clarke at Gloucester Place?"

"I was."

"Was the establishment kept up at great expense?"

"It certainly was. There were sometimes three men cooks at dinner, and if there was anything found fault with by His Royal Highness she would send for another cook."

"Was Mrs. Clarke in the habit of receiving visits from other gentlemen?"

"Yes, gentlemen came backwards and forwards."

"Before Samuel Carter came to live with Mrs. Clarke as footman did he come in company with a Captain Sutton?"

"Captain Sutton brought him along certainly, but he didn't take Sam into the parlour."

"Do you know if Mrs. Clarke ever lived with a gentleman called Ogilvie?"

"I've seen Mr. Ogilvie, but she didn't live with him. He used to come to Tavistock Place, a lusty gentleman."

"Do you know a man called Walmsley?"

"Why do you want to bring that up?"

Martha, flushed and indignant, stared resentfully at the Attorney-General. Sir Vicary Gibbs leant forward. So . . . another lover to add to the list of Mrs. Clarke's conquests?

The name Walmsley buzzed across the benches. A Shropshire Walmsley shook his head and turned scarlet. The Attorney-General held up his hand for silence. "If," he said to Martha, "you have anything to bring forward about a Mr. Walmsley I shall be very glad to hear it."

Martha fumbled for a handkerchief. Supposing she did not tell the truth, the Attorney-General might put her in prison.

"Mrs. Clarke knows about it," she answered. "I was married to the man, and he was a married man all the time. He deceived me but I didn't know it—I wouldn't live with him when I got to hear of it, and I didn't cohabit with him again. I was married to him at Woolwich church. He was a coal merchant and Mrs. Clarke told me not to have him, but I wouldn't listen."

A shout of laughter rang through the House, and the Attorney-General, with a glance at Mr. Perceval, allowed his bewildered witness to depart, and called Mrs. Mary Anne Clarke for her final examination.

"Did you know about Walmsley?"

"Yes. I heard of the man a dozen times. I heard he was a thief, and I was missing some soup plates, and my servants thought he had stolen them. He was a man of very bad character, and the Duke thought it was best for her to leave my service."

"How long was it before you took her into your service again?"

"I did not take her until I wanted her very much. Mrs. Favoury is necessary to me, and knows all my affairs, and I believe she keeps my secrets, and I have never found her dishonest."

"You abide by your former evidence that you once received a long list of names for promotion that you showed His Royal Highness?"

"Yes, I do. He put the list away in his pocketbook, and later I saw the list with some of the names scratched through. I only mention this because I have heard a gentleman on my right hand here just say that I might have picked his pocket."

She glanced in accusation at the offending Tory Member, and there were mocking calls of "Shame" from the Opposition benches.

The Attorney-General consulted a note in his hand.

"You said in former evidence you knew Major Dodd. When did you last see him?"

"I don't remember. I'm not ashamed of Major Dodd, nor, I dare say, is Major Dodd ashamed of me. Except perhaps at this moment."

"Do you know a Mr. Ogilvie?"

"Yes."

"How long have you known him?"

"I don't recollect. Some years."

"Four years?"

"Perhaps."

"Six years?"

"I don't think so."

"How long did you know Mr. Ogilvie before you lived with the Duke of York?"

"A few months. He was just failing in his business and his books were being made up when I knew him."

"Did you ever live with him?"

"I have lived with no man but the Duke of York."

Cheers and whistles sounded through the House. The witness listened to them with composure. The Attorney-

General shrugged his shoulders. Lord Folkestone stared at his feet. Colonel Wardle mopped his brow. And then, to the disappointment of the whole House, the Attorney-General intimated that he had no further questions to put to the witness.

There was little more to come. The proceedings were terminated by the evidence of two military spokesmen for the Government—the Secretary for War, and the Right Honourable Sir Arthur Wellesley.

"In respect of the state of the Army," said Sir Arthur Wellesley, "I can say from my own knowledge of it, which is intimate, that it has materially improved in every way. The discipline of the soldiers is improved, the officers are improved in knowledge, the Staff is better than it was and much more complete, the officers of the cavalry are better than they were, the whole system of the management of the clothing of the Army, the interior economy of the regiments, and everything that relates to the military discipline of the soldiers and the military efficiency of the Army have been greatly improved since His Royal Highness the Duke of York was appointed Commander-in-Chief."

The evidence having been finally concluded, Mr. Perceval suggested that, as the whole of the Minutes would be printed by the following Monday, the report should be taken into consideration on Tuesday next. Colonel Wardle agreed.

The Investigation into the conduct of the Duke of York was over. The debate, which was to last from Thursday, February twenty-third, until Friday, March seventeenth, was yet to come.

SEVEN: She sat in the drawing-room of Westbourne Place with a sense of anticlimax, of depression. The Investigation, hateful though it had been, had served as a challenge. Now there was nothing to do but wait for the verdict. Which way it went did not seem to matter.

She had no resentment now, no sort of anger. Even the Court Martial had been forgotten. Adam was to blame for it all—Adam and Greenwood.

She picked up the morning paper and read the letter the Duke of York had sent to the House of Commons;

Sir,

I have waited with the greatest anxiety until the Committee appointed by the House of Commons to enquire into my conduct as Commander-in-Chief of His Majesty's Army had closed its examinations, and I now hope that it will not be deemed improper to address this letter through you to the House of Commons.

I observe with the deepest concern that in the course of the enquiry my name has been coupled with transactions the most criminal and disgraceful, and I must ever regret and lament that a connection should ever have existed which has thus exposed my character and honour to public animadversion.

All right, she thought, lament it. You didn't once. You didn't lament it when you swore you loved me. You didn't lament it when you promised to provide for the children. You only lamented it when your jaded eye fell upon Mrs. Carey and I was a nuisance. And then, had you kept your promise, I would have spared you. She picked up the paper and read the letter through to the end.

With respect to my alleged offence, connected with the

discharge of my official duties, I do, in the most solemn manner, upon my honour as a Prince, distinctly assert my innocence, not only by denying all corrupt participation in any of the infamous transactions which have appeared in evidence at the bar of the House of Commons, or any connivance at their existence, but also the slightest knowledge or suspicion that they existed at all.

Oh, God forgive you. What about those earrings, the ones I got from Parker's, and the horses, and the carriages, and my gowns, and the coat-of-arms stamped on all the silver? Do you think I paid for them with the eighty pounds a month that you allowed me?

My consciousness of innocence leads me confidently to hope that the House of Commons will not, upon such evidence as they have heard, adopt any proceedings prejudicial to my honour and character; but if, upon such testimony as has been adduced against me, the House of Commons can think my innocence questionable, I claim of their justice that I shall not be condemned without trial, or be deprived of the benefit and protection which is afforded to every British subject by those sanctions, under which alone evidence is received in ordinary administration of the law.

I am, Sir, yours, Frederick

Written by himself? In all probability. Or drafted by his private secretary Herbert Taylor, with Adam, possibly, hovering in the background.

It had not made much impression, according to Folkestone. There had been talk of the privileges of the House having been attacked—she did not understand it and cared even less.

"Well, what's going to happen now?"

She put this to the conspirators when they called, the conspirators being Wardle, Dodd, and Glennie, the bunch who had set the business going. "We can't plan ahead," said Wardle, turned suddenly pompous; "your future, and ours as well, depends on the House. The next few weeks I shall be exceedingly busy. The whole weight of the debate will fall on my shoulders."

"Won't you get support from the rest of the Opposition?"

"Of course. But as instigator of the charges, I am the man responsible. I'm in the forefront, everyone waits on me."

"Which is just what you like, my smooth and immaculate patriot."

"Dear lady, the acid tongue does not become you."

"You admired it in the House."

"That was rather different. You employed it against the Government; we are your friends."

"And speaking of the Government . . ." chipped in Dodd, and she saw the two men exchange glances of understanding. "We were talking of you last night to Sir Richard Phillips."

"The publisher in Bridge Street?"

"That's the man. A great admirer of yours, or so he told us."

"Oh? What does he want?"

"Why 'want'? He praised your charm."

"Experience, Major Dodd, has long informed me that no man ever expresses admiration unless he wants something out of the person admired."

"That's a very cynical view."

"I'm a cynical woman."

Colonel Wardle interrupted. "The point at issue was really connected with Phillips's particular business. You're so much in the public eye—all of London's talking—that he's hoping you're going to sit down and write your memoirs. The demand would be enormous, according to him."

"My memoirs? . . . Memoirs of what?"

"Of your life with the Duke, of all the people you've met, all the gossip and scandal. You'd make a fortune, of course. You'd be wealthy for life."

"But I thought you already had that fixed and settled? That the Duke of Kent has a pension up his sleeve?"

There was a strange silence, an awkward pause. Then Dodd again: "Of course, that's all in the air, until the debate is over in the House and we know what's going to happen. In the meanwhile you've everything to gain, and nothing to lose, by getting out a book as soon as possible."

"With your talent," said Wardle, "your wit, your charm, your ease of expression, the business would only take you a matter of weeks. Phillips knows a hack who'd pull it into shape. Someone called Gillingham."

"I'll be willing to help you myself," said Major Dodd. "I've quite a turn with my pen; my wife used to say if I only had the time I could write a novel. His Royal Highness the Duke of Kent has said the same."

"Why not write his memoirs, then? They'd sell better than mine. How he first met Madame de Laurent, with all the details. And how the troops at Gibraltar burnt him as Guy Fawkes."

"The object of the book, if you write your memoirs," said Colonel Wardle, trying to change the subject, "would be, of course, in the main to sully York, but at the same time to attack the present Government. Rake up the private gossip, and so strike a blow for freedom and for all of us."

"Wash the Government's dirty linen, and save you the trouble?"

"I'm a busy man. I haven't the time to write."

Good God! How she despised the lot of them. Using her as a tool to further their plans. It did not matter how she smirched herself, their hands would stay clean—as long as they kept their distance.

"I tell you what," she said. "I might write a book on the private lives of all the men I've known. Including you, and also Major Dodd."

"Dear lady, our lives would bear investigation. Ask our wives."

"All right. What about the pseudonym 'Mr. Brown'? And the coffeehouse at the end of Cadogan Square?"

Colonel Wardle turned bright puce and blinked his eyes.

"What exactly do you mean?"

"Search your conscience, if you've got one. I don't know. The chambermaid takes tea in the kitchen with Martha. As for Major Dodd, there's a chophouse in Drury Lane, with a red-haired girl who sits behind the counter. My brother dines there sometimes—he's fond of the theatre."

Major Glennie tittered. "And what do you know about me?"

"I merely wonder how you wangled your present safe appointment as teacher of mathematics down at Woolwich. I thought all artillery experts were needed in Spain?"

Silence. Then hearty laughter, very forced, and glances at watches—they must all go home.

"If you do think about the memoirs, Mrs. Clarke, then Sir Richard is your man, a very live publisher."

So live that an ardent request to see her came by the very next post, which proved connivance. She had an interview with Sir Richard in his office in Bridge Street, and, looking about her, thought of ten years back, when, not in his office but in others similar, she had traded her scraps of gossip to halfpenny pamphlets.

Ten shillings a column those days, for Joseph to sneak round the corner and spend in the taverns. Mr. Jones, in Paternoster Row: "It's not smutty enough, the public want something that sizzles, to ginger the palate." But now the red carpet was down and the shillings were thousands.

Sir Richard Phillips began by praising her evidence.

"My dear Mrs. Clarke, you had the whole House at your feet."

"With the possible exception of the Attorney-General. And the Leader of the House never got to his knees. Nor did I observe the Government benches stripped of sitting figures—they seemed unmoved."

"But impressed all the same, I assure you. You're far too modest. Now, what about these memoirs?"

"What about them?"

"Have you anything yet on paper?"

"Not a line."

"But I understand that before the Investigation, some time last year in the summer, you made some notes about your recollections of life at Gloucester Place, conversations with the Duke, private matters relating to the Royal Family, etc., etc. Now that's the stuff I'm after. Could I see it?"

"That rather depends on what you intend to do with it."

"Why, publish it, of course, with certain embellishments. Just a master touch here and there by a professional hack,

303

while you supply the material and the letters. Pretty hot, I have no doubt. I know these princes—it's the German blood, they've no idea of restraint. I'd pay you well for the copyright, Mrs. Clarke."

"I'm not selling any copyright, Sir Richard."

"Not selling . . . but what are you after?"

"You can print it, and sell the book as you please, but you stay the vendor. The copyright won't go out of my possession."

"In that case, Mrs. Clarke, we can't do business."

"I'm sorry. I'll find someone else, I'm in no hurry."

She rose to leave, but he pressed her to stay a moment. "If I don't do the book myself I can put you in touch with an excellent man who's about to become a publisher, a Mr. Gillet, who's been some time in the trade. As a matter of fact he's here, I'll introduce him." She recognised the racket. Wheels within wheels. There was somebody else who had "just dropped in by chance," but who had actually waited about for the touch of a bell.

"And as it happens there's a bookseller here from Kent, with a flourishing business in Maidstone, a man called Sullivan. One glimpse at you, Mrs. Clarke, and he'll give an order. Strike while the iron is hot is my favourite motto."

Enter Mr. Gillet and Mr. Sullivan. More flattering speeches were made and tributes paid to her charm, after which they began to scribble figures on paper.

"A first edition of twelve thousand copies, I reckon we'd get that subscribed in a very few weeks."

"A portrait of the author as a frontispiece? The head by Mr. Buck that was in the papers? And signed, of course— no value unless it's signed."

"What about over in Ireland, the Dublin market?"

"The Micks don't pay so high, but they'd want the book. I'd say Mrs. Clarke would pocket two thousand guineas."

She listened to them in silence, then put in a question.

"How about some money before the book is started?"

No bids. A deathly silence. Then Mr. Gillet: "It's customary to deliver the manuscript first," his protest backed up by the Maidstone hawker and Sir Richard.

"I see. Well, I'd better go home and start to write it."

Her words brought relief to all concerned. The interview was over, with nothing committed in ink on either side—no signatures to agreements, nothing binding, but a literary future assured and a fortune promised. She'd believe them when she held the cash in her hands; then all their charming speeches might make sense. So back to Westbourne Place and a sheet of foolscap. And then . . . ? *Memoirs of M. A. Clarke*—would that be the title? It sounded dry as dust, like a teacher's manual. *My Rise and Fall* would come more *à propos*, but the rise would take some telling and cause some flutters. Let sleeping dogs stay put, and draw the veil until the girls were married and George was a general.

My Life with the Duke? It was all in the Minutes already, being pulled about at the moment in the Commons. A lot they wouldn't find, of course, in that. What he wore (or didn't wear), his taste in food, the mood at breakfast, the singing in the washtub, the dislike of a warming-pan, the midnight yawn. They would say she was lying, no doubt—that was the trouble—and put her into court for misrepresentation. The book, to be really convincing, must give his letters: they couldn't be denied or explained away. She had them all in that box tied up with ribbon, except the few she had taken to the House, and the letters were what the public really wanted. Not the *billets-doux*, like those they had read in the Commons, but the notes where he'd spilt the beans about the Family.

The King playing whist in his dressing-gown (nicknamed Snuffy) while the Premier, Mr. Pitt, awaited his audience . . . The Queen's determined insistence on protocol . . . The Household flat on their faces at her approach . . . The Princess of Wales's confinement, with strange repercussions . . . The habits and tastes of his brothers, especially Cumberland, with mirrors all over St. James's and odd-looking valets . . .

Yes, those letters were worth a good deal, one way and another, once they'd been bound up in calf with gold lettering proudly displayed. But whether Sir Richard, Gillet, or the hawker of Maidstone would pay quite as much for possession as the royal hand that had penned them was open to question—and to enquiry, too.

It was amusing, the general sense of discomfort that seemed to attack so many of her friends. James Fitzgerald, from Ireland, was one of the most agitated—with reason, what was more, when she thought of his letters. He wasn't the only one who wrote imploring that if she should ever consider writing her memoirs—the rumour had spread, then, across to Dublin already—she would not, for old friendship's sake, she would not include him. If his letters had not been burnt, would she kindly return them? She couldn't return them, or burn them, in point of fact. They'd been part of the bundle that Nichols had found up at Hampstead, and were now reposing in the House of Commons.

This news had the result of sending Willie, his son, to her house at six in the morning with tears in his eyes.

"What in heaven's the matter? Is your father dead?"

Curtains were hastily drawn, the fire kindled, hot coffee and eggs put before him, herself in a wrapper.

"Mary Anne, we're faced with ruin. Only you can help us."

"I've scarcely got five guineas in the house. I'll send round to my upholsterer, he'll oblige me."

"Not that. Not money . . ."

"Then what the devil is it?"

He looked like a raving lunatic from Bedlam. He even had straws in his hair (the boat from Dublin), he hadn't shaved or cleaned his fingernails. "My father got your note five days ago. I've come at once . . . you *must* get those letters back."

"How can I? They're under seal at the House of Commons."

"You must appeal to Perceval without delay."

"He wouldn't listen. He's probably broken the seal and is reading the lot."

"Don't you realise our position if we're disgraced? My father will never lift his head again, my sister will have to break off her engagement, and as for myself . . ."

"I know, it is rather distressing. There's one letter where James asks to be my agent in Ireland, written, if I remember rightly, around 1805, and saying he could whip up the prices for ensigns. It will look rather bad if it's read before the committee."

"You sit there and smile . . ."

"There's nothing else I can do. I haven't the letters. Go and ask Perceval yourself, but he'll hardly listen to you until the debate is over."

"Meanwhile, you won't mention us in your memoirs?"

"Meanwhile, I promise nothing. Eat your breakfast."

How could she ever have thought him amusing at Worthing? It must have been his youthful blond appearance, coupled with being bored and a hot July.

"I tell you what you can do"—a thought suddenly striking her—"you told me you knew the Earl of Moira well, and the Earl of Chichester too. I met them with you. My name will be mud to them now, but never mind. They've long been personal friends of the Duke of York. Put it about that I'm going to publish my memoirs, including all the letters of the Duke, but I might change my mind if somebody cared to persuade me."

That surely was fair enough, and left every door open.

And during those weeks in March, while the debate continued, day after day, with long, interminable speeches —the For, the Against, the Praise and the Slander, the lauding to heaven and the hurling in the mud—the Chief Witness for Wardle's charges scribbled in notebooks; confessions, impressions, digressions, and everything else. There was no time for any intrusion, not even for the children (who were safely away in the country with her mother), not a moment either for Bill, over at Uxbridge, tending his elderly father seized with a stroke.

Only once in a while did she pause—when his Radical Lordship, hot from debate in the House, paid a clandestine call. Then she heard all the news. How the war of ideals was progressing, how someone had called her a witch and another a wanton, and a third a poor woman misjudged who craved mercy from heaven.

"Who's winning?"

"It's close."

"Will it be neck-and-neck at the finish?"

"No, a Government lead, with a margin they won't care to look at."

"Which means?"

"Resignation."

"For whom?"

"For your gallant Commander-in-Chief."

She had no moment of joy, no elation, no sense of triumph—only a pain in the heart and a feeling of shame. I will repay, saith the Lord—so the words ran in her mother's worn Bible; but all that revenge had achieved was a taste in the mouth.

"Can I stay?"

"If you like."

And even that was indifferent, a tribute unwanted. The same old experience shared without fervour or folly.

The House sat through the night of March sixteenth, before they came to division and the heads were counted. The debate that had lasted three weeks was wound up at last, and the concluding speeches showed how the House might divide.

First the Leader of the House and the Attorney-General gave it as their opinion that no necessity existed for removing His Royal Highness from the station he held at present, which he was so well qualified to fill. Could Mrs. Clarke be believed, then the charges were proved, but her testimony had appeared a tissue of fabrication. It was the duty of the House to acquit him of the foul charges that had been made against him.

Sir Francis Burdett, for the Opposition, said he had been astonished to find the Leader of the House, Mr. Perceval, who also held the post of Chancellor of the Exchequer, Sir Vicary Gibbs, the Attorney-General, and all the Crown lawyers, whose duty it was to punish public delinquencies, arraying themselves this time upon the side of the party accused.

The principle had been to do away with the evidence of Mrs. Clarke, but the amazing thing had been the truly consistent manner in which she had given it. All those who endeavoured to trap her, or make her discredit herself, had found themselves constantly foiled. His Majesty's Attorney-General had been continually defeated.

As to the Duke of York's high principles, he had felt no remorse in shaking off his mistress, and exposing her to poverty and infamy. The annuity, when applied for, had been refused, which spoke much for royal promises. The high rank of the Prince was immaterial in this case. For the case was the justice of England, and the people of England looked to the House for justice. It seemed to him impossible, after all that had been heard during the past weeks in the House of Commons, that the Duke of York could retain his situation at the head of the Army.

Amid scenes of intense excitement the House divided, and the result was as Lord Folkestone had prophesied. Although the Duke of York was acquitted both of personal corruption and of connivance, the majority in his favour was no more than eighty-two.

On paper, and in terms of figures, the charges had been disproved; but in the eyes of public opinion the Duke of York had been convicted, and the result was a triumph for the Opposition.

When the news became known on the Friday evening there was shouting and rejoicing in the streets of London. Colonel Wardle became a national hero, Mrs. Clarke a benefactress to the British people, and instead of the street boys throwing bricks at her drawing-room window there was now a mob from the back lanes of Chelsea and Kensington waiting for her to appear on her doorstep and smile at them.

That night she attended the Opera House in the Haymarket, where a benefit performance was being given for the actors and actresses of Drury Lane. Charley was with her, May Taylor, and Lord Folkestone; and when they came into the box and were seen by the audience cheers and loud applause rang out through the theatre.

"This makes up for what you went through with the Attorney-General, doesn't it?" whispered Charley.

Her sister smiled, and bowed, and waved her hand in acknowledgement to the crowd. "No," she said, and smiled and waved again.

"What will you try for next, then? A public apology?"

She laughed. "I shall bide my time," she answered. "You wait and see. One of these days I'll get even with Vicary Gibbs."

"If you get these tributes now," murmured Lord Folkestone as the clapping died away and the audience settled, "what will it be when you bring out the promised memoirs?"

"An author is read, not observed," whispered Mary Anne. "Besides, it's very possible I won't publish them."

"But you must . . ." He looked astounded. "I heard through Sir Richard Phillips that the whole thing was settled. The book will put another spoke in the Government's wheel and bring more popularity to the Opposition."

Mary Anne shrugged her shoulders. The lights went dim.

If you think I care a damn for either side," she said, "you are mistaken. Fight your own quarrels."

"Then what has the battle been for?"

"My children's future."

The curtain rose and a hush came over the house. The title of the piece was *Honey-moon*. The audience rose and shouted halfway through when one of the leading actors, concluding a speech, was obliged to say, "It will be rather awkward, to be sure, to resign at the end of the month, but like other great men in office I must make the most of my time, and retire with a good grace to avoid being turned out."

Once again all heads turned to the right-hand box and waved and laughed and shouted. Triumph was complete.

On the Saturday morning His Royal Highness the Duke of York tendered his resignation as Commander-in-Chief of the Army, which His Majesty was graciously pleased to accept. The excitement that followed lasted over Easter, and speeches by the Opposition at Westminster Hall were cheered wildly. On April first Colonel Wardle was voted a Freeman of the City of London, and the Lord Mayor, who had spoken against the suggestion, was howled at by the mob and mud thrown at his carriage.

On that same day the chief witness for the colonel's charges against the Duke of York had a meeting with three gentlemen—the Earl of Moira, the Earl of Chichester, and Sir Herbert Taylor, private secretary to His Royal Highness the Duke of York.

At this meeting Mrs. Clarke, attended by her lawyer

Mr. Comrie, her brother Captain Thompson, and two friends, Mr. William Dowler and Mr. William Coxhead-Marsh, agreed to suppress her memoirs, parts of which had already been printed to the tune of several thousand copies and were in the hands of the publisher Mr. Gillett, who would receive fifteen hundred pounds indemnity as soon as he had destroyed every single copy.

For the suppression of the memoirs, and for agreeing to hand over to the Earl of Chichester all the letters from the Duke of York that were still in her possession, Mrs. Clarke was to receive the sum of ten thousand pounds, with an annuity for life of four hundred pounds, and two hundred pounds for each of her daughters. Her own annuity was to pass to her daughters on her death. The three gentlemen who attended Mrs. Clarke would be trustees for her annuity; and the Earl of Chichester and Mr. Cox, of Cox and Greenwood, guaranteed the payment.

Mrs. Mary Anne Clarke then sat down and signed the following agreement:

In consideration of the Terms proposed and agreed to, I, Mary Anne Clarke, of 2 Westbourn Place, London, promise to deliver up every Letter, Paper, Memorandum and Writing, in my power or custody, respecting the Duke of York or any other of the Royal Family, and particularly all Letters, Memorandums or other Writings written or signed by the Duke. I also promise to procure all the letters not in my custody entrusted to me by others, and deliver them to the Duke's friend.

I also agree that I will, when required, make a solemn declaration on oath that I have delivered up all the Letters and other Writings from the Duke to me, as far as is in my power or possession, and that I know of no other, and I promise to procure from the Printer, and the persons employed to print a publication of my Life, every document in their possession, and all such parts of the work as may have been printed.

I further promise not to write, print, or publish any article respecting the connection between me and the Duke, or any anecdote, either written or verbal, that may have come to my knowledge from the Duke.

I further consent that, on failure of my complying with the several stipulations above stated, the Annuity agreed to be paid to myself for my life, and to my daughters after my decease, shall become absolutely forfeited.

I will deliver up all the Letters, but the Manuscripts and all that is printed thereof shall be burnt before any person appointed for that purpose. I also promise to keep no copy, or copies, of any of the Duke of York's letters, or of any Manuscripts, or of any part thereof. Dated this first day of April, 1809.

Signed: Mary Anne Clarke

Her lawyer, Mr. James Comrie, witnessed the document.

She drove home to Westbourne Place and gave a party . . . but thought of the empty chair at the Horse Guards office.

When her friends had all gone she stood at the drawing room window. Only Bill remained, and Charley, and May Taylor. Bill came and stood beside her, and took her arm.

"The end of an era," he said. "Forget all about it. An unfortunate side of your life that's over and done with."

"Not over and done with at all. What of the future?"

"You've got what you wanted. The children are secure."

"I'm not thinking of that. I'm thinking of Wardle's promises."

"What did he promise you?"

"Castles and coaches-and-four, with the Duke of Kent as a driver holding the whip."

She laughed and would say no more. They finished the wine—the last of Mr. Illingworth's handsome present.

"Did you notice," she said, "a very strange omission in that pompous document I signed today? I promised I would not publish a word about myself and the Duke and our life together. But the promise bound only myself, and not my heirs."

She shrugged her shoulders.

"Do you think the children . . ." began Bill.

"I find the omission intriguing," she said, "that's all."

She drank a toast to the future, and drained the glass.

312

PART FOUR

ONE: They came to her in turn, heaping recrimination on her head: Wardle, Dodd, Folkestone, and lastly, of course, Will Ogilvie—all asking the same question, "Why? What for?"

To each of them she answered, "Security. The children."

"But we held the cards," persisted Wardle. "Our triumph was complete, and the publication of your memoirs, including the Duke's letters, would have been an enormous advantage to our cause."

She shrugged her shoulders.

"Your cause does not interest me," she said. "I fought for you on the floor of the House, and that was enough."

"The letters," moaned Major Dodd, "the precious letters! The bare hint you gave me of their contents would have degraded the Duke of York for life in the eyes of the public, not to mention his own family. The Duke of Kent would have stepped into his shoes, and because of his sober, upright character turned overnight into a revered and adulated figure, whereas now . . ."

"Whereas now," she said, "he's still sitting on his backside down at Ealing, and Sir David Dundas has the job of C.-in-C."

His Radical lordship, solicitous and tender, bent close to her, shaking a doubtful head.

"You promised you would consult me on every point," he said reproachfully. "I understand your longing for security, but to throw away that ace was utter madness. The publication of those memoirs and the letters could have a profound effect upon political life, not only splitting the entire Tory party, dividing the Ministry, and bringing welcome Republican breath on to the benches, where . . ."

"Where, good God, a change of air is needed," she finished for him. "Sweep your House clean, but do it for yourselves. I'm not, and never want to be, a politician. Go home. Your faces bore me."

They went and left her alone, solitude bringing, as it did too often, a swing of the pendulum and aftermath. No doubt she had been a fool—only time could tell—but at least there was money in the bank for Mary and Ellen, and a nest-egg for herself. She was no longer dependent on male magnanimity. The eternal fear was banished, and forever. But what remained? Sit back, and do damn all at thirty-three? Doubt took possession of the shifting mood, clashing, as it did so, with Will Ogilvie.

He said at once, without preliminaries, "You've let me down."

She answered, "I told you long ago—whatever I do in life I do for my children."

"Rubbish! You'd have made a packet from your memoirs and turned the girls into little heiresses. Now you've merely secured them two hundred each for life, a beggarly pittance; and as for your own ten thousand, knowing the way you live and your eye for colour, you'll run through the whole amount in a couple of years. As to the larger issue . . ."

"The larger issue being Buck House empty and the Brunswicks scattered?"

"Put it like that if you choose."

"Quite frankly, Will, I like my pageantry. Red coats and bright cuirasses, polished brass, the King with a crown upon his head—even if he's dotty and wears straws beneath it. I'm romantic about blue blood and God's annointed."

"Oh no, you're not. That's simply your excuse. In the depths of your feminine soul you want him back."

"Want who?"

"Your Duke of York. That's why you gave up the letters and burnt the memoirs. You think, in your devious, womanly way, that by doing this you've made some sort of gesture. That his heart will be touched, that he'll shed

316

a nostalgic tear, and that one of these days his carriage will stop at your door and he'll pull the bell."

"It isn't true."

"Don't lie. I know all your thoughts. Well, put that bonfire out and stamp on it fairly quick. He won't come back; he's sick at the sound of your name. Disgraced in the eyes of the world, and all through you."

This set the light to temper and sent it flaring.

"Advised by a blackmailing, bankrupt army agent . . . My God, you've meddled enough in my affairs. I wish to heaven I'd never set eyes on you."

"And where would you be now if you had not? On your back at Brighton, in some squalid lodging? Thrice nightly, to tipsy week-enders, five bob a time? Or, *faute de mieux,* installed by the faithful Dowler in a hide-out near his home, very pinched and poky? Doing the cooking yourself, become rather blousy, begrudging poor Dowler his dues on a Saturday night."

"On the contrary, I'd have cut out Mrs. Fitz and queened it at Carlton House—or gone out of business. Oh heaven, I hate you, Will, you've been my devil."

"I've been your saviour, but you won't admit it. The question is, what next?"

"Rest on my laurels. Teach my daughters manners."

"And marry them to parsons with twopence a year. Your blameless life will pall . . . What about lovers?"

"I don't need 'em with ten thousand down and four hundred per annum. Beside's, I'm sick of men, they're too demanding."

"Meaning his Radical lordship?"

"Meaning no one—only the race in general. I've won my security through my own sweet efforts, no thanks to you, or Wardle. Where, incidentally, is the promised bonus? The turreted mansion and the coach-and-four?"

"You'd better ask the Member for Okehampton. He'll say, as I do, that you've let him down, and by suppressing those memoirs at this vital moment thrown away weapon one, on which he depended. In other words, you're no further use to him."

"And Kent?"

"Oh, Kent's in a holy terror that he'll be unmasked. I

317

admit I misjudged the man, I thought he had quality, but it's all run to his boots in Germanic fashion. He won't get his brother's job or anybody else's."

"So we're all where we were before?"

"You've hit it precisely. Though Wardle's a popular hero, and you're notorious . . . If not the face that launched a thousand ships, at least your features are stamped on Staffordshire jugs. Cartooned, in bed, in every printer's shop—what more do you ask?"

"A word of thanks for filling the House of Commons. For taking people's minds off the war in Spain."

"You've done that most successfully. All credit to you. The whole of England rings to the name of Clarke. The pity is, it's not going to ring much longer. With the memoirs burnt, you'll merely fade from fashion. There's nothing so dull as living in retirement."

She watched the impassive eyes that never flickered. How much did he say to draw her, to egg her on, what genius lay in his mind for brewing poison?

"I hate ingratitude," she said, "and broken promises."

"When sworn by fools," he suggested, "with swollen heads."

So he disliked Wardle too? She understood. His game had not come out, his plan had miscarried. Somewhere, amidst the turmoil of intrigue, Wardle had blundered badly; and Ogilvie, weaving his spider's web in secret, had seen the grubs escape . . . The web was shattered.

"If," she said, "you'd only be active yourself, instead of employing pawns, you might be successful."

"My physical make-up is such that it irks me to move."

"Is that it? I've often wondered . . ."

But no admissions would follow, no revelations of the hidden life. Where did he go for pleasure or fulfillment? At least, she thought resentfully, never here. Which made at once a bond—and a division. Perhaps, as was his habit, he read her thoughts, for he laughed, and kissed her hand, and said good-night.

"All right, I forgive you," he said, "for burning the memoirs. But ten thousand down has a way of disappearing. Try and double it while you have the chance. Besides,

318

you've only provided for your daughters. Don't the whole of the clan Mackenzie need largesse?"

And with this he took his leave. But he'd pinned her mood, and turned it to the angle opportune, most useful for his purpose, and she knew it.

The turbulent thoughts he had left her with ended in a shadowy, sleepless night, salts in the morning, angry words with Martha.

"The blue gown, not the white."

"The blue gown's torn."

"Then why the devil haven't you had it mended?"

"There's been no time, ma'am, when you wore it yesterday."

"The blue silk, not the satin . . . Don't take my tray, I haven't finished yet. Has the post come? Who's called? Where are my letters?"

"All here, ma'am. On the tray. You'd pushed them aside."

"I thought they were bills. They are bills. Take them away. What, may I ask, is this bunch of withered daisies?"

"Flowers from Mr. Fitzgerald, come this morning."

"Fitzgerald father or son?"

"Mr. William, ma'am."

"At twenty-six he ought to do better than that. His father used to send roses. The stocks declining or Irish blood's run cold, one or the other. Has no one called?"

"Mr. Wright's below."

"Wright the upholsterer?"

"Yes, ma'am. Been here since seven."

"Whom did he think he'd catch at that unchaste hour?"

"He didn't say . . . He said something about Colonel Wardle."

"God forbid I'd keep him here till seven. Have you ever seen Colonel Wardle on my pillow?"

"No never, ma'am . . . How shocking . . ."

"Shocking's the word. One touch of his hand would give me *rigor mortis*. You can tell Wright so, with all my compliments. Now go and fill my bath and stop your gossiping."

Francis Wright had read the papers like everyone else.

Ten thousand pounds paid down to Mrs. Clarke. All snug and safe and secure, said the *Morning Post.* So trade was brisk, or at any rate looking up, and he had not yet been paid for all the furniture.

She floated into the drawing-room, hands extended.

"Dear Mr. Wright, what can I do for you?"

"Well, Mrs. Clarke, it's really about the house."

"About the house?"

"You've had it now five months."

"I know. It suits me well."

"I thought perhaps, with the change in your circumstances, you might want something larger, something grander?"

"Oh no . . . My tastes are humble, as you know. Besides, there's been no change. Only a little pin-money for my daughters."

"I see. Well, if that's the case . . ." He produced his bill. Pages and pages, all the items neatly printed. "This is going back to October of last year, not to mention, of course, the storage before that. Would you like me to read the details one by one?"

"I should hate you to lose your voice, you sound rather husky. That comes of walking abroad at an early hour— quite fatal to queasy throats. You must have some wine."

Mr. Wright was not used to wine at a quarter to ten. By half-past he was puffy and apoplectic, bemused, and talking of boyhood days at Greenwich, the bill thrust back in his waistcoat pocket. And yet he had called for something. Had called for what? He stared at his customer, puzzled, and struggled for words.

"My brother and I agree we must have our dues."

"Your brother's entirely right, and you have my backing. Apply to Colonel Wardle, he promised to pay you. Wasn't there some agreement with a wine merchant called Illingworth?"

"There was. But it's not been honoured."

"How very remiss . . . I can tell you in the strictest confidence, *entre nous*, that Colonel Wardle has acted disgracefully, and not only to you. He has not kept a single promise he made to me. You remember all he said in November last?"

"I think I do. I can't be very sure."

"Oh yes, you can. Those influential friends, a new day to dawn for England—you must remember?"

"I believe he admired the furniture in my store, but he said it was very expensive, I recollect that."

"Expensive, perhaps, but vital to my needs and to the rôle he wished me to play. That's why he promised to pay, and gave you his word."

Wright shook his head. His brain was beginning to clear. "I'm doubtful if we'll get a penny out of him."

"Are you willing to go to law?"

"If our case is clean."

"Of course it's clean. Open and honest-to-God. Write and demand your money, and if he refuses you leave it to me. I'll see that he won't get away. The popular lion, Mr. Wright, is due for a fall."

Mr. Wright was dismissed, declining further sherry. The next caller was Doctor Metcalfe, her physician. He'd attended her on and off for the past ten months, and seen her through the strain of the Investigation, besides hearing bits on the side during moments of stress.

"Mrs. Clarke, your servant, ma'am. Congratulations."

"But on what?"

"On this morning's news. I see that some friends of the Duke have paid you ten thousand pounds, and an annuity for life for you and the girls."

"Oh, that . . . A fleabite in trust, to keep us from starving."

"I see. Not quite what you hoped. How disappointing. The fact is . . ."

"Yes?"

"I'd pinned faith on your future myself. You told me some months ago you had expectations, or shall we say hopes, of rather a different kind, in which I might have a share when they came to pass."

Heaven take all doctors with a bedside manner. A touch of migraine, a four-poster bed changed every sickroom to a confessional. She remembered now the moments of indiscretion, hints dropped because of a sympathetic voice, murmurs of Dodd and Wardle, the Duke of Kent—a rosy future for all her intimate friends. She'd even asked him

321

to dine one January night, he and his wife, to meet both Dodd and Wardle. There'd been some talk of affluence—the wine flowing freely—of patronage, a stir in the medical world. Doctor Metcalfe had seen himself no longer a humble practitioner bringing forth babies, but installed at Windsor, stethoscope to the lungs of grateful princesses.

"I'm sorry," she said. "The truth is, we've been duped. Not only you and I, but others too. Those promises made before the Investigation were merely to get me to the House of Commons; without me they had no case, which they knew very well. And now it's all over they choose to forget their promises. They've no further use for me, or for my friends."

"But, my dear Mrs. Clarke, Major Dodd assured me himself."

"He assured me a hundred things, but not on paper. The human voice, Doctor Metcalfe, can never be proven; only the printed word has legal value. I fancy I have some notes from him upstairs that will make him quake a little, one of these days."

"And Colonel Wardle?"

"Is the public idol. But only for the moment—the phase will pass. There's nothing like a little ridicule to bring a popular favourite to his knees and turn the crowd against him—you leave it to me."

"But my prospects, Mrs. Clarke, my dwindling practice? I admit I've let things slide the past few months, with such high hopes for the future, and then my wife, she's not in good health as you know, so many expenses . . ."

The old, old story. The pill with the sugar coating. They were all going to flock like vultures to seize the pickings. She hastily scribbled a cheque and passed it to him, saw him to the door, and patted his shoulder. Will Ogilvie was right again, as usual. Ten thousand was a beggarly sum, it should have been twenty.

The next visitor was Charley, frowning, disgruntled, kicking the legs of the furniture not yet paid for.

"Now it's all over, what's going to happen to me?"

"I'll see that you get a job."

"But what sort of job? I won't lick anyone's boots, I won't be dependent. What about all that talk of reinstatement, quashing the Court Martial verdict, a new commission?"

"Darling, we've got to face it. The brutes were bluffing."

"Well, can't you do something about it, show them up?"

"I haven't had time to think . . . For the Lord's sake, leave me. First Wright, then Metcalfe, then you, all begging assistance. I thought Coxshead-Marsh had invited you down to Loughton?"

"He said something about a job as estate agent, under his bailiff—the sort of thing for a servant. I'm trained as a soldier. I'm damned if I'm going to accept some menial position, when, with my qualifications, I ought to command. Surely there's someone you know who would pull a few strings? By the way, I want some money. I haven't a penny."

Thank heaven May Taylor was fixed—a public subscription for her and her sister Sarah had been started in the House by Samuel Whitbread, and subscribed to by all the Opposition members.

And lastly George, no longer a Chelsea cadet, his uniform, loved and prized, packed away in a trunk, his blue eyes, large and trusting, fixed on his mother.

"I don't quite see what all the row's about. Why have I got to go to some other school?"

"Because, my angel, there's been a big military scandal. His Royal Highness is no longer Commander-in-Chief, and therefore no longer head of the Chelsea Asylum. Your connection with him is known, and it just wouldn't do. I must send you somewhere else where there won't be gossip."

She saw a look of Charley, sulky, obstinate, more dreams of the clan Mackenzie bruised or shattered.

"I bet you spoilt things with your silly quarrel. Nothing's been the same since Gloucester Place."

"I know, my pet. But Mother can't explain. One day, perhaps, when you're older, you'll know what happened."

His answer was a drooping lip, a sullen boyish shrug, and suddenly the first glance of mistrust, of doubt, of apprehension in the eyes.

"I can still go into the Army? You promised me that. On my fifth birthday you sat on my bed and swore it."

"I swear it still. I'll never break my word."

Prison, the rack, the pillory, any ordeal—she would go to the stake for George, and his heart's desire.

In the meantime, though, to business, and satisfaction from Wardle, Dodd and Co. Both gentlemen, summoned to dine, proved very evasive, stayed for an hour, then hurriedly made their escape. When pressed to call again they were noncommittal. She gave them three weeks' grace, then penned her letter, despatched on May fourteenth to Colonel Wardle:

Dear sir,

When I sent for you the other day and you were accompanied by Major Dodd, to enquire what were your intentions with respect to putting your promises into execution, you seemed unwilling to admit that they were made unconditionally—I say they were.

The only construction I can put upon it is this, that you felt yourself under a heavy responsibility to me, which both you and Major Dodd thought to get rid of by future promises as futile as they were evasive.

I will here put you once more in mind of those promises and of my expectations, which, if you value yourselves as men of honour, you cannot but accede to, nor can you think I require anything but what I am fully entitled to— nothing less than five hundred a year; and as my children have been equal sufferers with myself in the public opinion, as being the daughters of so indiscreet a mother, they demand from me every thing I can or ought to command. Therefore as five hundred a year for my own life, which may be short, would be of no advantage to them, I think that by letting you off for ten thousand pounds is not half your promises to me. I expect you and Major Dodd to enter into a joint bond as you did into joint promises, for ten thousand pounds, to be paid within two years, and till that be accomplished, to pay me five hundred a year, commencing from March last, and to pay Wright the remainder of his bill.

This is all, and surely it is not half the value of the promises made to me, which were these! As my son was then under the protection of the Duke of York, and of course would lose that protection as soon as I began on the Duke's ruin, he was to have equal protection from the Duke of Kent. I withdrew my son, and I have him now on my hands.

The next was a situation for Captain Thompson, in some way, or enough to keep him, or in the event of the Duke of Kent coming in as Commander-in-Chief, to get him reinstated in the army. He still remains as he was! The next, the payment of the arrears of annuity, as promised me by the Duke of York, and the annuity to be continued to me during my life of four hundred; my debts to be paid, those contracted while I lived with the Duke of York and those since.

The debt of twelve hundred pounds which is owing to Mr. Comrie, my lawyer, for which he stops my jewels. My present house and furniture to be paid for, of which a part only is paid by you and Dodd.

Now, let me ask, if the ten thousand pounds is equal to half these promises, and for the fulfillment of which you pledged yourself in the most solemn manner to see performed? I shall add but little more, but even were this sum to come out of your own pocket, in view of the character you have acquired through my means it would not be more than I am fully entitled to. Take a fortnight to consider. After that time do not depend upon my secrecy. I shall consider myself at liberty to make what use I please of the copy of this letter.

> I remain, dear Sir,
> Yours, etc., etc.,
> Mary Anne Clarke

And that, she thought, Mr. Freeman of London City, you can put in your golden casket, or anywhere else, but you won't feel so smug when you see it in print in the *Times*.

T W O : "What have you done to Wardle?"

"Why do you ask?"

"I saw him in the House before coming here. I happened to mention your name and he turned pale grey, muttered a word I can't repeat, and disappeared."

"A word beginning with *b* and ending with *h?*"

"Well, yes—since you're so perceptive. I nearly attacked him. After all you've done for the fellow. I can't understand it. His absurd popularity's due entirely to you, and the least he can do is to show some sense of feeling."

"That's the trouble. He feels too much. I don't wonder he's pale."

"You mean he wants to make love and you've turned him down?"

Lord Folkestone, his eyes on sticks, shifted position. He was one of those men who looked better fully clothed. A certain angularity of outline put him to disadvantage when in drawers. And yet in a velvet coat at about half-past ten, his shoulders well padded, standing in a drawing-room ... imagination painted a brighter picture.

"No. Nothing of the sort. He owes me money."

She turned on her side and yawned, then drank some water. His Radical lordship realised with disappointment that his night was over. *Rien ne va plus, la suite au prochain numéro* . . .

"Then you *were* his mistress?"

"Never in this world. He knew he couldn't win his case without me. The same goes for all His Majesty's Opposition, which said such pretty things two months ago, yourself, William Pleydell-Bouverie, included."

So that's how the land was lying. How very distressing. "If you'd only published your memoirs . . ." he began.

"My memoirs have nothing to do with promises made."

"Did Wardle really give you some guarantee?"

She leant on her elbow, turning up the lamp. "Now listen, my youthful protagonist. Was I likely to get myself smirched with the dirt of ages, to have my reputation torn to shreds, my personal history hiccoughed in every ale-house, unless I had something to gain when the thing was done?"

His sharp thin face looked surprised in the sudden lamp-light.

"Well, no . . . But I thought some motive of revenge, your treatment by the Duke, and a common cause . . ."

"What cause, ye gods?"

"The British people's welfare, the future of England . . ."

"Future of England, nonsense! My future, you mean. L.s.d., plus a bonus, for Mary Anne Clarke. Thank God I'm not a hypocrite, like the rest of you. I know what I've always wanted, and tried to get it. At times I've succeeded with a splash, then taken a beating. I backed your friend Colonel Wardle, thinking it paid me. Now he's ratted, like his master, the Duke of Kent."

His eager eyes lit up. In an instant the dishevelled hair was smoothed and immaculate, the vest buttoned over his narrow chest. Charm began to return—alas, too late.

"Good God! Then the tale *was* true!"

"Of course it was true. And only idealists like you and Francis Burdett swallowed the line of talk about England's freedom. The thing was a put-up job from the very beginning. Kent hoped to sit at the Horse Guards as C.-in-C., with dear Colonel Wardle Secretary for War. As for Dodd, I really don't know! Some perquisite, with a pension. For myself, any number of houses, carriages, coaches, thousands of pounds in the bank and more business than ever."

He was dressed. He was ready to go. The enchantment was over, the world of ideals crashing about his ears. It was just as well the House would soon rise for the summer recess. The rumours would then blow over and be forgotten, and he himself have a moment to feel his position. It would never do to be connected with any sort of scandal that might arise.

"Are you going to take any action?" He put on his coat.

"Ask Colonel Wardle. You said he was looking pale."

"Then you are. You mean to publish this in the papers?"

She smiled and rested her hands behind her head. "I'm not yet sure. He hasn't answered my letter."

"I can swear, in perfect honesty, I am innocent. My only thought has been for the public good."

He stood by the door, fully dressed and exceedingly nervous.

"Your only thought? But what about compassion? Surely faith in a fallen woman came in somewhere?"

She looked at him and laughed. He opened the door, but dignity was ruined by stockinged feet. He'd left his shoes in the hall as a matter of prudence . . .

"When shall I see you again?"

He seemed embarrassed. "I have to go to the country very soon."

"I'm sure you have. June is always delightful. Gardens and roses and strawberries—how I adore them."

"I'll write, of course."

"But isn't that rather risky? I might take it into my head to publish your letters."

He was gone. She heard him tittup down the stairs, grope for his shoes in the dark, and creep from the house.

Well, that was that. Another peer gone west, crossed off the slate and thrown in the paper-basket. Not that she really minded—the liaison bored her—but viscounts didn't grow on gooseberry bushes and contact was useful, giving a certain cachet. Moreover the future Earl of Radnor was a widower. However, there it was, never count the losses.

In the meantime, not a word from Colonel Wardle. Francis Wright reported that when he called, with a humble request to see the popular Member, the servant had slammed the door, saying his master knew no upholsterer of the name of Wright and was busily engaged on Parliament business.

"So what do I do now?" asked the anxious tradesman.

"Send in your bill, Mr. Wright, with this note enclosed."

The following note was left at the colonel's house:

Francis Wright's respectful compliments to the Colonel, and he has taken the liberty to enclose his bill. As the articles were to be charged for ready money, having met with a most serious disappointment, will thank him to settle the balance, and for that purpose will call upon him tomorrow morning at eleven o'clock.

No answer, and no admittance. The Member for Okehampton was not at home.

"What now, ma'am?"

"Off with the gloves and see a lawyer."

Mr. Stokes, a partner in the firm of Comrie, Stokes & Son, known to Mrs. Clarke for many years, was ready to oblige. The case was clear. If dirty linen was washed, it would all be Wardle's.

On the second day of June, Francis Wright, upholsterer, sent notice of an action to be brought against Gwyllym Lloyd Wardle, of St. James's Street, for recovery of the sum of two thousand pounds, owing him for furniture bought and delivered to Mrs. M. A. Clarke, of Westbourne Place, and ordered by the aforesaid Gwyllym Wardle. The case was appointed to be heard at Westminster Hall, the following month, on the third day of July.

Confusion, panic, and horror sprang up in St. James's Street. The news-hawks blazoned the story in the papers. The lion of the British public trembled, seeing his popularity vanish in vapour, and the British public itself rubbed a puzzled eye. Could it be that the conqueror of corruption, who had battled for honour and truth, had feet of clay? That the people's darling, Freeman of London City, had tried to sneak out of paying a tradesman's bill? Forget the Peninsular War, here was juice for the jaded. The news brought an outraged Dowler up from Uxbridge.

"Mary Anne . . . You must be insane."

"Why so? What's the matter?"

"Plunging into publicity once again, just when you had the chance to let scandal die."

"But I've nothing to lose, and the poor brothers Wright want their money."

"That isn't the point. Their bill could be paid from your trust—Coxhead-Marsh and myself could have settled it all in an instant."

"Pay Wright from the trust? Good God, what a frightful suggestion, when somebody else can be tapped. I don't owe

329

Wright a penny. It was Wardle who ordered the furniture, all you see here, mirrors and carpets and curtains, it was none of my doing?"

"My dearest girl, you expect me to swallow that story?"

"It's the truth, and my lawyer can prove it."

"With you in the box?"

"Of course, if I'm called. I didn't do badly before. Besides, the cream of the joke . . . no, I don't think I'll tell you!"

"There's no joke in the business at all, the action's disgraceful. I've been down at Uxbridge—my poor father's practically dying—and my one consolation was thinking of you and the children, now happily settled without any worries or troubles, and perhaps in the autumn, I thought, I might find a cottage, not far from my home, where you could be all quietly installed. And then, in the long winter evenings . . ."

"Shut up, or I'll scream. I'm *not* happily settled, I *won't* lose myself in the country, and as for the long winter evenings I'm damned if I'll spend them mooning around like a moron and yawning my head off."

"Very well. Then don't call upon me when you find you're in trouble."

"I shall call upon you just when, and as often, as I choose. Now come over here and sit down, and stop pulling that face—you look like a curate about to finish the Lesson. Doesn't anyone rumple your hair in the backwoods of Uxbridge?"

Apparently not. It was one of the pleasures discarded, belonging to happier times and the high spots of Hampstead. No more was therefore said about the action. Bill Dowler returned to Uxbridge mute but mellow. And, she kept the cream of the joke to taste alone, which was, of course, that the Prosecutor against Wardle, in the course of his usual duties upon King's Bench, would be her late antagonist—the Attorney-General.

The introduction to his chambers in Lincoln's Inn—her lawyer, Mr. Comrie, by her side, with Francis and Daniel Wright in their Sunday clothes—made up for every distress in the House of Commons. Sir Vicary Gibbs, his pince-nez on his nose, received them with cordial grace.

Formalities passed. Questions were asked and answered. Notes were taken. Legal matters were tossed between legal minds.

Mr. Comrie, having another appointment at five, took his leave at four, with his partner Mr. Stokes, followed almost at once by the brothers Wright. The chief witness for the prosecution lingered. The Attorney-General closed his door, and smiled, and rose to the top of his height, which was five foot four.

"A master stroke," he said: "my congratulations." And removing his pince-nez he opened a bottle of brandy. "Too early in the day?"

"No, rather too late. I could have done with some of that on the first of February."

"I'd have sent you round a bottle had I known. But I thought you were well supplied by the Opposition?"

"They never got further than coffee and glasses of water."

"That's the worst of the Whigs, they won't put their hands in their pockets. Surely Folkestone treated you well?"

"He said it with flowers."

"No use on an empty stomach, with nerves in pieces. No Radical has the smallest ounce of perception; but I'm rather surprised at Folkestone, brought up in France. I'd have said he'd conduct his business with more finesse. The fault of youth, these things need a riper judgement."

"*Si jeunesse pouvait . . .*"

"Oh, can't it? How very lamentable. I thought that was youth's only possible stock-in-trade. The Tories will be delighted. May I quote you?

"Rather unfair, don't you think? We all have our failings."

"To give them their due, the Whigs usually have the muscle. We muster the brains, that's why we govern the country. Tell me, were you exhausted by your ordeal in the House?"

"I lost half a stone."

"I don't wonder. We kept you hard at it and gave you no quarter. I was fairly exhausted myself—but you look very well."

"I have powers of resilience."

331

"You must have. I used to know Barrymore—where is he now?"

"Dear Cripplegate? Somewhere in Ireland. Bogged down by marriage, of course, and harnessed to horses."

"Jamie Fitzgerald's another I used to know well."

"James is disgruntled. He lives in perpetual panic that I'm going to publish his letters and keeps writing from Dublin."

"Would they be entertaining?"

"To the Government, not to the public. The Protestant outlook, as seen by an Irish M.P."

"Try Christie's. I'll put in a bid."

"He's got most of them back. I'm not grasping by nature, it's that I've children to keep."

"More brandy?"

"Why not?"

A knock at the door of the chambers. Sir Vicary Gibbs readjusted his gown and wig.

"Who's there?"

A voice from without, "Lord Chief Justice Ellenborough, sir, below in his carriage, come to collect you. You're dining with him in the Lords, he says have you forgotten?"

"No, no . . . Tell his Lordship to go, I shall follow on foot."

He turned to his visitor. "Can you give me a lift in your carriage? It's all on your way back to Chelsea, if it's not inconvenient."

"Delighted. Whenever you please."

"That's exceedingly good of you. The bishops are giving a dinner in honour of Ellenborough. I mustn't be late, but as long as I'm there by six-thirty . . . It's not every day that I have an encounter like this."

He glanced at the clock on the mantelpiece and finished his brandy.

"This upholsterer business," he said, "is it all above-board?"

"We've got Wardle on toast," she replied, "he can't wriggle out of it."

"Did he promise to pay?"

"There was no limit to his promises last November."

"The earth and its contents, oh, quite . . . but the matter before us?"

"I used what finesse I possess, and so fixed him completely."

"That's fine, all is well. I imagine he'll give us no trouble. A verdict for Wright, and the popular patriot deflated. There's nothing in it for you, I'm afraid, except more notoriety. Is that why you do it?"

"Good God, no. I've had all I need."

"Then why?"

She put down her glass, smoothed her gown, and glanced out of the window.

"I wanted to meet you," she said. "There was no other way. Mrs. Clarke and Sir Vicary Gibbs make a good combination."

The Attorney-General was half an hour late at the Lords . . .

As June progressed, the Member for Okehampton endeavoured to settle the action out of court. He was unsuccessful; Plaintiff would not withdraw. And Plaintiff's witness found preparation pleasant, the visits to Lincoln's Inn extremely rewarding. All things considered, the summer proved amusing; it was a novel event to provide light relief for the Bench. And far less fatiguing than punching those pillows for Folkestone. His Radical lordship still styled himself an admirer, but wrote from a distance—pen-friendship was safe, within limits.

He forgot it was always incautious to write after dinner. The pen ran more freely, the thoughts flowed at ease and at random. A note scrawled at midnight was never the same in the morning, when read at breakfast by a lady who kept correspondence, and that letter of June twenty-seventh might damn him one day. Her discerning eye passed rapidly over the pages, written from Coleshill House one idle evening.

. . . I wish I had some news to send you in return for your entertaining letter, but from this sequestered spot you can expect none, indeed since I came here I have done nothing but wander about the fields by myself, and eat strawberries, things which are very wholesome, but altogether uninteresting to relate. Your letter, on the con-

trary, is full of interesting matter, whereon such a hermit as I am at this place, whether he be of a contemplative turn of mind or not, might chew the cud of reflection for many a day. I think, from what you say, there will be hell to pay, when the matter comes on for trial. The whole affair must out, and the Royal Brother, Dodd, and Wardle will be exposed. I lament that they do not foresee this, and prevent the éclat. I do not guess what Wardle means to do, I suppose he will trust to his popularity to bear him through, but that will not do—for after all, though his part has not been so base as that of the other two, it has been a dirty one, and he has suffered himself to be made an instrument of by them.

The thing, however, will do no good to the Royal Family in general, for though the Duke's friends will attempt to invalidate your testimony, there is so much evidence in your statements, so many corroborating circumstances, and so many people know so many instances of this kind, that the public will not be induced to believe your testimony false.

I suppose the public prints will endeavour to mix me up with the prenamed trio, but this is quite impossible. Whitbread, Burdett, and myself can in no degree be involved —at least I have no doubt but that they are as clear as I know myself to be.

I could contemplate with amusement, and observe all these intrigues at work, with philosophical indifference, were I not fearful you would be the sufferer. I tremble for the settlement of your affairs, which I should presume to be now more distant than ever?

I am afraid that you will be tired of this scrawl, which is nearly illegible. Pray let me hear from you again when anything occurs, and you have a moment for writing. Your letters sent to Harley Street, as usual, will meet me. Adieu!

Ever sincerely yours—Folkestone.

Into the box with the others, and tied up with tape.

On the third of July, at the Court of Common Pleas, Westminster Hall, before the Lord Chief Justice, the action Wright versus Wardle was heard and tried. Excitement was in the air. The court was packed. It might have been Drury Lane on an opening night.

Mrs. Clarke, in white, with a hat of flimsy straw cocked at an angle, made her appearance to subdued applause. Her audience, mostly male—for daughters and wives were still struggling in the queue in Palace Yard—leant forward, eyes agleam and shoulders touching (they were chiefly Members of the House of Commons, and Tory ones at that), but what surprised them was the Attorney-General's strangely youthful bearing. The man had lost twenty years, had become debonair. A dog with a dozen tails could not surpass him. As he rose to open the case for the Prosecution he might have been Lancelot himself at Lyonesse. The voice that had sent a chill to so many spines, hard and forbidding, held a new liquid quality. Lush notes came forth like a nightingale in spring.

"An honest, working tradesman has been defrauded. A woman and mother has been wronged."

Good heavens! Lord Chief Justice Ellenborough wiped his forehead. Had old Vinegar Gibbs got religion, or was he dreaming? A hot July, of course—he might have been drinking. But what was all this about rats and feminine frailty? Asps at Cleopatra's bosom . . . venom . . . ingratitude? Women who gave their all? Babes in the gutter? The Lord Chief Justice winced—what a *volte-face*. How different from February last, in the House of Commons. His friend the Attorney-General must be slipping. Rhetoric passed to banter, and His Lordship relaxed. This was more like it, the old familiar sneering, covert suggestions, polishing of the pince-nez, a tongue like a two-edged dagger probing defences. The wretched defendant had shrunk to the size of a sparrow, and serve him right for bringing those shocking charges—the fellow deserved to be horse-whipped and sent from the country—but even so it pained the Lord Chief Justice to see the Attorney-General so flamboyant, so lavish of eye and of gesture, a peacock in plummage; it lowered the tone of the Bench and was rather distasteful. If this was the result of contact with the Plaintiff's chief witness, an encounter or two prior to action, the Judge disapproved. And those grins from spectators, those nudges and diggings of elbows suggested a spirit of levity highly misplaced.

His Lordship called "Order," tapped sharply, and made himself felt. A frown at Sir Vicary Gibbs brought the speech to a close. A word or two later in chambers would settle ill-feeling, and in the meantime the Court must observe that the Judge held the scales. An opening sting to the witness would show his position, and perhaps bring a blush to her cheeks, and so restore balance.

She flaunted her way to the box amid smiles of approval, whispers, and murmurs, then somebody shouted, "Go get him."

The Lord Chief Justice stiffened, tapped again.

"The Court will be cleared unless there is absolute silence."

The murmurs died down. The witness was sworn and stood waiting. His Lordship observed her, and said with emphasis, "Under whose protection, madam, are you now?"

The witness raised her eyes and answered softly, "I thought, my Lord, that I was under yours."

It was this, more than anything else, that settled the action. Laughter, led by the Jury, set the tone, and the case, like a river in spate, rippled on to conclusion.

The Attorney-General spooned his witness bait, fed her with frivolous sop . . . The Court applauded. The Lord Chief Justice could not interrupt them. The pair were playing a game that defied intervention, they were matched like reel and rod and there was no unwinding. They juggled in jargon, dabbled in *doubles-entendres*, wallowed in each other's witticisms, and all at the expense of the Defendant.

Colonel Wardle went to the warehouse, Mrs. Clarke? Then tell us about him, what was the furniture chosen? Colonel Wardle praised a sideboard—was it mirrored? And what about the bronze and scarlet carpet that Colonel Wardle insisted on for the bedroom? It was too large for Westbourne Place—alterations were needed, a piece cut off the end on Colonel Wardle's orders. Some trouble with the bed? The legs were missing. Colonel Wardle suggested lampstands upside down. It was perfectly safe

336

if pressure was not used. Had Francis Wright concurred in the suggestion? Francis Wright was unmarried and lived with his brother, Daniel; they both slept in single beds, and could not say. But Colonel Wardle knew that lamp-stands served, he had stayed in a coffeehouse in Cadogan Square—*persona grata*—where such things were used. With ordinary precautions, there could be no disaster. Had Colonel Wardle admired a marble statue? Yes, Aphrodite rising from the foam, and a miniature one in bronze of Leda's swan. Both were highly ornamental to a mantel-piece, when viewed from the side, or so Colonel Wardle said. Mrs. Clarke was reluctant to have them, because of the children—young minds were so quick to seize upon ideas—but Colonel Wardle was exceedingly temperamental and couldn't compose a speech without inspiration.

Then Westbourne Place had been a home from home? Oh, very decidedly. Not at the request of the witness. The colonel was always appearing at awkward hours. He was found by the maid one morning at eight o'clock examining Leda's swan with a microscope. And so on, until the outraged Lord Chief Justice raised his hand for silence and cleared the Court.

The witness withdrew and the proceedings settled down. Brother Daniel Wright gave sober, solemn evidence, and when the Defending Counsel, Mr. Park, rose to speak, he knew he had lost. His client was beaten before he reached the box. Colonel Wardle faltered, fumbled, failed; his "That I deny," repeated again and again, was scarcely heard.

Notes of despair were passed between the lawyers. Witnesses Glennie and Dodd were never called—their evidence was deemed too damaging to help the cause, when the cause was already dead. The concluding speeches were brief; there was no need for eloquence. The scales were tipped and His Lordship threw in his hand.

The Jury gave a verdict for Francis Wright. His Lordship found the Defendant, Gwyllym Wardle, guilty of owing the Plaintiff two thousand pounds, this sum to be paid within three months.

The patriot had lost and Old Palace Yard, the scene of his former triumph, was deserted. The crowds that had cheered him in April had all gone home. Colonel Wardle drove away, his carriage closed.

The Attorney-General escorted his witness to chambers.

"He'll appeal, of course, or bring a case against you."

"What then?"

"I shall defend you."

"How can you, if you're Public Prosecutor?"

"My dear, I do as I please. I can switch my rôle."

"But isn't that rather unfair?"

"It makes for variety."

"Attorney-General turned into Learned Counsel?"

"Yes, it mellows the mood, and helps to broaden judgement. If you'd rather have someone else by all means do so."

"Oh no . . . united we stand. Shall we get the same Judge?"

"Eddie Ellenborough? Very probably. And if we do we'll have to mind our manners. We mightn't be so successful a second time. As it is, I foresee a certain coolness coming; it was only his Tory principles today that prevented him leading the Jury in favour of Wardle."

"Those shaggy eyebrows . . . What is he like at home?"

"Petulant and proud, and damned intolerant."

"Perhaps that's just a façade and he needs understanding."

"You're welcome to try your powers, he's a frigid old fellow."

"All judges must be cold-blooded, it goes with their nature. If they weren't, there wouldn't be any British justice. I suppose when they're promoted to the Bench they turn monastic . . . Now, when a man takes silk . . ."

"Must we discuss it now? Am I taking you home?"

"But I love legal chat . . ."

"I detest it. My question's repeated."

"Your question was not understood. You must alter the phrasing."

"Does Witness permit Learned Counsel to give her instruction?"

"*Chez vous,* or *chez moi?*"

"*Chez* wherever you please."

"Then how about coming to dine at Westbourne Place and giving Counsel's opinion on Leda's swan?"

In St. James's Street the defendant, Gwyllym Wardle, alone and embittered, sat down to compose a letter, which he addressed to the people of the United Kingdom.

THREE: *Honoured as my Parliamentary conduct has been by the approbation of so many of my countrymen, I feel myself called upon, in consequence of an event that yesterday took place, immediately to address you, and that in vindication of my character, rendered open to attack from the verdict of the Jury, upon the evidence of Mrs. Clarke and Mr. Wright, the brother of the Upholsterer, in a cause in which I was defendant, in the Court of King's Bench.*

The detail of the evidence the public prints will afford. It is with me to state that my Counsel, satisfied in their own minds that the jury would not, upon such testimony as had been given by the plaintiff's brother and Mrs. Clarke alone, find a verdict against me, did not comply with my earnest entreaty, repeated to them in writing during the trial, in the strongest terms, that Major Dodd and Mr. Glennie and other respectable witnesses might be examined, as I knew their testimony would be founded in truth, and in direct contradiction to what had been sworn against me.

Under such circumstances the verdict was obtained.

There only remains for me now, before my God and my Country, to declare that it was obtained by perjury alone; and I do pledge myself to prove that fact the earliest moment the forms of the law will allow me to do so.

Anxiously, therefore, do I look forward to that period; and I trust that till then the public will suspend their judgement upon the case. With sentiments of the deepest gratitude and respect, I remain your ever faithfully devoted Servant,

G. L. Wardle.

The letter was published in every newspaper on July fifth, and at once discussed with avidity. The question was, would anyone reply?

On the sixteenth of the month, Mrs. M. A. Clarke published an address in the *National Register:*

To the People of the United Kingdom.

Honoured as my testimony before the House of Commons has been with the confidence of the country at large, and sanctioned as my evidence has been in a recent instance by a jury of my Countrymen, I feel myself called upon (after affording time for the most deliberate reflection) to address you, in consequence of a circumstance which has arisen out of the Cause in which Mr. Wright, an Upholsterer, was plaintiff; Colonel Wardle, defendant; and Mr. Daniel Wright, brother of the plaintiff, and myself were witnesses.

In this Cause it is well known that Colonel Wardle was cast, to the satisfaction of every honest tradesman, and indeed of everybody in the Court.

The detail of evidence the public prints will afford: as for my testimony, these details are somewhat inaccurate, but they are sufficiently correct to have enabled the public to strengthen this verdict with an almost universal approbation.

Colonel Wardle, inflated by a popularity the extent of which was as unexpected as it will be found to have been undeserved, had vainly flattered himself that this same popularity would protect him against the justice of his country: disappointed at the verdict, he has lost his prudence with his temper, and without giving himself time for reflection, has made an unusual Appeal to the People of the United Kingdom against the Verdict of a Jury.

If he had been content to throw the blame of his failure upon Counsel, it would have been no business of mine, they are able to defend themselves; but to be charged with a crime so disgraceful, so low, so contemptible, and by a person who of all men best knows how abhorrent to my nature is anything like falsehood—to be charged with perjury is really too bad.

It only remains for me to declare before God and my country that the evidence I gave was strictly true, and

*that my intimacy with Colonel Wardle merely related to
my evidence and his promises.*

*Most anxiously therefore do I look forward to the
period when the futility of Colonel Wardle's attempts to
prove the contrary will recoil upon himself and others. I
trust that till then the public will suspend their judgement
upon Colonel Wardle's intemperate accusation.*

*Although it may not be equally proper in me, as in
Colonel Wardle, to state the gratitude and respect I feel
for the public approbation, yet I hope it is not denied
even unto me to express the anguish of mind I should endure, if upon such an occasion, and in such a manner, I
had really deserved their disapprobation.*

I have the honour to be,

With the greatest respect,
M. A. Clarke

Whether the British public really cared one way or the
other was very doubtful. But the subject made lively chat
at a dinner table. Hostesses—with the fish—plunged into
discussion, and when the port was passed and the ladies
had risen, the topic was seized on again and went well
with the brandy. I wonder who's keeping her now? made
diverting debate. What with Parliament risen for the summer recess and the Members scattered, it was small wonder the windows were shuttered at Westbourne Place. Has
she gone out of town? I don't know, they say she's at
Brighton. Is that so? Tubby Clifton declares she was seen
at Southampton. On shore or at sea? In the Solent, a pen-
chant for prawning . . . No rocks, most unlikely. What's
the betting she's found in a frigate? Pooh! The fleet's at
Gibraltar, not so much as a pinnace at Portsmouth . . .

As a matter of fact, Mrs. Clarke was at Cowes with the
children. The air on the island was healthy—Spithead in
the offing—and what with the yachts in the roads and in
the Medina, excursions to Ventnor and picknicking parties
at Wootten, the long summer days proved refreshing, except for letters.

James Fitzgerald kept pestering from Ireland. He hoped
to see her in August. Was it true she had kept a few
scraps of his indiscreet letters, or would she swear faithfully they'd all been returned to his son? As for Willie,

the father was worried; the boy had got into some scrape, had she heard any rumours?

She had. She had spent a whole evening before leaving town, with Willie in tears in the drawing-room, begging assistance. A young lady was in trouble—her condition becoming suspicious; pills had been taken *ad nauseam*, but nothing had happened and the young lady's husband was due any day from abroad. Did Mrs. Clarke know of a doctor? What were his charges?

She immediately summoned the Metcalfes and swore them to silence. The young lady was offered asylum, but Willie was refused, the young lady's condition being such as commanded abstention—all this with the children arriving, and packing for Cowes.

"The things I do for my friends!" said Mary Anne, the young lady packed up in blankets and put in a post-chaise, with Mrs. Metcalfe in charge—and two minutes later the girls in a carriage with Martha, their faces glued to the window and all of them waving.

"Scrape's the word," she wrote from Cowes to James Fitzgerald. "Forget the letters you scribbled me in 1805 and keep a watch on Willie, he merits attention . . ." If she cared to spill the beans on the feckless Fitzgeralds, the results would fill a volume—but no one would print it.

The repercussions from the Wright versus Wardle action continued to fill the papers. It seemed very likely, viewed from the shelter of Cowes, that the autumn would prove vindictive: no time had been lost by Colonel Wardle in filing a counter-action. An Action for Conspiracy, Wardle versus Wright and Clarke, was due to be heard on King's Bench in early December. So it was essential to hold the right cards and to play them. Thus it was an amazing stroke of fortune that Lord Chief Justice Ellenborough suffered a rupture and sent for a physician—his own was away—and the locum turned out to be Doctor Thomas Metcalfe.

The bedside manner, with successful treatment, worked wonders in a week and was duly reported and seized upon with glee, of course, at Cowes. Hope springs eternal . . . Much might be accomplished. Strings in the legal world lay between the fingers, if his Lordship was now a patron of the doctor's.

A letter was dashed off from Cowes to Thomas Metcalfe:

. . . I have hit on a plan, which if you think well of proposing to your friend and patron, might put you in the way of exercising your abilities in your profession, and otherwise make you comfortable. If put into practice or not, you will see the confidence I place in you by penning it, and of course it must ever be a secret between ourselves; but if once or twice in your patron's company, I am certain of succeeding, for all I want is his interest in an affair of mine, and this is not to be gained without making myself very pleasant, and so on.

Now if he, as your friend, will take you a small house and furnish it, which will not cost him more than five hundred pounds (and what is that trifle to him?) I will either be your lodger, inmate or patient, and for which I will pay you as much as will enable Mrs. M. with her economy to keep your house, and you shall have the use of my carriage, for a doctor is nothing without one.

All he has to do, with your permission, is to call once or twice a week, when it is dusk, and play a game or two of piquet, or any other game with which His Worship is au fait!

Think of this well, will you? And fail not writing to me to-morrow.

Yours truly,
M. A. Clarke

Your patron would not meet with such a disinterested offer every day—he is old now, you know—but it is so pleasant to have a great man or two in tow.

It was more pleasant still to have the Judge on her side and keep the Attorney-General on his toes.

On Monday, December eleventh at Westminster Hall, the action Wardle versus Wright and Clarke was held before the Lord Chief Justice Ellenborough. The parties at piquet had proved successful.

Counsel for the Defence was the Attorney-General, whose curious legal switch caused excited chatter. Those in the know said politics was the reason—the case was not Wardle versus Clarke but Whig versus Tory, and the Ministry couldn't afford to let Wardle win. But what depressed the spectators in the gallery, who had hoped for a repetition of the scenes in July, was the fact that Mrs. Clarke was not called as a witness. She sat, discreetly veiled, beside her Counsel, and spent the day passing notes to him under her mantle.

Mr. Alley, who opened the case for the Prosecution, started off with a bang about Scylla and Charybdis, vicarious quicksands and navigators' perils, and passed from them to a woman who, he alleged, had lived with Englishmen, Irishmen, Scotsmen, Welshmen, soldiers, sailors, agents, lords, and commoners—Mrs. Clarke was observed to be counting on her fingers—and, after a lengthy reprise of past events that had taken place in England since the Conquest, he proceeded to talk of corruption, and Corsican bandits, and jugglers who aspired to the highest places.

At this point the Lord Chief Justice interrupted.

"Pray, Mr. Alley, do you think this bears upon the question under consideration?"

"I really think it does, My Lord. With great deference I am endeavouring to show that this case originated in corruption."

Lord Ellenborough sighed. "Why, Mr. Alley, if you really think that going over the history of Bonaparte and the present state of Europe has any bearing upon the issue, I shall hear you, but to my mind the connection seems somewhat remote."

Mr. Alley continued for a further twenty minutes and ended with the words, "The safety of the British Empire is at this moment entrusted to the twelve gentlemen now in that box; I have no doubt they will act upon the dying words of our immortal hero, 'England expects every man to do his duty.' "

He sat down, perspiration pouring. No applause. The Attorney-General leapt to his feet in a second.

"Before this case is gone into, I should wish my learned friend Mr. Alley to inform me whom he meant by the arch-juggler who aspires to a situation to which neither his birth nor his education entitles him?"

Mrs. Clarke was head to whisper, "Don't be touchy."

The Lord Chief Justice frowned and shook his head.

"I do not think," he said, "that I can in this state of the proceedings call upon the Learned Counsel for an explanation."

The trial went on. Minutes of the action were read at length. Colonel Wardle was called, the same old ground was covered, the warehouse visit, the choosing of curtains and carpets—but this time the lighter side was left untouched. Sir Vicary Gibbs introduced a sterner note. The name of the Duke of Kent was constantly mentioned.

"On your first visit to Mrs. Clarke last November, did you not tell her the Duke of Kent was acquainted with the proceedings against the Duke of York?"

"Neither on my first visit nor on my second."

"Do you swear that the name of His Royal Highness the Duke of Kent was unconnected with your proceedings against His Royal Highness the Duke of York?"

"I swear it was wholly unconnnected."

"Can you inform me whether Major Dodd held any situation under the Duke of Kent?"

"I believe he did."

"What situation?"

"I believe he was a private secretary."

"Wasn't that a very confidential situation?"

"Most certainly."

"You and Major Dodd and Major Glennie took Mrs. Clarke with you on a visit to the Martello Towers?"

"Yes."

"Your object then was to procure information about the Duke of York?"

"It was."

"You had no other object in mind?"

"No."

"Did Mrs. Clarke mention the Duke of Kent?"

"She frequently mentioned many of the Royal Family, but not the Duke of Kent as knowing of the enquiry."

"The name of the Duke of Kent was not used by you as attached to any promise, or as interested in any promise, to Mrs. Clarke?"

"Never."

"Did you ever give Mrs. Clarke money?"

"When she said she would give me some papers, I

346

gave her a hundred pounds to pay her butcher and baker."

"You gave her no promises besides?"

"None, but that if she would be a steady friend to the public I would be a steady friend to her."

"Can you mean gravely to say that no other promises were held out to her but public acknowledgement as a great and public benefactress?"

"I made her none other whatever."

Colonel Wardle was suffered to withdraw, and Major Dodd was examined in his place. He gave evidence to the effect that neither he nor Colonel Wardle had made promises to Mrs. Clarke, and that as far as he knew Colonel Wardle had never undertaken to pay for the furniture at Westbourne Place. The Attorney-General listened with folded arms and eyes closed: he did not even bother to cross-examine the witness himself, but motioned to his junior counsel to do so.

"I believe you held a high situation under His Royal Highness the Duke of Kent?"

"I was His Royal Highness's private secretary."

"Do you hold that situation now?"

"I do not."

"About what time were you deprived of it?"

"I cannot say on what day I relinquished my situation; I feel it unsuitable to do so."

"When you first met Mrs. Clarke had you not constant access to His Royal Highness? Were you not backwards and forwards from Westbourne Place to His Royal Highness, and from his Royal Highness to Westbourne Place?"

"Yes, I was frequently with his Royal Highness, and at Westbourne Place."

"Did you never inform His Royal Highness you were engaged on the business with Colonel Wardle?"

"No, I did not."

"Had he not the least suspicion of it, or that you were daily consulted about the matter?"

"No, I thought it would have been indelicate to mention the subject to His Royal Highness."

Counsel turned to the Lord Chief Justice.

"If it is thought necessary to go into an enquiry why this gentleman was dismissed from his situation we are ready to do so."

Lord Ellenborough looked grave.

"That is a thing which I cannot permit. It cannot possibly have any bearing upon this case."

Major Dodd withdrew and Major Glennie was called.

"You came accidentally into this business?" Counsel enquired.

"I understood Colonel Wardle wanted information from the lady. He wished to put a stop to corrupt practices in the Army."

"Then you wished to see corruption put down also. Did you go down to criticise the Martello Towers?"

"I went to satisfy myself of their utility, not to criticise. I had published a book on dockyard fortifications."

"You took notes when you went on this expedition?"

"Yes, I did."

"On the Martello Towers?"

"No, on another subject."

"On what subject?"

"Well, to put it plainly, on what Mrs. Clarke said about the Royal Family."

"You did not omit to register a single thing which you thought might be offensive to those concerned?"

"They were about making baronets and peers, and different incidents which happened in the Royal Family."

Major Glennie, to his own surprise and disappointment —the *éclat* of being a witness had rather fired him—was directed to withdraw, and after other witnesses had been examined and cross-examined, amongst them Illingworth the wine merchant and Sir Richard Phillips the publisher, the case for the Prosecution closed.

The Attorney-General rose to speak for the Defence, and having gone over the preceding evidence, he then produced his single witness and trump-card, Mrs. Clarke's own lawyer, Mr. Stokes.

Mr. Stokes, known to the Prosecution, the Defence, and the Court in general as a lawyer of impeccable integrity, stated that during the proceedings in the House of Commons last February he had had an interview with Colonel Wardle as to the advisability or non-advisability of summoning Francis Wright as a witness on the part of Mrs. Clarke; and that he, Mr. Stokes, had strongly advised against it, as during cross-examination it would be very probable that Colonel Wardle's having furnished a house for Mrs. Clarke would come out, which would be seized upon by the Government as bribery, and therefore heap immediate discredit on Colonel Wardle's cause. Mr. Stokes said he had no doubt whatsoever that Colonel Wardle had undertaken to furnish and pay for the house in Westbourne Place.

A sensation was produced in Court by the lawyer's evidence, and the Prosecuting Counsel, Mr. Alley, rose to his feet in perplexity.

"I beg to submit to Your Lordship that the evidence just given by Mr. Stokes was totally unexpected, not only by myself, but I believe by the whole Court. I must entreat Your Lordship's indulgence for five minutes that I may send for Colonel Wardle."

The Lord Chief Justice granted the request and Colonel Wardle appeared for re-examination by his Counsel. He said he perfectly well remembered an interview with Mr. Stokes during the time of the Investigation, and that the reason why Francis Wright was not called to the bar of the House of Commons was because his evidence might have been dangerous to Mrs. Clarke, and certainly not because it might have been dangerous to him, Colonel Wardle.

The Attorney-General now addressed the Court again.

"May it please Your Lordship, Gentleman of the Jury. They have now called Colonel Wardle to contradict Mr. Stokes. Compare the manner in which these two witnesses have given their testimony. Carry in your recollection the clear and reflecting manner in which Mr. Stokes has given his evidence respecting his memory, by referring to the documents which he produced, and which certainly tended to confirm his evidence. That Colonel Wardle should have contradicted Mr. Stokes is perfectly natural. If he had not been ready to contradict him he had better have gone into Yorkshire.

"You have heard the evidence of Mr. Stokes, and after hearing that, I think it impossible that you should hesitate in believing either his evidence or the evidence of Mr. Wright, and you also carry in your recollection that all this occurred long before any dispute arose between Francis Wright and Colonel Wardle."

Mr. Alley, for the Prosecution, made a long and impassioned address in defence of his client, ending with the following words:

"The extraordinary length to which this trial has been protracted renders me unable to say all that I might have said on the present occasion in support of the Prosecution; from that circumstance, added to the lateness of the hour, I shalll decline adding more than the expression of my thanks for the patient indulgence with which I have been heard by His Lordship, and by the Gentlemen of the Jury. I shall only add this one observation—the eyes of the United Kingdom are upon you."

The eyes of the Lord Chief Justice had been closed, but he opened them at the conclusion of Counsel's speech.

His summing up could hardly be called impartial. The scales were heavily tipped against Colonel Wardle. His Lordship observed that it was difficult to conjecture why Colonel Wardle had ever gone to the upholsterer's warehouse. If a man did not go to such a place with a lady with the view of being paymaster, it was certainly a dangerous situation in which to trust himself. His Lordship told the Gentlemen of the Jury that the important issue between the parties lay in their hands, and he had no doubt they would do justice to both.

The Jury, after a consultation of ten minutes, returned a verdict of "Not Guilty" for Francis Wright and Mrs. M. A. Clarke.

For the second time within five calendar months the Member for Okehampton had been vanquished. The fêting was all forgotten; the tide had turned. The fickle public thumbed its nose and yawned. Nothing remained for Gwyllym Lloyd Wardle but the back benches of His Majesty's Opposition, from which obscurity he had so lately sprung.

"And you?" the Attorney-General asked his client. "Have you had your fill of the Courts, or do you want more?"

She smiled and shrugged her shoulders.

"That depends upon my friends and how they treat me."

"At least the verdict was a Christmas present."

"But thanks to Mr. Stokes."

"Not your Learned Counsel?"

"The arch-juggler? Yes, perhaps . . . and the Lord Chief Justice. And some of it also to Scylla and Charybdis, and vicarious quicksands and navigators' perils. I'm glad poor Francis Wright will get his money, but I'm no better off—which is rather a pity."

"I thought you had vast sums from memoirs expunged."

"Not vast enough . . . I sometimes regret the deal. Which gives me a sudden idea—you can advise me. Would the Government take it amiss if I published the facts that came out at the trial today about Dodd and Wardle? And the way I was bribed to appear at the House of Commons?"

"A blow to the Opposition—they'd be delighted. But your Whig friends will be furious, I warn you."

"I don't give a damn for them, except for Folkestone. And he's become very cool and needs a lesson."

"Then do your worst. The Ministry will stay mum."

In January 1810 a board "To Let" appeared above the door at Westbourne Place. The trustees for Mrs. Clarke and her two daughters had decided she could not afford so large a house. Expenses must be cut. She must retrench.

A cottage at Uxbridge? No, but a cottage at Putney, not far from Fulham Lodge, might prove amusing. The Duke still loaned the lodge to current favourites and exercised his horses on Putney heath, and no one could tell what stray nostalgic echo might cause him to take an early morning ride. Not that she had much hope, but the thought was distracting.

She settled down—ear cocked for the sound of hoofbeats—with paper and pen and a tin box full of letters, and late in the spring the result was printed and published by Mr. Chapple, 66 Pall Mall.

Title: *The Rival Princes*, by Mary Anne Clarke.

F O U R :   The first edition of *The Rival Princes* was exhausted within three weeks. A second followed, with further remarks and additional letters, and a foreword thanking the gentlemen of the press for taking up the cause of an injured woman without any reference to party politics. The editors of the *Times,* the *Post,* the *Sun,* the *Courier,* and the *Pilot* received their dues; Mr. Bell, of the *Weekly Messenger,* a blast, this editor having said that the scandalous volume deserved to be put to the flames by the common hangman. Mr. Bell, retorted the author, had never before been known to discharge a debt until he had been arrested. Colonel Wardle was therefore lucky in getting paid. The author knew several anecdotes, all of them curious, about the personal history of Mr. Bell, and if further provoked she might be induced to publish them—which was one sort of method of dealing with bad reviews.

The book had been fun to write. No one was spared. Messrs. Wardle, Dodd, and Glennie cut ludicrous figures; Sir Richard Phillips of Bridge Street fumed and fretted; the wine merchant, Illingworth, was caricatured. The visits to Romney Marsh, and the Martello Towers, and evenings at Westbourne Place were fully described. There were peeps behind the scenes at the Investigation, and the friendship of his Radical lordship was lightly sketched. The book began with the first encounter with Wardle, and ended with his defeat at Westminster Hall.

The Duke of York was alluded to in the preface, but in such a way that no offence could be taken and thus the ten thousand pounds were still secure. The author said that her late royal friend was indebted for all his disasters to the descendant of one misled by Eve, in days long past, by means of an apple. She would mention no names, but the Household might think as they pleased. An envenomed tongue had poisoned the royal ear, for the royal heart was incapable of injuring anyone. The author had been forced to stand up for her rights, or else perish at the feet of her infant children.

His Royal Highness the Duke of Kent was not so spared. In answer to Mary Anne's allegations, he published at large *A Declaration*, consisting of questions put to Major Dodd, late in his employ as private secretary.

In this *Declaration* Major Dodd denied ever having mentioned his master's name as encouraging any attack upon his brother. In fact the private secretary, now discharged, agreed that in his service of ten years, whatever the wounded feelings might have been, H.R.H. had never uttered a word of complaint. When pamphlets had censured his brother and praised himself, the Duke of Kent had shuddered and bowed his head. As to sanctioning measures to injure his brother's honour, as described in a recent book *The Rival Princes*, such a foul aspersion could not remain unnoticed and must make every honest man recoil with horror.

In the first edition a single letter only was printed from Lord Folkestone to the author, but this was enough to frighten his Radical lordship, who immediately scribbled a note of regret to Wardle, saying he had not read the work itself but that any opinion he may have expressed last year he wished now to disavow completely. Representations made by Mrs. Clarke were to blame for those opinions. He hoped that Major Dodd would understand, and though he hated to see his name in the public prints, both gentlemen might make use of his present letter. It was published the following day, June thirteenth, 1810, in the *Morning Chronicle*.

He did not publish a second, more intimate note, written the very same day to his friend Mr. Creevy. An excerpt ran as follows: "Is the letter she printed a damned foolish one? Does it make me appear ridiculous? Is it the one where I say 'It will do no good to the Family?' Do other people think much of it, and do you? Pardon these enquiries, but after the excessive nervousness you witnessed last December you will not wonder at them.

Does the bitch hint at my sleeping with her, or say anything else about me?"

It was just as well for his Radical lordship that the author never set eyes upon that, or he might have suffered. As it was, the *Morning Chronicle* caught her eye, and in the second edition of her book she printed nine more letters from Lord Folkestone, with some cryptic comments of explanation.

The second edition of *The Rival Princes* was snapped up even more quickly than the first, the interest being not in the Wardle story but in who had been shown up and torn to pieces. Dog-eared copies were smuggled on to back benches, scanned in smoke-rooms, sniggered at in closets, and, though full fire was turned on the Opposition, Government members did not escape unscathed. Not a word was said against Sir Vicary Gibbs; but the Secretary to the Admiralty, Mr. Croker, who with the Attorney-General had shown himself most hostile to the author in 1809, received a twelve-page blast, exposing his humble origins and the odium into which he had come as a result of his unsavoury activities as a tax collector in Ireland.

For three or four months the book was discussed and applauded—though derided by many as being in execrable taste—and then, as is the way with ephemeral topics, interest died and the subject was completely forgotten. Other matters arose to claim attention—the progress of the war and, in royal circles, the death of the King's favourite daughter, the Princess Amelia. This was the last straw in the wavering monarch. His Majesty George the Third was pronounced insane, and in 1811 the Prince of Wales became Regent. One of the earliest measures he put into force was to restore the Duke of York as Commander-in-Chief.

The Investigation, the lawsuits, *The Rival Princes* became stale news and nobody cared any more. Like last year's comic song or a summer fashion, the scandal had had its day and could now be buried. The only person to regret interment was Mrs. Clarke herself. It made life dull.

She said, "I've got letters in my old tin box to provide a dozen volumes and make a fortune. Why let them go to waste, and not to posterity?"

This was before a meeting of trustees, including Messrs. Dowler and Coxhead-Marsh. The ten thousand pounds had dwindled down to five; in a couple of years there wouldn't be anything left.

"A sound reason for making authorship my profession. The girls will live on the income of the annuity, and I can rake in royalties. Don't you agree?"

Charley Thompson nodded his head. He was third trustee. Anything that augmented the sisterly funds had his brotherly approbation—she gave him half.

Messrs. Dowler and Coxhead-Marsh held a different opinion. Shocked to the core and aghast at *The Rival Princes*—a libel on every page—they feared repetition. She had got away with it once, but she wouldn't again. There were heavy odds against hitting a target twice. Besides, no man was spared by her pen, and who knew what foolish scribbles from themselves reposed in that same tin box, tied up with ribbon?

"I think," said Coxhead-Marsh, "you'd be better advised to lie low for a while and attend to the girls' education."

"That excellent school at Uxbridge," said Bill Dowler, "only fifteen pounds a term, with French included."

"Sums can be advanced for scholastic purposes, but not for a splash in society," said Coxhead-Marsh. "Both Dowler and I are agreed upon that. If you want the girls to marry, and marry well, attention drawn to yourself will blot their chances. As it is . . ."

"As it is," said Dowler, interrupting, "what happened in 1809 may tell against them. In fact, as I've told you over and over again, a quiet retreat to the country is your answer. A cottage at Chalfont St. Peter's . . ."

She turned to blast him. "Are there courses for conjugal life at the school in Uxbridge? I'd rather prepare them myself, with French included . . . The girls must live in London, and so must I, with a *pied-à-Terre* at Brighton, or possibly Ramsgate, and when George goes into the Army we'll follow after him—there'll be cornets twelve a penny for Mary and Ellen, and some dashing cavalry colonel for myself."

There was silence at the mention of George's name, but a glance between the trustees was unmistakable.

355

She said, "Why, what's the matter?"

Bill did not answer. Charley shrugged his shoulders. It was left for Coxhead-Marsh to break the pause.

"I might pull a string in the City," he began, "and get George into some business. There's plenty of time."

"George is going into the Army," she replied. "It's his wish, and a standing promise."

"It won't be easy."

"Why not?"

"The reason's obvious. The son of the woman who broke the Commander-in-Chief isn't likely to find a welcome in any regiment. Applications will be turned down. He hasn't a hope."

"I warned you," said Charley. "I failed, and so will he. The Investigation ruined both our chances. If George cares to change his name he might strike lucky, but not in His Majesty's Army, that's very certain."

Sudden fury seized her. Incompetent idiots, all of them.

"If anyone stands in the way I know how to fight. I've a letter from the Duke of York himself promising George a commission at fifteen. What if I produce it in open Court?"

The trustees sighed. Back to King's Bench again and Westminster Hall? Publicity—damaging, dangerous, fatal to everyone. It would be the wreckage of George's chances, and the girls.' Could nobody persuade her to keep silent?

"If you attempt any sort of threat," said Coxhead-Marsh, "you'll utterly destroy your children's future. The annuity for yourself and for the girls will be withdrawn and you'll be left without a penny."

"Except what I know I can earn with my wits and my pen, which might be considerably more than any annuity."

She stormed her way out of the building and left them haggling. They could do what they liked with the funds of the dwindling capital, pinch and scrape and invest in the three per cents; no one could launch an attack except herself.

It was not until she got home and searched through her box that she remembered—the letter referring to George

356

from the Duke was no longer in her possession. She had sent it, ages ago, to James Fitzgerald for safekeeping.

She had heard nothing from either Fitzgerald for several months. James had retired from politics only that year and Willie had leapt into prominence very swiftly, becoming Chancellor of the Irish Exchequer and a member of the English Privy Council. She wrote to them at once. They were both in Ireland, Parliament having risen for the summer recess, and she had little doubt that Willie, in his new position, could obtain a commission for George against all opposition.

No answer from father or son. She wrote again. A few curt words from James arrived at last. "The letter to which you allude has long been destroyed."

Destroyed, that most precious of her possessions! Did he think it would contaminate him? Or was he terrified of retaining a scrap of evidence of his relations with the notorious Mrs. Clarke?

A further appeal to Willie was unsuccessful, and a message implied that William Fitzgerald, Chancellor, had no wish to be remembered by Mrs. Clarke. Any acquaintance they may have had in the distant past was best forgotten by both, and not resumed. In addition, the Irish Chancellor refused to take action regarding the future of Mrs. Clarke's son.

At first she was stunned. She couldn't believe the truth. It wasn't humanly possible that the Fitzgeralds, close friends of ten years' standing, could turn against her, after so many secrets had been shared, and so many worries. Willie, who'd told her his troubles since Oxford days, running for help and assistance, as Charley had; James, who'd unburdened his heart on a hundred occasions, spilling political beans and personal problems. No wish for further acquaintance . . . a chapter closed . . . and nothing done for George—George was abandoned.

Emotion turned to anger, anger to fury, and fury to blind instinct for revenge. As in the past, she turned for advice to Ogilvie.

"What shall I do? How can I hit them hardest?"

During the past four years much had miscarried. Ogilvie's hopes had failed him one by one. The Regency had damped all expectations of a country divided in two, of a

357

revolution. The Tories were still in power with no prospect of change, and thus any weapon would serve if it discredited ministers. Ill-feeling betwen England and Ireland might be fostered; dissension always served a useful purpose, and here was something to seize upon and encourage.

"I told you," he said, "when you published *The Rival Princes*, that you ought to have made it stronger. Now's your chance. Start on a series of pamphlets attacking the Government, beginning with William Fitzgerald. Show him up. There'll be an appalling outcry—he'll have to resign. Remember what a fool you made of Croker? There was bitter disappointment in the country that you never followed it up by damning the rest."

"You think what I say carries weight?"

"Of course it does. When you wrote *The Rival Princes* you'd got the public. But you let the moment slip, and so you lost them. You don't realise the power you have in your pen, and for that matter in your tongue as well. Two men fell to disgrace because of you, the Duke of York and Wardle. Try for the third. Get the Irish Chancellor booted—the public will back you."

The words were honey to her avid ears. Will told her all the things she longed to hear. His suggestion stirred her, excited her. A series of pamphlets attacking her world, the world she had known; once more a chance to prove she was not forgotten, that she still had the power to break a man.

The battle was on again, the *ideé fixe*—men were a race apart to be subjected. She shut herself up in her room and began to write . . .

The letter to the Right Honourable William Fitzgerald consisted of some twenty pages or so, and was printed in pamphlet form by a Mr. Mitchell. Mr. Chapple of Pall Mall had turned it down. He advised against publication, scenting danger, but the author of *The Rival Princes* would not listen.

"Danger to William Fitzgerald, not to me."

Mr. Chapple shook his head. The letter was vitriol, without the grace of humour, or of wit:

I am anxious to caution the Irish nation against one of

the most vicious and profligate of men, who at present most mysteriously presides over the finances of that nation, and who is to be its organ in the Imperial Parliament.

I am guided by the general principle that has regulated my whole life; never to suffer ingratitude, one of the blackest of crimes, to go unpunished, or hypocrisy unexposed. You, Mr. Fitzgerald, shall afford an additional example that none, be his rank ever so exalted, shall with impunity trifle with my feelings to suit his private convenience, and I wish to impress it upon your memory that when stung by injury I would enforce redress not only from the son of the King, but from the King himself. As yet I have shown up no one who did not richly deserve to be exposed to the public; this is the only revenge I am desirous of taking on those by whom I am ill-treated.

The following circumstance affords us a striking illustration of the baseness and treachery of that subtle intriguer, your father, to whom I entrusted a letter from the Duke of York, written soon after our separation, in which he pledged himself by everything sacred to educate, protect and provide for my son as long as he lived.

I wrote to your father requesting him to restore this letter. To this application he returned for answer: "I have destroyed it."

Words are inadequate to express the indignation which I feel at this traitorous conduct to an innocent child whose sole dependence for provision in life was upon that letter, and who was now basely deprived of this his only guarantee; to say nothing of his flagrant ingratitude to myself who had saved him and you with all your family from ignominy and utter ruin by secreting his venal correspondence.

After these few remarks on the character of your insidious father I shall now direct my attention to your own.

Your impaired sight, which your father believes to be a hereditary infirmity, is due to to your incessant nocturnal practice of gambling; inexcusable on your part, as no pecuniary necessity draws you to the game-table. Apart from this ruling passion of your life what would the world in general think of a man who deliberately seduces the wife of his intimate friend, and by the exertion of corrupt *influence causes the husband to be sent to an unhealthy clime in the flattering hope that disease will speedily sweep him into the grave; who then indulges his licentious passion without restraint; and who, when its effects are likely to become apparent, drugs the unconscious victim of his debauchery, that at the risk of her life he may relieve his apprehensions by destroying the innocent witness of his guilt, and spare his avarice the sacrifice of a pittance for its support? It was not long before a still-born infant, a spectacle so frightful that even a medical pen would recoil with horror from the description, attested the virulence of the fatal potion by which the unhappy mother herself was brought to the brink of the grave.*

You protested that you could not marry a woman so disgraced, even though you yourself were the cause of her dishonour, nor could you debase the blood of the Fitzgeralds by an alliance with one of the daughters of Lord Dillon, because they were bastards, and that the same objection had induced you to decline a similar offer from Marquis Wellesley.

But where is your birth, or rank, or talents, that authorise you thus to spurn with contempt the children of the noblest families? You who are destitute of all this— you whose grandfather, roguish Billy Fitzgerald of Ennis, was a poor pettifogging attorney; whose father owes his advancement in life not to merit but to the dirty arts of political intrigue; whose aunt is a common street-walker, and whose cousin was hanged for horse-stealing—you whose whole conduct since your first entry into the world has been a tissue of infamy and complicated guilt?

I shall show by what means you acquired the blushing honours which you now wear so thick upon you, and which according to report are to be swelled with a peerage. You imagine perhaps that the ermine will be a convenient cloak for your moral deformities, and that the possession of a coronet will compensate for the want of every kind of merit, but give me leave to ask whether you will ever be able to look at the animal which forms your appropriate crest without calling to mind your grovelling origin?

I now append the letters from your father and yourself which are still in my possession, and it remains to be seen, Sir, whether the people of Great Britain and Ireland, with the knowledge of your genuine character, will suffer such a profligate upstart to lord it over them with patience. It remains to be seen whether they will applaud the selection of a needy political adventurer to fill some of the highest and most lucrative offices in the State, or whether they will judge that the financial correspondence of an essential portion of the Empire might not have been committed to abler and purer hands than those of one whose nights are committed to the gaming-table, and who stands convicted as the deliberate destroyer of his own un-born.

This was the general tone of the published letter, and she added a footnote, promising more to come. Who next for the coconut-shy, three shots a penny?

I here announce my intention of submitting to the public in a very short time two or three volumes, which may be followed by others, as opportunity shall suit, or circumstances require. The Author.

Certain of His Majesty's faithful Commons found themselves uneasy at the prospect. One or two of the Lords were chilled. The Cabinet murmured. Lord Liverpool himself was heard to say, "Suppress the woman before she does more harm. We'll all be out of office if this continues."

The first victim consulted his legal advisors, and served a writ.

On Monday the seventh of February 1814, Mrs. Mary Anne Clarke was indicted for publishing libel upon the Chancellor of the Irish Exchequer, the Right Honourable William Fitzgerald, M.P. for Ennis.

She sat for the third and last time in the Court of King's Bench, watching the sea of faces turned towards her; but Sir Vicary Gibbs was no longer there to defend her. He'd become a judge exactly two years before.

Lord Chief Justice Ellenborough was absent. His place was taken by Mr. Justice Le Blanc. No parties at piquet before this trial. No chats in Lincoln's Inn, no Leda's swan.

"Get hold of Henry Brougham and damn the cost," the ex-Attorney-General told the author. "I abhor his politics, but he's the only chap in the world who may get you off. I shall warn him, however, that he won't have an easy brief."

On advice of Counsel, Defendant pleaded guilty. Mary Anne had overreached herself at last.

FIVE: Proceedings were brief. Witnesses were not summoned. The letter to the Right Honourable William Fitzgerald was read aloud in Court and heard in silence.

The defendant gave no evidence whatsoever, but put in a sworn affidavit, pleading in extenuation of her offence the treacherous conduct of the Fitzgeralds, in that they had destroyed many valuable papers which she had entrusted to their keeping, among them one from a person in high authority promising to provide for her only son; and throwing herself, in these words, upon the mercy of the Court:

That this deponent hath two daughters, one of them approaching the age of womanhood; that she hath hitherto under many adverse circumstances and misfortunes given them an education and brought them up in honour and virtue, and that should this honourable Court in its wisdom deprive her said daughters of her protection, they would be left totally destitute; and she humbly hopes that these circumstances and the state of her health, and that in the present case she has been actuated by no news of a political nature but solely by the treatment received from the Prosecutor in his private capacity, will be taken into consideration by this honourable Court.

The Attorney-General—who had now prosecuted for two years in place of Sir Vicary Gibbs—characterised the libel as the most flagrant that had ever appeared in the Court of Justice.

He said there was no doubt that it was directly meant for the purpose of extorting money—indeed, revenge was stated to be the motive of the pamphlet. He hoped that the sentence of the Court would at least teach the Defendant to hold her hand and to refrain from the publication of future libels.

Mr. Henry Brougham (who six years later was to defend Queen Caroline) addressed the Court in mitigation of the Defendant's punishment, but he knew that there was little he could do for Mrs. Clarke.

"This is not the case," he protested warmly, "of a wanton and unprovoked attack upon the private character of an individual, for the sake of ministering to the public appetite for domestic slander. The publication of that letter arose out of a long connection between the parties, a connection of fourteen years' standing.

"My Lords, I do not urge any extenuation of the offence because the person who yielded to these feelings of provocation was a woman, lest it is said that when the sex no longer imposes restraint it ceases to afford protection, but I will entreat Your Lordships to reflect on the effects of her punishment on those she has brought up in honour and virtue, by giving them that education and those habits of which she may live to feel the want, if she had not already.

"When the Court takes these things into account, I hope and trust Your Lordships will mingle the appointment of justice that the facts may demand with a merciful regard to the interests of the guiltless."

Mr. Brougham had done his best. But the Court was hostile. Their Lordships felt, and not without cause, that a woman who would write such accusations against persons in high places should be muzzled. It certainly would not do to let her loose. A few weeks' grace, and she would begin again. Only five years earlier a Prince of the Blood had been broken by her. Women of her type were dangerous.

The Defendant had shown her usual lightheartedness, even during proceedings that very day. She had laughed at the aged appearance of Mr. Mitchell, the seventy-year-old printer and Co-defendant, and had gone so far as to curtsey in mocking fashion at the conclusion of the Attorney-General's speech. Mr. Justice Le Blanc was determined to be severe.

"There is no doubt," he said sternly, "of the libellous

tendency of the publication, and there can be as little doubt that the motive in which it originated, and which induced the threat of those further volumes which the Defendant has herself stated to have in meditation, was the desire to raise money by the papers, or by their suppression. Let this be a warning to the world how they form hasty and imprudent connections, and for the Defendant herself I trust that the solitude and confinement to which it is the duty of the Court to sentence her will induce her to review her past life and repent of those errors which have brought her to her present situation.

"It is always painful to be obliged to visit the sins of the fathers upon the children, but in some cases the separation of the latter from the former may be attended with beneficial results. Whether it may be so in this instance, it is not for the Court to enquire.

"Taking all the circumstances into consideration, the Court does order and adjudge that the Defendant Mary Anne Clark shall be committed to the custody of the King's Bench Prison for the space of nine calendar months, and at the end of that period she shall enter into surety to keep the peace for three years, under a recognisance herself of £200, and two sureties of £100 each, and to be further imprisoned until that surety be given."

All eyes turned to the Defendant Mrs. Clarke as she stood in the box to receive the sentence. Her Counsel, Henry Brougham, had hinted prison but never for one moment had she believed him. Damages, perhaps a few thousand pounds, the trust stock sold to meet the sums demanded; and then there would be a sequel to *The Rival Princes*, authentic and trenchant—but vetted for libel first.

But prison for nine months! The children deserted, and George's sixteenth birthday a week from today! She looked around, unbelieving. No faces smiled. Charley was there with Bill, their eyes on the ground. It was true, then. No escape. No mitigation. Jangling keys, cold walls and a prison cell. She dug her nails into her hand to keep command. The *Times* reporter jotted his final phrase. "When Mr. Justice Le Blanc came to speak of imprisonment, her gaiety failed her, and she shed a few tears."

Her friends were allowed to say good-bye to her before

she was driven away to King's Bench Prison. She blinked the tears aside and came smiling to them.

"I always intended to diet, and here's my chance. It's so good for the face and figure at thirty-eight. The Marshalsea waters are so much better than Bath, and the lodgings at half the expense . . . Will you please tell Martha to pack necessities for a few days only, until I've inspected my quarters? I can't help feeling I shan't need evening gowns, but woollens only. Books? Who'll feed me with books? I rely on you all. Gibbon's *Decline and Fall* ought to see me through, and Homer's *Odyssey* . . . Any more suggestions? I shall be at home on Tuesday's and Fridays for certain. All callers welcomed, but bring your own stools and chairs. Coxy, look after the girls and ask them to Loughton, and for heaven's sake try and find Charley a job. Bill, kiss me, darling, quick, and then disappear. I might make a fool of myself, which would disgrace you. You know what to do about George, and break it gently. Say he's not to worry at all, and I'm highly amused—can't wait, in fact, to explore the inside of a prison. Is Mr. Brougham there? I want to thank him."

Henry Brougham went to her side and took her hand. He saw through the gay façade and guessed the strain. He sent her friends away and she relaxed.

"It's going to be hard," he said. "I must prepare you."

"Yes," she answered; "tell me the worst at once."

"How strong are you?"

"I don't know. I've not been tested. I've never been ill."

"You'll be given a room in time, or the share of a room. I take it your friends will be able to pay for that. But at first there won't be any question of it. Solitary confinement is the sentence."

"What does that mean exactly?"

"There are two small cells, or dungeons, in King's Bench Prison. The Court has decreed that you shall be placed in one of them."

"Will it be quite dark? Shall I be able to read or write?"

"I understand there is a small window high in the wall."

"Is there anything to lie on in the cell?"

"Nothing at the moment. Only straw. You will be allowed to send for a bed—I've given instructions."

"Any coverings?"

"Tonight you shall have my own carriage rugs. I shall do everything I can to forward a bed and blankets from your home tomorrow."

"Who governs the prison?"

"The present marshal is a Mr. Jones, but I understand nobody ever sees him and the prison is run by his clerk, a man called Brooshooft."

"Brooshooft or Brushoff, it's all the same to me. Do I make myself nice to him?"

"Possibly later on, but not at present. Are you ready? The carriage is waiting."

"Don't I go in a tumbril?"

"You're spared that in England. Counsel is permitted to conduct the prisoner."

She stepped into his carriage, still clutching his hand.

"We ought to have gone by water—so much more romantic. Is there no Traitor's Gate at King's Bench Prison?"

"Unfortunately, no. It's not on the river. It's the other side of the bridge, not far from Southwark."

"A quarter I hardly know . . . Is it much frequented?"

"By ragpickers and beggars, nobody else. Except of course the debtors in the prison."

"Shall I catch a glimpse of the Thames? I adore the river."

"I'm afraid you won't. The prison is rather hemmed in . . . By the way, have you got a doctor within call?"

"My beloved Doctor Metcalfe's gone to the Midlands. But I'm sure I could whistle him home in any emergency. Why?"

"There is no medical attendance at King's Bench Prison. None of any kind. Nor is there any infirmary."

"What happens if a person is suddenly ill?"

"Unless one of the inmates has medical knowledge, I am told, precisely nothing. That's why I warned you."

"Forewarned is forearmed. Martha must send me my pills . . . Which reminds me, how exactly is the sanitation?"

"I'm informed there are certain scavengers paid by the marshal, but they don't come every day. It depends on the refuse. When the quantity reaches above a certain height the scavengers make a profit, and so it's removed."

"There's logic for you . . . Aren't there any drains?"

"Apparently not. The waste is collected in tubs."

"Which constantly overflow like the falls of Niagara? Martha will get a list as long as my arm . . . What about food, Mr. Brougham?"

"There is a dining-room in King's Bench Prison, which is generally used by the poorer sort of debtor who can't afford to send out for what he wants. Butcher's meat can be bought about twice a week, but from what I've heard it's not to be recommended."

"Then food can be sent in?"

"Yes, at a price. The turnkeys will arrange it. We'll have to find out. I believe a lot of drinking goes on inside which is winked at by the marshal, but that won't interest you. You'll have to stop your ears against the racket."

"Is this it? This great gate?"

"Yes, we drive inside and draw up in the inner court. If anyone shouts or tries to insult you, don't take any notice; the poorer debtors always collect in the court. You'd better wait here in the carriage while I make enquiries."

She folded the carriage rugs upon her arm. "In Bowling Inn Alley," she thought, "the blankets were thinner, but I did have a bed, and Charley to keep me warm. Besides, it was thirty years back, and I wasn't so brittle . . ." She leant out of the carriage window and called to Brougham.

"Order a large four-poster and dinner for two, and I *must* have the champagne iced . . ." He waved his hand.

As soon as he had disappeared into the prison, the debtors came and crowded round the carriage. They thrust their hands in the window with slips of paper.

"Chum tickets for sale. Ten shillings a night. Bed to yourself, only four persons in a room . . . Eight shillings, lady, I can offer eight shillings, and mattress new three months ago . . . Four shillings to you, madam, for part share of a bed, occupant very clean young person of twenty-eight . . . A guinea a night for a room to yourself, madam, best offer in the whole of King's Bench, you wouldn't find the like in either the Fleet or the Marshalsea, guinea a night, and slops collected every morning extra."

A pity she wasn't a debtor instead of a criminal.

"Very kind of you all," she said, "to take so much trouble. But the business has been arranged. I've a room to myself."

They stared back at her, faces blank.

"Some mistake, lady. There ain't no single rooms unoccupied."

"Ah! But there are. Ones you don't know about. The marshal has a beauty up his sleeve."

Henry Brougham came back. The debtors cleared a path, still talking loudly, arguing the point.

"I'm sorry," Brougham said, "it's rather worse than I thought."

"What's rather worse? These people have been very kind."

"Your quarters. They're very small."

"But I have them alone?"

"You have them alone." He looked at her with compassion.

"Do I come with you now?"

"If you please." He took her arm and led her inside the door. "I've paid your commitment fees, which were ten and sixpence. In the ordinary way that would entitle you to what they call, in slang phrase, a chumming ticket."

"I know, they offered me one."

"It's no use in your case—you're committed for libel. It means the cell, as I told you. This is Mr. Brooshooft, the marshal's clerk."

A square pot-bellied man advanced towards her, hat on the back of his head. She smiled and curtseyed. He did not take any notice but turned to Brougham.

"Has she brought a bed?"

"The bed will be sent in the morning. And blankets, of course, and and a table and a chair, and any other things that may be necessary."

"No room for anything except the bed. The cell's only nine feet square. Has she got any candles?"

"Are candles not provided?"

"Nothing's provided. Only the straw, and that was fresh this morning."

"Where can I buy candles?"

"The coffeehouse master may have some. That's not my province. And don't forget she's here on a criminal charge. I've had my instructions, no privileges allowed. Only the prison fare from the dining-room."

"What would that be?"

The marshal's clerk shrugged his shoulders. "Gruel for breakfast, soup for midday dinner. It varies from day to day, the cooks arrange it. The debtors can buy what they want from the coffeehouse depending upon their means ... Her case is different."

Henry Brougham turned to his client. She waved her hand.

"What did I say? *Régime pour embonpoint*. I'll come out like a willow wand and set the fashion."

The marshal's clerk had beckoned to a turnkey. "Conduct the prisoner to Number 2. Her bed's being sent tomorrow, no other privs."

"No chits to the coffeehouse?"

"It's not on orders."

The marshal's clerk permitted his bulbous eye to fall upon the prisoner with indifference.

"If you do fall sick," he said, "you can always complain. Send up a written notice to the marshal, and it's put on the books and is shown when the prison's inspected."

"How often is that?" asked Brougham.

"Supposed to be twice a year, by the Crown Office, but it don't always follow—next visit's due in June. If a prisoner's dying, of course, I have power to shift him, but the relatives or friends are obliged to pay. I've made a concession in this case, as it's happened, the prisoner being a female and over thirty. Number 2 strong-room has a wooden floor; Number 1 is stone, and no glass to the window."

The prisoner smiled and gathered up her rugs.

"How very thoughtful and kind. What do I owe you?"

"That's up to your friends, I don't take money direct. Against the regulations, counts as offence. Will you follow the turnkey? Loitering's not allowed unless you're committed for debt or have served three months of sentence. Good afternoon."

He nodded to Henry Brougham and disappeared. Counsel took the rugs from his client's arm, and together they followed the turnkey along the passage.

"What a pity," she said, "we're not arriving in Brighton, with lodgings on the front and a party tonight."

Henry Brougham held tight to her arm. He did not answer. The turnkey led them through a maze of passages, bordered at corners by stairways where people loitered. These were the meeting-places of the debtors. Men and women and children sprawled on the stairs, the adults eating or drinking, the children playing. A game of dice was in progress on one of the stairways, on another a game of skittles, with broken bottles. The walls of the prison echoed; shouting and screaming, laughter and raucous singing filled the air.

"There's one thing at least—I shan't complain of the silence. But I'm rather afraid the scavengers haven't called. I don't like the look of those tubs without any lids on . . ."

The stench in the passage was worse than anything known in Bowling Inn Alley days. Or had she forgotten? Could it be there was something familiar in the smell? Unemptied slops of neighbours . . . leaking floors . . . wet walls and finger-marks . . . suggestive stains . . . even the shrieks of the children round the corner might have been Charley and Eddie playing marbles.

"Do you remember Mary Stuart?"

"Why Mary Stuart?"

" 'In my end,' she said, 'is my beginning.' Perhaps it applies to us all . . . I think we've arrived."

The turnkey had stopped at the farthest end of the passage and was wrestling with his key in a double lock. He opened the heavy door and flung it wide.

The marshal's clerk had not exaggerated: the cell was nine feet square, no more, no less. A window, high in the wall, barricaded by iron and covered with cobwebs, gave three feet of light. The floor was of wooden planks, and in a corner, against the wall, was a pallet heaped with straw. A small tub, like those observed along the passages, stood beside the door, without a lid.

The prisoner measured the cell with her arms extended.

"The trouble is," she said, "when I get my bed there literally won't be room for anything else. I shall have to wash, and dress, and take my meals straddled across it or standing on one leg—a new exercise in deportment, *la flamingo*."

She gave a demonstration, lifting her gown. The turnkey stared. She threw him a dazzling smile.

"Since we're bound to see a lot of each other," she said, "let's begin as we mean to go on. I hope we'll be friends."

She shook his hand and gave him a couple of guineas.

"Now what about those candles, Mr. Brougham? In half an hour the room will be black as pitch. And rather cold —I see I have no fireplace. So candles will give an atmosphere of fête. What with the straw and your rugs I'll be rather cosy, and soup from the debtor's dining-room piping hot. What *is* the soup this evening, tomato or turtle?"

The turnkey, puzzled, gazed at his latest charge.

"It's always the same," he said, "a kind of gravy, potato peelings on top, and a slice of bread."

"*Potage parmentier*, I've had it at Almack's . . . Now, Mr. Brougham, I think it's time you went."

Her Counsel took her hand, bowed, and kissed it.

"If there's any mortal thing that I can do to get you out of this hole and into a room, it shall be done—I promise you most faithfully."

"Thank you a thousand times. Will you come and see me?"

"Whenever it's permitted. By the way, I think I ought to have that doctor's address . . ."

"Bill Dowler's got it."

"Is there anything else you want? I mean—immediately?"

"Candles from the coffeehouse; and if they stock them, ink and pens and paper."

"Not another letter, I hope, to Mr. Fitzgerald?"

"No. A report on King's Bench Prison, as seen at firsthand. To be shown, if need be, to the House of Commons."

He laughed and shook his head.

"I think you're incorrigible."

"Good God, I hope so. Otherwise why live?"

The turnkey opened the door and he and Henry Brougham stepped outside. The door shut to with a clang. The key was turned. The prisoner's face appeared at the little grille. She had thrown her hat on the straw, and round her shoulders she was wearing one of her Counsel's carriage rugs.

"Just one last word," Mr. Brougham said, "I'm so terribly sorry . . ."

She looked at him and smiled. One blue eye winked. She murmured in broadest cockney, learnt in the alley,

"You pays yer money, and you takes yer choice."

She heard their footsteps echo in the passage, then merge into the distant prison sounds, the shouting and the screaming and the laughter. At ten o'clock that night, as the candles guttered, the turnkey unlocked the cell and brought her a letter. It had been sent by King's messenger to the marshal's office, with orders to give it direct, the turnkey said.

She stretched out her hand from the straw and took it from him. The letter had no beginning and no ending, but the paper was headed Horse Guards, at Whitehall, and dated the seventh of February 1814.

The message was very brief, and ran as follows:

His Majesty has been pleased to grant a commission to George Noel Clarke, in the 17th Light Dragoons. The appointment will date from the 17th of March, four weeks after the officer's sixteenth birthday, when Cornet Clarke is ordered to report for duty.

H.R.H. the Commander-in-Chief had remembered his promise.

SIX: They were always moving. No house was home for long. An eternal restlessness filled her heart and spirit —what Ellen used to call "Mother's divine discontent"— so that once again trunks would be clasped and corded and boxes packed, and the three of them set forth on another pilgrimage, in search of some unattainable El Dorado. Brussels perhaps today; Paris tomorrow; or, fancy seizing her for some place yet untried, they'd rumble along the dusty roads of France humped in a diligence, the window closed, her questing face pressed hard against a pane, enthusiasm riper than her daughters'.

"Hôtel de la Tête d'Or, that's where we'll stay"—simply because a cobbled square held mystery, and women washed their linen by a stream, and peasants in cobalt blue flashed sunburnt smiles. Besides, hard by was a château on a hill, lived in by some baron or seedy count, who might be called upon and prove amusing, for nothing daunted her, no Gallic protocol—she'd wave a *carte de visite* in her hand and claim acquaintance with the stiffest stranger.

Her suffering daughters would sit with downcast eyes, pride turning them to mutes, while their smiling mother, rippling in a French of no known origin, accent impeccable and grammar crude, made her introduction with lavish gestures.

"Ravie de faire votre connaissance, monsieur!" And Monsieur, not so *ravi*, clicked and bowed—his château hitherto impregnable except to maiden aunts and ancient curés but now defenceless, conquered by piercing eyes that swept his rooms and priced his *objects d'art*—and shame upon shame to the anguished daughters, the hiss behind the hand, the stage aside, "A widower. Might do for one of you."

Plombières-les-Bains, Nancy, Dieppe, watering-places pinpricked on a map because of something heard two years ago, forgotten, and then remembered. "Who lives at Nancy? The Marquis de Videlange? A heavenly creature who sat next to me once at dinner and never uttered the words *ancien régime*—we'll look him up." And Mary and Ellen, exchanging a glance of horror, cried, "Mother, we *can't*, he'll find out who you are."

"But darlings, what if he does? It makes it amusing."

And out would come the well-worn quips and stories, the scandals of days gone by, the fun and folly, the life of London twenty years ago—now lost and scarce overshadowed by an image of prison walls, of horror beyond description, of someone white and wan who could not stand, whose eyes were glazed, who stared without recognition when carried out of hell into the world.

Was it true what the doctors said to Uncle Bill—that the mind aways blotted out what it feared to remember? Or did she never speak of those hidden months because she *knew*, and wished to spare them pain? Even between themselves it was never mentioned, and when their mother launched into the past, spilling the anecdotes she loved, ridiculing the Court of a vanished age, a momentary panic held them taut. But if a tactless stranger touched upon it, murmured the word "imprisonment," what then? Would floodgates open up a turbid memory? The girls were never sure.

So let her indulge her fancy, roam the Continent, avid for new scenes and fresh experience, a summer here, a winter somewhere else, because, she would say to the girls, you never know . . . A Spanish duke might feast his eyes on Mary, or a Russian prince cast roubles in Ellen's lap.

On, then, from lodging to lodging, vagabounding, the three annuities stretched to the furthest limit. A moonlight flit; bills often left unpaid; relics from the past pressed into service, rings handed over counters, bracelets sold, and sordid bargains struck with doubting jewellers.

"I assure you that necklace belonged to the late Queen Charlotte."

"Madame, je regrette infiniment . . ."

"How much then will you give me?"

Fifty louis! Fifty louis for a necklace worth five hundred? The French were a race of robbers, the scum of the earth, they never washed, their very houses stank. But once in the street the money was quickly counted, the coins rung in case they were counterfeit, and then there'd be a smile, a wave of a parasol, a passing fiacre hailed to conduct them home—home for the moment being a small hotel, *prix modéré*, in the Faubourg Poissonière. "Darlings, we're rich again, let's spend our all!" Dresses would be ordered, a dinner party given, a furnished apartment taken for two months.

"But mother, we can't afford it!"

"Does it matter?"

The French were no longer thieves and the scum of the earth, but angels with melting eyes, sworn to her service. Her life history was told at once to concierges, her love affairs were discussed with the *femme-de-chambre*, Paris was the only city in the world—until the money went and they moved again. And still no Spanish dukes or Russian princes appeared, with Mary delicate and Ellen bookish. She saw them fated both to spinsterhood and talked about them as "my vestal virgins," delighting riffraff friends and old acquaintances but scaring off prospective sons-in-law. George, become very pompous, disapproved.

"The girls will never marry until you settle. And Paris is not at all the place to choose. I don't like to think of you roaming about without me."

Possessed and bossed by her son, she gazed, adoring. How handsome he looked in his beautiful uniform, and always the most distinguished of his regiment! "My son's in the 17th Lancers. He's doing well—only just twenty-seven, and a captain." But what pleased her best at the moment—he had no eyes for women; there were no frightful daughters-in-law to share his leave; his mother was supreme in his life. Long might it last.

But the girls—she'd go on hoping for belted earls, or foreigners with millions, or merely men. (They did turn up in the end, but both without prospects. A fellow called Bowles for Mary, who loved her and left her, and a Frenchman *sans-souci* for Ellen called Busson du Maurier.)

The trouble was that as she reached middle age, *déracinée*, an exile on alien soil, however much she plunged into the present, took active interest in the day-by-day, watched seasons pass, gave parties, wrote to friends, her thoughts went sweeping back to other days.

I remember . . . Then she'd stop herself. The young are bored with reminiscences. Who minded whether dandies in Vauxhall had stood on tiptoe once to watch her pass? What did it matter if a gaping crowd had climbed her carriage wheels in Palace Yard? Or that she'd queened it in the House of Commons, the only woman in that world of men? Those things are best forgotten, George had told her; everyone's very decent in the regiment, so why not draw a veil? She took the hint. But sometimes, in the night, and no one with her, a strange nostalgic yearning came for the past; and baffled by the silence, oddly lonely, a church clock in Boulogne chiming the hour, she thought, "There's no one left who gives a damn. The world I knew has gone. This is tomorrow."

If so, were all things lost? Did nothing remain? Did no stray fragment cling to a shadowed corner and stay there to be gathered by other hands? One moment her brother Charley was a boy, dragging at her skirt in Bowling Inn Alley; the next, a bill for some seventy pounds came in a lawyer's letter: "Dear Madam, there were costs to the above amount incurred in proving the death and the identity of Charles Farquhar Thompson."

Which of these two was Charley, known and loved? And what relation did a battered body found near a Thames-side sewer bear to a boy?

Bill, fetching her from prison, holding her hands, arranging the passage to France, unaltered, unchanging, saying, "Whenever you need me, I'll come at once." What sense, then, in those words, when he couldn't keep them? And Bill, so strong, dependable, becoming "Your late dear friend who was taken from us suddenly . . . Held in respect by all . . . The town of Uxbridge . . . Mourning rings, of course, to be transmitted." Where was all the tenderness and patience? Gone with the "late lamented" to the grave, or about her in the darkness, bright and steadfast?

"Mother dyes her hair. I wish she wouldn't."

"It makes her look so cheap. George ought to stop her."

"A woman should grow old gracefully, accept her age."

She overheard this conversation between Mary and Ellen. But what was grace, and when was a person old? The mornings smelt the same, dew-fresh and exciting, and the sea at Boulogne sparkled as it used to do at Brighton. Kick off the slippers. Sand between the toes. Dabble the feet in water. Shrieks of *"Mother!"* the vestal virgins rushing with parasols . . . But that was life, that sudden ecstacy, that upsurge of the spirit for no reason, calling the blood at eight, or fifty-two. It came upon her now, as it always had done: a happy flood of feeling, a wild unrest. This moment counts. This moment, and no other. The Grande Rue in Boulogne is Ludgate Hill, is Brighton Crescent, is Bond Street in the morning; she'd go and buy a hat in the market-place, or a basket of pears, or a ball of coloured string. The point was people, people and their faces.

That old man with a crutch, that woman crying, the boy with a spinning top, those lovers smiling; they were part of something known and shared and remembered, an oft-recurring, richly coloured pattern. The child who fell in the gutter was herself, and so was the girl who waved from an upper window. "This was what I was once, I've been them all"—that aching heart, that burst of sudden laughter, those angry tears, that bubble of desire.

Life was still an adventure, even now. Forget tomorrow and the lonely hours. There might be a letter from England in the morning, there might be English news and English papers. There might be someone passing through on his way to Paris. "What's happening? What's the gossip, the latest scandal? Is it true? Does it go on still? Does he look very old? But I remember . . ." Back to the past again, the life that used to be, the days that were. "What fun we had. How long the summer seemed." And so on, till nearly midnight, when the visitor, glancing at the clock, caught the coach to Paris.

An odd sort of empty feeling came when he'd gone, tempered with perplexity and surprise. Last seen as a gay young sprig with a roving eye, he was now bull-necked and stout, with greying hair. Something had gone amiss. Some link was broken. That ageing bachelor wasn't the boy she knew. Were all her friends and contemporaries just as heavy, slow-chewing of their food, pompous, deliberate? Had the vital spark been extinguished with the years? If that was the case, then better be blown like a candle, snuffed in an instant, lost in the empty air. Cast a lovely light for one brief moment only, an incandescent glow; then out—and finish.

One January morning the papers arrived from England, solemn and black-edged, the columns lined; and Mary and Ellen, quick and intuitive, wished to keep them from her so as to spare emotion, the sudden switch of mood they knew and feared. It was no use. Those searching eyes had seen the darkened print and guessed what it had to tell— rumours had reached her—but even so the news came as shock, and she went and sat upstairs, alone in her bedroom, locked the door, and opened up her *Times*.

> *January 5th 1827*
>
> *At ten minutes past nine o'clock last night in Rutland House, Arlington Street, died His Royal Highness Frederick, Duke of York and Albany, in the 64th year of his age.*

Just that, and nothing else. And thinking back, she remembered how in the old days she would scan that page and see some brief announcement of his programme. "His Royal Highness, the Commander-in-Chief, today inspected the 14th Light Dragoons, and later called up His Majesty" —and later still, she used to tell him, laughing, on Mrs. M. A. Clarke at Gloucester Place. She had dozens of scrapbooks somewhere with those cuttings, and, underneath, additions by herself scribbled in pen and ink and unrepeatable.

She turned to the summing-up, the final judgement.

> *The deceased Prince, whose kindness of disposition rendered him popular in his lifetime and will make him generally lamented, had been what is termed a good liver.*
>
> *He liked wine, he loved play, and he had other tastes unfortunately too often indulged in, of which the cultivation is more excusable in many other walks of life than in that of a Prince.*
>
> *Besides the Duke of York's attachment to the pleasures of the table, to gambling on the Turf and elsewhere, and to another class of immoral indulgence which, without be-*

379

ing named, may be sufficiently comprehended, His Royal Highness was weakly—we are bound to say culpably as well as most unhappily—insensible of the real use of money. We should hardly here have touched upon the painful Investigation in which the Commons of England were unfortunately engaged seventeen years ago, were it not, first, that the singular occurrence to which we allude must, in spite of us, live in our history and blot our Parliamentary records; and second, that the result proved strikingly beneficial to the Army, and to the kingdom at large. Disappointment itself has ceased to clamour, and envy to whisper, that promotions have been obtained through secret and impure interference.

The Duke of York in private society was warmly and justifiably beloved; cheerful, affable, open, generous, a steady and cordial friend, grateful for kindness, placable in his few resentments, human and compassionate to all whose distresses he had the means of relieving.

The memory of His Royal Highness will long be dear to all who take serious interest in the honour, welfare and efficiency of the British Army.

A later edition gave a further item.

The King's Guard at the King's Palace, St. James's, mounted and dismounted in solemn silence, for thousands were in attendance in consequence of the demise of the Duke of York.

We understand the remains of the Royal Duke are to lie in state two days in the King's Palace, St. James's, and the days are to be Thursday and Friday the 18th and 19th instant, and the following day the remains are to be removed to Windsor, to be interred in the royal vault. The funeral of the lamented Duke will be conducted as Heir Presumptive to the Throne and Commander-in-Chief, and not as Field Marshal.

She told neither Mary nor Ellen of her plan. They would have tried to prevent her. That ban on England, imposed by the trustees, adhered to ever since leaving King's Bench Prison, mattered no longer. Charley had gone alone to his suicide's grave, and Bill to rest with his parents in Uxbridge village; Will Ogilvie, shot in the back by an unknown hand, had passed without a prayer; but this was different.

Some stubborn, fundamental English pride drove her to cross the Channel once again, to brave the tossing sea and the leaden skies, call herself Madame Chambres, assume an accent, mask the face that no one would remember with a long mourning veil and widow's weeds.

She lost identity among the crowds, swayed backwards, forwards, pushed and fought and struggled. No one controlled the people in Pall Mall, the plunging horses, the broken line of carriages; all were confusion, turmoil and distress. Ten thousand men and women, twenty thousand, and still they came and would not be turned back, and bobbing amongst the heads were the sombre banners inscribed with the words "The Soldier's Friend," in purple, followed by marching soldiers, followed by the cadets from the Chelsea school, five hundred little boys, white-faced and solemn, the younger children accompanied by their nurses, wearing their black straw hats and scarlet gowns like those Martha used to wear in 1805.

She felt herself borne forward towards St. James's, and now her shawl was slipping, her veil had gone, while somebody was shouting in her ear and a fainting child was lifted overhead, followed by another and another, and a woman in stockinged feet was trodden down.

A murmur rose from behind. "They'll close the doors . . . they'll never let us in." More panic, confusion, heads turned in all directions, bodies swaying . . . "Go on . . . turn back . . . they're calling out the Guards . . ." And still she fought her way towards the front, her shawl torn from her back one shoe missing, not caring, set, determined. "Let 'em call!"

Now they were in the courtyard of St. James's, surging towards the stairs. The stairs were lined with mutes and soldiers. Yeomen of the Guard, crêpe on their hats and halberds, crêpe on their swords.

The crowd became strangely hushed, became strangely solemn, and in St. James's Palace all was still, the state apartment dimly lit by candles. She found herself staring suddenly at his sword. It lay on the pall with his coronet and baton, but they were regal things, belonging to duty; the sword was personal, part of the man she'd known.

She thought, "I used to hold that in my hands," and found herself surprised at recognition, for it looked forbidding there by candlelight, austere and oddly lonely, out of place.

She heard it clanking down the stairs at breakfast time, or sounding in the hall, or tossed aside; she saw it thrown to Ludovick to clean, or standing upright in the dressing-room, or taken from its sheath to show to George. It had no business there upon the pall—the sword was part of life and not of mourning.

There were his Orders, there was his Garter ribbon, but somebody pushed her past and she could not turn. There were too many people pressing, urging her forward—on with a hundred others down the stairs. One glimpse of his sword, and no more . . . a strange farewell.

She found herself in the open air once again, carried by aimless crowds towards Charing Cross, and she thought, "What now? I've done what I came to do. There's nothing left to stay for, the visit's over."

She went and sat on the steps of St. Martin's Church, hemmed in by grumbling men and weary women, crying children pressing against her knees, all of them huddled together for greather warmth, defeating the gusts of wind and the slanting rain.

A woman beside her offered her bread-and-cheese, and a man on the other side a swig of beer. "Here's luck all round," she said, and somebody laughed, and the sun came out and one of them started singing. She thought of her vestal virgins in Boulogne and George in his regimentals, stiff and pompous, and suddenly none of them mattered, not even George; she was home where she belonged, in the heart of London.

"Come far?" asked her next-door neighbour, sucking an orange.

"Only from round the corner," she said, "from Bowling Inn Alley."

The bells of St. Martin's began to toll, but she went on sitting there, eating her bread-and-cheese, tossing the rind to the pigeons that spattered the steps, and watching a million starlings span the sky.

Menabilly
March-September, 1953